Caught Dead Handed

Books by Carol J. Perry

Caught Dead Handed

Caught Dead Handed

CAROL J. PERRY

KENSINGTON PUBLISHING CORP.
http://www.kensingtonbooks.com

KENSINGTON BOOKS are published by

Kensington Publishing Corp.
119 West 40th Street
New York, NY 10018

All Kensington titles, imprints, and distributed lines are available at special quantity discounts for bulk purchases for sales promotions, premiums, fund-raising, and educational or institutional use. Special book excerpts or customized printings can also be created to fit specific needs. For details, write or phone the office of the Kensington Special Sales Manager: Kensington Publishing Corp., 119 West 40th Street, New York, NY 10018, Attn: Special Sales Department, Phone: 1-800-221-2647.

Kensington and the K logo Reg. U.S. Pat. & TM Off.

ISBN-13: 978-1-61773-369-7
ISBN-10: 1-61773-369-5
First Kensington Mass Market Edition: September 2014

eISBN-13: 978-1-61773-370-3
eISBN-10: 1-61773-370-9
First Kensington Electronic Edition: September 2014

10 9 8 7 6 5 4 3 2 1

Printed in the United States of America

For Dan, my husband and best friend.

ACKNOWLEDGMENTS

A big thank-you to my critique group—Adele, Laura, and Liz—for their keen eyes, editing skills, friendship, and support. Special thanks to Rose and Mim of Plum Island, Massachusetts, for providing me with a calm and quiet place to write, and to my daughter Debbie for providing the same in Florida. Much appreciation to Linda Bennett, a real-life radio call-in psychic who taught me about crystals and golden-white light, and to my editor, Esi Sogah, for her gentle and perceptive suggestions and patient understanding of my technical shortcomings. And, of course, eternal gratitude to my parents for having the good sense to raise me in the magical city of Salem.

'Tis now the very witching time of night,
When churchyards yawn and hell itself breathes out
Contagion to this world.

William Shakespeare

CHAPTER 1

After parking the borrowed Buick in a space marked VISITOR, I pulled down the visor mirror and smoothed a couple of strands of red hair into place. I stepped out beside a granite seawall onto a sparse, brittle strip of grass that was already winter-killed, although it was only October. Hiking the strap of my handbag over the shoulder of a new green wool suit, I took a deep breath of salty air. A dingy, mouse-colored sky hung over Salem Harbor, threatening but not yet raining on the sprawling New England city I used to call home.

Ducking the chill wind by staying close to the weathered brick structure housing WICH-TV, I rounded the corner of the building. The Salem cable channel's ad for a field reporter had come along at just the right time for me. Dodging a page of soggy newspaper cartwheeling across the parking lot like so much urban tumbleweed, I dashed up three broad marble steps to a gracefully arched doorway.

Some things don't change. The old streets are still messy, and the old buildings are still beautiful.

Some things *do* change. Ten years can be a long time in the life of a city. Or of a person. Half a lifetime ago I'd walked along this same street on my way to school—teenage Maralee Kowolski with big dreams of becoming an actress, a star. Now I was back. Thirty-year-old Lee Barrett, unemployed, with hardly any dreams left, Salem born, orphaned early, married once, widowed young. Just yesterday I'd flown here from Florida. I'd come home to the place where I was raised, my aunt Ibby's big old house on Winter Street, exchanging sunshine and theme parks for Salem's unpredictable weather and historic architecture.

The station's lobby featured an old-fashioned black-and-white tile floor and a brass-doored vintage elevator, which growled its way slowly upward. At the end of the second-floor corridor I found the office I was looking for. Gilt lettering across the glass spelled out WICH-TV. No tile floor here. A turquoise carpet vied for attention with purple leather and chrome furniture. A curved reception desk was topped with a towering arrangement of silk lilacs. A brunette receptionist looked in my direction. Her name tag said RHONDA, with the *o* in the form of a heart. I glanced at the gold sunburst clock. It was a couple of minutes before nine. I was right on time for my interview with the station manager. I felt almost confident.

"Good morning," I said, trying to modulate my normally throaty voice. "I'm Lee Barrett. I have a nine o'clock appointment with Mr. Doan."

That voice had become sort of a trademark for me, first as a weather girl on a Miami cable station and more recently as a show host on a Central Florida TV home-shopping program.

I mentally crossed my fingers. If this interview went well, there'd be no more cumulus clouds or cubic zirconia in my future. I'd have a *real* TV job.

Rhonda consulted an open notebook. "Mr. Doan said that if you showed up, I should tell you that he's very sorry. The job you applied for has already been filled."

"What do you mean, if I showed up?" I reached into my handbag and pulled out a letter. "Here!" I waved the paper, signed with the station manager's name. "Mr. Doan specifically said that I was under serious consideration for the field reporter's job. I flew here from Florida for this interview!"

She arched black-penciled eyebrows and shrugged. "Sorry. He hired somebody else. Some guy."

Some guy.

"Some guy," I repeated. "Well, that's just great! Please tell Mr. Doan thanks a lot for his consideration."

"Sure." If she'd caught my sarcasm, she didn't show it.

I've been told that I have the typical redhead's temper, but I've learned to control it pretty well. Too angry to say anything else, and close to tears, I headed down the long corridor toward the elevator. Rows of framed photographs lined the walls. I recognized Phil Archer. He'd been an anchor on WICH-TV since I was a little kid. A cute blonde was posed in front of a weather map, and an athletic-looking guy held a football. There was one blank space with a dusty outline of an oblong frame.

Must be reserved for the photo of the next field reporter. Some guy.

"Damn," I whispered. "Damn. Damn. Damn."

"Bad day?" The voice came from just over my shoulder. I turned and looked into brown eyes, just about level with my own green ones. The man was slim and wiry, probably in his mid-forties, with a prominent nose and dark hair graying at the temples.

"A really bad day," I agreed. "One of the worst."

The door of the office I'd just left burst open, and a red-faced man stormed out.

"Cancel my appointments, Rhonda," he shouted. "That sow! She can't do this! I'll sue the bitch! She has a contract!"

He stepped in front of me and punched the already lit call button.

"Problem, Mr. Doan?" Brown Eyes spoke softly.

"Huh? Oh, hello, George. Yeah." Doan ran a hand through thinning hair. "Seems the psychic walked out in the middle of last night's show. Just like that. And now the bitch isn't answering her phone. Walked out! She'd better never show her fat face around here again!"

The elevator rattled to a stop, and sliding gates slowly began to part. Doan pounded on them, then seemed to notice me for the first time.

"You going up?"

"Down," I said.

"Well, I'm taking this one up." The doors clanged shut, and the elevator growled upward.

"Nice guy," I muttered. "What was that all about?"

"Seems our late-show psychic has resigned suddenly," George said.

"Psychic?"

He nodded. "Right. Ariel Constellation. WICH-TV's late-night movie host and call-in psychic."

I smothered a laugh. "Ariel Constellation?"

"Yep." He tapped one of the frames. "There she is."

It was one of those coy, hand-under-the-chin poses. A round face was topped by an enormous platinum beehive. An arrangement of shiny stars and moons decorated the lacquered hair. A star-shaped beauty mark on her cheek accented lavender-lidded eyes, and the large onyx ring on her extended pinkie finger was set with a five-pointed star at its center. A big yellow striped cat snuggled against an ample, satin-clad shoulder and stared, golden-eyed, into the camera.

"Wow," I said, pointing at the symbol on the ring. "Does she think she's a witch?"

"So they say." He smiled. "She always wears that witch's pentagram. I think it's just part of the act. A Salem thing."

The elevator doors slid open once more, and we stepped inside.

"You've really never seen Ariel?" he asked. "You must be the only person in Salem who doesn't watch *Nightshades*."

"I've been away for quite a while. What does Ariel Constellation do, exactly?"

"She hosts *Nightshades,* our late-night show. It's mostly old *Twilight Zone*s and *Outer Limits* and some of the classic horror films. Stuff like that," he said. "In between commercial breaks she takes phone calls. Live. She answers questions. Gives advice."

"Like Miss Cleo? And the old Psychic Friends

Network? I thought that sort of thing had been pretty much discredited."

"Only because they used to charge for it. Advice is free on *Nightshades*."

"Neat programming idea," I said. "Is she good?"

He shrugged, smiling. "I don't care much for that kind of baloney myself, but the audience seems to love it. The ratings are amazing for that time of night. She beats *The Tonight Show* sometimes."

"No kidding? Do you think she really quit?"

"Might have. She and Doan never got along. And she's managed to get on the wrong side of Mrs. Doan somehow, too. Anyway, Ariel's kind of an old hippie. Lost in the sixties," he said. "She always talked about going back to California. Maybe that's what she did."

When we reached the ground floor, he stuck out his hand. "I'm George Valen," he said. "Cameraman. I didn't get your name."

I shook his hand. He had a good grip. "Lee," I said. "Lee Barrett."

"Well, so long, Lee. I hope your day gets better."

"Thanks." I gave a brief wave, pulled the car keys from my handbag, and stepped out the front door onto Derby Street. I turned the corner of the building and headed along the edge of the paved lot toward the wall where I'd parked Aunt Ibby's Buick. The seawall beside the car was a little more than knee-high, and a fine mist of salt spray fanned out over the top of it with each slowly rolling wave. I could taste it on my lips. The cries of seagulls and the soft *slap-slap* of waves against rough stone had a calming effect, and I paused there for a moment, just listening.

I could sure use some calming down right about now, I thought, anger rising again. *I wanted that job. I deserved that job. Maybe working for the unpleasant Doan wouldn't have been much fun, after all, but what am I supposed to do now?*

Then there was another sound. One that didn't fit in. A tiny buzzing noise. It seemed to come from the top of the wall. I bent toward the buzz and identified it immediately. Someone had dropped a slim cell phone, and it vibrated there, wedged between two of the huge granite slabs.

I leaned cautiously, reaching for it. Below the wall a tangle of seaweed drifted, mixed up with Styrofoam cups and beer cans, all the usual debris the tide brings ashore every day. There was a bright orange glove down there, the kind that lobstermen use. There was even a big lavender sofa cushion.

But sofa cushions don't have platinum hair, do they? Or a hand? A strangely discolored hand that seemed to wave in a languid motion as tiny fishes bumped and nibbled at the shiny ring on a plump finger.

CHAPTER 2

I turned to run. To get help. To tell somebody. I stumbled over a large yellow cat and fell forward, scraping my knees and palms on the pebble-strewn pavement. I scrambled to my feet, pulse throbbing in my ears. Breaking into a run, I fumbled in the unfamiliar depths of the new handbag. A blank screen on the cell phone reminded me too late of the charger still in my suitcase. I shoved the station door open and crashed into a tall blond woman.

"Whoa, Red." She grabbed my arm. "In a hurry?"

"Dead." I gasped. "In the water. Call 911."

"Slow down. What's dead in the water? Your boat?"

"Look," I tried to speak slowly. "There's a body back there. Somebody should call the police."

"A body?" The blonde gripped my arm more tightly. "A dead body? Are you sure?"

I nodded, seeing again the platinum hair floating beneath the surface like so much pale seaweed, the tiny fishes nibbling at that hand with its witch's ring.

"I'm sure."

"Okay. Come on." She headed for a door marked

STAIRS. "Damned elevator takes too long." The stairwell was gray and dingy, with metal treads curving toward a solid green door.

"Janice Valen," my companion announced as we pounded around a triangular landing halfway up.

"Huh?"

"I'm Janice Valen. Program director. You?"

"Oh. Lee. Lee Barrett."

Another Valen?

We tumbled out into the corridor, with its gallery of photos, and arrived at the glass door together. If we hadn't been there to announce a death, it probably would have been funny. Like a Laurel and Hardy entrance.

"Dial 911, Rhonda," Janice shouted to the brunette. "Quick."

Rhonda blinked and dropped her *People* magazine. "911? Why?"

"Oh, for Chrissake!" The blonde stretched a long, slim arm across the purple countertop and grabbed the telephone. "Here. I'll do it." She punched in the number.

Janice Valen gave her name and the address of the station. I walked over to a tall window overlooking the parking lot, half expecting to see a crowd gathering where I'd seen the body. But there was just the granite wall. The blue-gray water. The stunted brown grass. The yellow cat.

"I don't know. Just a minute." Janice covered the mouthpiece. "Hey, Red. Lee."

"What?"

"Man? Or woman?"

"I think it's a woman."

Should I tell them I think it's their missing psychic? What if I'm wrong?

"Woman," Janice repeated. "Better hurry. Tide's going." She hung up. "Stick around, Lee. The cops want to talk to you."

Rhonda looked at me with new interest. "You found a body? Wow. Cool."

"Rhonda, call my brother. Tell him to get down to the seawall," Janice commanded. "We need to get a camera down there before the cops come."

Of course. Cameras. This is a TV station, after all. And George is her brother.

Rhonda picked up a pencil and poked a few buttons on the phone with the eraser. Janice headed for the office marked MANAGER.

"Hey, Doan," she called. "Guess what?"

I glanced around, not knowing what to do next. Down below, the once-empty vista was becoming crowded. Sirens and flashing lights heralded the arrival of police. The WICH-TV truck and camera crew arrived. I recognized George and wondered if the tall guy with him was the new field reporter.

That should be me out there, getting ready to do the live shot. But then I wouldn't have found the body, and poor Ariel . . . if it is Ariel . . . might have disappeared with the outgoing tide.

The next hour was a blur of activity. Two uniformed officers hovered around Rhonda, asking about who had been working at the station the previous day. Another officer disappeared into the manager's office. A tall, broad-shouldered man identified himself as Detective Mondello and joined me at the window.

A tall, broad-shouldered, good-looking man.

The thought surprised me. I hadn't paid much attention to that sort of thing since Johnny's death.

Poor Johnny. Poor me.

The detective made notes as he took my statement about hearing the phone and finding the body. "Did you touch the phone?"

"No. I guess it must still be there."

He nodded. "Just how did you happen to be here in the first place, Miss Barrett?"

"I was here applying for a job, and my car is parked next to the seawall."

Janice had come back into the room and stood next to the detective. Her brown eyes seemed to study me closely, and a surprised expression crossed her face. She snapped her fingers. "Barrett. Of course! I should have recognized you from the audition tape you sent! You're very good."

"Thanks." I didn't voice the obvious question. Then why didn't I get the job?

Detective Mondello looked from one of us to the other. "So you're a new employee here, Miss Barrett?"

"No. They hired someone else."

"I see." He was silent for a moment, scribbling in his notebook, and I turned back to the scene at the water's edge. As I watched, wet-suited divers placed their heavy burden, mercifully covered by a tarp, onto a wheeled gurney.

"Miss Valen?" The detective faced Janice. "We understand that there's a station employee missing."

"An employee?" Janice looked puzzled. "Oh, yes. Ariel . . . the night-show host, left last night in the middle of her show. Oh no! You think it could be . . ."

She looked at me. "You said it was a woman. Oh my God!"

"Were you able to distinguish any features of the person you saw in the water, Miss Barrett?"

"Not really. I couldn't see the face. But she had blond hair. And a big ring on her hand."

"Jesus! It's Ariel. I have to tell Doan." Janice turned, pushing her way past the officers, hurrying to the station manager's office.

The detective grew silent again, watching Janice's retreating back. Down below, the new field reporter was on camera. He stood next to a long white van, doors open to receive the drowned woman, and the large yellow cat I'd tripped over sat beneath a nearly leafless tree, licking his paws with seeming unconcern as the body of his late mistress was trundled by.

"Miss Barrett, were you acquainted with the missing employee at all?"

"What? Oh, no," I answered. "No. I've never even seen her TV show. I just arrived from St. Petersburg last night."

"I see." He continued making notes. "And you say you came to Salem for a job interview?"

"Yes. Well, also I have family here."

"You weren't hired."

"That's right."

"Will you be returning to Florida soon, then?"

"I don't think so."

Returning to what? Johnny was gone. My job was gone. And I'd signed a two-year rental agreement on my condo in St. Petersburg.

"I see," he said again. "Do you have a local number?

Somewhere you can be reached if we have further questions?"

I gave him the numbers for my cell and Aunt Ibby's house, and he snapped his notebook shut.

"Thank you, Miss Barrett."

"You're welcome, Detective."

He strode to the reception desk, pulled out the notebook again, and began speaking in low tones to Rhonda, who seemed to enjoy the attention. The scene in the parking lot had changed again. The white van was gone, and yellow tape was festooned along the wall. A mobile unit from one of the Boston TV stations had pulled into the lot, and the crowd had grown.

"Is that your Buick? Right in the middle of all the action?" Janice Valen spoke from behind me.

"Yes. Well, it's my aunt's car."

"You might want to stick around here for a while," she said. "You'll walk straight into that mess if you try to leave now."

She was right. I certainly didn't want to be interviewed as the one who'd discovered poor drowned Ariel's body.

"Come on into my office. I want to talk to you, anyway."

Janice Valen's office was, thankfully, different from the turquoise and purple decor of the reception area. The walls were a soft golden color. The Scandinavian modern furniture was sleek and stylish. *Like Janice,* I thought.

There were a few nice prints of old Salem sailing vessels on the walls. On the desk was a small framed nightclub souvenir–type photo of a sparsely clad, slender woman wearing the tall feather-and-sequin headdress of a showgirl. Stamped across the bottom in purple metallic ink was *The Purple Dragon, London, New Year's Eve 2005.*

"Looking at the evidence of my misspent youth?"

"It's lovely," I said. "You looked beautiful."

"Thanks."

"You're an actress?"

"Was. That was taken in London back when the skinny, anorexic Diana look was still in."

"London. That must have been exciting."

"It was okay. Here. Please sit down."

The chair was soft and comfortable, and I realized just how tired I was. For the first time I noticed that my hands were scraped, my knees bloody, and my hose ripped. I tried to pull the green skirt down to cover the damage.

"Look, I'm sorry I didn't recognize you right off," she said. "What with all the excitement, I didn't make the connection until you started talking to the cute cop."

"That's all right," I said. "No reason you should have."

She shook her head, and her short, fine hair flared out, then fell perfectly back into place. Mine never does that.

"Really, I should have picked up on it. You're the Emerson grad. Best school in the world for theater arts. You have great TV experience, too. Doan was supposed to interview you this morning."

"Yep. That was me." *So if I'm so darned qualified, why'd you hire some guy? Where is this conversation leading, anyway?* I tried changing the subject.

"How did Mr. Doan take the news? About Ariel?"

She shrugged, a slight lift of one elegant shoulder. "Doan is Doan. He said it was her own fault, always going down to the wall to sneak a smoke during the movie. He said a woman of her size ought to know better than to get too close to the edge—especially since she couldn't swim a stroke. He's mostly ticked off because now he has no late-show host."

"That seems cold," I said. The anger was back. "And so was the way he hired that man without even giving me the courtesy of an interview."

Again the ladylike shrug. "He decided to grab the other guy. Scott Palmer."

"So I gathered." That sounded snarky. I didn't care.

"I don't blame you for being mad," she said. "But Palmer had another appointment with a Boston station, and Doan didn't want to lose him."

"Is he all that good? How did Mr. Doan figure that I might not be better?"

"You don't do sports."

"Excuse me?" Nobody had said anything about sports.

"He compared résumés. It was down to you two. You can do weather and shopping. Palmer used to do sports. Doan figured since he already has a weather girl and we don't do shopping, he'll get more for his money with Palmer. Our regular sports guy does only the pro teams. Sox, Bruins, Celts, Pats." She gave a soft laugh. "He's going to get Palmer to cover the high school basketball and football games. Two talents for the price of one."

So the station manager isn't only rude, but he's cheap, too.
It was my turn to shrug. "I suppose that makes a

certain amount of sense, but it was still a rotten way to treat me after I came all this way for an interview."

"I know it was, but listen. Are you still interested in working here?"

The question surprised me. "Why? Doing what?"

"Look," she said. "Doan told me to find a replacement for Ariel, pronto. Like, in time for next Monday's show. Tonight we'll probably do some kind of Ariel tribute or something, and we don't do *Nightshades* on the weekend. Doan said, 'I don't care how you do it. Just do it!' How in hell am I supposed to do that?" She spread her hands in a hopeless gesture.

"Beats me."

"Yours is the only résumé I have that even remotely approaches the qualifications for show host."

"Well, thanks, but no thanks." I almost laughed out loud. "I'm not the least bit psychic."

"So what? Neither was Ariel. They're all a bunch of fakes. It doesn't matter. I mean, you have an acting background. You've hosted a show before. You look good on camera. You know how to pitch a product. That's all it takes."

"It can't be that simple. George told me that *Night-shades* is one of your top-rated shows."

"You know George? My brother?"

"Not really. We met earlier this morning. In the corridor."

She shook the perfect hair again. "George does make friends easily. But listen, Lee. Help me out here. Where else am I going to find a good-looking Emerson grad with TV credits and a brain in a couple of days?" She lowered her voice to a conspiratorial whisper. "And it gets you into the station. Of course, it's not as much money as the field reporter job, but it's not as many hours, either."

"Miss Valen," I said. "Thanks, anyway. . . ."

"Janice. Call me Janice."

"All right then. Janice. Mr. Doan has seen my tapes, and he's already turned me down once today. Besides, I've never even seen *Nightshades*."

"Look at it this way, Lee. You don't have to sign a contract if you don't want to. And if a better position opens up, or if the Palmer guy falls on his face, why, there you'll be!"

She had a point there. "True. But I'm not sure I can pull off the psychic thing."

"Oh, it's not that difficult. It's mostly just introducing old movies and reading a few commercials. I'll give you a couple of DVDs of Ariel's old shows, and you can see how she handled the callers. It won't take too long to watch it. No movies, just the calls and a few commercials."

"Give me a couple of hours to think it over," I said. "I'll get back to you this afternoon."

"Good. Thanks. I appreciate this." There was relief in her voice. "By the way, were you able to help the cops out any?"

"I doubt it. The detective just asked me to describe what I saw."

"Sorry you had to be the one who found her. Must have been a shock. I'm going to call downstairs. Get one of the uniforms to escort you to your car, keep the vultures away from you."

"Thanks."

Within a few minutes I was behind the wheel of the

Buick, driving carefully away from the yellow tape, the gray harbor, and the gawking strangers.

The yellow cat still sat under the tree. He stretched and yawned as I passed, then trotted to the curb. Head cocked to one side, he seemed to watch with interest as I turned onto Derby Street and headed for home.

CHAPTER 3

I rolled the Buick carefully into the garage behind Aunt Ibby's house, dutifully waiting for the tennis ball suspended from the ceiling to tap the windshield. Opening a black iron gate, I cut through the garden, where late season marigolds and winter geraniums still nodded, defying the chill autumn air. I hurried up the back steps and pushed my key into the center of the brass doorknob.

"I'm in the den, Maralee," my aunt called. "Come tell me all about the job." The den in the Winter Street house was my aunt's favorite room. The furnishings were appropriate to the style and age of the fine old home, but the giant TV, the computers, printers, speakers, fax machine and other communication devices were strictly state of the art.

"It didn't turn out exactly the way I'd thought it might," I said. "But they did offer me one."

"Good," she said. "Sit right down. You must tell me all about it. But first, let's watch the noon news. Seems they've found a body in the harbor!"

I wasn't surprised by the response. My aunt Isobel

Russell, a youthful sixty-five-year-old, semiretired research librarian, voracious reader, and computer whiz, is a true TV addict. To her, the invention of the remote control ranks right up there with the wheel and the safety pin.

I sat and felt some of the tension of the morning slipping away.

"I know." My voice sounded shaky. "I . . . sort of . . . found the body. It was a woman who worked at the station."

She dropped the control and faced me. "My dear! How horrible! And look at your poor knees. And your hands. What on earth happened to you?"

"Oh, that. I'm all right. Just tripped over a cat. Anyway, I'd parked down by the seawall. I was about to leave when I heard something that made me look down into the water. There was a body floating there. They say it's one of the show hosts. A woman called Ariel Constellation."

We each grew silent when, like an eerie echo, the same name sounded from the TV.

"Ariel Constellation was the victim of an apparent accidental drowning." The announcer spoke solemnly about the dead woman. "The body of the popular WICH-TV night-show host was discovered just hours ago near the seawall adjacent to the building that houses this station." The newsman recited some facts about Ariel, probably hastily culled from her personnel file.

"Her real name was Gladys Renquist, but her many fans have known her as Ariel Constellation for the nearly a decade she has worked here. Ms. Renquist was unmarried and apparently has no relatives in the

Salem area. We go now to field reporter Scott Palmer, at the scene of the accident. Scott?" A rugged-looking guy faced the camera. He looked like a jock. Obviously, that nose had been broken a time or two.

He looks nervous. I'll bet he's not used to doing a stand-up. That could just as well be me. And I know enough to use extra hair spray in that wind.

I couldn't resist a tiny speck of satisfaction that the new field reporter's first day's tapings would show him with that nice wavy hair standing darned near straight up.

"The police have removed the lifeless body of this station's popular nighttime host from Salem Harbor. The medical examiner has not yet determined the cause of Ariel Constellation's death, although it appears to be an accidental drowning. Station officials have told police that due to WICH-TV's no smoking policy, Ms. Constellation often stepped outside for a cigarette while the feature was running. Here's what was recorded earlier, when the victim was removed from the water."

The scene was the same, except for the Buick parked by the wall, the white van with rear doors open, and a wheeled gurney with its grim burden.

"Look, Aunt Ibby." I pointed at the screen. "There's the cat I tripped over."

"That's Ariel's cat," she said. "She has him on the show sometimes."

I was surprised. "You watch *Nightshades?*"

"Well, I've certainly never called and asked for her advice, but, yes. I guess you might say I'm a fan. I love all those old movies and TV shows. Why, in the last couple of months Ariel showed twenty episodes of

Dark Shadows back to back. The real *Dark Shadows.* Not that movie thing." She wrinkled her nose. "Whatever will they do now that she's gone? Do you suppose they'll find someone to take her place?"

"That's what the plan is. And they've offered me the job."

"Oh, dear." My aunt looked genuinely distressed. "You can't be serious! You aren't the least bit psychic." Her eyes widened. "Or are you?"

"Of course not!" I had to smile. "Neither was Ariel, according to the program director. It's all an act. But it is a foot in the door at the station. And, as she told me, if the field reporter they hired doesn't work out, why, there I'll be!"

"I see. So that good-looking young fellow doing the report about Ariel has the job you applied for?"

I glanced again at the screen. "You think he's good-looking?" Then, not waiting for an answer, I explained as well as I could about Mr. Doan's habit of hiring people who could do more than one job. "And," I added, "I told them I'd decide in a couple of hours about taking over *Nightshades.*"

"That's awfully short notice, isn't it?"

Before I could answer, the phone rang. Aunt Ibby picked it up. Handing it to me, she put her hand over the mouthpiece and whispered, "Better think fast. It's that program director. Janice somebody."

So I thought fast.

"Hello, Janice."

"Hi, Lee. Look. I don't mean to pressure you, but Doan is getting antsy."

I pictured the red-faced man I'd seen at the elevator. "I can imagine."

"Well, have you thought about it?"

"I think I might like to try it. I have enough of an acting background. But I'll need time to watch the DVDs you gave me to see how the show's supposed to run."

Behind me, I heard Aunt Ibby's sharp intake of breath.

Janice was clearly relieved by my answer. "Whew, Lee. You have no idea how much I appreciate this. Can you possibly come in tomorrow and look over the *Nightshades* set just to get the feel of it? And then maybe sometime this weekend you can do a test video."

What the hell was I thinking? How could anyone prepare a show that fast? Back when I was doing weather reports, I had a week of rehearsals just to learn how the green screen works!

But I heard myself say, quite calmly, "Yes. I could do that."

Janice hadn't finished. "Now, you'll have to think up a name for yourself, and I guess you need to work out some kind of fashion statement. Ariel's costumes obviously won't fit you. Anyway, I don't see you as the 'lavender satin with crystal stars and moons' type."

"You're right." I smiled, picturing my red hair teased into a beehive, lacquered stiff, and decorated Ariel style. "No crystal stars or silver moons! I presume there's a wardrobe budget?"

"There is, but maybe you can just throw something together for the test. Then, when you get the okay from Doan, we'll set you up with all that stuff."

"I'll find something to wear. I come from a long line of women who never throw anything away. It's all here in my aunt's attic." I turned and grinned at Aunt Ibby, who was clearly hanging on every word.

"Super," Janice said. "Just call Rhonda and set up some times. And, Lee, thanks."

"Good-bye," I said, but she had already hung up. "That's that." I faced Aunt Ibby. "I start Monday."

"Doesn't give you much time to prepare, does it? What was all that about crystal moons?"

"Oh, Ariel's costumes. I need . . . Wait a minute. Say that again."

"Say what?"

"Crystal moon."

"Very well. Crystal moon."

"I like it. I think that's my new name. Crystal Moon."

She nodded. "It does have a certain New Age ring to it."

"Can we go up to the attic and see if we can throw together some kind of costume to get me started in the psychic business?"

She frowned. "I'm sure we can. But aren't they asking a bit much? Wanting you to take on a job on short notice, then expecting you to provide your own wardrobe?"

"It'll be just for the weekend. After that, if Mr. Doan approves my test video, the station buys the costumes for Crystal Moon."

"You always did love going to the attic to play dress up."

"True. Let's go see what we can find. I'm thinking of a sort of Gypsy look."

"Just a minute, young lady!" She sounded exactly the way she had when I was a kid. "If you're determined to go through with this, first you hop upstairs and take a nice shower," she ordered. "Put some antibiotic on those scrapes and get into some comfortable clothes. Now shoo!"

She was right, of course. I gave her a hug, picked up the handbag from where I'd tossed it on the floor, and headed up the curving oak stairs. They gleamed with lemon oil polish and the patina of years of meticulous care from a series of housekeepers. It would feel good to get out of the suit and heels.

The warm shower was soothing. I felt some of the tension from that strange morning's happenings wash away. I dutifully applied healing lotion and adhesive bandages to hands and knees, then pulled on comfortable jeans and a blue T-shirt. I plugged in the cell phone, and within twenty minutes I was back downstairs, anxious to clothe my new persona, Crystal Moon.

Aunt Ibby was quiet as we climbed the first- and second-floor stairways. We approached the door leading to the attic. "You don't need to rush into anything, you know." The matter-of-fact voice held reassurance. "There's no financial need for you to work at all."

I knew that. The income from my parents' estate totaled far more than my salary at WICH-TV would ever be. I had used some of the money to pay my way through college, then had left the rest to Aunt Ibby's financial advisers to manage. I'd made my own way since graduation, and Johnny Barrett, a rising star on the NASCAR racing circuit, had earned more than enough to keep us nicely during our too-short time together. Not many knew it, but I was, by anybody's standards, a wealthy woman.

"And you know, too," she continued, "you're welcome to stay here as long as you like."

The idea of staying indefinitely at the Winter Street house held some appeal. It had been, after all, my childhood home. When I was five, I'd stayed with Aunt Ibby for the weekend, while my parents took a trip to Maine in Daddy's bright yellow Piper Cub. There'd been a crash, and they'd never returned. I'd just stayed on with Aunt Ibby, walking across the common to school when I was little, later taking the bus to Salem High School, and then commuting by train to Boston's Emerson College, where I'd learned the skills that landed me on TV.

Aunt Ibby produced a large, round ring with a jangling assortment of keys. She inserted one into the lock at the foot of the narrow staircase leading to the attic, and we climbed up into the long, slant-ceilinged room.

"I'm sure we can piece together a costume," she said, "but piecing together a character on short notice is quite another matter."

"I know. But it's worth a try. If I mess up, I'm no worse off than I was in the first place."

"Can't argue with that logic." She opened the curved lid of a 1925 Louis Vuitton trunk and began removing tissue-wrapped parcels. "Here. This red skirt might do. It was mine back when I was about your size."

Unfolding the colorful circle of fabric, I held the skirt to my waist. "This'll do fine."

She pulled another parcel from the trunk. "This blouse was your mother's. Try it on."

After removing the blue T-shirt, I slipped the silky embroidered blouse over my head, then pulled the elasticized neckline down over Florida-tanned shoulders. Then I hastily drew it up again, looking at my reflection in the dusty, and slightly wavy, surface of an oak-framed oval mirror.

My aunt smiled. "She never could decide which way to wear it, either."

"I wish I could really remember her. Daddy too. Sometimes it seems as if I'm remembering something—there'll be a picture in my mind, like a freeze-frame from a movie—and I can see them. But I don't know." I frowned into the mirror. "Probably they're just times you've told me about, or maybe snapshots I've seen in one of your old albums." I tugged at the blouse, exposing one shoulder. "I like it that this was hers, though. Maybe it'll bring me luck. It looks kind of Gypsyish, don't you think?"

"Quite. How about jewelry? You'll need gold earrings, it seems to me, and maybe some beads?" She pulled the top drawer from a small mahogany bureau and dumped its contents onto the seat of a rocking chair. "Prowl through these," she advised. "There must be some hoop earrings in there somewhere."

I sorted through the jumble of costume jewelry. "No earrings in this pile." I tugged at the second drawer. "This one is stuck. What's in it?"

"I don't remember. Try the next one."

I selected a pair of dangly hoop earrings, a strand of blue glass beads, and a couple of chunky rings from the third drawer of the little bureau and placed them on top of the red skirt. "That should about do it," I said.

"Look. Here's a shawl that belonged to Great-grandmother Forbes .She brought it back from Spain in the twenties. It used to be on top of her grand piano. You could drape it around your hips."

I tied the deeply fringed square loosely over one hip. I turned slowly. "Dum-dum-da-da-da-dum-dum-da." I hummed the repetitive rhythm of "Habanera." "What do you think? Would I make a good Carmen? Or maybe Esmeralda, the goat girl?"

"I hope not." Aunt Ibby returned the last of the tissue-wrapped parcels to the trunk and closed the lid. "Carmen was stabbed to death by her lover, and they hanged poor little Esmeralda as a witch."

CHAPTER 4

With blouse and skirt spinning in the washing machine and my great-grandmother's shawl fluffing in the dryer, Aunt Ibby and I returned to the den. I popped one of the disks Janice had given me into the DVD player. The image of a large blond woman in flowing purple satin filled the TV screen. I listened carefully as Ariel delivered a commercial for a local New Age bookstore. The psychic had good diction and a soothing voice.

"She'll take some calls after this commercial," Aunt Ibby promised. "Watch."

"Go ahead, caller," said Ariel. "You're on the air." She leaned forward, looking directly into the camera. "Go ahead," she repeated. "You're on the air with Ariel. Your first name and your question please."

"Ariel?" came the hesitant reply.

The psychic nodded, hair decorations bobbing and shimmering.

"Your first name and your question please. We have to move right along. There are other callers waiting."

"She sounds a little testy," I said.

Aunt Ibby grinned. "That's half the fun of watching her. Some nights she's sweet as cream, but other times she's downright bitchy."

"My name is Donna." The girl sounded very young. "Will my boyfriend and I get married?"

"His first name?" Ariel pressed the middle finger of her left hand to the center of her forehead, closing purple-lidded eyes.

"Mark. His name is Mark."

Ariel's eyes remained closed, heavily blackened false eyelashes dark against plump cheeks. "I feel that Mark may be a good friend for you, but nothing more. There will be a number of other men in your life before you find your true soul mate."

"Well, uh, thanks, Ariel."

"Just a moment." Ariel tilted her head back dramatically.

"I see another man," she said. "A very handsome, tall man. He is coming to you from a . . . It seems to be a large building. It's a . . . yes, it's a school. Perhaps a college. Are you planning to go to college, Donna?"

"Well, maybe."

"Try to, if you possibly can," Ariel counseled. "There you will find the metaphysical key to your best future."

"She always does that," Aunt Ibby said.

"Does what?"

"Finds some way to tell the young-sounding ones to stay in school or to get jobs or look for other relationships."

"Good idea. I could do that."

Ariel gazed into the camera. "Do we have another caller on the line? Hello, caller?"

There was an audible buzzing sound. Ariel's brows knotted. "We've apparently lost that one. Could you people in the control room stay awake?" There was a decidedly unpleasant edge to her voice. "My calls are important."

"Oh, good." Aunt Ibby leaned closer to the screen. "She's going to be nasty."

"Shall we try again?" The tone showed barely concealed exasperation. "Hello, caller. Your first name and your question please."

The voice was thin, almost a whisper.

"I . . . I don't know what to do about my husband. I think I want to leave him. I'm not sure what I should do."

"Your first name, please?"

"Oh. It's Mavis."

"Your birthday?"

The woman gave a December date.

"And your husband's name and date of birth?"

"Do I have to tell? If he found out . . . he wouldn't like it."

"No. You don't have to tell, Mavis." Ariel's voice was softer. "I sense that he has mistreated you."

"Yes."

"Physically hurt you. I can feel your pain." Ariel's forehead furrowed, and she pressed the fingers of both hands against her temples.

She's good. I'll try to learn some of those moves.

Again came the caller's answer. "Yes."

"I see you putting great distance between yourself and this man." Ariel moved her hands apart.

"Then you think that I should leave him?"

"That's not for me to say." Ariel's eyes were closed

again. "I can only tell you about impressions that I receive. You are a child of the universe, Mavis. You will determine your own path."

"But you said—"

"I see you moving away from this man. I see you becoming stronger as the distance becomes greater. Are there children involved, Mavis?"

"No. No kids. Thank you, Ariel. You've helped a lot."

"Love and light to you, Mavis."

"Love and light to you, Ariel."

"Does she do much marriage counseling over the phone? I mean, did she?" It was hard to speak of her in the past tense. The TV image was so alive.

"Yes. She often did it. And quite well, don't you think? If it seems as though the woman is being abused, as this poor soul obviously was, Ariel usually 'sees' her leaving. If it's just a whiner, she might suggest counseling."

The next caller was Bill, a Gemini worried about his relationship with his sister. Ariel advised him to meditate with rose quartz crystals—providing a neat segue into a promo for a sale on healing crystals at an Essex Street shop. A woman thinking of moving and another contemplating the sale of property followed. Ariel advised each of them to wait until after the full moon to make any decisions regarding real estate. Then she announced the next night's movie, read a commercial for natural vitamins, and wished her audience pleasant dreams.

"Want to watch another? I have those *Dark Shadows* episodes," my aunt said. "Or should we stop for lunch?"

"Lunch please." I realized that I was really hungry.

"And I think I'll do a little basic research. Do we still have a copy of *Linda Goodman's Sun Signs*?"

"Nonfiction. One-thirty-three point five," said my librarian aunt.

Not too many home bookshelves are organized by the Dewey decimal system, but ours was.

As Aunt Ibby pointed the remote toward the TV set, a close-up of Ariel's face filled the screen. She nodded slightly, and the image was gone. It seemed to me just then that the little nod might be one of approval.

For Crystal Moon.

I made a quick trip to the upstairs study while Aunt Ibby busied herself with lunch preparations. Then, pulling a stool up to the kitchen counter, I propped the copy of *Linda Goodman's Sun Signs* against an apple-shaped cookie jar. A grilled cheese sandwich and a steaming mug of tomato soup, my favorite childhood comfort foods, appeared beside me.

"Thanks, Aunt Ibby. You're going to spoil me."

"My pleasure," she said. "Why the astrology book?"

"I noticed that Ariel sometimes asked for a caller's birth date. This is a crash course."

She reached over and touched my hand. "You know, Maralee, you don't have to rush into this job. You could wait a bit and find something a bit more . . . mainstream."

"I know." I closed the book. "I need to work, Aunt Ibby. I need to keep busy. It's been almost a year since Johnny . . ."

"I wish I'd had a chance to know him better." She spoke softly. "I wish now I'd visited you in Florida more often. And I always enjoyed so much the times the two of you stayed here when Johnny raced up in New Hampshire .But we just don't think about how fragile life is, do we? First, your parents, too young. Then your Johnny. And now poor Ariel. It's all so sad."

"Sometimes, when I first wake up, I forget that he's not there beside me." I blinked back tears.

"It's still hard for you to talk about, isn't it? Such a tragic accident. But it *was* an accident, Maralee! It wasn't your fault. Not one bit your fault!"

"I know. Everyone says that. But I was driving. I was the one behind the wheel. I can't help thinking if my reflexes had been faster . . . if I had been more alert . . ."

"My dear child." Aunt Ibby looked into my eyes. "It was a black car . . . on a pitch-black night. Traveling without lights. Speeding. The driver was drunk. There was nothing anyone could do."

I tried to blot out the vision of that terrible moment. "I know. And I'm lucky to be alive."

"Indeed you are." Aunt Ibby squeezed my hand, then abruptly, and wisely, changed the subject. "Now, about this horoscope nonsense. Naturally it's all bunk. You agree?"

"Sure I do. See?" I flipped the book open. "It says here I'm a very agreeable person."

"Very funny." She peered over my shoulder. "And it does not."

"I know. But I do need to do some studying. I wonder if they'd let me borrow some of those books and things Ariel had displayed on the *Nightshades* set."

"I don't see why not."

"I think I'll go back over this afternoon. I need to get everything done by Monday night."

"I have to put in a few hours at the library today," Aunt Ibby said. "I can drop you off if you like."

"No. Thanks just the same. I'll just grab a cab. I'll probably be back before you are."

Before long, lunch finished, dishes washed, hair combed, and clothes changed, I was on the front steps as a green-and-white cab pulled up. The driver raced around the vehicle and held the door for me. "Thanks," I said and gave him the TV station's address as I climbed into the backseat. It smelled of cigarette smoke and air freshener. I rolled the window down, and we headed east on Winter Street. Within seconds sirens sounded, and we pulled over as two police cars, lights flashing, sped past.

"Uh-oh," the cabbie muttered. "I should have gone the other way. Cops are keeping busy. They don't usually get two stiffs in one day."

"What do you mean? What happened?"

"Well, there was that floater this morning over by the TV station. . . . Say, that's where you're headed, ain't it?"

"Yes. What do you mean, two?"

"Oh, some dame down the other end of Derby Street went and got herself iced. Landlady found the body. Hope you ain't in a big hurry. Two dead bodies in one day, both on the same street, makes kind of a mess for drivin'."

CHAPTER 5

Traffic had slowed to a near halt as we approached the lights at the intersection of Derby Street.

"When did this happen?" I asked. "I was watching TV only a little while ago. They didn't mention any second death."

"Just came over the police scanner. Our dispatcher listens to it all day. Loves all that cop stuff."

I saw the WICH-TV remote unit move into the line of traffic heading north. The new field reporter was having a busy day for himself. *I wonder if his new boss will want him to cover a high school football game later.*

I couldn't help smiling at the thought.

Some cars had pulled over and were double-parked for a better look at whatever was going on. Figuring that I might as well join the lookie-loos, I moved over to the left side of the cab and rolled down that window, too, giving me a better view of the old street.

"What did the dispatcher say happened to the lady who was . . . Did you say she was murdered?"

The driver caught my eye in the rearview mirror and slowly drew his finger across his throat.

"One of our drivers is a part-time deputy. Says she got her throat cut. They're looking for her old man. Had a bunch of domestic violence calls from that address before."

"Uh-oh. Guess that happens everywhere."

"Yeah, well, here we are at the station. Looks like the excitement has died down some."

"Seems like it." I added a generous tip to the amount shown on the meter. "Well, thanks." I glanced at the identification card posted on the visor. "Thanks, Mr. Litka. I'll probably call back soon for a ride back home."

"You do that. Just ask for Jim Litka."

I hurried along the sidewalk toward the front door. A row of seagulls stood motionless on the roof, watching with small bright eyes as I passed.

"Mind your own business," I muttered, stepping inside and punching the elevator's UP button.

Rhonda registered mild surprise at seeing me again so soon.

"Janice says you're going to start working here Monday night. That's cool."

"Thanks. Is she here?"

"Janice? Nope. She left already."

"She said I should check with you about times for a test video and a rehearsal."

"Okay. Sure. Wait a sec."

Rhonda pulled a notebook from a drawer and consulted a laptop computer on her desk.

"Would it be all right if I borrow some of Ariel's props from the *Nightshades* set? Especially the books?"

"Fine with me. I'll check the schedules and see who can do the test and stuff. You know your way?"

"Sorry. No."

"Come on. I'll show you."

I followed the swaying hips of the brunette down a short corridor and through a set of double doors.

"Newsroom," Rhonda said, deadpan expression in place. She pointed past a huge glass window to a cluster of desks. A bank of color monitors on one wall showed the current WICH-TV programming, a film on whales. A wire-service printer clicked loudly, and somewhere a phone rang. In the far corner of the room two men and a woman were gathered around a glowing screen.

An image of the three witches from *Macbeth* popped into my mind.

I followed Rhonda through another scarred metal door. The walls of the studio were painted black. It was a long room with high ceilings and no windows that I could see. Several sets were positioned around the perimeter of the place. I recognized Ariel's *Nightshades* background right away. Blue curtains with silvery outlines of several constellations hung behind a curved turquoise couch. A long, low table held some of the psychic's props.

A giant cluster of quartz crystals rested on a wooden base. A deck of tarot cards lay facedown, and a stack of books displayed such titles as *The Art and Practice of Astral Projection* and *Past-Life Therapy in Action.* In the center of the table was a large black ball mounted on an ornate brass stand.

"Well, this is it." Rhonda spread her arms. "All Ariel's stuff."

"Impressive," I said, glancing around the set. "What? No crystal ball?"

"Oh, she used to have one of those, too, but George said it reflected the lights too much. So she got that black one. Say, I gotta get back. You okay down here alone?"

"I'm fine. I won't be long. Thanks, Rhonda."

I heard the door swing shut as I picked a card from the top of the tarot deck and turned it faceup.

The Nine of Cups.

I was just beginning to realize how truly clueless I was about the psychic business. Studying the titles on Ariel's stack of books, I reached for *The Complete Guide to the Tarot*. I flipped through the colorful pages. The cups were apparently, a suit of cards, like diamonds or clubs or spades. I found only one meaning for the nine.

You get your wish.

I'd made so many wishes lately, I didn't know which one that might be, but at least it sounded positive. I put the tarot book back and checked out some of the other titles. There were several books on crystals that looked interesting, and even one on cats. I wondered where Ariel's cat was, and hoped he'd be taken care of now that she was gone.

I reached across the table and gingerly touched the black sphere.

This has to go. I hate black.

The surface reflected tiny pinpoints of brightness from the few lights illuminating the studio. I leaned closer to the thing and saw that it seemed to have misty colors swirling around inside it. An instant later I pushed the table away from the couch and jumped to my feet.

"Who did that?" I screamed, my voice echoing in

the empty studio. Then, feeling foolish, I sat down, took a deep breath, and forced myself to look at the ball again.

The pinpoints of light were still reflected there. Nothing more. Yet I knew that seconds earlier I had looked into that glistening blackness and had plainly seen the form of a woman. She lay facedown on a kitchen floor. A bright spray of red splattered the floor, the range, and the refrigerator.

"What the hell is going on in here? And who the Christ are you?" The speaker was one of the people I'd just passed in the newsroom. The gray-haired woman pushed the door open.

"I . . . I'm sorry," I stammered. "I thought I saw something. . . ."

"Probably just a rat." Gray curls bobbing, she approached the couch and sat beside me. "Place is full of 'em. So close to the water, you know."

A man appeared in the doorway. I recognized Phil Archer, one of the news anchors. "Everything okay in here?" He squinted in the dim light. "Oh, you must be the new psychic. Janice said you'd be stopping by. What's all the screaming about?"

My newfound companion gave a dismissive wave. "Just saw a rat, is all."

As the newsman left, she turned to face me. "That right? You the new psychic? The one that found Ariel?"

"I am," I admitted, extending my hand. "Lee Barrett."

"Marty McCarthy," she said. Her grip was firm. "Camerawoman. I'll be doing your show."

"Good to meet you," I said. "Sorry about the interruption."

"No problem. Damn rats." She glanced around the

studio, as though expecting to see rodents in the shadows. "But we keep a cat around. He keeps them in check pretty well."

"I didn't actually see a rat. It was something else."

"What do you mean?"

Hesitantly, and without going into detail, I explained as well as I could that I'd seen something disturbing in the black ball.

"Oh, that. It must have been a reflection from the overhead monitor." She pointed to a blank screen above the *Nightshades* set and jerked a thumb toward the newsroom. "We were next door editing a live feed from the murder down the street. You heard about that?" She didn't wait for an answer. "Someone must have transmitted to your set by mistake."

I felt relieved and a bit foolish. "It just startled me for a minute."

"I'll bet it did!" Her smile crinkled the corners of her eyes. "You must have thought that old bowling ball of Ariel's really worked."

Still a little shaken, I returned her smile. "You say you'll be working on *Nightshades*?"

"Yep. I've been camera on that show since the very first one."

"Then you were here when . . ."

"When poor Ariel took a header into the drink? I sure was. See, whenever she went out for a smoke, I'd call her cell when it was time for a commercial break. Oh, I knew something was wrong when she didn't answer. Everyone around here said she probably just walked. She'd had a fight with Doan. Nothing new there. She had a fight with Doan at least once a week. I knew there was something wrong when she didn't come back in." The gray curls quivered as she shook her head. "I put her number on redial and tried it all night. This morning, too."

"I suppose someone checked to see if her car was still there?"

"Nope. See, that's a problem. Ariel didn't drive. Had a couple of DUIs and never got her license back. She used to take a cab or bum a ride."

"I see. That confuses things."

Marty shrugged. "Ariel was a confusing person."

"She'll be missed around here, I'm sure," I said.

"Yeah. Well, I guess so. The audience loved her." She looked me up and down. "But you'll do all right. Weird, isn't it? This morning you find her body, and in a couple of days you'll be doing her job."

"It's awfully strange to me."

"Ariel would say it's karma. You thought up a name yet? Or are you going to use your own?"

"I'm going to be Crystal Moon."

"Crystal Moon!" Her laugh was hearty. "Christ, what a moniker. Worse than Ariel Constellation. Crystal Moon. It's perfect!"

"I kind of like it. Janice said I could do some kind of on-camera dress rehearsal this weekend. Will you be here for that?"

"I guess. Probably tomorrow. You can set it up with Rhonda. You've had a pretty full day for yourself, haven't you? Finding Ariel and all." She gave me a sideways glance. "How did you happen to, uh, find the body?"

"I heard her phone ringing, and when I followed the sound, I saw her in the water."

"Probably me calling."

"Probably," I agreed. "Say, you haven't been here all night, have you?"

"Yeah. See, I thought she might come back. Thought she might have started drinking again and wandered off. Thought all kinds of things. But I never thought she'd drowned."

She looked so sad, I almost wanted to put my arm around her slim shoulders. Instead, I said, "Where did you sleep?"

"I dozed off right here on this couch. Woke up about a hundred times, every time I heard a footstep or a bump or a thump or a creak. Washed up this morning in the john, grabbed a clean WICH-TV T-shirt out of George's locker, and made a pot of coffee in the break room, just in time for the cops to barge in and ask me a bunch of stupid questions."

"Talk about a full day! You must be exhausted."

"I'm fine. And if you're okay, I've still got to get next door and help those guys get that video in shape to go on the air in . . ." She looked at her watch. "Cripes! Five minutes!"

"I'm good. You go right ahead."

"If you want, I'll turn your monitor back on so you can see the story they just filed from down the street."

"Sure. And thanks for warning me this time."

"Okay." She headed for the door, then turned with a mischievous grin. "But watch out for those rats."

"I'll trust the big yellow cat to catch them."

She paused in the doorway and frowned slightly. "Funny thing about that cat. He refuses to come back inside. He lives here at the station, you know. Walks around like he owns the place. I tried to call him in this morning, but he won't set foot in the building."

The door closed, and once again I was alone in the long, black-walled studio. Alone with Ariel's books and crystals and with my own thoughts and plans.

And maybe with a rat or two.

CHAPTER 6

I fanned Ariel's books out on the table. Bright graphics on the covers showed crystals, pyramids, astral charts, tarot cards—there was even a unicorn on a field of stars. Clearly, I had a lot of studying to do if I was going to pass as a credible replacement for the drowned woman.

The overhead monitor clicked to life, and Phil Archer's face appeared on-screen.

"It's not an ordinary happening here in Salem when two unusual deaths are discovered on the same day, on the same street," he began. "As many of you already know, WICH-TV's own Ariel Constellation was the victim of an apparent accidental drowning in the harbor, just behind this station's Derby Street headquarters. There has been another death on Derby Street, this one under suspicious circumstances. Scott Palmer filed this report a short time ago."

"We're on Derby Street, at the home where the body of a woman was discovered this morning." The field reporter spoke in hushed tones. "Here's Police Chief Whaley to update us on the situation."

A makeshift podium had been set up in front of a four-story, wooden tenement-style house. The chief adjusted a microphone, which squealed briefly, and began speaking.

"This morning, at approximately eleven a.m., a 911 call was received reporting the discovery of an unresponsive woman in a first-floor Derby Street apartment. The victim is a white female in her forties. Identification is being withheld pending notification of next of kin. We are treating the death as a homicide. The victim had sustained upper body trauma. A weapon has been recovered that may be associated with this case. That's all the information I can give you at this time."

He turned away from the microphone and cameras and headed for a nearby police vehicle amid cries from the press of "Chief! Hey, Chief!" and "Who found the body?"

Whaley paused before climbing into the car. "It was the landlady."

The reporters persisted.

"Where did you find the weapon, Chief?"

"In a pile of trash," he said. "But we're not sure it *is* the weapon."

The cruiser sped away. A second officer stepped forward. "No more questions right now, folks. We're waiting on the medical examiner. We'll call a news conference as soon as we have something to report."

"That was it for word from the chief," Scott Palmer announced. "But stay tuned as WICH-TV brings you an exclusive interview with the man who discovered what may be the murder weapon."

The next shot showed the field reporter with a

handheld mike, standing next to a shabbily dressed man. In the background yellow tape surrounded a trash-strewn area, a large rusted Dumpster at its center. The reporter looked into the camera, his expression serious.

"Ladies and gentlemen, this is Vergil Henry. After the chief's remarks, as the WICH-TV crew was putting away the camera equipment and preparing to return to the station, Mr. Henry approached us." He extended the mike toward the man. "Mr. Henry, would you tell our audience what you found here this morning?"

The fellow smiled, revealing missing teeth. "Well, sir, I was looking for aluminum cans in that there trash bin. It was early morn, y'know. Just turnin' light. Well, I seen this nice green plastic raincoat, all folded up neat like. I pick it up, 'cause, you know, I could use something like that, what with the rainy weather we've been gettin'." The old man paused, staring into the camera, as though he'd lost his train of thought.

Scott Palmer nodded and spoke quickly. "Yes, indeed. What happened after you saw the raincoat?"

"Oh, yeah. I pick it up, you know, and it feels kinda heavy, like there was something wrapped up in it. Well, sir, I unwrap it, and it's got one of them old-fashioned razors in it."

"A razor?"

"Yep. One of them old kind that flips out, like a switchblade knife."

"A straight razor."

"Right. And it's all wrapped up nice and neat in that raincoat. But it's a good thing I wear gloves when I'm looking for cans."

"Why is that?" Scott Palmer asked.

"The durned thing had blood on it. I don't like blood."

"So, did you just leave it there?"

"Course not. I figure the thing has to be worth something, even if some danged fool cut hisself shavin' with it. I tossed it in my shopping cart, along with the cans and stuff."

"I see." The reporter looked into the camera and then back toward the old man. "So when did you tell the police about it?"

"Soon's I heard about that lady getting herself killed over here. They was glad I kept my gloves on. Case there's some fingerprints on the thing."

"Thanks, Mr. Henry." Scott stepped away from the trash-strewn area. "Stay tuned to WICH-TV, folks, for the latest information on this tragic death. This is Scott Palmer, reporting from the scene of an apparent murder on Derby Street in Salem."

The sound clicked off, and Marty McCarthy reentered the studio. "Pretty exciting stuff, huh? The new guy did a good job, finding that old homeless dude. Looks like none of the other stations got to him yet."

"He did okay, I guess."

"You don't sound too thrilled. Can't say I blame you. I heard that you'd applied for that job, too. Tough luck." Her expression was sympathetic. "Anyway, welcome to WICH-TV."

"Thanks. Say, did you have to edit a lot in Palmer's report? It looked a little choppy in spots." I remembered the graphic scene I'd seen reflected in the black ball.

Much too gory for daytime TV.

"Yeah. We had to cut out some stuff. Palmer got a

little too close to the house, like you could see the house number in one shot. And that old guy tended to wander a little in his story. We cut some of that."

She turned, as though to leave the studio. "Oh. And naturally, we cut the part about that bloody raincoat having a WICH-TV logo on it."

I was just about to question Marty about the raincoat, and what connection the station might have to the murdered woman, when Rhonda appeared in the doorway with Aunt Ibby in tow.

"Hello, dear. I finished up at the library and thought you might like a ride home." She nodded to the brunette. "Thank you, Rhonda. It's nice to see you again."

I looked from my aunt to the receptionist. "You two know each other?"

"A reference librarian gets to know just about every high school student who needs to write a report or use a computer."

Rhonda smiled, flashing dimples I hadn't seen before. "Nice to see you, too, Miss Russell." She gave a little wave. "Gotta get back to my desk. And, Ms. Barrett, George says he can do a test taping tomorrow morning, around ten, if that's okay with you."

"That'll be fine. Thanks, Rhonda."

I introduced Aunt Ibby to Marty, and as they exchanged pleasantries, I put the tarot cards and most of the books into a pile.

"Have you collected all the things you need, Maralee?" my aunt asked.

"I think so, but I guess I should have brought a bag."

"No problem," Marty said. "We'll just grab a canvas bag from George's locker."

"Will he mind?"

"Oh, no. They're not his. Just some station give-aways. He's got a slew of 'em. Wait a sec."

She disappeared into the shadows for a moment and reappeared with a good-size canvas bag.

"This ought to do. It's plenty sturdy. You can even fit that obsidian ball in it."

"No," I said, refusing quickly. "I won't need it."

"Obsidian," said Aunt Ibby. "A most interesting material. It's really glass, volcanic in nature, you know."

I didn't know, and I didn't want to look at the thing again. "Yes," I agreed. "Interesting."

Marty chuckled. "Your niece here thought she was seeing pictures in it, until I explained that they were just reflections."

"Is that so, Maralee?" Aunt Ibby looked concerned. "Did you see pictures in it?"

"Not really," I said. "It was just a reflection from the TV monitor." I gestured to the screen overhead. "But I admit it was . . ." I reached for a word. "Unsettling."

"Yes, I imagine it might be. Are you sure you have everything you need?" She glanced around, looking at the things on the table and finally peering behind the couch. "Nothing back here except a bag of cat food. Guess it must belong to the yellow cat. By the way, what's going to become of him now that Ariel's gone?" Aunt Ibby frowned. "Did she take him home with her at night?"

Marty shook her head. "No. He didn't really belong to Ariel. He just showed up at the back door of the studio one day. Somebody let him in, and he's just stayed here. Doesn't really belong to anybody."

Aunt Ibby sighed. "Poor thing."

"I know." Marty repeated her concern about the cat, who had refused to come inside the building. "Janice put a bowl of cat food out for him this morning, but he just sniffed at it and ran away."

"What's the cat's name, anyway?" I asked.

"Ariel called him Orion."

"O'Ryan?"

"Yes. Like the constellation."

"Oh, I was thinking O'Ryan, like the Irish name."

"Cute. That suits him better." Marty smiled. "But I do worry about him. Cold weather's coming, and if he refuses to come inside, I'm afraid he'll freeze out there. Even worse, he could get run over. This is a busy street. I'd take him myself, but my apartment doesn't allow pets."

Aunt Ibby looked thoughtful. "I wonder if the station manager would let us take him to our house. I've always been good with cats, and he'd be safe there."

She was right. I remembered a series of fat, happy tabby cats during my growing-up years on Winter Street. None of them had ever run away.

"You could ask Mr. Doan," Marty said. "I'm pretty sure it'd be okay. He doesn't like cats, anyway."

"But a cat's really useful for keeping the rat population in check," I said.

"Not if he won't come inside," Marty offered reasonably. "Want me to call Doan for you?"

"Would you? I haven't officially met him yet. Seems a little soon for me to be asking for favors."

"Sure." She pulled a cell phone from her pocket. "Rhonda? Marty. Ring Doan for me, will you?" She gave me a thumbs-up. "Mr. Doan? Marty McCarthy here. Yeah. Say, look. I've found a home for that old yellow cat. Okay with you? It is? Okay. Thanks."

She put the phone away. "Piece of cake."

"Lovely!" Aunt Ibby said. "I saw the poor animal just sitting by himself under a tree. I'm going to try to coax him to come to me."

"He may not want to leave," I warned. "After all, he thinks this is his home."

"See you outside." Aunt Ibby waved my concern away and headed for the exit. I knew that determined walk. The poor cat didn't have a chance. I finished stuffing books and a couple of pamphlets into the sturdy bag and slung it over one shoulder, my handbag on the other.

"Thanks, Marty," I said, "for all your help."

"I'll come outside with you. I want to see if your aunt has corralled O'Ryan."

"I'd bet on it," I told her.

I was right. Beneath a tree stood Aunt Ibby, looking pleased, the big cat purring in her arms.

"How about that?" Marty shook her head. "Listen. I've got to get ready to shoot the cooking show. *Cool Weather Cooking with Wanda the Weather Girl.*"

I had to laugh. "Does everyone here wear two hats?"

"Pretty much. Say, why don't you run in and pick up another bag and grab that cat food? The lockers are behind the sports desk, and George's is the biggest one. It's never locked."

I did as she said, and located the locker she'd described. The locker door, marked GEORGE VALEN, stood ajar. The light was dim, but I could easily make out a pile of T-shirts, a stack of coffee mugs, and a package of canvas bags. There was a carton half full of folded

green plastic raincoats, too. Each item bore the
WICH-TV logo. I selected a bag and loaded the cat
food into it.

I looked back at the obsidian ball on the nearly
empty table. *Don't be silly. It's a chunk of volcanic glass!*

"What the hell," I muttered. I picked the thing up
and tossed it into the bag.

CHAPTER 7

I had ambitious plans for what was left of the day. I'd watch the rest of that first Ariel DVD, begin studying some of the borrowed books, and maybe finish unpacking. Not that I'd brought much with me. My Florida wardrobe wasn't suitable for fall in New England, let alone winter. I'd donated cartons of clothes to a women's shelter before I left, which meant I had some serious shopping to look forward to.

When we arrived at the Winter Street house, Aunt Ibby carried O'Ryan into the kitchen. I brought the canvas bags into the dining room and dropped them onto the long mahogany table, where there'd be plenty of room to sort through everything later.

We watched the big cat as he explored the kitchen, making a leisurely inspection of every corner of the room.

"Do you think he needs a litter box?" I wondered aloud. "Maybe that's what he's looking for."

"Nonsense. All our cats did their business in the back garden. He will, too." She sounded convinced. "I'll just take the latch off the cat door. He'll be fine.

But he must be hungry. I'll open a nice can of tuna for him. And a lovely saucer of milk."

"There's part of a package of cat food in one of the bags in the dining room. Shall I get it?"

"Oh, he doesn't want that old dry stuff, do you, O'Ryan?"

The cat gave me a disdainful "What are you thinking?" look, then curled himself around Aunt Ibby's ankles at the first whir of the can opener. He ate hungrily, took a few pink-tongued laps of the milk, and then headed straight for the old cat door, as though he'd done it all his life.

"What if he climbs over the garden wall and runs away?" I said.

"He won't. He likes it here."

Feeling slightly voyeuristic, we peeked out the kitchen window into the brick-walled garden. Sure enough, O'Ryan sniffed around Aunt Ibby's carefully tended chives, rosemary, and basil plants, then dug a neat hole under a little cedar tree and efficiently accomplished his mission. When he looked directly at the window, we both ducked behind the curtains and pretended nonchalance as the cat door creaked open. Barely glancing at us, he trotted down the hall toward the living room, where he curled up on a blue velvet throw pillow, blinked golden eyes a couple of times, and went to sleep.

"I think I'll head upstairs," I said. "I have some studying to do."

"I'll send out for pizza. It's not too late to change your mind about this job, you know."

"I know. Don't worry about me. Pizza sounds good." I returned to the dining room, selected a book on crystals, retrieved the Ariel DVDs, and headed up the stairs, filled with good intentions.

My old bedroom looked much as it had when I'd left Salem nearly ten years ago. The four-poster bed faced a fireplace, flanked by two tall bay windows, each with its own comfortable window seat. Over the white-painted mantel, where a Tom Hill painting of Yellowstone had once hung, was a new flat-screen TV. The closet held plenty of hangers, an ironing board, and iron, and the French Provincial dresser had fresh lavender-scented liners in each drawer. Aunt Ibby, as usual, had thought of everything.

Some multitasking was in order. I'd get my clothes pressed, hung, and folded while watching a few more *Nightshades* episodes. I set up the ironing board and started the Ariel DVD I'd watched before, fast-forwarding past the program we'd seen earlier. Ariel's theme music, "The Night Has a Thousand Eyes," played as the WICH-TV credits rolled.

I aimed spray starch at a cotton shirt and listened to the first caller. She said her name was Evie and she was calling to thank Ariel for some advice she'd received on a previous show.

"I feel so much better about everything now, Ariel," she said. "The kids and I are better off without him, what with him bein' so mean and all. I just want to thank you. You were so right."

"You and your boys deserve happiness, Evie. Be sure to meditate every day."

"I will, Ariel. Blessed be."

"Blessed be, Evie."

The next caller was Herbert, who gave a November

birth date and was contemplating leaving his job to work full-time as a writer.

"Have you published anything yet?" Ariel asked, silver hair ornaments bobbing. "I mean, has anyone paid you for your work yet?"

"Well, no. Not yet. But I'm working on a novel, and I think if I could spend more time on it, I can sell it for a lot of money."

I folded my one cashmere sweater carefully and watched as Ariel touched her forehead with her left hand in a meditative pose.

"Herbert, I don't see you leaving your place of employment just yet. Perhaps you already know this. You have Scorpio's mystical penetration into the secrets of the universe. You know your time will come. I feel that through your present job, you may make an important contact in the publishing business."

"I never thought about that before. We do see a lot of people there."

"Meanwhile, Herbert, if you can write just one page a day, you'll have a three-hundred-and-sixty-five-page book at the end of a year."

Once again, I was impressed with the way the psychic gave plain, commonsense answers, delivered with a sprinkling of astrological terms and metaphysical trivia.

Ariel delivered a commercial for one of the shops on Pickering Wharf, I put my Tampa Bay Buccaneers shirt on a hanger, and Aunt Ibby tiptoed into the room, bearing two big slices of pizza and a generous glass of red wine. I thanked her, nibbled and sipped, and continued ironing and folding, sorting and hanging. On the big screen Ariel's soothing voice dispelled the fears of William, who wanted to move out of his mother's house; encouraged Alicia, who wanted to go to college; and suggested that Jean and her husband get some counseling. O'Ryan appeared on-screen occasionally, sometimes sleeping on Ariel's ample lap, other times prowling about, batting at a bowl of crystals on the table or stalking along the back of the turquoise couch.

Unpacking chores complete, and with the *Nightshades* end credits rolling, I put on pajama bottoms and one of Johnny's old T-shirts and climbed into bed. Relaxing against a soft pile of pillows, I shut off the TV and picked up the book on crystals. Flipping through the pages, I found a paragraph that jumped out at me as though it had been highlighted.

When the crystal ball is not in use, it read, *it should always be covered. The purpose of the cover is not only to protect the surface from dust, but, even more importantly, to prevent random reflections, which would disturb the ball's rest period. A black silk handkerchief makes an excellent cover.*

Having recently viewed a "random reflection," I was happy to find such a quick solution to that particular problem. I'd intended to do more studying, but between that day's strange activities and the wine, I knew I couldn't stay awake much longer. Just as I began to doze off, the bed shook gently. A moist nose nudged my hand, and purring loudly, O'Ryan curled up beside me. An apologetic pink-tongued lick tickled my bandaged palm, and the unblinking golden eyes looked into mine for a long, oddly comforting moment.

CHAPTER 8

Once in a while in New England in October, there's a picture-perfect day, and I awoke to one of them. It was barely seven o'clock, and already the rising sun revealed a cloudless cerulean-blue sky. Gone was the drizzle and the dull gray of the day before, and the leaves remaining on the old maple tree outside my window seemed to glow in shades of red and gold. I'd slept surprisingly well, a deep, dreamless night's rest.

The familiar craving for morning coffee sent me padding downstairs. O'Ryan, an early riser, was already happily relaxed on the cushioned seat of a captain's chair. Before long, full coffee mug in hand, I headed for the dining room to face the contents of the canvas bags. The one with the cat's food in it would be the easiest to deal with. I carried it into the kitchen, and O'Ryan raised his head and blinked at the sound of nuggets of food being poured into a bowl. I placed it on the floor, and he sniffed at it.

He looked at me, looked at the bowl and back at me again. *Can cats sneer?* Clearly, he wasn't having any part of this menu. I dumped the food back into the open bag and folded it shut.

"Well, Mr. Fussy," I told him, "somehow my aunt has spoiled you already with a couple of cans of tuna."

With O'Ryan purring over a bowl of crabmeat chunks—we were out of tuna—and with a fresh mug of coffee in one hand and the canvas bag in the other, I returned to the dining room. Sitting down, I explored the contents of the first bag. Mostly hardcover books, a few paperbacks, tarot cards, and a small mesh bag of colorful crystals. The second bag now held only the obsidian ball. Forcing myself to look directly at its smooth black surface, I placed the ball on the table.

It's just a chunk of shiny rock. Volcanic glass.

There was a twinkling reflection of light from the chandelier overhead. Nothing more. I relaxed, leaned back in the chair, and reached for the top book in the pile. *Crystallomancy.*

I opened the purple cover and began to read.

To develop your mental powers and to learn the secrets of crystal gazing, first you must obtain a crystal ball. Now retire to a quiet room and place your crystal on a table.

So far, so good, I thought.

Your crystal ball is capable of producing a variety of visions. They may result from your own imagination. Some might be of events long forgotten, visions of past happenings. Some of these could even be occurrences unknown to the viewer. Some visions can show present or future events.

I put the book down and, resisting an urge to look at the black ball again, stared out the window. Dry leaves swirled in the brick-walled courtyard, and the yellow cat, apparently finished with his morning meal, batted at them kitten-like.

Content for the moment with the few basic facts about crystal, and wondering if obsidian even operated under the same rules, I selected another book. *A Student's Guide to the Tarot.*

I'd already learned that most of the deck was divided into suits. Cups, wands, swords, and pentacles. There was even a card called the Fool, which seemed to be a lot like the joker in modern card games. But besides these, there was a bewildering assortment of pictures and symbols, with names like Death and Judgment. I counted seventy-eight cards in Ariel's deck, none of which made the least bit of sense to me. Under the heading "The Mystery of the Tarot," I read,

The tarot is a symbolic record of human experience. Through mystic powers they provide important insight, wise counsel, and accurate divination.

"Gobbledygook," I said aloud, closing the book. No way was I going to accomplish miracles of psychological insight with a quick read.

Aunt Ibby poked her head into the room. "Did you say something, Maralee?"

"Nothing important," I said. "Good morning. I didn't hear you come down. I made coffee."

"I smelled it. Already poured a cup. You're up early."

"Doing a little studying," I said. "Say, are there any tarot card readers around?"

"In Salem? During Halloween month?" She came into the room and sat next to me. "Every self-styled witch and charlatan for miles around has set up shop in Salem, hoping to make a fortune from the tourists. Why?"

"I was just thinking, since I'm supposed to be a Gypsy of sorts, I'll need a vague idea of what a card reader does." I gestured toward the book. "This book isn't much help. I think I might get my cards read and maybe pick up a little lingo."

"I suppose . . ." Her voice trailed off as she looked at the things I'd lined up on the table. She put her coffee cup down. She picked up the purple book. "Do you really have to read all this stuff? I don't like this, Maralee. I don't like this a bit."

Surprised at her tone, I felt a little pang of guilt. Something like the way I'd felt at ten, when she'd caught me reading *The Adventurers*. But back then she'd only looked disapproving. Now she looked . . . stricken.

"Must you read this dreadful nonsense?" She waved toward my display of books. Her hand brushed against the black ball, and she pulled away, as though she'd been burned.

"Why did you bring this thing home?" She pointed a French-manicured fingertip. Her voice quavered slightly.

Alarmed, I stood up. "What's wrong? I've never

seen you like this." Kneeling beside her, I put my arm around her shoulders. She was trembling.

"I'm sorry. I'm fine." She sat up straight and patted my arm. "It's just . . . you shouldn't have brought that ball home." She looked into my eyes. "Maybe that—what happened in the studio—was just what they said. A reflection. A coincidence. But please, get rid of it. Black reflective things like that, they're bad. Bad for you."

"*Bad* for me? I don't understand."

"Are you seeing things in it? Is that why you're reading this?" She shook the purple book. "Don't bother with this skinny little thing. I have volumes on the subject."

"But why? And how did you know? Did . . . do you see things in it, too?"

Her head shake was vehement. "No! Never! And with all I've read, I've never understood why you could."

"What are you talking about?" I demanded. "And what do you think I've seen?"

"I don't know how it works. I've just always hoped it would never come back."

"That what would never come back? Do you think I really saw a murder scene in the ball?"

"Oh, my dear! Is that what you believe you saw? How horrible! It's that job. Just leave the station. Get rid of that horrid black thing."

She buried her face in her hands. The only sound was a slight creak from the cat door as O'Ryan came inside. After a moment my aunt stood slowly, extending her hand toward me. "Come with me to the study, child. I have several books you should see. We should have talked about this sooner, I know. I just . . . hoped it had gone away for good. This dreadful gift of yours."

"Gift? I don't understand."

"A gift . . . or a curse maybe . . . Hush. Come along."

I followed her from the dining room, through the kitchen, and out into the long front hall. A recent vacuuming had left neat tracks in the plush surface of a burgundy rug. My thoughts were a jumble. I concentrated on the gently curving indentations and dutifully followed my aunt upstairs, into the book-lined study.

I sat at the big mahogany desk that had belonged to Great-grandfather Forbes. I rubbed my palms along the smooth polished edges of the desktop, then folded my hands like a schoolchild. And waited.

Aunt Ibby pushed aside several volumes of *Encyclopædia Britannica,* revealing a hidden row of books at the back of the shelf. Soon the only sound was the ticking of a brass ship's clock on the wall and the intermittent *swoosh* as she slid each slim book across the desk. Soon four of them were spread in front of me.

"Here," my aunt said. "Look these over. Then we'll talk."

I read the titles. *Mirror Visions, Crystal Enlightenment, Gazers World, The Mirror and the Man.*

Questions crowded my mind. "But what—"

"Read," she said. "Just skim through them. It won't take long."

I began to read. At some point I became aware of a new sound. Purring. O'Ryan had crept into the room and was curled up at my feet. I read on.

At last I closed the fourth book. "So," I said, "you think there may be something to it? The seeing of visions, or whatever they are? Is that why you collected these?"

"Not just these," she admitted. "A lot more."

"But why? You think I . . . people . . . actually see things in crystals? In mirrors? In obsidian?"

"Particularly obsidian, in your case. Does looking into that cursed ball remind you of anything? Bring back any memories?"

I frowned and shook my head. "I don't know. I don't think so. And yet . . . there's something. Something kind of nibbling at the corners of my mind. I just can't seem to bring it into focus."

"I never wanted to have to tell you this," Aunt Ibby said. "But I think I must. You've had these visions before, Maralee. When you were a child. And they were real. I'm afraid this gift, or curse or whatever it is, may be coming back."

"I don't get it." I reached down and patted O'Ryan's soft fur. "I don't remember anything about crystals when I was a child. I don't remember any visions."

"Thing is, of course, we didn't believe you. We thought you just had an unusual imagination." She seemed to be talking to herself. "The pictures you told us about. The pictures you saw only on Sunday. You thought it was some kind of special TV."

She laughed, a small, mirthless sound. "You were only five. A cute little girl all dressed up for Sunday school. Seeing pictures grown-ups couldn't see."

I hesitated, then reached a hand toward my aunt.

"Aunt Ibby, are you all right? Maybe we'd better talk about this some other time."

"No. No, I'm fine." She stood, holding herself erect. "Come on. I've saved something all these years. Something I think you need to see. Perhaps it'll help explain what's happening to you. Maybe together we can make some sense out of all this."

Again, I followed my aunt upstairs. We walked past my room and several guest rooms to the door leading to the attic. Aunt Ibby unlocked it, and I felt in the dark for the smooth glass pull that would light the bare bulb at the head of the stairs.

"What are we looking for? Aren't you going to tell me?"

"I think I'd better show you. It may help you to remember."

We ducked our heads, avoiding the low slanted beams. Aunt Ibby knelt in front of the small bureau where I'd selected jewelry for Crystal Moon's debut.

"We went through these drawers, except for the one that was stuck," I protested. "There's not room for anything as big as a crystal ball." I looked around.

"No crystal ball. But you've seen the books. I think you are what they call a 'scryer.' Some call people who can do . . . what you do . . . 'gazers.' And gazers throughout history, all the way back to Nostradamus, even the ancient Aztecs, have used mirrors, bowls of water, sword handles, whatever was handy to do . . . what they did." Aunt Ibby opened the top drawer and removed a small key on a striped ribbon. "Apparently, a smooth polished surface is all it takes for some. Like you, I'm afraid."

"But I'm sure that over the years I've looked at a

zillion shiny surfaces. Nothing weird happened. Why now?"

She inserted the little key into the brass keyhole of the second drawer and sighed. "I don't know, Maralee. I don't know. And I just hope I'm doing the right thing."

I knelt beside my aunt and looked into the open drawer. There was a small shoe box inside.

A shoe box?

I reached down and carefully lifted the oblong cardboard box. There were cartoon animals in bright colors on the lid. I sat back on my heels. "Should I open it?"

"You must." Aunt Ibby put a protective arm around my shoulders. "I think you need to remember some things if you're ever going to make sense of what's happening to you now."

I removed the lid and pushed aside blue tissue paper.

The tiny black patent-leather shoes were still shiny.

Little Maralee Kowolski loved Sundays. She and Daddy and Mommy and Aunt Ibby would get all dressed up and go to church. Sometimes it was Daddy's church, with the pretty colored windows and the man who said funny-sounding words. Sometimes it was Aunt Ibby's church, with the plain windows and the man in the black suit. It didn't matter to Maralee. She liked both churches. The music was nice, and, anyway, if she didn't want to listen to the man talk, she could watch the pictures in the toes of her Sunday shoes.

Then one day Mommy and Daddy went on vacation. Maralee stayed at Aunt Ibby's house. On Sunday morning

*Aunt Ibby helped her get dressed in her prettiest dress. Maralee
wore ankle socks with lace on them and her shiny patent-
leather shoes.*

*"You may sit on the front steps, Maralee," said Aunt Ibby,
"while I bring the car around. Don't get dirty, will you?"*

*The little girl sat quietly and, to pass the time, looked to
see what pictures might be in her shoes. First, she saw the little
cloud. That always came first. Then the swirling colors and
twinkling lights. Then the pictures. The child clapped her
hands together in delight when she saw the image of a yellow
airplane.*

"Daddy! Mommy!" she whispered happily.

She saw the cliff. "Watch out, Daddy!" she cried.

She saw the flames.

I screamed, just as little Maralee had screamed all
those years ago. Aunt Ibby held me close, whispering
comforting words. She had done the same thing back
then, not comprehending the horror I had witnessed
in the shiny surface of my shoes.

They say that when you're drowning, your whole
life flashes before you. That moment in the attic was
like that for me, as soon as I looked at those shoes.
Long-forgotten scenes rolled by, along with glimpses
of recent events.

Again, I saw the yellow plane bursting into flames.
I saw my mother's face, mouth open in a silent
scream. I saw sad-faced people and big bouquets of
flowers. I saw my five-year-old self curled up in my
bed, unable to speak. Scenes of school days, childhood friends flashed by. I saw my wedding day. I saw
Johnny at Daytona, proudly hoisting a trophy. I

saw the black car careening toward me out of the night, and I watched my own hands on the steering wheel as I tried to get out of the way. And again, I saw Ariel's hand, floating, beckoning from the water.

I threw the shoes onto the dusty attic floor. Maybe I fainted then. I'm not sure. The screaming had stopped, and I was crying, great gulping sobs against Aunt Ibby's shoulder.

I was vaguely aware of walking downstairs, sipping a cup of hot tea, patting the yellow cat, who'd climbed into my lap. Slowly, reality returned, and I felt self-control kicking in.

"Feeling better?" Aunt Ibby's face mirrored her concern.

"Yes," I said. "Sorry I kind of lost it there."

"Oh, Maralee, forgive me. I never should have told you."

"You were right to tell me, Aunt Ibby," I assured her. "It's just so overwhelming. Things I'd forgotten are all crowding into my mind at once. I just need to sort it all out. Especially the gazing thing."

"I wish I knew how to help," she said. "From what I've read, some gazers are able to control the visions."

"Well," I said, "if I really have it, it's apparently been under control for all these years. Maybe it'll go away again."

"Maybe." She didn't sound convinced. "After it happened . . ." Her voice dropped to a near whisper. "After it happened, and you told me what you'd seen in your shoes, I still thought it was your imagination. Then the phone call came, and I knew it was real. But I didn't tell anyone about your . . . *vision*. Not a soul."

She paused, looked away, and then continued.

"After the funeral you stopped talking. Didn't speak a word for nearly six months. You walked and you ate and you looked at your books, but you couldn't be coaxed to speak. Then, one day, you began to talk again. You knew your parents were gone, of course, and you were sad about that. But you never said anything about what you had seen. Naturally, I put the shoes away and made sure you never had another pair of Mary Janes, but other shiny things, mirrors and the like, didn't seem to bother you at all. I thought . . . I hoped . . . this *thing,* whatever it is, was gone for good."

I patted her hand. "Maybe it'll never happen again. And probably what I saw in the ball was really just a reflection."

"I hope so, Maralee. I truly hope so. But you saw something in the shoes again just now, didn't you? Do you want to talk about it?"

I tried to describe what I had seen. "It went by so fast. It was all blurred together. But it was very real." The admission came with difficulty. "I'm afraid you may be right. About me being a gazer."

"I'm sure you understand now why I've tried to discourage you from taking on this psychic thing at the station. It's not a good idea. Please be sensible and tell them you won't be hosting *Nightshades.*"

"No," I said, surprising myself with the firm sound of the word. "No," I repeated in a softer tone. "What did you tell me just yesterday, before I drove to the station, when I admitted I'm still terrified every time I get behind the wheel of a car?"

Her smile was brief and wistful. "I handed you the keys to the Buick and told you to face your fear."

"And you were right. I know I have to face my fear of this . . . ability I seem to have. But I'm still struggling. I'm not sure how to handle it."

"I understand. But what are you going to do about it?"

"I don't know," I admitted. "It's too new. I'm afraid to even think about using it for anything. But I'm going to try to keep the *Nightshades* job. It's just an acting gig, after all, and it won't be forever. I'm sure something better will open up before too long."

The ringing of the telephone interrupted my thoughts of what "something better" might possibly be.

"It's for you, Maralee," my aunt stage-whispered. "And it's the *police!*"

She handed me the phone.

"Ms. Barrett? Pete Mondello. I spoke to you yesterday?"

"Yes, Detective. I remember you."

"Uh, Ms. Barrett, the chief asked me to call you about some items you removed from the station."

"I beg your pardon?"

"The chief is on his way over to the studio, and, well, it would be a good idea if you brought all that stuff you took back. Save an officer from going to your house. With the neighbors watching and all."

What on earth is this man talking about?

"Of course I'll return the books and cards," I told him. "And the obsidian ball."

"You're coming over right away?"

What is the big rush about some cheap books and a chunk of glass?

"Yes, sure." I tried to keep the annoyance out of my

voice and was not sure I'd succeeded. "I'll be right along." I hung up.

"What was that all about?" Aunt Ibby wanted to know.

"It was that detective who interviewed me yesterday. Mondello," I said. "I have no idea what he was talking about, but apparently, they're in a big hurry to get Ariel's things back."

"The police need Ariel's things? Do you suppose they're thinking she didn't fall in by accident? That she was pushed—"

"I don't know what they think," I interrupted. "And you read too many mysteries! I'll pick up Ariel's stuff and get down there."

"Want me to come along?" She looked worried.

"If you really want to."

"I do," she said. "Let's go."

We dressed quickly for the cool October morning. I dumped Ariel's things into a WICH-TV canvas bag and looked around to make sure I hadn't missed anything. "Not much point in returning half a bag of cat food, I guess."

"I'll take it to the animal shelter later," Aunt Ibby said, "where the cats aren't so picky. I certainly hope they don't think I'll be returning the cat! Come on. I'll drive."

CHAPTER 9

As Aunt Ibby approached the green expanse of Salem Common, she slowed the Buick and pointed. "Look, Maralee."

A huge striped tent now covered the area from the wrought-iron fence to the bandstand. A sign proclaimed PSYCHIC FAIR – THREE DAYS ONLY – 12 PSYCHICS – NO WAITING – READINGS ONLY $25 EACH!

"Maybe I can pick up all the psychic lingo I'll need with one twenty-five-dollar stop," I said.

"Worth a try," Aunt Ibby agreed. "Maybe you can walk over later today."

When we reached the WICH-TV parking lot, police cars with lights flashing barred both entrances, so we circled the block and found a space on a nearby side street. I grabbed the canvas bag, and we walked the short distance to the station.

With every driveway and even the front doorway blocked, I had no idea what I was supposed to do next. I glanced around, looking for Detective Mondello. A uniformed officer standing beside one of the patrol cars noticed my confusion.

"Can I help you, miss?"

"I'm Lee Barrett," I said. "Detective Mondello is expecting me."

"You got ID?"

I pulled out my wallet and handed him my Florida driver's license. He squinted at it for a long moment, then handed it back. He nodded toward Aunt Ibby.

"You with her, Miss Russell?"

Library buddy? Facebook friend? Does she know everybody?

"She's my niece, Patrick. How's your mother?"

"She's fine, thanks. Go on back, you two. Chief Whaley's waiting down by the water."

"Patrick's mom is in my Zumba class," my aunt explained as we crossed the lot.

Chief Tom Whaley was a big cop. I'm five-eight, close to six feet in heels, and he towered over me.

"Ms. Barrett?"

"Yes, sir."

He looked at Aunt Ibby. "And you are . . . ?"

"Isobel Russell. Maralee is my niece."

"You work at the library. I've seen you there."

"Yes. What's all this about?"

He consulted a notebook, and I looked around. Everything seemed a lot different than it had the day before. Felt different, too. The yellow tape now read CRIME SCENE, instead of DO NOT CROSS. A paneled truck marked CSI was parked nearby, and several jumpsuited technicians had congregated beside the wall, close to the spot where I'd found the buzzing phone. A few yards away stood a group of people in lab coats. At their feet, in a neat, still row, were the bodies of five dead seagulls.

I nudged Aunt Ibby.

A few dead birds in a parking lot hardly constitute a crime scene!

My aunt put my thought into words. "Chief Whaley, it's certainly a shame about those poor birds, but killing birds isn't a real crime, is it?"

He snapped the notebook shut. "Of course not. We're investigating a homicide here."

"You mean . . . Ariel?" I asked.

He ignored my question. "Do I understand that you have been hired to replace the deceased, uh, psychic?"

"Yes. That is . . . ," I stammered. "I think I have the job. I don't have a contract yet."

"You spoke with someone about that job within a few hours of the discovery of the body?"

"Yes. Janice Valen."

Once again he consulted the notebook. "And you were the person who discovered the body?"

"Yes."

"At approximately what time did you discover it?"

"A little past nine."

He scribbled in the notebook. "And how did you happen to be in this area?"

"Well, as I explained to Detective Mondello yesterday, I'd just been told that the job I wanted had already been filled. So I came down here for my car." I gestured toward the space where the Buick had been. "That's when I heard a phone buzzing. I went to the wall to see what it was, and then I saw the body."

His uh-huh sounded skeptical. He lifted the yellow tape so the three of us could duck under. The CSI people paused as we approached. One motioned to the chief.

"What's up?" the chief asked, frowning.

"There's a trace of blood on the pavement here," was the reply. "We're swabbing it now."

Aunt Ibby couldn't remain silent any longer. "So Ariel's drowning wasn't an accident?"

"No, ma'am. We don't think so."

Aunt Ibby persisted. "Why?"

"I guess there's no harm in telling you. It will be in all the papers. The fingers on both of her hands were broken. As though someone had stepped on them. With heavy boots." He looked pointedly at my booted feet and then directly into my eyes. "Does that bag contain the articles you took from the *Nightshades* set?"

I handed him the bag. "I didn't *take* anything. I borrowed a few props—with permission."

"I see." His tone was almost casual. "Can you account for your whereabouts at around midnight the night before last?"

"Of course I can," I snapped. "My aunt picked me up at Logan Airport around eleven. I flew nonstop from Tampa. It took about forty minutes to get to our house. Then we sat up and talked for a while."

"That right?" He faced Aunt Ibby, who looked ready to explode.

"Of course it's right! Why are you interrogating my niece?"

"Just routine, ma'am," he said in the same tone. He motioned to a uniformed officer and handed the canvas bag to the man. "Take this inside and give it to Mondello to inventory."

"So," he said, looking down at me with that stern

expression on his craggy face. "Miss Russell here can vouch for your whereabouts during the night of the murder."

"Yes," I said, trying hard to mask my resentment. "She will. Why are you asking? You can't seriously think that I had anything to do with Ariel's death."

"Just routine," he said again, and again consulted the notebook. Aunt Ibby and I stood there in silence. A wrinkled tarpaulin had been placed over the dead birds, and a chill wind stirred up the harbor. Whaley looked toward the sky, where dark clouds marred the lovely blue I'd admired earlier.

"Rain on the way," he said. "We'll finish up inside." He opened a heavy door in the side of the building leading to the black-walled studio. It took a moment for my eyes to adjust to the gloom. I took Aunt Ibby's arm, and we followed him to the *Nightshades* set.

Detective Mondello was there, along with George Valen. I made quick introductions to my aunt. The cards and books and the black ball were once again arranged on Ariel's table.

"Are these the items you returned, Ms. Barrett?" the chief asked.

"Yes," I said. "They're all there."

He flipped a page of the notebook. "It says here that you took a bag of cat food and a cat."

Aunt Ibby assumed a hands-on-the-hips position, which I recognized. She was irate. "The station manager gave me the cat!" she said.

The chief held up his hand. "Don't worry, Miss Russell. No one wants the cat back." He returned his attention to me. "Where's the bag of cat food now?"

"It's at my aunt's house," I said. "The cat wouldn't eat it. I didn't think it was important to bring it back."

"I'll send an officer to pick it up. Now, is there anything else you want to tell me? Any more items you might have borrowed from the station?"

"No, sir. But there is one thing I think you need to know."

"What's that?" Once more the pencil was poised over the notebook.

I extended my hands, palms up, exposing the adhesive bandages covering scraped and bruised skin.

"I'm afraid the bloodstains out there in the parking lot might be mine."

CHAPTER 10

I explained how I'd tripped over the cat, cutting and scraping both hands and knees. The chief, expressionless, wrote in his notebook, then glanced down at me. "Any witnesses to this, uh, fall?"

"I don't think so," I admitted.

"Say, Chief," Detective Mondello said, "I think I was the first one to interview Ms. Barrett here after she found the body, and, well, I noticed that her, um, stockings were ripped."

"Was that in your report, Detective?"

"No, sir. It didn't seem important."

"How did you happen to notice this seemingly unimportant detail, Detective?"

Mondello colored slightly. "I was, well, looking at her legs, sir—"

George interrupted. "I saw her before she found the body, Chief. Definitely no rips then."

"Looking at her legs, too, were you, Mr. Valen?"

"Right," the cameraman said. "Guilty."

Aunt Ibby spoke up. "Chief Whaley, I can vouch for the fact that my niece left the house for her interview with her hose perfectly intact. She returned with scraped hands and knees. That should put the matter to rest. Am I correct?"

Whaley snapped his notebook shut, nodding in my aunt's direction. "Yes, ma'am." He turned to face me. "We'll ask you to allow us to swab your mouth for a matchup. And we may as well take a set of fingerprints at the same time. Permission?"

"Okay," I agreed, but he was already phoning the CSI techs, ordering swab and print kits. In less than a minute, two of the jumpsuited techs appeared. One stuck a skinny swab into my mouth, sealed the thing in a plastic tube, slapped a label on it, and put it in a poly bag marked EVIDENCE. At the same time the other one inked my fingers and pressed each one onto a pad.

George Valen watched, unsmiling. "Look, Chief," he said, "we have to prepare a show, and we only have a couple of days to do it. Can we use this set? Is it all right to handle Ariel's props or not?"

"We'll probably be finished up in here late today or early tomorrow," Whaley said. "Then it's all yours." He turned toward Mondello. "Tape this area, Pete. I'll be down the street at the other murder site if you need me."

George motioned for Aunt Ibby and me to follow him toward the double doors leading to the newsroom. "Lee, want to do a test video today and get it over with? We can use another set and fake up a couple of props."

"Well, sure. I guess. Costume and all?"

"Yep. I know I'm rushing you. You've had a busy couple of days." He pushed open the doors.

"She sure has!" The click of high heels and a whiff of J'adore announced Janice Valen's presence. "How're you guys doing? Rhonda says Whaley looked steamed when he came in."

"He was really annoyed about the stuff I borrowed from the set. And they think Ariel was murdered," I said.

"I know. That's why I came in. This was supposed to be my morning off." She sounded testy. "Doan's not too happy about all this, either. Seems Whaley questioned him for about half an hour last night about that stupid WICH-TV raincoat. Are we going to be able to do Lee's test? Doan wants it ASAP."

"Just now trying to schedule it," George said. "We'll have to use another set, though. The cops are still messing around with Ariel's."

"Great. The whole damned city's going to be festooned with yellow tape by Halloween, what with the murder down the street and Ariel taking a header off the wall." Janice nodded toward Aunt Ibby. "You must be Lee's aunt. Rhonda told me about you. Sorry you have to be involved in all this."

"How do you do?" Aunt Ibby offered her hand. Janice shook it briefly, then turned her attention back to George. "I've called Marty to come in and help deal with this mess. She'll be able to mouse up some kind of set for the test. I'll sweet-talk the cops into clearing the regular one in time for the show."

"Good idea," George said. "We're going to shoot the test today. Can you stick around to make some fake calls for Lee . . . Crystal Moon . . . to answer?"

"Oh, all right. Just call when you need me." She

waved a hand toward me. "And don't worry about
Doan liking the test. He'll like it fine."

"I hope so," I said. "Will he find a red-haired Gypsy
believable?"

"Red-haired and overqualified. Doesn't matter. Too
late for him to find anyone else. Just go for it."

"And what's so wrong about being overqualified?"
Aunt Ibby wanted to know.

"They always think you'll want more than they're
willing to pay," George explained. "And that you'll
leave the minute something better comes along."

"I'm not too worried about the money part," I said,
"but I was really hoping for something better. I came
here in the first place to audition for the field reporter's job, you know, but that Palmer guy beat me
to it."

The green door opened, and Scott Palmer strode
toward us.

"Well, speak of the devil! Hi, Scotty!" Janice was
suddenly all smiles. "We're figuring out how to make
a temporary *Nightshades* set for the overqualified,
red-haired Gypsy here." She pointed an accusing
finger in his direction. "Seems you grabbed the job
she wanted, so you can help."

Scott shook his head, clearly confused. "Sure. Glad
to help out." He moved closer and stared at me intently. "Who are you? And how did I grab your job?"

George made the quick introductions. "Didn't realize you two hadn't met yet, with all the excitement
around here. Lee Barrett, aka Crystal Moon, Scott
Palmer. And this lady is Lee's aunt, Ms. Russell."

There was a chorus of "Hi there" and "Glad to meet you" and "How do you do?"

George wasn't going to waste a minute with any further niceties. "Okay. Let's get started. Lee, want to run home and pick up whatever you're planning to wear?"

"Good idea." Janice smoothed her butter-soft tan leather skirt over slim hips and turned slowly, pausing to study each shadowy set in the long room. "Can we get some lights on in here?" She gestured toward the ceiling.

"Got it!" came an answering voice. Lights flooded the studio as Marty moved toward us, clipboard in hand. "What's up?"

Does she never sleep? Doan was certainly getting more than the requisite two jobs from the gray-haired camerawoman.

"We can't use Ariel's set for Lee's test. Need to fix one up, pronto," Janice said. "Can do?"

"Can do." Marty moved quickly down the center aisle. "The sports desk will work. It's pretty plain. A hunk of cloth over the table and a little bit of hocus-pocus crap on top should do the trick."

"Sounds good. Do it." With that carefully practiced model's walk, Janice left the studio.

"Maralee, why don't I just run along home and pick up your outfit? You stay and help get things ready here," Aunt Ibby offered.

Made sense to me. "Okay. Thanks." I waved a quick good-bye to my aunt, wondering how helpful I might be to the superefficient Marty or the very professional George. And Scott Palmer probably didn't know any more about what a psychic's temporary surroundings should look like than I did.

In the end, it wasn't that difficult. George tossed a length of yellow velvet fabric over the sports desk, explaining that it was the skirt to the annual lobby Christmas tree. Marty provided a potted silk chrysanthemum for seasonal color, along with a ceramic black cat. Scott and I tacked up a couple of posters advertising the upcoming Halloween Witches Ball, neatly covering the sports logos on the backdrop.

"Good enough," George said. "All we need for Doan is general effect. The *Nightshades* regulars want to see a bunch of mystical tchotchkes like Ariel has . . . had." His nice smile had disappeared. He looked almost angry. "They really swallow that psychic crap, hook, line, and sinker."

"Seems you don't think much of it," Scott said.

"I was raised with it. My mother didn't make a move without checking her horoscope, talking to her quartz crystals, and reading her tea leaves. And God only knows how much money she spent on séances, card readings, and astrological charts and other stupid shit. Drove us kids nuts."

"A real believer, huh?" Scott said. "Your dad, too?"

"Nope. She finally drove him off altogether. Some nutcase card reader told her that true love was in her future. So she dumped the old man."

"Did she ever find it? True love?" I asked.

"Of course not." He laughed. "And Sarge was probably glad to have a reason to leave for good."

"Sarge?"

"Yeah. Our dad was career army. We were army

brats. Moved around from base to base. State to state. Country to country."

"My folks moved around a little," Scott said. "But nothing like your family did. Did you enjoy it?"

"What was that like? Having all that travel opportunity?" I wondered aloud. "I had the same address until after I'd finished college."

George paused for a long moment, adjusting the velvet drapery. "I liked taking pictures everywhere we went. That's how I knew I wanted to be a photographer. My mother gave me my first camera when I was twelve. There are albums full of shots I took when I was a kid. But I hated changing schools, leaving friends, that part."

"And Janice?" I asked.

He shrugged. "She was pretty young. She doesn't seem to remember much about those days. She—" His buzzing cell phone interrupted. "Yes, Rhonda? What's up? Sure. Bring it down, will you?" He tucked the phone back into his shirt pocket. "Lee, your aunt dropped off your clothes. Says to call her when you need a ride home."

Things were moving fast. Rhonda dashed into the studio, tossed a garment bag toward one of the tall stools behind the sports desk. "Gotta run," she gasped. "Doan's on a tear."

Marty rescued the bag as it began to slide toward the floor. "Look, you guys, I'll hang this in the dressing room and fool around with the set a little more." She looked at her watch. "Why don't you three grab lunch somewhere and we can shoot this thing when you get back?"

"Good idea. I'm starving." George gave the velvet cloth a final tug.

"Me too," Scott said with a broad wink. "Maybe Lee will tell me how I got a reputation as a job grabber."

"Don't worry about it. No big deal," I said. "And, Marty, won't you please come with us?"

"Nah." She waved the invitation aside. "I brought a sandwich. Anyway, I'd rather putz around here, make sure everything is ready."

"Come on. Let's go." George was already on his way to the outside exit. "Marty loves this place. She'd never leave if she didn't have to. Isn't that right, Marty?"

The reply was a dismissive "Get outta here!"

I remembered Marty's story about sleeping on Ariel's couch the night of the murder, getting a clean shirt from George's locker, and making coffee in the break room. I wondered if she was in the habit of sleeping here, just like O'Ryan used to.

"We'll be over at the bar if you need me," George told her.

"Won't need you. Nothing here I can't handle." Marty was firm.

"Okay." George looked at Scott and me. "The Pig's Eye isn't really just a bar. They have great sandwiches. Everybody from the station goes there. It's close, and the food is always good."

"I'm sorry Marty isn't coming," I said. "She's so sad about Ariel. I'm sure you all are."

"Not so much." George's laugh was short and unfunny. "She'd made some enemies here. Doan will miss the ratings and the revenue. That's about it."

In A Pig's Eye was just a couple of blocks down

Derby Street. The three of us walked briskly, facing into an increasingly chill northeast wind, with George leading the way. Scott and I followed along the narrow sidewalk, dodging wind-borne dry leaves. The warm, food-fragrant atmosphere of the cozy restaurant was welcoming and friendly.

"Service is faster at the bar," George said, shepherding us toward tall stools.

"Hi, George," said the pretty barmaid. "You're early. Brought along some friends today, I see."

"Yep. Couple of new hires at the station. Lee and Scott. Thought we'd beat the lunch-hour rush. Can we see some menus?"

"Sure thing." She slid three menus across the polished wood surface. "Can I get you folks something to drink?"

George ordered a beer, Scott asked for black coffee, and I opted for sweet tea. Studying the menu did away with the necessity for small talk, and I had just taken my first sip of tea when George's phone buzzed.

"Yes, Mr. Doan." I could hear the rumbling tone of the station manager's voice but couldn't make out the words. "Yes, sir. Right away," George said. "Palmer's right here with me. We're on our way."

"What's going on?" Scott asked, already on his feet.

"Jesus! Come on, Scotty. Let's roll! Something's happening at the station." George headed for the door, Scott close behind. "Lee! Tell the girl to put those drinks on my tab."

I could only nod wordlessly. The restaurant door swung open, and an instant later the two men passed the mullioned windows, both at a dead run toward the station.

In a few minutes I was headed in that direction myself, wind at my back, wondering what could have caused the hasty exit. But then, George and Scott were newspeople and had to be ready to jump and run at a moment's notice.

That could just as well have been me. I would have been glad to jump and run.

I looked down at my high-heeled boots. Well, maybe I couldn't run quite as fast. But I would be a good news reporter. And maybe it would have been Mr. Scott Palmer leaving a tip for the barmaid and tagging along behind. My smile at that thought faded as I crossed Derby Street and approached the station.

What now?

The police cars were back, lights flashing, blocking the entrance to the parking lot. I climbed the granite stairs to the station's front door, entered the lobby, and began the slow elevator ride to the second floor. I pushed open the glass door.

"Rhonda? You here?"

"Over here. Jeez! Look at that, will ya?"

I circled the curved reception desk and joined Rhonda at the window. "What's going on out there? George and Scott took off like a couple of Indy cars."

"Yep. They're both down there already. Camera rolling. See 'em?"

She pointed. Scott faced George's camera. But it was what was going on behind Scott, out in the harbor, that made me gasp.

"What is that? Who are they? My God, what are they doing?"

Just beyond the seawall, almost in a direct line from where I'd first seen Ariel's floating body, was a long, gray barge-like vessel. And along a low rail running the length of the thing stood a row of black-clad figures.

"Who are they?" I asked again, my voice dropping to a whisper. "It looks like they're throwing something in the water."

"Herbs," came Marty's voice from behind me. "Potions. Bats' wings. Eyes of newt. Who knows what the crazies are polluting the harbor with."

"But why?" I couldn't take my eyes from the spectacle below.

"They look like witches," Rhonda said. "Real witches."

"It must be about Ariel somehow." I tried to piece things together.

"It's her coven," Marty announced. "Ariel was their queen."

CHAPTER 11

Marty's announcement just sort of hung there in the purple and turquoise atmosphere. Rhonda, eyes wide, gasped and brought both hands to her mouth. I focused my attention on the strange assemblage bobbing on the waves in their barge-like boat. Thoughts of Ariel, her pentagram ring on a broken finger, her crystals and books and the obsidian ball, crowded my mind.

What have I gotten myself into?

I broke the silence. "Are they filming this down there?" I looked toward the blank monitor behind Rhonda's desk. "Is it on the air?"

"Sure. I guess so. The noon news should be on." The receptionist reached for a button on her console. The screen came to life, and Scott's voice, with the cries of seagulls in the background, filled the room.

"And what can you tell us about these . . . er . . . witches?" Scott stood in front of the now drooping yellow tape, facing a young woman. She wore a black robe, similar to those on the vessel-borne people in the background.

"Well," she replied, "I belong to a different coven, but I knew Ariel. She was very important in the Wiccan community."

"I see," said Scott, not sounding as though he really did. "Is there a large Wiccan community here in Salem?"

She gave him a "you've got to be kidding" look. "In Salem? Sure. There are about two or three thousand of us living here. And naturally, near Halloween, a lot more come to visit."

"Do you know what those folks out there"—he gestured toward the boat—"are doing exactly?"

"Yes. They're sanctifying the site of Ariel's crossing over."

"Sanctifying? How?"

"With certain herbs and potions and spells. To help her cross over, you know. We're all trying to help, but it's so difficult."

"Difficult? How so?"

"She won't be able to reach the light until whoever killed her is caught and punished." She smiled. "To be honest, she probably doesn't want to."

"Well, thank you for talking to us." Scott ended the interview abruptly.

Don't end it there, dummy! I wanted to shout at the screen. *Ask more questions! Ask her why she thinks Ariel doesn't want to reach the light—whatever that means.* I should have his job instead of this Gypsy masquerade. It should be me down there talking to a witch. I was positive of that.

"Uh-oh. Here comes the Coast Guard." Marty pointed toward the upper left corner of the screen. An orange and white boat sped toward the witches. It had obviously attracted Scott's attention, too, accounting for the quick dismissal of the young witch.

Okay, so maybe you're not a dummy.

There was a chiming sound. Rhonda returned to her desk and punched a lighted button.

George's voice crackled over the speaker.

"Tell Marty to grab a camera and get down here! All hell is breaking loose. The Coast Guard is on the way, and there's a bunch of church people across the street, yelling about something. I can't cover it all, and Scotty is going nuts trying to keep up with it."

Marty took off running, and Tim Walker, the noon anchor, cut in from the newsroom. "Stay tuned, folks, as this story continues to develop." A thirty-second commercial was followed by a split-screen view from the WICH-TV parking lot. On the left screen was Scott, the witch barge, and the Coast Guard boat. On the right a small crowd of men and women carrying signs paraded on the sidewalk across the street. The anchor rambled on, giving George, Marty, and Scott time to figure out the best way to cover the chaos.

"This station's late-night host, known locally as Ariel Constellation, drowned under questionable circumstances in Salem Harbor. Police suspect foul play, and an investigation of the area continues. During the past half hour a group of people tentatively identified as members of a Wiccan organization have positioned a boat close to shore, and now the vessel has been boarded by Coast Guard personnel. At the same time a group of citizens has gathered on a sidewalk in front of the station, carrying protest signs. Now back to field reporter Scott Palmer. Bring us up to date, Scott, if you can, on what's going on out there."

"Thanks, Tim. It's quite a scene here. Neither of the groups appears to have crossed police lines, and Salem Coast Guard reports that the Wiccans have the correct number of life preservers and proper vessel documentation. But they've thrown unidentified substances into the harbor, which is a violation of the Massachusetts Clean Water Act, and they're being cited for that. The protestors on the sidewalk claim to be members of a fundamentalist church and seem to be assembling peacefully. We'll update you as the story unfolds."

The left side of the screen showed the witch barge moving slowly away from shore. The camera on the right scanned the sidewalk crowd. A large woman in the foreground, wearing a purple hat, brandished a hand-lettered sign that read THOU SHALT NOT SUFFER A WITCH TO LIVE. Next to her a man waved one that advised CAST OUT DEMONS.

"Oh boy!" Rhonda cried. "There's Mrs. Doan!"

I looked from right to left on the split screen. "Mrs. Doan? Where?" Could the boss's wife possibly be a witch? Or was she one of the fundamentalist sign wavers?

"The one in the purple hat." Rhonda pointed at the screen. "See? She loves purple. She decorated this place."

That explains a lot, I thought, glancing around at the purple-toned flower arrangement and the purple leather furniture.

Scott had brought the young witch into camera range again. "What about those signs?" he asked. "Does this sort of protest happen often?"

She sighed. "It does. Especially around Halloween.

Sometimes they come here by the busload. They march in front of the Salem Witch Museum and the magic shops. Some of the psychics and card readers hire security guards to keep them from scaring customers away."

Will a big phony psychic like Crystal Moon need a security guard?

Scott moved closer to the witch. "Do they frighten you?"

"Not really. I don't think they mean to harm us. But they don't seem to realize that Wicca is a recognized religion. This is America! We have as much right to our religion as they do to theirs!"

"Wow!" Rhonda pointed to the monitor. "Marty must have recognized Mrs. Doan. Look at that close-up!"

She was right. The purple-hatted woman's face filled the screen on the right, features distorted into a grimace. The sound was indistinct, but it was easy to read the thin lips.

"The witch is dead. Praise God."

"There's Mr. Doan!" Rhonda pointed again at the screen. "He sure got down there in a hurry!"

The station manager had moved into the picture, approaching his wife. He put one arm around her shoulders and, with the other arm, waved the camera away. Marty quickly shifted to another protester, whose sign proclaimed A SORCERESS SHALL BE PUT TO DEATH.

"How did he get down there so fast?" I was puzzled. "I thought he was in his office."

"So did I." Rhonda snorted a little laugh. "He probably used his secret staircase. He does that sometimes when he's in a hurry. Or ducking someone he doesn't want to see."

"A secret staircase? Like the one in the House of the Seven Gables?" Thoughts of school excursions to the old Salem home made famous by Nathaniel Hawthorne popped into my mind. Climbing up and down the crooked hidden staircase was always the high point of the field trips.

"No. Nothing that interesting. Just an old flight of stairs that goes to a door at the back of the building. Janice says that it was probably an old-fashioned fire escape."

"No kidding. What does it look like?"

"I don't know." She shrugged. "He always keeps the door to it locked."

Tim Walker's image returned to the screen, and the waterfront and sidewalk scenes disappeared. A "Breaking News" crawl appeared at the top of the picture.

"Chief Whaley of the Salem Police Department has just issued a statement regarding the murder of Yvette Pelletier," Walker announced. "A witness has given a description of a man seen in the vicinity of the Pelletier apartment on the evening of the Salem woman's death. The man, who police are calling 'a person of interest,' was wearing what the witness describes as a military-style camouflage suit with a hood-type head covering. Police have requested tapes from surveillance cameras along Derby Street in hopes that one or more of them might have captured a view of this man. Anyone with information about this person, or anything unusual you might have observed in the area on Thursday afternoon or evening, is asked to call the number at the bottom of your screen. Tune in to the WICH-TV six o'clock news for the latest on this and other stories."

"I suppose the police already have the video of the parking lot here," I said, "because of what happened to Ariel."

"I don't know anything about it," Rhonda said. "You'll have to ask George or Janice. The computer that records all that security stuff is in the control room." She clicked off the sound but not the picture on the monitor. The regular programming had resumed with a network feature on rescue pets. "Doan likes this thing on all day, but it gets really annoying after a while. I'm not allowed to watch any other channels. Like the ones with the good soaps."

Click. Away went the cute puppies and kitties.

I mumbled a noncommittal "Uh-huh" and returned to the window. The witch barge was no longer in sight, and the Coast Guard boat was a dot on the horizon. George and Scott were gone. If the protesters had left, too, Marty was probably already in the studio, waiting for me.

I was right. The dressing room door stood open. My skirt and blouse hung on a rolling rack, and I could see the folded shawl and bright jewelry neatly arranged on a tabletop. Aunt Ibby had sent along the astrology book, too, and it was propped against a large makeup kit. The redecorated sports area was fully lighted. A papier-mâché jack-o'-lantern had been added to the set, casting an orange glow onto the desk. A couple of plastic bats, dangling from invisible wires, added to the Halloween theme.

"Look okay to you?" Marty appeared from behind the poster-covered backdrop.

"Looks great."

"Hop into your Gypsy rig, then, and let's get this show on the road. Want Rhonda to do your makeup?"

"Rhonda?"

"Yeah. She's a Mary Kay rep. Does a damn good job, too. She does Wanda the Weather Girl and most of the guys."

So even Rhonda has two jobs. Wonder what Doan will think up for me?

"Thanks, anyway. I'm used to doing my own."

"That's fine. Ariel did her own, too."

I dressed quickly, brushed my hair and gave it a quick spray, patted on some matte makeup, added a generous amount of mascara and eyeliner, and applied bright red lipstick. Gold earrings and a few strands of beads completed the look. I turned from side to side in front of the mirror. *Not bad for a hurry-up job.* I stepped out into the studio.

"Start out standing in front of the set so Doan can get a good look at you," Marty advised. "Then you can sit behind the desk for the rest of the show if you want to."

"That'll work," I said. "I've got a book here I might want to peek at. Thought I'd keep it on my lap, out of camera range." I put the book on a tall stool behind the desk, then positioned myself in front of the Halloween display. "How's this?"

"Good. Here's the plan. Introduce yourself. Say something nice about Ariel. Read a commercial off the teleprompter. I picked an easy one. No tricky words." She looked pleased about that. "Read the intro to the movie. Then you'll take a couple of fake calls. Piece of cake."

"Piece of cake," I repeated, hoping I sounded as confident as she did.

Marty looked into her camera, then back at me. "Say, does that blouse come down off the shoulders?"

"Uh, yes."

"Pull it down more. Doan likes to see skin." She ducked back behind the camera and quickly popped back out again. "On the good-looking ones. Not Ariel."

I thought about Mrs. Doan, with scorn for the dead psychic showing plainly on her face, and about her husband, with a protective arm around her shoulders amid the waving of hateful signs.

What sort of people am I mixed up with?

I tugged the blouse a little lower and faced the camera, waiting. The red light winked on. I leaned forward slightly, cocked my head at an angle I knew would emphasize my cheekbones and accent my eyes.

"Good evening, friends of *Nightshades*. My name is Crystal Moon. I'm here to guide you as we search together for universal truth and answers to the many mysteries of this and other worlds. As you know, our dear Ariel has crossed over. I am sure that she wishes to send her message of love and light to all of you."

Focusing my attention on the teleprompter, I read a thirty-second commercial for a New Age bookstore. Marty indicated approval, raising her hand to give me the okay sign. Encouraged, I moved on to the introduction of the movie.

"Prepare to be terrified, friends of the night. Did you ever wish that you could know what was going to happen in the near future? Think again as we prepare to watch *Torture Garden*. You may change your mind after you see this 1967 classic. Burgess Meredith stars as Dr. Diablo. Enjoy."

The red light winked off.

"So far, so good," Marty said. "Ready for some phony phone calls?"

"I guess so." I moved to the seat behind the desk, then opened the book on my lap.

There'd be no teleprompter for this. What kind of questions would there be? All I had to go on was my brief viewing of one of Ariel's DVDs.

"Janice?" Marty used a throat mike, and her voice reverberated in the long room. "You ready to be the caller?"

"Ready." Janice's disembodied voice was amplified, too. "Crystal, a flasher on the console will let you know when there's a caller on the line. Just press the green button when you're ready. Got it?"

The console was close to my right hand. I'd used similar models on the shopping channel back in Florida.

"Got it," I said, and all of a sudden getting this silly little job seemed very important.

The flasher blinked. I took a deep breath. With my scraped hand shaking ever so slightly, I pressed the green button.

CHAPTER 12

"Hello, caller," I said. "Your first name and your question please."

"'Ello, ducks." It was Janice with a broad Cockney accent. "This is Audrey."

"Hello, Audrey. Do you have a question?"

"Yes, indeed, luv." She sounded like Eliza Doolittle before the elocution lessons. "Me daughter is datin' a bloke I don't like much. What do you think will come of it?"

"His name?" I pressed my fingers to my temples and closed my eyes, Ariel fashion.

"Oh, 'is name is 'Erbie."

Fighting an urge to smile, I opened my eyes and spoke carefully. "Audrey, your first impression of this man may be correct. But I feel that your daughter resents your interference. Yes?"

She sighed. "Don't they all, though?"

"Well, perhaps if you can stop criticizing Herbie so much, your daughter may get bored with him and explore the universe further. I feel that her true soul mate has yet to find her."

"That makes sense, luv. I'll give it a try. Thank you, Crystal."

"You're welcome, Audrey. Peace and love to you and your daughter."

The next voice was so convincing, I almost forgot that I was talking to Janice. This time she pretended to be a teenage boy named Paul.

"Hey, Crystal," he said. "Hi. Listen. I got a chance to take an afternoon job at the Stop & Shop. Baggin' groceries, y'know? But my mom says I should be spendin' that time on my schoolwork. But I need the money to buy a car. So what's up with that?"

"I understand, Paul," I said. "When is your birthday?"

"My birthday? Uh, May thirtieth. Why?"

Mostly to give me time to think.

I flipped the book in my lap open to the chapter on Gemini. "Because, Paul, your zodiac sign tells me that you change your mind very often about what you want to do. Are your marks in school important to you?"

"Sure. I have to get into college. I only have another year of high school."

"Is getting into college next year more important than having a car right now?"

"I guess so."

"Mom may be right on this one, Paul. Think about it carefully. Love and light to you."

Janice made one more call, this time as a woman who wanted to know if Crystal Moon could help her find her lost dog. I told her that I felt that her pet was being cared for, and suggested that she contact the Salem Animal Rescue League for assistance.

"Okay. That's a wrap." Marty rolled her camera away from the set. "Nice goin', kid."

"Thanks. I hope Mr. Doan likes it." I stood, glad to stretch tense muscles. "Can I thank Janice for her help? The calls were great."

"Sure. Janice, you still there?"

"I'm here," came the amplified voice.

"Can you come down here for a minute?"

"No can do, Marty. I'm talking to you from home sweet home. Wicked headache. What's up?"

"Lee here wanted to thank you."

"Put her on."

Marty handed me her mike. "Thanks, Janice," I said. "Sorry you're not feeling well. You're awfully good with voices. Audrey was divine!"

"That one was easy. We lived in London for years, you know. Georgie and I are practically honorary Brits!" She laughed shortly; then her voice took a more serious tone. "Listen, Lee, are you all set with how the phones work? We may be kind of rushed Monday night, getting the eleven o'clock news squared away and all. If you have any questions, now's the time to ask."

"You seem to be pretty sure I'll be here Monday night."

"I'm sure. Look, there's a five-second lag between the time the call comes in and the time it gets on the air."

I was familiar with the time delay from my stint as a shopping-show host and nearly said, "I know," but caught myself. Better to let her explain it.

"It lets us cut off the crazies," Janice said, "and the religious nuts and the heavy breathers."

"Did Ariel get many crank calls?"

"Uh-huh. But usually we can head them off at the control room. See, somebody always mans the phones and screens all the calls."

"I see. And you'll be doing it Monday?"

"That's usually my night off. But yes, I'll try to be there for your first show. I'm there most nights, anyway, so often the regulars who call know my voice."

"Are there many regulars?"

"Some of them would be on every night if we let them. But you'll be fine. There's always someone there who knows how to handle everything."

"Okay. If you say so. Thanks again, Janice. Marty is signaling me to cut this short. Bye." I handed the mike to the frantically hand-signaling woman. "What's wrong?"

"Nothing wrong. Sorry to rush you, but George is back and we're ready to button things up here. He's going to put the sports set back together, and I want to run this tape up to Doan. Scott had to leave in a hurry. The chief called another presser down at the police station. Seems they found some kind of ID on that straight razor."

"Good," I said. "I hope they catch the guy soon."

"I know." Marty headed for the door. "No one likes to think about some murdering nut job wandering around loose in Salem."

Back in the dressing room, I changed into jeans and sweater, put the Crystal Moon costume back into the garment bag, tucked the astronomy book under my arm, and called my aunt.

"Give me a few minutes, Maralee," she said. "There's

a policeman here to pick up that cat food. I'll call when I get close to the station."

I nearly ran into Detective Mondello as I left the dressing room.

"Oh, hi, Ms. Barrett. I was looking for you."

"How can I help you, Detective?"

"We've finished up back there." He motioned toward the *Nightshades* set. "You folks can get back to work now."

"Thanks," I said, looking around the long studio. "I don't see George around, and I really have no authority here. Maybe you should tell somebody upstairs."

"I will," he said. "Want to take a look and be sure we put everything back the way it's supposed to be?"

"I guess I could do that."

I followed him down the aisle toward the set. With Mondello standing next to me, I surveyed the items arranged on the table. The books were laid out so that all the titles were visible. The bowl of crystals and the obsidian ball were there, both showing dustlike residue left over from a fingerprinting examination. As I added my copy of *Linda Goodman's Sun Signs* to the pile of books, I noticed something different. A dust-covered paperback I hadn't seen before. I pointed.

"I don't think that one belongs here," I said. "At least it wasn't there when I borrowed the others."

He read the title aloud. "*Dissociative Disorders.* Yeah. We found it between the couch cushions. Figured it must be one of hers."

"Must be. Well, thanks for finishing so quickly."

"No problem." He smiled. "I'll be watching for you on TV."

"If I get the job," I said. "It's not for sure yet."

"Bet you do." He gave a little salute and headed for the parking lot.

I sat on the couch and began to arrange the books, as well as I could remember, into their original positions. I reached into my handbag for a tissue and gingerly flicked some of the dust from the black ball. Immediately I saw the pinpoints of light. Then the swirling colors. I tried to look away.

A pair of boots. Not dressy, high-heeled boots like mine. Not cowboy boots or fishermen's boots, either. These were big, sturdy boots. The kind that workmen or soldiers might wear. There was a bright spray of red across the toes, and beneath the soles I saw a pair of pale hands clutching, clawing at a granite surface. The vision faded until all that was visible was a flash of gold in the shape of a pentagram.

This time I didn't scream or cry or faint. I sat there on Ariel's turquoise couch, staring at her obsidian ball, trying to make some sense of what I had seen seconds ago in the smooth black glass.

The vision, or whatever it was, had to do with her death.

Her murder.

The chief had said that heavy boots had broken Ariel's fingers. So the images had simply reinforced something I already knew. The picture I'd seen in the ball earlier, the one of the figure in the blood-spattered kitchen, seemed to represent the other murdered woman, Yvette Pelletier. The taxi driver had told me her throat was cut, so again, that scene had shown something I already knew. And what about the pictures I'd seen in the little shoes in the attic? All those things were from my own past. Again, things I knew about.

"So," I muttered, "tell me something I don't know."

The pinpoints of light, the swirling colors appeared in an instant. Again, I saw the rough, heavy boots. Then it seemed as though a camera was slowly pulling back, broadening my field of vision. Just before the colors faded, I saw the tops of the boots, where the pants legs were tucked inside. The worn fabric of the pants bore the random spot design called camouflage.

That's the guy they're looking for in the murder down the street. Could the same man have something to do with both deaths?

My first instinct was to chase Detective Mondello, to tell him. . . . *To tell him what? That the same man is involved in both crimes? And when he asks me why I think so, I can tell him that a fake psychic thinks she sees his picture in a fake crystal ball.*

Scratch that idea.

If I could just see some of the footage of the surveillance videos they'd been collecting, at least I'd know if the man was wearing boots or not. That made sense. I'd just ask Marty. She seemed to have access to all things camera related.

I picked up my garment bag and purse and headed up to the office. Detective Mondello was there, talking with Rhonda. They both looked up, halting their conversation.

"Oh, you still here?" Rhonda asked. "I thought you'd gone. This place emptied out like Fenway Park in a rain delay."

"Where is everybody?" I asked.

She held up a well-manicured hand and began counting on cerise nail-polished fingers. "Well, let's see. George and Scott are at the police station. Marty's down the street, at that murder thing. They even had me call Old Sam to come in and cover the picketers across the street."

"Old Sam?" That was a new name to me.

"Yeah. Part-time camera guy. He's over there, trying to sort out the witch protesters from the PETA people."

"PETA? What's their problem—"

Mondello interrupted. "Let me guess. The dead seagulls, right?"

Rhonda nodded. "Right. Five seagulls. Dead from poison."

"No kidding," I said. "*Poison?* Things around here just keep getting weirder!"

"Tell me about it!" Rhonda consulted her notebook. "But, hey. Good news. Mr. Doan says you can start Monday on *Nightshades* and see how it goes."

"See? I knew you'd get it!" The detective offered a high five.

"Thanks," I said, tapping his big hand. "That was fast. I wonder if he even watched the test video."

"He just watched the beginning," Rhonda said. "I guess that's all he needed to see."

Remembering the deliberately lowered neckline and the forward leaning pose, I wasn't surprised. So I had a job. Sort of. No contract, no personal interview, and no mention of money yet, but it was something. And after all, everyone at the station seemed pretty busy with more important things than their new psychic's future.

I realized that Mondello was still watching me, with what seemed like more than professional interest. Maybe, if I asked in just the right way, he'd tell me something that would help to explain the pictures in the obsidian ball.

"Detective Mondello," I began.

"Pete."

"Pete." I smiled my sweetest smile. "I was just wondering, did that man in the camouflage suit show up on any of the surveillance films?"

His interested look became totally professional. "Funny you should mention that. I was just asking Rhonda here about the footage from this station's outdoor cameras." His eyes narrowed slightly. "Seems the guy showed up on cameras all the way down Derby Street. Right up to the building next door."

I didn't see a logical opening there for my question about the boots, so I offered a noncommittal "Oh?"

"It's weird, you know," Rhonda said. "There's a whole chunk of video missing. There's no pictures of Ariel going outside, and there's no pictures of the camo dude walking by. It's an old camera, but it's always worked okay. There should be something on it, shouldn't there?"

"That *is* strange." I agreed with Rhonda. "How is that possible, Detective . . . uh . . . Pete?"

"We're working on it. Seems to be a computer problem."

The buzzing of my cell saved me from having to respond to this latest bombshell.

"Hello. Aunt Ibby?"

"Maralee? I'm on my way to pick you up. The policeman just left with the bag of O'Ryan's old cat food. And, my dear, thank God he didn't eat it. They think it's full of rat poison!"

CHAPTER 13

I spotted the Buick at a parking meter across the street from the station, motor running and Aunt Ibby leaning out of the window, talking to one of the PETA protesters. I made my way to the passenger side and climbed in, tossing the garment bag onto the back-seat.

"One of your library friends?" I asked as my aunt waved a cheery good-bye to the sign-carrying woman.

"Yes, indeed. She and the others are very upset about those dead seagulls."

"I heard. Poisoned, apparently."

"Yes. And the police think it was the cat food."

"Could be," I said, "but I'm sure nobody meant to harm the birds. When Janice fixed a big bowl of it for him the morning after Ariel died, she certainly didn't know there was anything wrong with it."

"A good thing he's not easily enticed."

I laughed. "You're a fine one to talk! You've been enticing that cat with gourmet goodies from the start."

"True." She sounded pleased with herself. "I had that bag of nasty stuff in the garage, along with some old blankets and things I was going to take over to the animal shelter, when that policeman showed up, put on rubber gloves, and put the whole package into a big red plastic bag and took it away. I hope the neighbors weren't looking. What must they think?"

"I don't even know what I think," I admitted.

But if the poison wasn't meant for the gulls, does that mean someone wants O'Ryan dead? Why?

I shook the thought away. "I hope the police don't bother you again."

"No bother. Actually, it's kind of exciting being part of something mysterious." She reached over and patted my hand. "But enough about me. Tell me all about your test run. When will you know if Mr. Doan approves of you as Ariel's replacement?"

"The test went well, and according to Rhonda, he's already approved the video. I can start Monday and 'see how it goes.' Whatever that means."

"I don't know whether to be pleased for you or frightened of the whole psychic thing because of . . . you know."

"Yes, I know."

Shall I tell her about the latest picture in the ball? Or would it be kinder—and wiser—to keep it to myself?

We approached the common, where the striped tent had attracted a good-size group of people.

"Why don't you just drop me off here?" I said. "I'll walk home."

"All right. If you think it will be useful." She sounded unconvinced but pulled the Buick over to the curb, and I stepped out onto the narrow brick sidewalk.

"Please don't worry. It'll be fun. I'll be home soon."

There was a line outside the tent, so clearly the "no waiting" promise wasn't going to work out. But considering the city's well-advertised monthlong celebration of Halloween, it was a relatively short queue.

At the tent entrance a tall man wearing a pointed hat straight out of *Harry Potter* seemed to be performing some sort of triage. "Fortune-teller? Crystal gazer? Tarot card reader? Dearly departed contact? Tea leaf reader?" Depending on each visitor's preference, he or she was quickly directed to a particular roped-off area.

I paused for just a moment, and at my hesitation he tapped a pointed red shoe. "Well, what'll it be, lady? Fortune? Crystal? Cards? Dead people? Tea?"

I knew I didn't want to look at that crystal ball. Having my fortune told held some appeal. I thought about Ariel's books and decided.

"Tarot," I said. "Definitely tarot."

There were three tables at the end of my rope line. I studied one of the readers. The black robe she'd worn earlier had been replaced with jeans and a yellow sweater. She looked different, but it was the same young witch Scott Palmer had interviewed. I selected the folding chair opposite the girl.

"I recognize you," I said, handing her my twenty-five dollars. "I saw you on TV."

She smiled and began to place colorful tarot cards, one by one, in a pattern on the tabletop.

"I recognize you, too," she said. "The Queen of Wands."

"Oh, have we met?"

Recognizes me? I know we haven't. But then, she's a witch.

She continued arranging cards, chattering in a

friendly way. "The Queen of Wands. I knew you by the green eyes, and the copper hair, of course."

Have I traveled through the looking glass? What in hell is a Queen of Wands?

I searched my memory. *Wands. Pentacles. Cups. Swords.*

"The tarot cards," I said aloud.

She looked up. "Yes. The tarot is my gift."

"And you're a witch, too?"

She glanced around, speaking softly. "I am. But they asked us not to wear our robes or say anything about that. They don't want the picketers messing up the common."

"I see. What's your name?"

"River North."

"Really?"

"No," she said, smiling. "Not really. What's yours?"

I smiled back. "Crystal Moon."

"Really?"

"No. Not really." We both laughed.

"Okay, Crystal. Let's get started on your reading."

"Yes, please, River."

She moved her hands gracefully over the surface of the cards. "The Seven of Swords is reversed in your sixth house. You are good at giving advice."

"Interesting," I said, "and a very useful thing to know right now."

"Is it? Good. But remember, less is more. Know when to be quiet. Avoid TMI."

"TMI?"

"Too much information."

"I'll try. You said on TV that you knew Ariel Constellation. Was the tarot her gift, too?"

"Ariel had many gifts." She returned to studying the cards she'd arranged on the table.

"Listen closely, Crystal." She leaned forward. "You have to be careful. The King of Cups is reversed in your twelfth house." She looked at me expectantly. "Any idea who it is?"

"I don't know what it *means,* River."

"Oh, sorry. It means you have a secret enemy. A man. He probably seems calm. Cool. But watch out. He has two faces. Underneath he's fierce. Maybe violent."

"Great. That's all I need."

"Don't worry too much. Just be careful around men."

"I always am. Anything else?"

"Hmmm." She passed her hands over the cards again. "Do you live with your mother?"

"My mother? No. My mother's dead. I'm staying with my aunt. Why?"

"There's a woman close to you. The Queen of Cups. She's often a mother."

"Aunt Ibby's really the only mother I've ever known. She raised me."

"That explains the card. Keep her close. She's a good protector." She nodded several times, as though pleased with the reading. "Do you have questions?"

"Anything there about a job?"

"Do you have one now?"

"Sort of. I'm not sure it will last, though."

She touched a card. "It won't."

"How do you know that?"

"It's all here," she said, tapping the card. "The Five of Pentacles. You'll be out of work within a month."

"Wow. You're full of good news, aren't you?"

"It's not me, Crystal." She reached across the table and took my hand. "Really. It's the cards." She lowered her voice. "There's more here you need to know. They only allow a few minutes with each client. Need to keep the lines moving." She handed me a business card. "Please call me. Soon. I think it may be important."

"I will. And thanks, River. It was very . . . instructive."

"You're welcome, Crystal. Good-bye. Be safe."

I headed for the exit and passed a black-draped souvenir stand. Postcards, T-shirts, medallions, crystals, and Styrofoam gargoyles vied for space with staffs, broomsticks, pointed hats, and rows and rows of books. I found the boxed sets of tarot cards among Ouija boards and glitter filled magic wands. Feeling just a little foolish, I bought one.

Once outside the tent, I headed for one of the cement benches spaced around the perimeter of the park. I opened the box and sorted through the colorful oblong cards until I found the one marked Queen of Wands. I placed it in my lap and put the rest of the deck back into the box. I gazed around the old familiar Salem Common, not really focusing on anything in particular, then slowly lifted the card to eye level.

The red-haired queen carried a staff in her right hand. In the other hand she held a tall sunflower, a black ball in its center. In the foreground, with its back to the throne, sat a golden-eyed cat.

CHAPTER 14

Crossing Washington Square, I passed the huge stone Civil War monument that marks the corner of Winter Street. I crossed the street and, walking carefully, stepped over the curb in front of the house. Vintage brick and cobblestone sidewalks might be charming to look at, but they can be hazardous to wearers of high heels!

Turning my key in the lock, I smiled at O'Ryan, whose pink nose was pressed against one of the tall windows beside the front door. He greeted my entrance with something that sounded like a happy combination of a purr and meow.

"Why all the attention, O'Ryan?" I leaned down and scratched between his ears. "Not that it isn't welcome."

Aunt Ibby appeared in the dining-room doorway. "Are you talking to me, dear?"

"Nope. Just having a chat with O'Ryan."

"He's been quite talkative today—meowing

and purring ever since I came in. How was your bargain-priced psychic experience?"

"Brief, but interesting," I said. "I had my cards read, and the reader was that young witch who was interviewed on TV this morning."

"Really? Did she give you the usual spiel? You are a caring and sensitive person? You have a handsome secret admirer? You are about to come into a large sum of money?"

"Not exactly. She says I talk too much, there's some man who secretly hates me, and I'm going to be out of work within a month."

"Oh, dear." Her eyes widened. "Of course you know it's all nonsense."

"I know," I said. "I'm not really worried about it. But I bought a set of tarot cards, anyway. I wish I still had Ariel's books about how to read them. Do we have any?" Seeing her look of disapproval, I added, "It might be useful on the show if I sounded as though I knew something about wands and cups and whatever."

"We probably have something. Look around in nonfiction. Maybe one-thirty-three point thirty-two."

"Thanks." I headed for the study, O'Ryan a few steps in front of me, as though he knew exactly where I was going.

"Have you had lunch?" my aunt called after me.

"Nope. Never got around to it."

"How about a nice salad?"

"Sounds good."

With the cat on my lap, I settled down behind the big desk with *A Beginner's Guide to the Tarot*. I skipped over the introduction and turned directly to the page showing the Queen of Wands. *If the woman is Caucasian,* I read, *she has red or brown hair and blue or green eyes.*

"That fits," I told the cat as I scanned the page further.

She has great sales ability.

"I did pretty well on the shopping shows," I said.

"Mrruff," said O'Ryan. He hopped up onto the desk, putting his paw on the part of the illustration that showed the cat in front of the seated queen.

"What about it? It says here the cat is supposed to protect the queen from harm. But look. You're supposed to be a black cat. Not all stripey and yellow."

O'Ryan put both paws across his nose and squeezed his eyes shut, seemingly dismissive of black cats in general, and resumed purring.

I looked up the Seven of Swords. River had told me it meant I was good at giving advice, as long as I didn't overdo it. The card showed a man who was apparently stealing some swords.

"What does sword stealing have to do with advice?" I wondered aloud. The printed explanation suggested that I might need to change my thinking to find a new approach to problems. That made some sense, since I'd be dealing with other people's problems, not mine, but the sword analogy still escaped me.

"It's all nonsense, you know." I repeated Aunt Ibby's words to the now-sleeping cat. "So let's see what the Five of Pentacles has to say about my soon-to-be unemployment."

I flipped through the pages until I found the card. "Uh-oh. This doesn't look good at all!"

O'Ryan's ears twitched, but he kept his eyes closed. "Don't want to look at it? I don't blame you. It's creepy."

The card showed two people dressed in rags, struggling through snow beside a church with stained-glass windows. Each window displayed a pentagram—like the one on Ariel's ring. The text told about forthcoming financial woes. *Change is coming,* it said. *Find your true purpose in life,* which, if River was right, was not the career of a call-in TV psychic.

I'd saved the King of Cups for last. The idea of a violent man who might be a secret enemy was frightening. Even if it was all nonsense.

The King of Cups didn't look like a bad guy at all. He was just sitting on his throne, holding a cup. The text suggested a father figure and mentioned maturity and creativity. But River had said that the King of Cups was reversed.

I read further. *The King of Cups reversed is an entirely different story. That king comes from a position of fear. He keeps information about himself hidden, while watching all the time to find another's weakness. He feels that he's been wronged somewhere along the line and is looking for revenge. His ability to find love or compassion has been forever changed, perhaps from something that happened early in his life.* I slammed the book shut.

The sound woke the sleeping cat. He stretched, yawned, and sat on the back cover of *A Beginner's Guide to the Tarot.* His tail pointed straight up, what might be interpreted as a cat version of a rude gesture.

"You're right," I told him. "It's total garbage. I haven't even been here long enough to tick anybody

off, let alone a king. Come on. Let's go get something
to eat."

The cell phone in my pocket began to vibrate. The
caller ID told me the call was from WICH-TV.

"Hello," I said. "Lee Barrett speaking."

"Hello." The male voice was familiar. "This is Scott
Palmer. We met this morning. At the station."

"Yes, of course, Mr. Palmer. How are you?" *And why
are you calling me?*

"Just fine, thanks. Look, I thought we were going to
have a chance to get acquainted at the restaurant
today. Maybe get that job thing smoothed over.
Dropped the ball there, I guess. So, I was wondering,
since we never got to eat, would you like to join me for
a late lunch?"

Boy, do I wish Janice hadn't made that job-grabbing crack!

"That's very kind of you, Mr. Palmer, but my aunt is
making lunch right now. I appreciate the invitation,
though."

"I'm disappointed," he said. "Maybe another time.
And please call me Scott."

"Okay, Scott. Thanks again. We'll probably run into
each other at the station."

"I hope so," he said. "It seems as if I've been out on
assignment ever since I got here."

Right. Those assignments that could have—should
have—been mine.

'Yes," I agreed. "You've been busy."

Polite. Noncommittal. Just right.

Then the proverbial lightbulb went off. If Pete
Mondello couldn't give me information about the
killer, maybe Scott Palmer could. I was pretty sure
he'd seen the surveillance tapes by now.

"Uh, Scott," I said. "Did anything interesting show up on those surveillance tapes? Like a better look at the man? What he was wearing?"

"There were a few shots of him as he moved along Derby Street. The videos are all pretty grainy, though. His face was covered by some kind of hood. About all you could really tell was that it was a guy wearing camo and boots."

Bingo. The killer wore boots. That was all I wanted to know. Time to end this conversation.

"I hope they catch him soon," I said. "It's just terrible about that poor woman. Dying that way on her own kitchen floor." I was ready to hang up. "So long, Scott. Thanks again for the invitation."

He was silent for a few seconds. "Okay. No lunch. But here's an idea. How'd you like to go to a football game tonight? Salem High is playing Swampscott. I scored a couple of fifty-yard-line tickets this afternoon."

He'd hit a soft spot. I love football. High school, college, pro—didn't matter. Aunt Ibby started taking me to New England Patriots games when I was six.

I couldn't resist asking. "Did Mr. Doan give you the tickets?"

"Yeah. He knew I used to play. Nice guy."

"Very nice," I said.

He's softening you up for your second job—announcing high school games!

"Well, how about it? Would you like to go? Rhonda says you're a native. You can help me find the stadium. We can grab a late supper after the game."

"I think you've sold me. Salem High is my alma mater. What time is the game?"

"Seven o'clock. Pick you up at six thirty."

"It sounds like fun." I gave him directions to Winter Street and hung up. "Was that a good idea? Making a date with a fellow employee?"

O'Ryan crawled under the desk.

"I know. I know. I haven't been out with a man since Johnny died."

A scratching sound from below.

"I mean, a high school football game isn't a *real* date."

"Mmfff," came the muffled reply.

"Oh, what do you know? You're a cat!" I put the tarot book back on the shelf and started for the door. "Come on, O'Ryan. Let's go downstairs."

A yellow paw snaked out from under the desk, causing River's business card to land neatly at my feet.

"Must have dropped that when I pulled out my phone." I picked it up and tucked it back into my pocket. "Maybe I'll give her a call."

O'Ryan trotted to the doorway and looked back at me, his tail this time forming a furry question mark.

"Soon," I promised. "I'll call her soon."

I followed the cat into the kitchen.

Aunt Ibby looked up from her *Boston Globe*. "Ready for a bite to eat? I've fixed a nice salad."

"A salad will be perfect."

"Did you find anything helpful about the tarot?" She smiled, but her tone was disapproving.

"Yes, thanks. *A Beginner's Guide.* I don't expect to get past beginner's status."

"I should think not. Ariel rarely referred to it, other than using a sprinkling of the vocabulary. Knaves and wands and such. Anyway, I'm glad if the book was helpful."

She opened the refrigerator and produced two bowls of crisp, colorful salad. "Looks yummy," I said.

O'Ryan, pink nose twitching, hopped onto a stool and put his front paws on the edge of the granite counter surface.

"This isn't for you, O'Ryan," I told him. "Scat!"

"He wants to sniff everything," Aunt Ibby said. "I think he heard me when I said that someone had put p-o-i-s-o-n in his food."

I had to laugh. "He isn't so smart that you have to spell in front of him."

She shrugged. "He might be."

I wasn't prepared to argue the point, and O'Ryan had apparently lost interest in both the food and the conversation. Within seconds the cat door creaked open.

We ate in silence for a while; then I put my fork down and took a deep breath.

"Is something wrong, dear?" my very perceptive aunt asked.

"I'm not sure. But there are a couple of things I'd like to talk to you about."

"Go ahead, dear. I'm listening."

"Okay. I saw . . . I think I saw . . . something else in that obsidian ball."

"Oh, God. I had hoped . . . What did you see?"

"I think I saw Ariel's killer," I said. "I saw him stepping on her hands. It was as though I was looking up at him, just the way Ariel must have."

"Lord! Who is he?"

"I didn't see his face. But I'm sure it's the same

man they're looking for in that other murder. The woman in her kitchen."

"Yvette Pelletier."

"Right." I explained about the camouflaged pants legs and the boots. "The clothes match the description of the man they're calling 'a person of interest.'"

"Did you tell the police?"

"Of course not. I wanted to, but what could I say? I sometimes see pictures in an old black ball? They'd think I'm nuts!"

She nodded her agreement. "You're right. I understand. But, Maralee, what *are* you going to do about it?"

"I don't know what I *can* do. I'll keep asking questions. Look at as many surveillance tapes as I can. Detective Mondello said the man showed up on cameras all the way down Derby Street. But there's no picture from outside the TV station. Strange, isn't it?"

"It is," she agreed. "I'm sure we'll see some of those tapes on TV soon. Probably today. They'll want people to be on the lookout for that man. Someone might be able to identify him."

"I hope so."

"Anyway, please don't look at that cursed ball anymore."

"I'll try not to," I promised. "That reminds me. Do you have a black silk handkerchief I can use to cover it?"

"I'm sure I do. Why black silk?"

"Instructions from *Crystal Enlightenment*. It's supposed to help it rest."

Her expression was grim. "May it rest in peace. You

said you had a couple of things to talk to me about. What else?"

"I have sort of a date. With a man."

"How nice! Anyone I know?"

"It's not a *real* date," I insisted. "I'm going to the Salem-Swampscott game tonight. With Scott Palmer."

"The good-looking reporter who took your job?"

"Yes. I know it's kind of crazy, but do you think it's okay?"

"I think it's fine, unless the station has some sort of policy against employees dating. But then, you're not officially employed yet, are you?"

"No, and, anyway, the card reader said I'd be out of work within a month. Remember?"

She made a face. "Foolishness."

I decided not to tell her that I planned to see River again.

CHAPTER 15

Even though I kept telling myself, *It's not a real date,* I took extra care in getting ready for the evening. I changed into dark blue jeans that were just a bit on the tight side and a creamy Irish knit pullover. I caught my hair back with a wide silver barrette and decided on the same boots I'd worn earlier. I wouldn't need my big leather purse at a football game, so I transferred wallet, lipstick, and comb to a smaller one. The purse also yielded several business cards I'd accumulated since I'd been in Salem. Contact information on Jim Litka, the cabdriver, Detective Pete Mondello, Janice Valen, and River North was quickly entered into my phone's memory. Recalling some chilly evenings at Bertram Field, I pulled a short leather jacket with a NASCAR logo on the sleeve from the closet and tossed it over my shoulders.

The doorbell rang at precisely six thirty. Scott Palmer's punctuality didn't surprise me. The time-ruled structures of radio and television made us that way. He looked taller than I'd remembered, and in jeans and a faded denim jacket over a close-fitting black T-shirt, he looked younger, too.

"Ready?" I could see approval in his eyes as he gave one of those up-and-down looks men do so well.

"Ready," I said, "but please come in and say hello to Aunt Ibby."

"Glad to. After you left, Rhonda told me a lot of good things about her."

"Rhonda seems to be a fountain of information."

"You bet." He grinned. "How do you think I got your phone number?"

Aunt Ibby was in the den, her laptop open on the Governor Winthrop desk. She extended her hand. "Mr. Palmer! What a pleasure to see you again. I'm enjoying your work at the station."

Scott shook her hand. "Thanks so much, Miss Russell. Don't let us interrupt your work."

"Just catching up with my Facebook friends," she said. "I'm afraid I've been neglecting them since my niece arrived home. You young people run along now. Don't be late for your game."

I hadn't seen or heard O'Ryan coming into the room, but there he was, in the center of the doorway. He approached Scott slowly and paused. Scott bent and patted the cat's head.

"Hello, big fella," he said. "Isn't this Ariel's cat? The one who witnessed the murder?"

"I hadn't thought of it quite that way," I said. "But yes, I guess he is."

"He's come to live with us now," said Aunt Ibby. "And apparently, he's none the worse for his experience. Do you like cats, Mr. Palmer?"

"They're okay, except for the litter box part."

"We haven't had to deal with that," I said. "O'Ryan uses a cat door and just takes himself outside whenever he likes."

"Good cat," Scott said and patted O'Ryan again. "We'd better get going, Lee. Don't want to miss the kickoff."

Scott's yellow Toyota was parked at the curb in front of the house. He held the door for me. *He's polite. Aunt Ibby would like that. I like it, too.* I pulled my jacket on and climbed in. He started the engine, then paused and looked down at the logo on my sleeve.

"NASCAR. Barrett. Florida. Oh, jeez. Johnny Barrett. You're Johnny Barrett's wife. Widow. I'm sorry. I mean . . ."

"It's okay," I said. "Yes. I was married to Johnny Barrett."

"Wow." He looked like a kid for a moment. "I was a fan. Used to do sports for a small cable station in Illinois."

Thought so.

"I saw him race once at the Chicagoland Speedway. He had a great career ahead of him."

"Yes, I know."

There was a moment's awkward silence as we approached the common, where there were still lines outside the tent.

"Look," I said. "It's a psychic fair. I ran into River there this afternoon."

"River?"

"River North. The witch you interviewed."

"Oh, yeah. River. What's she doing in there?"

"Telling fortunes."

"No kidding? Did she read your palm?"

"Nope. Read my cards—" The disembodied voice from the GPS on the dashboard interrupted with instructions to turn left in 1.5 miles. "So. You didn't really need me to help you find the football stadium," I teased.

"You've got me there." He smiled. "It seemed like a good excuse to ask you out."

We found a parking space not far from the entrance to Bertram Field, and we joined the crowd heading for the stands. The sound of the band tuning up and the smell of hot dogs and popcorn brought back happy memories.

"What a nostalgia rush!" I said. "I haven't been here in a dozen years, and it feels like yesterday."

The weather had cleared a bit, and the stadium lights gave the grass on the field a warm golden glow. A roar from the crowd announced the home team. Cheerleaders formed an arch with red-and-white shakers, and a dry ice–induced fog lent drama to the arrival of the young athletes. Cries of "Go, Salem Witches" rang loud and strong.

"It's a wonder those witch protesters aren't here to complain about the team name," Scott said, looking around as though he halfway expected to see the purple-hatted Mrs. Doan and her sign-waving minions marching into the stands.

"Wouldn't do them any good," I told him. "They've always been the Salem Witches. Salem likes it that way. Haven't you seen the statue of Samantha from *Bewitched* over near city hall?"

"You're kidding!"

"Nope. She's there, and most of Salem loves her."

A loud cheer from the bleachers across the field

announced the arrival of the Swampscott Big Blue. A coin was tossed; the kickoff positions were decided. Scott studied his program, making notes in pencil along the margins.

"That Roberts kid looks good," he said.

"How can you tell?"

"Read his stats this afternoon. I figured I might as well study up on the team. I expect Doan will recruit me for high school sports reporter."

"I heard that could happen."

"Yeah. Everyone seems to wear at least two hats at WICH-TV." He stuck the pencil behind his ear and turned toward me. "Wonder what he has in mind for your second job."

"Whoa!" I laughed. "He hasn't officially hired me for the first one yet. Anyway, River says I'll be out of work within a month."

His smile was warm. "I doubt that. At least I hope not. I'm counting on seeing you there. On-screen and off."

The much-admired Roberts kid returned the kick-off for a ninety-yard touchdown, and I found myself caught up in the excitement of the game, cheering and jumping up and down like the teenagers around us. At halftime we drank hot coffee and applauded the band and baton twirlers. When Salem kicked the winning field goal with seconds to spare, a spontaneous hug led to a brief awkward moment before we joined the crowd heading for the exit.

A light mist had turned into rain when we reached Scott's Toyota.

"I'm hungry," he said. "You up for a burger?"

"Sure."

"Better stick a raincoat over that nice leather jacket," Scott advised. "There're some in the glove box." He reached across and pressed the latch. "Help yourself."

Within the lighted compartment I saw several green plastic envelopes. "Thanks. There's one just like these in Aunt Ibby's glove box, too. George's supply of raincoats must be getting low."

"Marty says everyone in Salem must have at least two."

Including a murderer, I thought, remembering the blood-soaked raincoat in the Dumpster.

We rode in companionable silence, punctuated by the rhythmic whisper of the windshield wipers and the hum of tires on wet pavement, and before long we pulled into a crowded parking lot.

I wriggled into the raincoat as Scott hurried around and opened my door. We dashed for the entrance. The restaurant was warm and noisy. I slid into the red vinyl upholstered booth, and Scott went to the counter and ordered burgers and fries and milk shakes for both of us.

I was hungrier than I'd realized, and the food tasted wonderful. I was just enjoying the last sip of my chocolate milk shake when Scott reached across the table and took my hand.

"Lee," he said in a serious tone. "Lee, I wanted to talk to you tonight about more than a football game."

Uh-oh. I don't think I'm ready for this. Don't rush me.

Aloud, I said, "Oh?"

"It's about the Pelletier murder."

"Huh?" I pushed the straw into the empty plastic cup and stared at him. "The Pelletier murder?"

"Yes. How do you know so much about it?"

"Me? What are you talking about?"

"When I called you today, you said something about the woman dying on her own kitchen floor."

"Yes. So?"

Scott let go of my hand. "The murder scene. How did you know the body was in the kitchen?"

I frowned, annoyed. "TV, I guess. Same as everyone else." I recalled the vivid image.

"Can we talk about something else besides that poor woman's death? After all, we just ate."

"Come on, Lee. There is no footage of the murder scene. And even if there was, none of the stations could show it. So what made you think it was in the kitchen? Who told you that? Was it that Mondello guy?"

"No! I don't know anything about it. Really, I don't."

"If you've got connections . . . if you have a source with that kind of information . . . can you share it with a struggling reporter?"

My first reaction was a vague sense of embarrassment. He wanted to talk shop, and I'd imagined he had something more personal in mind. Embarrassment morphed into anger.

If I had inside connections on a murder case, I'd have your job, buster.

Of course, I knew exactly where I'd seen that sprawled body and the blood-smeared kitchen. It was inside the swirling depths of a black obsidian ball.

What could I say? If I told the truth—that I was apparently some kind of scryer, that I could see pictures no one else could see in shiny black things—he'd think I was nuts. And he might be right.

So I did the only thing I could think of. I told him a big, fat lie.

"You know," I said with all the sincerity I could muster, "you might be right. Maybe I did hear it from one of the detectives. I mean, maybe I *overheard* it. I mean, I wasn't *meant* to hear it. . . ."

He looked puzzled. "What *do* you mean?"

I took a deep breath. "Well, there was a lot of conversation going on around me, you know, after I found poor Ariel's body."

"Yeah. I imagine there was."

"Uh-huh. A lot of conversation." I thought back to that day. *May as well tell as much of the truth as possible.* "Anyway, they called me back to the station to return some of Ariel's books I'd borrowed, and the chief was on his cell, and the techs were all talking to each other. Detective Mondello was talking to a couple of the regular policemen, the ones in uniform. I'm pretty sure I heard somebody say, 'Blood all over the refrigerator.' That must be where I got the idea that the body was in the kitchen. Yes, I'm sure that must be it."

Another deep breath. Was he buying it?

He still had the puzzled look. "When was all this?"

"It was when I was getting swabbed and fingerprinted."

"You? Swabbed and fingerprinted? Why?"

"Because my blood showed up in the parking lot."

Scott's posture stiffened, and he moved back in his

seat. It didn't take a body language expert to realize that he was distancing himself from me.

Oh boy! This was a clear example of what River meant by TMI.

I explained quickly about tripping over O'Ryan and threw in the fact that I'd been on a Southwest jet between Tampa and Boston when the murder—or murders—occurred. Just in case he thought . . . you know.

He seemed to relax a little and leaned toward me again. It looked as though he was satisfied with my explanation about overhearing the cops. In fact, it sounded so plausible that I began to halfway believe it myself.

The ride home was pleasant enough. We made easy small talk about the football game, about the people we'd met at the station, about our backgrounds in broadcasting, our families. And, thankfully, neither of us mentioned the fact that he'd landed the job I'd wanted.

Scott walked with me to the front door. "Good night, Lee. I'll see you at work."

"Thanks, Scott. It was fun."

He stood there in the rain for a long moment, not speaking, just looking into my eyes.

"Yes," he said. "It really was, wasn't it?"

Then he dashed for his car, turning to wave briefly. I watched the Toyota until the taillights disappeared.

"Maralee?" Aunt Ibby called from the den. "Come in and tell me all about your date. Did you have fun?"

"The game was fun," I said, thinking about Scott's blatant pitch for information, "but it sure wasn't what I'd call a *real* date."

CHAPTER 16

During what was left of the weekend, I crammed as though I was preparing for final exams. *Linda Goodman's Sun Signs, A Beginner's Guide to the Tarot,* and *Crystal Enlightenment* were spread out on the study desk, along with the tarot deck, some blank index cards, and a couple of nice sharp number two pencils.

I played the first Ariel DVD again and fast-forwarded my way through a couple of Aunt Ibby's *Dark Shadows* episodes, writing down some of Ariel's phrases on the index cards. I practiced saying things like "Surround her with golden-white light" and "Blessed be." By Sunday afternoon I could recite with ease the directions for programming a quartz crystal. I'd also picked up some astrological lingo. I understood how the layout of the tarot cards worked, and I felt that I had a pretty good grasp of the kinds of calls I might get.

One more trip to the attic had yielded a couple more off-the-shoulder blouses and some full skirts left over from somebody's long-ago foray into square dancing—just in case the promised wardrobe budget wasn't forthcoming. I planned to wear the red skirt and my mother's blouse again for my first show, and I added a few more strands of beads and a couple of glitzy rings.

By Monday I felt almost confident.

I planned to get to the station well ahead of the time *Nightshades* was due to start. I turned down Aunt Ibby's offer of the Buick. It was her evening for book club with "the girls."

"I'm perfectly comfortable taking a cab," I told her. "But I hope you'll be home in time to watch my psychic debut!"

"Wouldn't miss it for the world," she promised. "But you come straight home after it's over. I don't want to be worrying about you being out so late at night with a murderer on the loose."

I called Jim Litka and asked if he'd be available for a late-night fare. I wanted to get to the station by nine thirty and to leave after my last live shot at around two thirty in the morning.

"Sure, miss," he said. "No problem. We're all working crazy hours this month, what with Halloween parties and goings-on. You can count on me."

At 9:15 p.m. the green-and-white cab pulled up in front of the house. I climbed into the backseat, carrying the garment bag, along with another bag containing the books I'd been studying, index cards, Aunt Ibby's black silk handkerchief and the tarot deck.

"Thanks for fitting me in, Mr. Litka," I said. "I know you're awfully busy."

"Just call me Jim," he said. "And it's never any trouble getting a pretty lady to where she's going."

We pulled up in front of the station, and I reached into my purse to pay the fare. No wallet.

"Oh, no! Mr. Litka . . . Jim, I changed purses, and I'm afraid I've left my wallet in the other one." I checked my watch. "Maybe we have time to go back and get it."

He waved a dismissive hand. "No worries, miss. I'll be picking you up later. We'll just settle up when I take you home tonight."

I thanked him and made a mental note to double the tip.

When I entered the office, I was surprised to see that Rhonda was still at her desk.

"You're working late, Rhonda," I said, glancing up at the sunburst-shaped clock. "What's up?"

"Mr. Doan asked me to stay for a while. He said somebody called in sick and I might have to sub."

"Oh? Who?"

She shrugged. "Dunno. I hope it's Wanda, though. I love doing the weather."

"Have you done it before?" I found it hard to believe that the station would use the inexperienced receptionist for on-air talent.

"Once," she said. "It was during a blizzard. We were snowed in, and Wanda couldn't make it. It was wild. Janice and I took turns doing the weather, and Mr. Doan did the news. Marty was the only camera. We lost the network feed for part of the day, so we just showed a lot of movies."

"I saw the enormous movie list. I'll have plenty of scary old movies to pick from."

"Awesome. Hey, listen. Marty's down on your set.

She wants you to see if you like the way she's fixed it up."

I hurried past the glass-walled newsroom, where Phil Archer pulled long paper pages from the news-line printer. Scott was there, too, his back to me, working at a battered desk. He didn't look up when I passed.

I stepped into the long, darkened studio. Stopping at the dressing room, I hung my costume on the rack, and then, carrying the other bag, I hurried toward the *Nightshades* set, where Marty was already positioned behind her camera.

"Hey, Moon! How was your weekend?" She didn't wait for an answer. "What do you think of this for an opening shot?" The camera was poised for a close-up of a picture of a cemetery. "It's a Halloween card. Nice and spooky. We'll play the theme music with a shot of this graveyard, then zoom in on the headstone in the front and roll titles on the stone. What d'ya think?" She stepped aside, motioning for me to take her place behind the camera.

"Looks good to me. Where'd you get the charming card?"

"Chamber of Commerce sent it. It's Ariel's invitation to the annual Witches Ball. Guess it's yours now."

"I probably won't use it."

"You ought to go. Two free tickets. It's an A-list party, and it's almost sold out. Maybe you could get another date with Scotty."

"What date? I mean . . . how do you know?"

"Rhonda. He called you from her phone. Nothing much gets by Rhonda."

Great. Nobody needs to be psychic around here. Rhonda sees all, hears all, tells all.

I changed the subject. "You wanted to show me something about the set?"

"Oh, yeah. The stuff on the table. It looks pretty much the way Ariel had it. Do you want to rearrange anything? Give it your own look?"

"Not yet," I said. "It looks okay the way it is." I added my three books to the grouping and placed the tarot deck and the index cards where I'd be able to get to them easily. The obsidian ball was in the center of the low table. I tried not to look directly at the thing as I reached into the bag for the black silk square. But the swirling colors were already there. I tossed the handkerchief as quickly as I could over the glowing surface, but not before I saw the image of a yellow cat, back arched, mouth open, teeth bared.

I looked at Marty. Had she seen anything in the black ball?

Of course not, dummy. No one sees this stuff but you.

Had she noticed any strange reaction on my part?

Do I even react to the pictures anymore? Or do I just accept them?

Marty's expression hadn't changed. "What's with the silk rag thing? You don't have to cover this one up. It doesn't glare like Ariel's old crystal one did."

"I know. It's not for glare. I've been reading up on crystals." I tapped the *Crystal Enlightenment* book. "You're supposed to keep the obsidian covered with black silk or velvet when you're not using it. I just thought in case anyone who really knows about this stuff is watching, they'd appreciate the authenticity."

"Sure. Okay. I see." Marty straightened the fabric so that it lay evenly over the globe. "Makes sense to me. Hey, you'd better get dressed for the show."

I left the set, happy to avoid any further discussion of the care and feeding of obsidian. Once inside the dressing room, I closed the door and sat in front of the mirror.

Why had I seen O'Ryan in the obsidian ball? Why the arched back? The bared teeth? I'd never seen him like that. Was that cat even O'Ryan? He was home alone. Was he all right?

I shook away the image, the bad thoughts. It was time to transform myself into Crystal Moon. I'd been an actress long enough to have learned the old "show must go on" discipline. I'd deal with visions later. I dressed carefully, adjusting the neckline of the blouse up and down several times, tying the fringed shawl just so, fiddling with the lengths of the colorful bead necklaces. I pressed powder onto my nose and fore-head, applied bright red lipstick, and added an extra coat of mascara. I ran my fingers through my hair for the tousled look Johnny had always loved. When the mirror finally reflected Crystal Moon the way I thought she should appear for her introduction to the *Nightshades* audience, I looked at my watch. The eleven o'clock news would be under way.

I pushed the door open and stepped out into the corridor. One of the ever-present overhead monitors displayed the news anchor's face, and closed-captioning showed his words.

Salem has been the scene of two violent deaths in recent days. Yvette Pelletier, forty-two, and WICH-TV's own Ariel Constellation, fifty, have each died under suspicious circumstances.

An artist's rendering of an open straight razor filled the screen.

A 1950s era straight razor was recovered near the Pelletier home, and police have indicated that it was the weapon used to kill the woman. Some indistinct scratches on it appear to be numerals. The instrument has been submitted to an MIT lab for further study.

A shot of Ariel, seated on the same turquoise couch I was about to occupy, was next.

The death of Ariel Constellation is under investigation. Police believe foul play is indicated. WICH-TV field reporter Scott Palmer talked earlier today with Salem police chief Tom Whaley.

Scott's image appeared on the screen. I'd seen the interview before, on the six o'clock broadcast. Hurrying to the *Nightshades* set, I sat on the couch, thumbed through my index cards once more, while Marty outlined the format we'd use for the show.

"Okay, Moon. You look good. Listen, first we use the graveyard bumper shot. Then we move in on you for your monologue, then cut to commercial. Then second commercial. Then back to you for intro to the movie. Then, midpoint in the flick, you take calls. Commercial, commercial, more calls. Then back to movie, commercial, commercial, then your close. Got it?"

"Got it. The only part I'm freaked out about is the calls. I'm glad Janice is screening for me. She won't let anything too weird get through."

"Oh yeah. About that. Janice got one of her migraine headaches. George had to take her home."

"Then who . . . ?" I remembered what Rhonda had said. "You mean on my first night I get Rhonda?"

"You got it, babe. Ready? Counting down. Ten. Nine. Eight . . ."

CHAPTER 17

The new *Nightshades* theme, Doppler's *Fantaisie*, boomed from the speakers, and the gloomy graveyard scene filled the screen. It was time to shake away worries about my surprise call screener and fears for my home-alone cat. The credits rolled, the music faded, and Marty moved in for a close-up. I'd decided not to dwell too much on Ariel. There'd been a long, sad retrospective on Saturday night, and of course, every newscast, day and night, kept viewers up to date on the progress of the investigation into the psychic's death. I moistened my lips and leaned toward the camera.

"Welcome, children of the night." I deliberately pitched my voice lower than usual, making use of the husky, sexy quality I'd cultivated over the years. "My name is Crystal Moon, and I'm your psychic and host for an adventure into the realms of the unknown. As you all know, our dear Ariel has crossed over, and I ask that you send her light and love to aid in her journey beyond."

I bowed my head for a couple of seconds. "Tonight

I invite you to join me in watching the 1944 mystery classic *Shadows in the Night*. Later, I'll be taking your calls. Let's get acquainted, my dear new friends."

The camera light winked off, and a recorded commercial showed a barrel of lentils. A professional voice-over recited the benefits of buying in bulk at a downtown health-food store. The next commercial was mine to read from the prompter. It was a promotion for one of Salem's many shops specializing in things mystic. I held a rose quartz crystal necklace toward the camera. Allowing each smooth, graduated bead to slip slowly through my fingers, I described the power of the crystals, the beauty of the lustrous pink color, and the fashionable appeal of the thing. All in all, it wasn't much different from selling jewelry on the home-shopping show I used to host in Florida. I leaned back against the turquoise cushions. *So far, so good*. It was time to introduce the movie.

"Tonight's thriller, *Shadows in the Night*, takes us into the terrifying dreams of a young designer. There are strange and ghostly happenings in an isolated mansion on a rocky shore. Watch with me, friends. I'll be back at intermission to take your personal calls. The number is at the bottom of your screen." The black-and-white image of a frightened Nina Foch struggling through a driving rain began the film.

Marty turned the sound off and gave me a thumbs-up. "Nice goin', kid," she said. "You're almost halfway home. Take a break, if you want. Or are you really going to watch the movie?"

"I don't think so. Watched it once when I was a kid, and it about scared me to death."

"Well, there's coffee in the break room, and I brought doughnuts. Help yourself."

"Thanks. Will you join me?"

"Nah. I've got stuff to do around here." She gestured broadly, indicating the entire studio.

"Me too. I think I need a little more studying." I reached for the book pile, randomly selecting *Witchcraft in Old Salem* and *Dissociative Disorders.*

"Okay. The movie runs sixty-seven minutes. So you've got about half an hour to kill before phone calls."

"I'll be here. Don't worry. Now, if I can just find the break room . . ."

She gave me quick directions, and I found the small, warm room. It was painted yellow, a nice change from turquoise and purple, and the fragrant coffee smelled good. I poured a cup, wiped a slight residue of fingerprint powder from the book covers, and opened the witchcraft volume. A corner of one page was turned down, making the book fall open to a chapter headed "Bridget Bishop."

Back in middle school, when we'd learned about Salem's history, we'd been taught that the victims of the "witchcraft delusion" were all innocent. But according to Ariel's book, the Bishop woman was really a witch. A thoroughly evil one at that. And she'd been the first one to die on Gallows Hill.

Someone—*Ariel?*—had highlighted a sentence in yellow.

The seventeenth-century medical doctor was likely to attribute symptoms he could not explain to witchcraft, much the way today's physician is apt to characterize

*whatever he cannot understand as a psychosomatic
problem.*

I puzzled over that for a moment, then closed the
book. There'd be time enough for Salem history later.
I checked my watch for about the twentieth time.
Couldn't afford to miss my cue for intermission
phone calls. Less than ten minutes had passed. I
reached for *Dissociative Disorders.* I didn't notice any
turned-down corners in this one, but a quick page flip
revealed quite a few yellow highlighted words.

"Hey. Hi, Lee!"

I looked up, startled. Scott Palmer stood in the
doorway. "Caught the first part of your show. Looking
good."

"Thanks. You're working late."

"Yeah, well, I guess I've become the official 'crime
reporter.' At least that's the way Archer introduced
me tonight."

"No kidding?" I stifled a smile. How many hats was
Scott going to be wearing? My single-purpose job was
beginning to look pretty good. "What was tonight's
crime report about? I missed it. Sorry."

"The alleged murder weapon. The razor the old
guy found. I got a look at it before it got sent to the
MIT lab."

"The early news said it had numbers on it."

"It does. They're real faint. Just kind of scratched
into the top part of the blade." He sat opposite me at
the table and pointed to the coffeemaker. "Is that
coffee still hot?"

"Sure. Help yourself. Have a doughnut, too. Marty brought them."

He poured a cup. Black. No sugar. Didn't take a doughnut. "Anyway, they think the lab can bring up the numbers so that they can read the whole sequence. Then maybe they'll make some sense. Maybe even provide an ID."

"Good. I hope they'll catch the guy soon." I checked my watch again. "Well, I have to get back to work. See you later."

"If you need a ride home, I could hang around. I noticed your car isn't in the parking lot."

So. He noticed. Wonder what he's after now.

"Thanks. That's really nice of you, but I've got a cab coming."

He smiled. "Okay, then. I'll just go home and watch you on TV. Maybe I'll call up and ask for help with my problems."

"Please don't! Rhonda's screening my calls. She'd probably put you right through, and I'd have to try to keep a straight face. Anyway, I doubt that you have many problems."

"You must really be psychic. You're right. I don't have many." Again, the nice smile. "But why Rhonda? Janice told me this morning that she'd be doing *Nightshades* herself tonight. Seemed to think it was important that she be here for your first show."

"I wish she could be, but Marty says she had a bad headache and George had to take her home."

"Bummer." He finished his coffee, rinsed the cup, and headed for the door. He stopped, turned back toward me, and gave another one of those long, quiet, deep-into-my-eyes looks.

I held my breath.

"Break a leg!" he said.

I hurried back to the *Nightshades* set, where Marty sat on the turquoise couch, feet on the table. She looked up from the book on her lap, then held it so that I could see the title.

Astral Projection in Thought and Action.

"You believe in this hocus-pocus?" she asked. "You think people can pass through walls and all that?"

"I've never really given it much thought," I admitted, "but I remember reading somewhere once that just because we don't understand something doesn't mean it isn't real."

"Yeah. Ariel used to say that all the time." She put the book back on the table, and I added the ones I'd borrowed to the stack. "Listen," she said, "if it's okay with you, I'm going to use some of these crystals and stuff for the bumper shot to lead into your call segment. I'll put it all back on the table during the first commercial."

"Well, uh, sure," I said, but she was already arranging the big quartz crystal cluster, a chunk of pyrite, the rose quartz beads I'd used in the earlier commercial, and a little silver figure of Buddha in front of the felt background where the cemetery card had been.

Then, before I could object, she folded the black handkerchief neatly and placed the obsidian ball right in the center of the tableau.

"Perfect," she said. "Like it?"

"It's lovely," I said. And it was. Except for the fact that the damned black ball was uncovered again.

I didn't want to see it, so I looked up at the monitor screen instead. There, the evil doctor was in a dark cave, trudging through murky water. Marty picked up a remote.

"Want me to turn on the sound so you can watch? Ariel always did that so she could say something to make the audience think she really watched all this dreck."

I thought about Aunt Ibby being among the faithful *Nightshades* viewers. "I like old movies," I said, "and I remember this one pretty well, but yes, I'd like to see where we're breaking. Thank you."

"Oops. Didn't know you liked 'em that much. Ariel couldn't stand the things. I thought you might feel the same way. I'm sorry."

The studio filled with the somber sound-track music and the evil doctor's voice as he cursed the darkness, realizing that crashing ocean waves lay just ahead.

The shot of Marty's crystal arrangement came next, followed by a canned commercial for a local auto dealership. Marty moved quickly, dismantling the display and putting everything back on the table just as it had been.

Except for the covering on the black ball.

The commercial ended. I made the obligatory comment about the sad plight of Nina Foch, and the call button on my console glowed green. With my hand shaking ever so slightly, I tapped it, anticipating Crystal Moon's very first call.

"Hello, caller. Your first name and your question please."

"Crystal?" The man's voice was thin and querulous. "You're better looking than the other one."

What would Ariel do with this guy?

"Inner beauty is all that is of importance," I said, with a silent vow to strangle Rhonda at the first opportunity. "Your name and your question please."

"Oh, I'm Marvin. Listen, Crystal. My children are trying to steal my money. They want to put me in a home so they can steal my house and my dogs and my collections."

Oh boy.

I pressed my fingers against my temples, Ariel style.

Damn. This isn't easy.

"Could you give me the first name of one of the children you say have made up this plan?"

"Sure. Albert. That ungrateful little snake."

"Marvin, you have it within your power to make sure that everything that happens between you and your children will be for the good," I told him. I hoped I sounded powerfully psychic. "I want you to meditate quietly and send golden-white light to Albert and the others. That way you can help them to make good decisions for you all."

"I can?"

"Yes."

"Thanks, honey," said Marvin. "You got great tits."

I smothered a laugh, hoping against hope that Rhonda had hit the dump button in time to keep Marvin's observation from the viewers.

The call button on the console glowed again. I

pressed it. "Hello, caller. Your first name and your question please."

In quick succession I fielded questions from a man looking for his lost wallet, a woman who wanted to reach her dead mother-in-law, and a man who wanted to know if his house was going to sell. I told the first one that I felt that he would get his wallet back, minus the money.

Nothing psychic about that. It usually works out that way.

To the viewer interested in contacting the dead, I gave the number of the mystic shop that had provided the rose quartz crystal necklace, suggesting that the people on the staff there could contact a psychic who specialized in that sort of thing.

Passing the buck while giving a sponsor an extra plug.

I told the prospective house seller that he might need to drop his price and exhibit patience.

Easy answer. The lousy state of the housing market was in the papers every day.

It was time for *Shadows in the Night* to resume. Marty wheeled the camera away and signaled that my live shot was over.

"Good job, kid."

"Thanks. That dirty old man's remark didn't go out over the air, did it?"

"'Fraid so. Rhonda's not real quick on the uptake, y'know."

"Great. Have I got time to go up and kill her before the movie ends?"

Marty shrugged. "Sure. Why not?"

Red skirt swirling, I headed for the sound booth. Killing her seemed a bit harsh, but Rhonda was going to get blistered ears, at least. I looked overhead, making sure the "on-the-air" light wasn't glowing, before I pushed the heavy door open.

"Rhonda!" I began. "What the hell . . ."

But it wasn't Rhonda I saw seated before the blinking lights and multiple screens of the control-room wall.

It was George Valen.

CHAPTER 18

"George? What . . . ? Why . . . ?"

He held both hands up in front of his face. "Whoa. Hold your fire! It wasn't me! I would never have let that caller get to you!"

I glanced around the room. "But . . . Rhonda?"

"I sent her home. I was watching the show, naturally. As soon as I heard what was happening, I jumped into the car and raced over here. Look. Pajamas." He unzipped a few inches of a Boston Red Sox jacket, revealing a striped pajama top.

I sat on a beige plastic-topped counter, furrowed with cigarette burns.

"Thanks. I really appreciate it. Between the dirty old man and the lady wanting to talk to the dead, this wasn't starting out well. I was really hoping the delay button was working on that one call."

"You mean the old fart who thought you had nice . . . um . . . you know."

"Uh-huh. Him."

"Don't worry. You handled it fine. Doan will be impressed."

"Thanks again, George. I'd better get back. Have to take another call or two at the end of the movie. I'm glad you're doing the screening."

"No problem. Glad to help out."

I started for the door and turned back. "I almost forgot to ask. How's Janice? Marty said she went home with a terrible headache."

"Yeah. Poor kid." He shook his head. "She's sound asleep. I loaded her up with her pain pills. She should be okay by morning. But I'll scram for home as soon as your show is over."

"You're a good guy," I said. "She's lucky to have such a nice brother to watch out for her."

After hurrying back to the *Nightshades* set, I checked my makeup, dabbed on a little more pressed powder, refreshed the lipstick, and fluffed up my hair. I returned to the turquoise couch, arranged the red skirt, and fiddled with the neckline of the blouse. Marty and I watched and listened together as Nina Foch regained her senses and justice triumphed over evil.

I read one more commercial, this one about the almost sold-out Halloween Witches Ball.

It sounded like fun. Maybe Marty was right. Maybe I should invite Scott to go with me. After all, free tickets for an A-list party . . .

The call button glowed.

"Hello, caller. Your first name and your question please."

"Hello, Crystal. William here. You're doing great.

Welcome to *Nightshades*." The voice was youthful, cultured, pleasant.

"Thank you. Do you have a question for me?"

"I'm having some problems with my mother."

"Your mother's name?"

"Lena."

"What do you want to know about Lena?"

"I just can't figure it out, Crystal. I do everything she asks me to do, and she's just never satisfied."

I used my fingers on the temples, brows furrowed pose.

"Do you live with your mother?"

"Yes. She watches everything I do. She makes me do things I don't want to do."

I pretended to concentrate on the cluster of crystals. What was this? A grown man still living with Mom and refusing to do his chores? Or was the old lady just unreasonable? I decided to ask. "Do you feel that she asks too much of you? Or could you perhaps try a little harder to help around the house?"

I looked past the crystal cluster, glanced at the obsidian ball, then quickly looked away. I smiled into the camera, waiting for his answer. There was a long pause. I could hear his breathing. When he spoke again, he sounded younger.

"I try to be good, Crystal. I really do."

"I'm sure you do, William."

Marty moved her hand in the circular motion, which meant "Speed it up."

"We're nearly out of time, William. I'm sorry. I feel that it may help if you and your mother can meditate together. There are some fine books on the subject at the Ultimate Journey Bookstore in downtown Salem."

"Okay, Crystal. Thanks. She wants me to get her a cat now. I guess I'll do it."

"That would be nice, William. A cat is good company."

A loud click, and he was gone.

Marty moved in for a close-up. "Thanks for watching, everyone," I said. "Please join us again tomorrow night for another edition of *Nightshades,* when we'll watch a classic tale of horror, Edgar Allen Poe's *The Pit and the Pendulum.*"

Marty gave the "cut" signal, and the camera light winked out. The phone lines ceased blinking, and the studio lights brightened. George Valen's voice came over the intercom.

"Good job, Crystal. Night, Marty. I'm buttoning up in here and switching over to network. See you guys tomorrow."

I looked at my watch. Nearly 2:15 a.m. Jim Litka's cab should be out front in a few minutes. "I've got to go, too," I said. "Are you leaving now, Marty?"

"You go along, Moon," she said. "I'll just get things tidied up around here. I'll be finished pretty soon."

"I hate to leave you alone here," I said.

"I'm fine. Anyway, I won't be alone. George is still here, and the cleaning man came on at two. Always on time."

"All right, then. But don't we have a security guard?"

"The cleaning man is the security guard."

"Of course he is. I should have known. Good night. See you tomorrow."

I headed for the dressing room and paused, looking back at the black ball. Its shiny surface was unblemished. No body. No boots. No snarling cat. I turned back, picked up the folded black handkerchief, and re-covered the thing.

There wasn't time to change. I tossed my jacket over the gypsy rig, stuffed my jeans, sweater, and boots into the garment bag, grabbed my purse, and took the clanging elevator down to the lobby. I waited inside, peeking from behind the glass pane in the front door every few seconds, searching for the green-and-white cab. I wasn't about to stand outside the TV station at two thirty in the morning.

Not with a killer out there somewhere.

The cab zoomed up to the curb exactly on time. I'd barely opened the door when a smiling Jim Litka came bounding up the stairs, took the garment bag with one hand and my elbow with the other, guiding me carefully to the waiting taxi.

"Can't have you standing around here alone at this hour," he said. "Not in this neighborhood. Did I keep you waiting at all?"

I climbed into the backseat. "Not at all, Jim. You're right on time."

"Whew. That's good. I was worried about you. Show go all right?"

"I think so," I said. "I think I did okay. For a first time, I mean."

"Aw, I'll bet you were great. Sorry I couldn't watch. It's been crazy out here. Parties all over the place. Leadin' up to the big one, I'm guessin'."

"The big one?"

"The Witches Ball."

"Everybody says that's a good one."

"You goin'?" He looked at me in the rearview

mirror as we pulled away from the curb and headed for Hawthorne Boulevard.

"Thinking about it," I admitted.

I was surprised to see the amount of traffic coming and going on Salem's darkened streets. There was pedestrian traffic, too, and the cab stopped at more than one intersection, allowing people to cross.

"I see what you mean about things being busy around here. Where are all these people going in the middle of the night?"

"Well, like I said, some of them are partiers. Headin' home from the bars. But a lot of them are night workers, like you and me. And besides them . . ." He caught my eye in the mirror again. "There's always the bad guys. The ones who need the dark to cover up what they're doin'."

We'd made the turn onto Winter Street, and even that familiar stretch of road, with its mellow brick sidewalks, fine old homes, and sturdy trees, had somehow been turned into a scary, alien place. Leafless branches clawed at a starless sky, and long, wavering shadows stretched from between darkened buildings. Unlike the other streets we'd traveled between the station and here, not a human was in sight and automobiles were few.

The cab pulled up in front of Aunt Ibby's house. The brightly illuminated doorway was a welcoming sight. With a promise to be right back with the money I owed, I hurried up the steps, my key in hand.

Aunt Ibby called out "Hello" from the living room as soon as I pushed the door open, and O'Ryan appeared, curling himself around my ankles and purring loudly. No arched back. No snarling. Just a big, soft yellow cat.

"You both waited up for me. How sweet!"

Aunt Ibby, in flowered housecoat and fuzzy slippers, joined me in the front hall, beaming.

"You were just wonderful, Maralee. And you looked so pretty! Come into the kitchen and tell me all about it. I'll make us some nice hot chocolate."

"That sounds great. I will. But first I have to run upstairs and get my wallet."

I explained about the cabdriver waiting out front and started up the stairs. Aunt Ibby headed for the kitchen, promising to get the hot chocolate started, with the cat hurrying along ahead of her. I heard the cat door creak, announcing that O'Ryan had left the building. I got the wallet and headed back downstairs. The silence was shattered by an earsplitting yowl, and I raced for the kitchen.

"What's wrong? Where's O'Ryan?"

Aunt Ibby had already hit the light switch for the outdoor floodlights and was looking out the kitchen window.

"Maralee! There's a man out there, and he's got O'Ryan. Oh dear! He's going over the wall!"

"Call 911," I yelled. "I'm going to chase him!"

The wall backed up to Winter Street, so I headed to the front door, threw it open, and scrambled down the steps. I could see the man, struggling with a large sack, running toward Salem Common.

"Mr. Litka! Help!" I called as I ran by the cab, slipping and stumbling in the silly gold sandals on the uneven brick sidewalk. "Help me catch that guy! He took my cat!" I pointed at the running man.

Jim Litka pounded past me and chased the fleeing thief across the street. They both disappeared behind the massive Civil War monument on the corner, and again I heard that frightful yowl. "Got your cat!" the cabdriver yelled, emerging from behind the monument, carrying the wiggling bag. "But the guy got away!"

By this time some lights had started to appear in upper-story windows along the street as people peered out to see what the commotion was about, and flashes of blue announced the arrival of the police.

Grinning, Jim Litka bounded onto the sidewalk and handed me the writhing bag—a pillowcase, actually—containing the frightened cat. Aunt Ibby was on the front steps, facing two uniformed policemen. We all began to talk at once.

"Calm down, everybody," commanded the tallest cop. "Can we step into the house?"

Aunt Ibby opened the door, and we filed inside.

"Now," he said, "one at a time please, can you tell us what's going on?" He looked at the pillowcase, which was quieter now, but still in motion. "And can you safely let whatever that is out?"

It was a good suggestion. Once freed, O'Ryan dashed up the front staircase to the second floor and safety. Aunt Ibby led the rest of us into the living room. What a strange-looking group we were! The burly cabdriver, the elderly housecoat-clad woman in fuzzy slippers, and the redhead in a gypsy costume showing far too much cleavage for the occasion. But the officers—who, because it was Halloween season in Salem, had probably seen stranger things that night—showed no surprise.

One at a time, we told our stories. They let Jim Litka talk first because, as he explained, he had to get back to work. He told them how he had picked me up from the TV station and had remained parked out front because I had to go inside to get my wallet. He described how I had run screaming from the house, and he said that was when he first saw the man with the bag running down the street, heading toward the common.

"When Ms. Barrett here yelled for me to help her," he said, "I jumped out of my cab and ran after the guy. He wasn't all that fast, y'know, and he was carrying that cat bag, so it wasn't too hard to catch him. I got him up against that big rock thing at the end of Winter Street, grabbed his arm, the one holding the bag, gave it a good twist, and he dropped the bag. I let go of him and picked it up, so's the cat wouldn't run away, y'know, and he took off runnin' over that way." He gestured in the direction of the common. "He got behind some of them big trees and that tent thing, and I lost sight of him."

Jim said that the man was of medium height, had a slim build, and was wearing some kind of uniform, gloves, and a dark-colored ski mask. Jim couldn't tell what color his eyes were.

"Anything else?" the tallest officer wanted to know.

Jim thought for a moment. "Yeah," he said. "You know what? He smelled of naphtha."

"Naphtha?"

"Yeah," Jim said. "Naphtha. It's in some of the chemicals they use to clean the upholstery in the cabs."

"It's in mothballs, too," Aunt Ibby offered.

Jim snapped his fingers. "Mothballs. That's it. He smelled like mothballs."

The other officer, who was taking notes, asked Jim for his phone number and told him he could leave. I paid the two fares, tripled the tip, and told him I'd call again soon.

Then it was Aunt Ibby's turn. She'd gone to the kitchen to make hot chocolate. O'Ryan had run on ahead of her and had gone out through the cat door. Within less than two minutes, she'd heard him yowl.

"I was standing right next to the light switch," she said. "The one that turns on the outdoor floodlights. He had O'Ryan by the scruff of his neck. Cats hate that, you know. Shoved the poor creature into a big cloth bag."

"Can you describe the man?" asked the note-taking officer.

"Well, as Mr. Litka said, he was medium height and slim. He was wearing one of those army outfits that look like camouflage. He had a brown ski mask on and brown gloves. And boots. Army boots perhaps. After he stuffed poor O'Ryan into that sack, he jumped over the stone wall. That's when my niece ran out the front door and chased after him." She stopped speaking and sniffed the air. "I think my hot chocolate is burning," she said and dashed for the kitchen.

It was my turn. The tallest officer turned to me, taking in the Gypsy outfit, not unappreciatively. The note-taking one spoke first. He asked my name, if I lived here, and if I had anything to add to what Aunt Ibby and Jim Litka had told them.

"Not really," I said. "I never got a good look at the

man. I was chasing him down the street in the dark, and I couldn't run very fast in these shoes."

He snapped the notebook shut. "That's okay, miss," he said. "I guess we've got all we need. We'll take a look over behind the monument and see if the guy dropped anything, and we'll take a look around the common, but he's pretty surely long gone by now."

"Do you think you'll be able to find out who he is?"

"Well, to tell you the truth, miss, we can't spend a lot of time on this one. After all, you got your cat back. No harm done."

Aunt Ibby returned to the living room, wooden stirring spoon still in hand.

The other officer spoke up. "Weird things happen around Halloween, miss. I'm thinking this guy was at a Halloween costume party where they had a scavenger hunt and he was supposed to bring back a cat. That's all. Probably drunk, too."

"I guess that's possible."

But why that *costume? Camo and army boots?* Aunt Ibby and I exchanged puzzled looks.

"Sure. Don't worry about it. Anyway, we've got a couple of murders on our hands now, too, so cat stealers aren't high priority."

"But, Officer," I said. "Didn't you know? O'Ryan was Ariel Constellation's cat."

CHAPTER 19

That information immediately increased the policemen's interest in the attempted cat-napping. One of the officers carefully picked up the discarded pillowcase, tucked it into an evidence bag, and left us. I considered calling Pete Mondello. He had, after all, told me to call anytime if I thought of anything that might help with the case. But would he appreciate a call at 3:00 a.m.? Probably not. With a relieved sigh, I closed the door behind the last officer.

"The camouflage suit and the boots cannot be a co-incidence," Aunt Ibby said as we headed for the kitchen for our long-delayed hot chocolate. "That man may be Ariel's killer."

"I know. He may be the Pelletier woman's killer, too. Surely the police must have made the connection."

"Do you think you ought to call that detective?"

"I thought about it. But look at the time!"

It turned out that someone else had thought it was important enough to wake Pete Mondello.

I'd barely had a sip of hot chocolate when the door

chimes sounded and the detective appeared in our foyer, leaving me wishing that I'd changed my clothes.

Mondello asked permission to check out the courtyard where the man had grabbed the cat, and within minutes a crew of techs was ruining what was left of Aunt Ibby's late-blooming geraniums and vacuuming the top of the wall where the thief had made his escape. Down the street another crew was swarming over the Civil War memorial site, while a few of the Winter Street neighbors, wide awake now and alerted by the commotion, stood along the curb.

I wasn't too sure exactly what was going on, so after a quick change into jeans and a sweater, and a much-needed face scrub, I caught up with the detective on the sidewalk in front of the house.

"Detective—" I began.

"Pete," he insisted with a smile.

I'll bet that smile gets him just about anything he wants.

"Pete, why all the interest in O'Ryan? I know he was Ariel's cat, but what would anyone gain by stealing him? Ransom?"

"Don't know. Doesn't make a lot of sense, does it? What we're interested in is what your aunt told us about the guy wearing boots. Ariel's killer wore boots. We're hoping to get a good casting in the soft dirt out in the garden or maybe down there by the monument."

"I have to admit that for one wild minute I thought it was because O'Ryan was a witness to Ariel's death!"

He laughed. "Yep. I thought of that, too. But unless the cat can communicate with humans, he wouldn't be much help."

I didn't laugh. I thought about the picture in the

obsidian ball of O'Ryan in distress. Had he arched his
back and snarled at his abductor, just as he had in
my vision? Could he communicate with humans?
With me?

And hadn't anyone but my aunt and I noticed that
the guy on all those surveillance cameras on Derby
Street was wearing camouflage?

I decided to ask.

"Pete," I said, "seriously, do you think the man
you're looking for in the Pelletier murder is the same
one who killed Ariel? And probably the same one who
just tried to steal our cat?"

His expression changed immediately into what I
recognized as his "cop face." I wasn't about to get any
information about police business, that was for sure.

Then, just as quickly, his expression softened.

"Yes, Lee. I do. And I don't like it that this creep
knows where you live. You haven't made any enemies
around here, have you?"

"Not that I know of."

*Not unless you count a guy sitting on a throne and hold-
ing a cup who lives in a deck of cards.*

By the time Pete and his crew left, it was far too late
to even think about going to bed. Anyway, I was wide
awake. Promising myself a good nap later, I headed
for the study for some *Nightshades* show prep. I jotted
down a few notes for my monologue and browsed
through a book on meditation techniques from Aunt
Ibby's secret stash.

Happily, O'Ryan showed no ill effects from his near
abduction. After hiding under my bed, behind the
dust ruffle, for an hour or so, he emerged, tail erect,
whiskers bristling, and joined me in the study. He

selected a pale pool of early morning sun in front of a bay window and proceeded to give himself a good washing.

"O'Ryan," I said, "do you really know who that man was?"

He paused in his fur-licking project, cocked his head to one side, and gave me a look that seemed to say, "Are you nuts? Of course I don't. I'm just a cat."

But then he winked.

I put the book and notes aside and thought about the mysterious man who'd run down the street, carrying the cat bag. Had he been waiting in the garden for O'Ryan to come outside via the cat door? Did he know that sooner or later the cat would appear? But the psychic's cat had been with Aunt Ibby and me for only a few days. How many people even knew about the cat door?

I could think of only one.

Before Scott Palmer and I had left for the football game, he'd mentioned that he liked cats all right but didn't like litter box duty. That was when I'd told him about the cat door. I was positive I had never mentioned it to another soul.

I didn't like the way I was thinking. It was definitely time for coffee. I headed for the kitchen, O'Ryan following close behind me.

When I passed the den, there was Aunt Ibby, dressed for the day, working at her computer.

"I thought you might have gone to bed, considering our all-nighter," I said. "But I'm glad you're here. I just had kind of a disturbing thought."

"What is it, dear?" She closed her laptop, looking at me with concern.

I told her about my cat door quandary. "Who knew about O'Ryan's bathroom habits besides you and me? And recently, Scott Palmer?" I asked. "I'm sure I've never mentioned it to anyone else. I hate to think that Scott . . ."

"Oops," said my aunt.

"Oops? What do you mean, oops?"

She tapped the closed lid of the laptop. "Facebook. I've been bragging to all my Facebook friends about how smart O'Ryan is. I even took pictures of him coming out of the cat door and posted them. Everyone loved them. Those pictures may have gone viral by now, they are so darned cute!"

"How many Facebook friends do you have?" I asked, relieved about Scott, but curious about who else might be on some kind of a short list of suspects.

"Oh, hundreds!" She waved a hand. "Lots of them. All over the world. Why, I was just talking to one of my old library friends in the UK. He earned a scholarship to Oxford, and he's with New Scotland Yard now. I'm blessed to have so many interesting friends."

"You are," I agreed. "Do any of those friends happen to be associated with WICH-TV?"

"Well, of course there's Rhonda."

Wonderful. Rhonda, of "sees all, knows all, tells all"
fame.

"No problem. But maybe we ought to tell Detective Mondello about those pictures of the cat door, anyway."

"Oh dear. Do you think it was wrong of me to post them?"

"Absolutely not. How would you know there was a catnapper lurking out there somewhere? But I promised to tell Pete any little thing that might be helpful."

"Pete?"

I could feel my face coloring. "Detective Mondello. His name is Pete."

My cell phone rang, so I didn't have to explain further.

"Hello?"

It was Rhonda. "Hi, Lee. Mr. Doan says to tell you he liked the show last night and he wants you to join him and Janice for lunch. He says for you to be at the old Lyceum restaurant at noon. Okay?"

The last-minute invitation, which ignored the fact that I'd worked until two in the morning, was typical of the high-handed manner of the station manager. But I knew I'd accept, because he was, at least for the time being, my boss.

I told Rhonda to tell Mr. Doan, "Thanks very much," and that I would be there at noon.

"What was that about?" my aunt wanted to know.

"I've been invited to lunch with the boss and Janice Valen. Apparently, Mr. Doan liked the show, and Janice must be feeling better."

"That's nice, dear. Where are you going to eat?"

"At the restaurant in the old Lyceum."

"A most interesting venue," she said. "Alexander Graham Bell gave the first public demonstration of the telephone there. Oh, and it's supposed to be haunted, you know."

"No kidding? By whom? Or what?"

"A witch," she said, "named Bridget Bishop."

So with thoughts of witches, good and bad, dancing in my head, and with O'Ryan stretched out beside me, I took a short nap. Somewhat refreshed, I got to the Lyceum at exactly noon. Janice had arrived ahead of me and was seated on a long bench with some other people.

"Hi, Lee." She moved over, patting the space next to her. "Come on. Sit down. George dropped me off. He doesn't like me to drive after I have one of my headaches." She wrinkled her perfect nose. "Even though I feel fine. Doan isn't here yet, but we'll get seated as soon as he arrives. They know him here."

She was stunning in a bright red suit and shoes that screamed Jimmy Choo. She certainly looked fully recovered from her headache. In fact, she looked as though she'd never been sick in her life. I was wearing the same green suit I'd worn for my ill-fated interview, and I hoped that my carefully applied makeup covered the fact that I hadn't really slept in about forty-eight hours.

"I'm glad you're feeling better," I said. "You look wonderful."

"I'm fine," she said again. "Big brother George always takes good care of me. But I'm truly sorry about not being there for your first show."

"Not your fault. But I'll admit it got pretty hairy there for a few minutes. I'm really grateful to George for bailing me out the way he did."

"You mean after the call from the old fart who thinks you have nice tits?"

"Uh . . . yes." I looked around, hoping none of our bench mates were listening.

"Well, don't worry about it. George says you handled everything perfectly. Doan was impressed. Anyway, you do."

"I do what?"

"Have nice tits." She looked down at her own chest. "I wish I did."

"Wish you did what?" It was Scott Palmer's voice. "Good show last night, Moon."

"Thanks," I said.

"Had nice tits," said Janice in a matter-of-fact tone.

I felt the color rising to my face. I looked at Scott through lowered lashes. He was red-faced, too.

"Everyone says it was a good show, Lee. I'm sorry I missed it." Janice seemed oblivious to the embarrassment she'd caused. "And, Scotty, I'm glad Doan invited you, too. He's really happy with your work. Especially that piece with the old guy who found that razor thing."

I welcomed the change of subject. "Scott, have they figured out what those numbers on the straight razor mean?"

"Not exactly. But the police think they could be old service numbers."

"Service numbers?"

"Yep. Back in the sixties everybody in the service had a number. Now they just keep track with Social Security numbers."

I thought about Aunt Ibby's description of the man she'd seen in the garden, and the surveillance videos of the "person of interest" in the Pelletier murder. "Do they think some old soldier has something to do with all this?"

"I don't know what the police think. They're not letting the media in on much."

Janice stood, pointing toward the sidewalk. "Here comes the great man now. About freakin' time. I'm starving."

A beaming hostess greeted the station manager by name and led us to a very good table. Janice was right. They knew him here.

Maybe he's a good tipper.

He stuck out his hand. "Glad to welcome you to WICH-TV, Ms. Barrett," he said. "I hope this is the beginning of a long and happy association."

Since we hadn't even discussed my salary yet and I hadn't given up my plans to land a *real* TV job, my reply was deliberately noncommittal.

"I'm pleased to meet you, sir." His handshake was surprisingly gentle for such a big man.

We were seated at a square table, Scott opposite me, and Doan and Janice facing each other. Bruce Doan aimed a smile in my direction.

"Looks as though you have the best seat in the house, Ms. Barrett," he said.

"Really?" I looked around.

"You're facing the staircase. That's where the ghost of the witch is supposed to appear."

"No kidding?" Scott leaned forward. "A real Salem witch ghost?"

"Her name was Bridget Bishop," Janice said. "Ariel always said she was a really evil witch. A very powerful one."

Doan made a snorting sound but didn't say anything.

Scott persisted with his questions. "Do you know of anyone who's really seen it?"

Doan looked annoyed. "Of course not. There's no such thing as ghosts."

"Ariel saw her once." Janice spoke softly.

"Ariel was a raving nutcase," Doan answered.

"You're just saying that because you hated her."

The station manager raised his voice. "Everybody hated her!"

"I didn't hate her. She was nice to me." Janice's eyes looked misty.

Heads began to turn in our direction. Had the two forgotten that Scott and I were there? I raised my menu to cover my face.

A waitress appeared to take our orders. Thankful for the interruption, I chose the daily lunch special. Scott and Mr. Doan did the same. Janice ordered a hearts of palm salad.

"Can we have a bottle of wine with lunch, Bruce?" she asked quite pleasantly. "After all, we're celebrating with our new friends."

Her change of demeanor didn't seem to surprise Doan at all. "Sure we can," he said and ordered a good merlot. "I'm real happy to have you two aboard."

"Glad to be here," I mumbled, and Scott said something similar. Our eyes met in a silent, if confused, communion.

The waitress delivered wineglasses, and Scott put his hand over his. "None for me, thanks. I'm still on company time. Might have to leave if anything interesting happens." I wished I had a similar excuse. Ditching this meeting looked more like an attractive option with every passing minute.

It was Scott's turn to change the subject. "Lee, the police notes mentioned some kind of little fracas in your neighborhood this morning. What's the story?"

I wasn't about to report on O'Ryan's adventure just yet. "Somebody said that they thought it might have been some kind of Halloween party scavenger hunt gone bad," I said. "I really don't know exactly what went on."

Sort of true. Anyway, I wasn't about to feed Scott information about anything!

We were only partway through our entrées when Scott's phone buzzed. He glanced at a text message, tossed his napkin on the table, and stood up. "Sorry, folks," he said. "Thanks for inviting me, Mr. Doan. Something's going on at the police station. Gotta run."

He actually did run, too. I couldn't help wondering if the message was really all that urgent or if he was just glad to get away.

"Oh, crap," Janice said. "If Scott has to go out on a story, that probably means George does, too. He won't be able to take me home. Now what am I going to do?" She made a pretty pout and drained her wineglass.

"I'd like to help you out, honey," said Doan, consulting his Rolex, "but I'm due to meet Mrs. Doan in half an hour. Some kind of church thing. How about you, Ms. Barrett? Or can I call you Lee? Will you give Janice a lift? She lives over near you."

Near me? I didn't know that.

"Yes, of course you may. And I'll be glad to drive Janice home."

"Great," he said. "Thanks. And, Janice, you'd better take the rest of the day off."

It was a good suggestion. And George was right about not letting her drive. She appeared to be getting quite smashed. Doan had had only one glass of wine, and I was still slowly sipping my first one. We all declined dessert, and I suggested to Janice that she sit on the bench in the lobby while I brought the car around. Doan signed the tab, and as he stood to leave, he reached into his suit coat pocket.

"Lee, here's a company credit card for you. Pick up a few costumes like the one you wore last night. Looked really good." His smile was darned near lascivious. "Oh yeah. Rhonda gave me this phone message for you." He handed me a wrinkled pink slip with a name and number on it. The message said, *Call me*.

It was from River North.

CHAPTER 20

I wished I could return River's call right away, but I was committed to driving the hammered program director home now. I tucked the pink slip into my purse with a vow to call the young witch as soon as I could.

Doan was right. Janice did live near me. Not in the same neighborhood, but about a mile away, on the opposite side of the common. If it wasn't for the trees and the striped tent, I'd probably be able to see her place from Aunt Ibby's front steps.

The house, which had been converted to condominiums, was a handsome old Federal-period mansion—probably once the home of some long-ago Salem ship captain. Janice tripped, losing and then regaining her balance, when she stepped out of the car. George had told me he'd "loaded her up with her pain pills" the night before. That, in combination with several glasses of wine, was undoubtedly having an exaggerated effect.

"Whoopsie." She giggled, steadying herself with a

hand on the Buick's hood. "I think I might be a teensy bit tiddly."

"It's okay," I told her. "Wait a sec. I'll give you a hand." I locked the car and took her arm, guiding her gently toward the house. At first she shook my hand away. After staggering a few steps, she allowed me to put a steadying arm around her waist and propel her forward and into the entryway of the place.

She retrieved a key from her Prada purse and, after a few stabs at the keyhole, opened the door to the first-floor condo. "Come on in, Leezy," she said. "Welcome to happy Valenville." Kicking off those expensive shoes in the high-ceilinged, chandeliered foyer, she lurched toward a spacious, gleaming state-of-the-art kitchen and dining area.

"See?" she said. "Georgie and I share this fine kitchen, and we each have our own bedroom, bathroom, and living room. Mine's in there." She pointed to the left, then, whirling unsteadily, pointed to the right. "Georgie lives in there. Come on to my house," she said, taking my hand, pulling me toward the doorway on the left.

Janice's living room was a surprising contrast to her starkly modern office at the station. It was furnished in traditional style. The chintz-patterned sofa and love seat were flanked by a Sheraton-style side table. *Probably the real thing*, I thought, observing the delicate reeded legs and simple hardware. Oil paintings on the cream damask-covered walls featured seaport scenes and portraits of men and women in period dress. The cushy maroon carpet was a perfect complement to the furnishings.

"Such a beautiful room, Janice," I said. "My aunt would love this."

"Bring her over sometime," she said. "Glad you like it. A decorator did the whole thing. Right down to the freakin' magazines on the coffee table and the books in the bookcases."

"It's lovely."

"George didn't want a decorator. Did his own place. Wanna see?"

"No thanks. I don't want to go into anybody's space uninvited."

Janice plopped down onto one of the flowered sofas. "Oh, I'm sure you'll be invited in there sooner or later. He thinks you're beautiful. He told me," she said. "And you've got those big boobs he likes."

What the hell is all this preoccupation with breast size?

Growing increasingly uncomfortable, I ignored the remark. But Janice wasn't through with the subject.

"Are yours real?"

So that's it. Janice must be thinking about getting implants!

"Yes, but quite a few of my friends in Florida have had implants, and they're all very happy with the results."

Janice shrank back against the bright cushions, and her face paled. "Oh, I could never do that! No doctor's going to use a knife on me!"

Oh boy! TMI again!

"Sorry," I said. "I didn't mean to upset you. I think your figure is just perfect the way it is."

"Thanks. Come on!" She jumped up, moving much faster than I thought possible in her condition. "I'll show you the pictures!"

Shoeless, she raced across the room, through the kitchen, and into the open entrance to her brother's half of the condo. By the time I caught up with her, she was in George's living room, kneeling in front of a plain, tan-colored wooden bureau. The bottom drawer was open, and Janice had pulled a large black photo album out from under a pile of neatly folded linens. She looked up at me with the expression of a mischievous child.

"Georgie doesn't know I look through his stuff all the time when he's not here," she said. "Come on. I want to show you something."

I knew I had no business in this man's private space. But as long as I was there, however reluctantly, I couldn't resist taking a quick glance around the room. The surroundings were far different from the decorator decor of his sister's quarters. A couch and two chairs were upholstered in striped mattress ticking. A glass-topped trunk served as a coffee table, and wooden side tables and a desk were all of simple construction—the kind people buy ready to finish in the big chain home stores. All of it was painted in shades of tan, in stark contrast to the navy-blue walls, which were covered with scores of neatly framed photographs hung in orderly rows.

Janice replaced the folded fabrics with swift efficiency. It was clear that she'd done this before. Closing the drawer, she scampered back across the kitchen and into her own living room. I hurried along behind her.

Pushing a few color-coordinated magazines aside, she placed the album carefully on the mahogany coffee table. "Come on. Sit with me. I'll show you the boobies Georgie likes."

"No, Janice. I don't want to. . . ."

Too late. She'd flipped the book open to an eight-by-ten matte-finished black-and-white photograph of a nude woman. It was a beautiful and tasteful pose. The woman stood in partial shade in a wooded area. She leaned against a tree, one hand above her head, touching the rough bark, her ample bosom thrust forward. Long dark hair framed her face.

"That's my mother," she said.

What are you supposed to say when someone shows you a naked picture of her mother?

"She's very beautiful," I said truthfully.

"Not is. Was. She's dead." Janice's voice was flat. Unemotional.

"I'm sorry," I said. "Was she a professional model?"

"Not really. She posed only for Georgie."

Jesus! What kind of a nest of weirdos have I wandered into?

She turned to another page, this one showing a pastoral scene. "You know," she said in a thoughtful tone, "they're quite good, aren't they? Imagine. He must have been only about fifteen when he took these."

"You'd better put that away." I grabbed my purse and headed for the door. "I've got to go."

Barely saying a quick good-bye, I dashed out of the building to my car, my mind buzzing.

Was George some kind of oedipal pervert? What was the message River North had for me? Should I invite Scott to the Witches Ball? Did I have enough time to finish my show prep for tonight's edition of *Nightshades?* Why would someone want to steal the cat?

There were only two things I was absolutely sure about.

I needed a shower, and I desperately needed a nap.

I began to feel better as soon as I'd parked the Buick in the garage. Hurrying up the brick pathway, I could smell Aunt Ibby's famous snickerdoodles before I'd even unlocked the back door. With a long spatula, she was arranging the fresh, hot cookies on a wire rack. I came up behind her and gave her a big hug.

"I love you, Aunt Ibby."

"Why, thank you, Maralee. I love you, too. But what have I done to earn such special attention?"

"I'm just glad to be home." I sat on a high stool and helped myself to a cookie. "It's been a strange day," I said, kicking off my shoes the way Janice had. Mine were not Jimmy Choos.

O'Ryan padded into the room and leapt up onto my lap. He turned around once, then settled down and closed his eyes. No doubt he was shedding yellow cat hairs all over the front of my green suit, but I was just too beat to care.

"Did you have a nice lunch?" She placed neat circles of dough onto a fresh cookie sheet. "The Lyceum is always pleasant, I think."

"The food was good, as usual, but Mr. Doan and Janice got into a row—something about witches. It was embarrassing. And Janice got a bit drunk. I think it was partly from the pills she'd taken for her migraine. Scott Palmer had to leave early for an assignment. . . ."

"You didn't mention that Scott was going to be there."

"I didn't know. But I'm sure he was glad to leave."

"That bad?"

"It was pretty awful. I had to drive Janice home. Her condo is gorgeous, by the way. You'd love it. The kitchen is fabulous, and Janice has some really nice antiques and paintings."

"Does she live alone?"

"No. She shares the place with her brother George." I explained briefly how the condo was divided into his and hers segments, separated by the *House Beautiful* kitchen.

"That makes a lot of sense, what with the high prices they get for condos these days. It's nice for families to share the space." She smiled. "Like you and me. I take it they're both single?"

"As far as I know."

"How old do you think Janice is?" my aunt asked.

"I don't know for sure. I saw a photo of her taken in London when she was an actress—maybe a showgirl. The date on it was 2005 and she looked as though she might be in her early twenties. So I'm guessing she's probably somewhere around my age."

"She's very attractive. How old do you think her brother might be?"

"George? Hard to tell. Could be forty-something. I get the impression that he feels responsible for his sister. He kind of hovers over her."

"Maybe she has health issues, what with the headaches and all."

"Maybe."

"You look tired, Maralee. Why don't you take a nice warm shower and try to sleep for a couple of hours? I'll wake you in plenty of time for tonight's show."

"Sounds good to me."

"And take the car tonight. I won't be needing it."

"Thanks. I will." I lifted the sleeping cat from my lap and put him on the floor, where he yawned and stretched. I picked up my shoes, reached for a warm cookie, and climbed the stairs, with O'Ryan trotting along behind me.

After a hot shower, and wrapped in a cozy terry robe, I headed for my room. O'Ryan was already there, curled up at the foot of the bed. I propped myself up on a few pillows and dialed the number on the pink slip Doan had given me.

River answered right away. "Oh, Crystal, I'm so glad you called. I watched your show last night. Why didn't you tell me you were a psychic?"

"I'm not really, River. Like the man says, 'I just play one on TV.'"

"Well, it's exciting that you're a TV star. I'd love to have a job like that."

"I'm hardly a star, River. What did you want to talk to me about?"

"While I was watching *Nightshades,* I laid the cards out for you again. There are some things you need to know. To be extra careful about."

"That doesn't sound too good." I tried to keep my tone light.

"Some of it is okay, but some of it might not be. Listen. It's mostly about your aunt. She's the only thing standing between you and the reversed King of Cups. Please tell her to be very careful."

"I will," I promised. "Should I make an appointment to see you again?"

"I'm all booked up for today, and I know you have

to work tonight. Could you come over to the tent sometime tomorrow afternoon? I'll be doing tea leaves."

"I can be there around two, if that's all right," I said. "Tea Leaves, huh? Another gift?"

"Two is good. And you don't need a gift to do tea. It's not hard, and people seem to like it."

"October must be an awfully busy time for you."

"You bet! I read the cards and the tea leaves most every day, along with some private readings. Then, a couple of times a week, I put on my pilgrim dress and do a few nighttime ghost tours. Have to go now. Here comes a customer. See you tomorrow. Bye!"

I patted the snoozing cat. "What do you think about that, O'Ryan? More bad news from the tarot." I picked up the remote and turned on the TV. "Let's see if I can stay awake long enough to catch the afternoon news. Maybe they'll be running whatever it was that made Scott run out on that delightful lunch!"

Police Chief Whaley's craggy face filled the screen. "MIT has completed their examination of the straight razor presumably used last week in the murder of Yvette Pelletier."

A split screen showed a studio portrait of the deceased woman on one side and an artist's sketch of a straight razor, blade exposed, on the other. Yvette Pelletier had been a rather pretty woman with large eyes and long dark hair. The razor, even in a drawing, looked lethal.

"The sequence of numerals scratched onto the weapon has been confirmed as a service number," the chief continued. "It was issued to a member of the United States armed forces during the Korean conflict. The number has been traced to a patient at a Florida veterans' hospital. A Salem detective is en route to Tampa to interview that individual. I'll take a few questions."

Scott asked the first question. "Do you know the man's name?"

Whaley shook his head. "Not releasing that information yet."

Scott asked another. "Any idea how the razor wound up in Salem?"

"No idea. It's an old item. Could have come from an antique store or pawnshop. We're checking all avenues."

One of the other reporters wanted to know when the media could get the name of the razor's original owner. The chief said he didn't know, announced that the press conference was over, and ignored shouted questions as he walked back inside the station.

Scott appeared on the screen. He promised to keep the WICH-TV audience posted on any breaks in the case and signed off, returning the viewers to the anchor desk at the studio. I turned off the set, leaned back onto my fluffy pillows, and wondered how Scott might look dressed as a Gypsy king at the Witches Ball. I dozed off smiling, picturing Scott in a white balloon-sleeved shirt open to the waist, with gold chains draped across a perfectly sculpted chest.

Within moments, my eyes flew open as another image intruded on those pleasant thoughts.

The televised portrait of Yvette Pelletier bore a striking resemblance to the woman in the photo in George Valen's album.

CHAPTER 21

I am always surprised by how much good a few hours of sound sleep can do. When Aunt Ibby woke me at around seven, I felt just fine. Shaking aside disturbing, but completely unfounded comparisons between the murdered woman and Janice's mother, I was wide awake and ready to get on with my *Nightshades* show prep. I'd already decided to open with the meditation advice I'd gleaned from one of Ariel's books. Then I'd introduce the 1961 version of *The Pit and the Pendulum,* with Vincent Price in the starring role. There were surely enough horrific revelations, ghostly appearances, and violent deaths packed into the old thriller to satisfy the late-show audience.

One of the attic outfits, a pink boatneck blouse and a ruffled blue square-dance skirt, would do for now, and I'd go costume shopping soon. Trying not to wake O'Ryan, I slipped out of bed and headed back to the study to print out my notes for the show.

It took only a few minutes for the cat to catch up with me. He hopped onto the desk, watching as I worked for an hour. Then, notes finished, we went downstairs together.

Aunt Ibby called from the kitchen. "I think you have time for a bite of supper. There's a nice pot roast simmering in the slow cooker."

"Sounds good. Smells good, too. I'll try to get to the station around nine thirty. That'll give me plenty of time to dress, do makeup, and look over the commercials," I said as I walked into the kitchen. "And to see who's screening my calls."

"That's turned out to be quite important," my aunt said as she filled my plate with a slice of tender roast, along with carrots and potatoes. "Considering last night's unfortunate editing error."

"That was awful. I was so relieved when George took over the board."

"This George seems to be a nice fellow. You say he isn't married?"

I shook a finger at her, the way she used to do to me when I was little. "Don't even go there!" I warned. "And as delicious as this food is, I'll have to eat and run."

I hurried back upstairs and dressed quickly in jeans and a sweater, hung the skirt and blouse in a garment bag, tossed in the gold sandals and a few strings of beads. O'Ryan had remained in the kitchen, finishing the scraps of my pot roast. I put on my NASCAR jacket, picked up my purse, makeup kit, and the costume, and headed for the garage.

"I'll be home right after the show," I told my aunt. "You don't have to wait up. You must be tired. . . . And, Aunt Ibby, you be careful," I said, thinking of River's message. "You take care of yourself, okay?"

"I'm fine," she said. "Don't worry about me. I'll see you when you get home. Anyway, I love Vincent Price!"

It was an easy drive to the station. The tent on the common was closed, and the lines at the Salem Witch Museum had disappeared. Traffic moved smoothly along Hawthorne Boulevard. I parked the Buick, choosing the spot closest to the station's front door.

Marty was already busy on the *Nightshades* set. "Hey, Moon," she called. "Check out the cool autumn flower arrangement. It's from the Doans. I guess you passed muster with the missus."

"Mrs. Doan? I've never even met her. Do they send flowers to every new hire?"

"Nope. Palmer didn't get any. Rhonda and Janice get them on their birthdays. That's about it. I don't get 'em. And Ariel sure didn't."

"Then, why me?" I admired the fall flowers in the tall copper-colored vase. Marty had placed the arrangement on the table, removing the obsidian ball to make room for it. I didn't ask where she'd put it. I was just glad it wasn't there.

"Dunno. But you must have made a good impression on her somehow. He doesn't do stuff like that without her say-so. Actually, he doesn't do much of anything without her say-so."

"Really? He seems so . . . in charge."

"It's just that he's so crazy about her. Spends every minute with her that he can." She gave a broad wink. "You know about the secret staircase?"

I nodded.

"He sneaks home sometimes in the afternoon. Thinks we don't notice."

"That's kind of sweet."

"Yep. We all think it's sorta cute. Otherwise, he's a pain in the ass."

I decided it was best not to comment. I tried to erase the mental picture of the Doans in bed, she in her purple hat.

"I didn't see Rhonda when I came in," I said. "Does that mean she's not screening my calls tonight?"

"Yeah. You're in luck. Janice is coming in."

"That's good," I said, not really sure whether it was or not. "I'd better get started turning myself into Crystal Moon." I headed for the dressing room, thinking maybe I needed to revise my first impressions of some of my fellow employees.

I'd thought George Valen was friendly and talented, but now he seemed a bit creepy. Bruce Doan came off as a rude, unpleasant bully. It turned out that he had a softer side. Loved his wife, was a generous tipper, and sent flowers to his employees. I'd figured Mrs. Doan for an eccentric busybody, but that may have been too hasty. Janice was still a puzzle. Was she the cool, confident program director or a nosy, pill-popping spoiled brat with a drinking problem? And I still wasn't sure about Scott Palmer.

I'd just put one last sweep of black mascara on my false eyelashes when Marty knocked on the dressing room door.

"Moon? You decent?"

"Sure. Come on in." I pulled the door open. "What's up?"

"You've got a call on the studio phone."

"Do you know who it is?"

"Oh, yeah." She smiled broadly. "It's Doan. You

know how he likes for everyone here to do more than one job?"

I nodded, following as she hurried toward the set.

"Well, honey, he's got a doozy for you!" She pointed to the console. "Line one."

I pressed the flashing button. "Yes, Mr. Doan. Can I help you?"

"Indeed you can, Lee. Indeed you can. I need a favor."

This probably explains the flowers.

"Yes, sir?"

"You may have observed that I like my employees to . . . wear more than one hat, so to speak."

"Yes, I noticed."

"They're quite well compensated for their efforts. Have you and I discussed your salary yet?"

"Not yet."

He mentioned a figure far exceeding what I'd expected a newly hired fake psychic might reasonably earn.

"That seems fair," I said, trying hard to keep the surprise out of my voice. "And I do want to thank you and Mrs. Doan for the lovely flowers."

"Good. Glad you like them. And, my dear, in addition to your nightly duties, I'm going to ask you to do a little traveling on behalf of the station."

Uh-oh. Here it comes.

"Traveling?"

"Do I understand that you recently lived in St. Petersburg?"

"Yes, I did."

"Are you familiar with the veterans' hospital there?"

"I know it well." I really did. Johnny and I used to

visit the patients there whenever we could. A lot of them are big NASCAR fans, and they loved talking to Johnny.

"Fine. Fine. I guess you know the police have the straight razor that killed the Pelletier woman. They've traced the numbers scratched on it to an old gentleman who's a patient in that hospital."

"Yes, I heard about that."

"They're not giving the man's name out yet, but we're pretty sure we can get it before noon tomorrow. Here's the plan. You'll fly down there on the early bird flight. So as soon as we get the name, you'll already be in place to get yourself in to see him, talk to him, get some video, and send everything back to us before anybody else around here has a shot at it."

"Me?"

"Sure. You can handle a little assignment like this! I believe you applied for a reporter's job in the first place?"

"I did. I mean, I can. But what about *Nightshades*? I don't see how I can go to Florida, do all that, and be back in time to do the show. And you already have a field reporter. Why not send Scott . . . Mr. Palmer?"

"He's got too much to do here. Anyway, you'd have better luck getting past the medical staff to see the old fellow. And we'll schedule a special event for *Nightshades*. A *Twilight Zone* marathon, or maybe we'll even show *Ghost* again, uninterrupted. They love that one. And you'll be back in time for the next night's show. Any questions?"

Yeah. Plenty. Like, how the hell am I going to pull this off? But all I said was, "What about a camera? Sound equipment?"

"Honey, we've got state-of-the-art high-res camcorders that will fit in your handbag."

"I see."

"We can count on you, then?"

If I was ever planning to become a full-fledged TV reporter, I'd have to be prepared to take on last-minute assignments, however weird they might be.

"Absolutely," I heard myself say. "What time does my plane leave?"

"Six fifteen tomorrow morning. Janice has already printed out your boarding pass, and you have your company credit card. A limo will pick you up at TPA and drive you directly to the VA hospital. You'll wait there for our call. Then it's up to you to get yourself in to see the old fellow."

"You must have been pretty sure I'd be up for this."

"Oh, we all agreed on it."

"All?"

"All of us. Mrs. Doan, of course, and Janice and George. Marty too. So, Lee, while tonight's movie is running, you just run up to the control room and Janice will fill you in on the details."

"Okay," I said as my mind raced.

When am I supposed to sleep? It'll be after two when I get home. I'll barely have time to throw a couple of outfits and a toothbrush into a bag. If Aunt Ibby can't drive me to the airport, I'm pretty sure I can get Jim Litka to do it.

The thoughts flew by so fast, I barely heard Doan's next proclamation.

"And don't worry about getting to the airport. George Valen has volunteered to take you. He'll pick you up at your house at four thirty tomorrow morning. Have a good trip!"

Time seemed compressed as I made the short walk back to the dressing room. By the time I was seated at the vanity, I'd mentally selected the clothes for the trip, packed my bag, and figured out how I might handle a half-hour early morning ride with George Valen.

I was glad I'd made index card notes for the show. It was going to be difficult to stay focused on Edgar Allen Poe, callers with lost dogs, and broken hearts while visions of straight razors and aged veterans, like sinister sugarplums, danced in my head. I tucked the stack of little cheat sheets into the pocket of the blue skirt and returned to the *Nightshades* set.

"Whataya think, kid? Going to take the Florida gig?" Marty wanted to know.

"Sure I am," I said, sitting on the turquoise couch and arranging my skirt for easy access to the pocket. "You never know where an assignment like that might lead."

"Damn right. Especially if the rumors are true about old Phil Archer retiring." She winked. "Guess you wouldn't mind leapfrogging over that guy who took your job if it means you get to be an anchor!"

I wanted to protest that Scott hadn't actually *taken* my job. It had been handed to him. I wanted to say that I hadn't even thought about the leapfrogging thing. But I had. And I definitely planned to take this assignment, this opportunity; and, to use one of Scott's sports-related expressions, knock one out of the park!

"Well," I said again, "you just never know."

"Yeah. Like Ariel used to say, 'If it's in the cards . . .'"

Cards! Tarot cards! I had an appointment with River I needed to break.

I interrupted Marty's reminiscence. "Marty, excuse me. I need to make a quick phone call. Be right back."

I dashed back to the dressing room, grabbed my phone, glad I'd put River's number in my cell phone's memory and hoping it wasn't too late to call. She answered on the first ring.

"Look, River. I don't have much time right now. The show starts in a few minutes." I explained as quickly as I could about the trip to Florida. "I'll be back the day after tomorrow. Can I see you then?"

"Of course you can." Her voice dropped to a near whisper. "Be careful, Crystal. Promise you'll be very careful. And please tell your aunt to do the same."

I promised. Then tucked her warnings into the very back of my mind, along with straight razors and old soldiers. It was showtime.

CHAPTER 22

Marty lit a candle in George's old papier-mâché jack-o'-lantern and placed it next to the fall flowers for an opening shot. Doppler's *Fantaisie* played in the background. The blue skirt was again carefully arranged, index cards for my intro handy but out of camera range. I opened the show, as I had planned, with meditation tips cribbed straight from Ariel's copy of *Meditation—The Road to Self-Discovery*.

"Welcome, dear friends of the dark, to *Nightshades*. My name is Crystal Moon, and I'll be your guide on our journey through life's mysteries, on film, in the imagination, and most of all, in our own everyday magical lives. I know that some of you meditate regularly. Good for you!" I dropped my voice for emphasis. "As our dear departed friend Ariel taught us, meditation will tune and train the mind, just as an athlete tunes and trains the body."

I gave a quick explanation of the breath-counting technique, favored by many experts. Breath counting sounds easy, but it's really fairly difficult to master. I'd learned it as a drama student to help with script memorization.

Maybe I should take my own advice and brush up on it.

"The goal is to do simply this," I told my audience. "Count breaths and nothing more. Next time we visit, I'll share some more tips on this ancient practice. But first, a word from one of our wonderful sponsors."

An ad from a local chiropractor appeared on the monitor. I flipped my cards to the notes I'd made on *The Pit and the Pendulum.* The light on Marty's camera signaled, and I launched into a tribute to Vincent Price, quoted some raves about the movie from Stephen King, and promised to return mid-film to take calls.

I watched the monitor as the credits rolled over the prologue scene of Francis Bernard's carriage arriving at the gloomy stone castle. In the background was the dismal, roiling ocean. For a fleeting moment, it reminded me of the news footage of the lone Buick parked next to the rough granite wall as storm clouds gathered over Salem Harbor.

Could it really have been only a few days ago?

Janice's voice came over the speaker. "You've got time for a cup of coffee, Lee. Come on up and we'll get the details of your trip worked out."

I pushed the control-room door open. The glow from multiple screens lit the room, and the coffee smelled good.

"Come on in." Janice waved a mug in my direction. "Coffee's ready, if Scotty here hasn't guzzled it all."

Seeing Scott was a surprise. I hadn't seen him, except on TV, since that strange lunch at the Lyceum.

"Hi, Janice. Hi, Scott."

Scott handed me a steaming yellow mug. "Here you go, Moon. Good show. You make being a psychic look easy."

"Thanks. You make doing live news look easy." I took a sip of the coffee. He'd remembered that I liked mine with cream, no sugar. "And the news around Salem is getting scarier than my old movies."

"It's kind of weird, all right," he agreed. "Janice says you'll be doing a little investigative reporting of your own down in Florida."

"Yes. I know the area pretty well."

What a lame answer!

"Home field advantage is always important." His expression was serious. "Well, you girls have some business to talk about. I'll see you later. Say, Moon. If you need a ride home, I could hang around until after the show."

"Thanks, Scott. That's awfully nice of you, but I have my car tonight."

"Oh, okay. See you when you get back. Have a good trip." He paused. "Say, Moon. You'll be home in time for that witches thing, won't you?"

"Witches thing?"

"That Witches Ball they have here every Halloween."

"Oh, that. Sure. That's not until Friday. Why?"

"I'm supposed to go over and do a couple of live shots for the news. Want to come along? I've got press passes."

And I'd been thinking about asking him!

"Thanks. Sounds like fun. I'll have to leave before midnight, though, for the show."

"Like Cinderella." He smiled. "No problem. See you when you get back from Florida."

"See you later, Scotty." Janice waved in his direction, not looking away from the bank of screens she faced.

The door closed behind him. "Good for you, Lee. Looks like you've scored a date with our cute new guy."

"Sure surprised me," I admitted. "And I have a couple of free tickets for the thing. Guess I won't need them. Say, can you use them?"

"Thanks. Maybe Georgie and I will get dressed up and go."

She's thinking of going with George? Why doesn't this beautiful woman have a man in her life besides her brother?

"I have the tickets in my purse. I'll bring them up after the show."

"Great. I have a few things for you, too. Look here."

Spread before Janice on the counter were a couple of envelopes and a small camcorder.

"Here you go, Lee. Your top-of-the-line HD camcorder with surround sound, your boarding pass for the flight to Tampa, and a nice eight-by-ten glossy of the murder weapon. You know how to use the camera?"

"I've used a similar one. This looks a little more complicated."

"The directions are in the box. George can answer any questions about it. Just shoot as much as you can of the old guy. Show him the picture and ask questions about the damned old razor. Then just upload it and send it to George. He'll edit and get it on the air. We'll scoop everybody."

"You make it sound easy."

Janice faced me. "You can do this. You can do this and more. We believe in you."

We? Who is we? The Doans? Janice and George?

I didn't ask. Maybe I didn't want to know the answer. I looked away from Janice's earnest expression and focused on the screens. The *Nightshades* movie was there, along with a couple of government alert channels. The local stations and Boston stations were there, too, and several black-and-white screens showing various parts of the WICH-TV building, inside and out.

"What's wrong with the two blank screens there?" I pointed.

"Oh, those. George hasn't gotten around to fixing a couple of the outdoor security camera connections. There's something wrong in there." She gestured toward a cabinet where a partly open door revealed a tangle of wires.

"I guess that's part of the job up here," I said.

"I know. I know. I should be able to handle it myself." She stretched out her long fingers and inspected a perfect manicure. "I don't even know when they stopped working. But it's more of a guy thing, you know, grubbing around down there with all that electrical mess."

"Uh-huh." I thought about all the hurry-up nail repairs I'd had after helping Johnny tear down an engine. I peered more closely at the screens. "Those must be the cameras that cover the parking lot and the back of the building."

She shrugged and pressed a button. A commercial for a vegan restaurant began to roll. "I guess. Oops.

There's your cue. Take your camera and stuff and go do your Gypsy thing."

A mad dash down the corridor to the set, a quick fluffing of hair, arranging of index cards, and I was ready to do my gypsy thing. I shared a little more trivia about Edgar Allen Poe and the making of the movie, then announced that the lines were open for callers. The console flasher began to blink.

"Hello, caller. Your first name and your question please."

"Hello, Crystal. Thanks so much for taking my call." The woman sounded delighted.

"You're welcome." I smiled into the camera. "Your first name and your question?"

"My name is Beverly," was the breathless reply, "and I want to know if Ariel's cat is okay. I'm used to seeing him on the couch with her, and, well, I just hope he's all right."

Easy question.

"He's just fine, Beverly. He has a new home, and he seems to be very happy there," I said. "Of course," I added, "I'm sure he misses Ariel very much, as we all do."

"Oh, I know. It was all so sudden. We miss her so much. And we miss the cat. And we miss Evie's calls, too. She was one of Ariel's regulars."

"Evie?"

"Sure. Evie. You know, Yvette Pelletier. The woman who died the same night as Ariel."

No, Beverly. I did not know that.

I glanced in Marty's direction. Her palms-up shoulder shrug indicated she'd never made the connection between the caller named Evie and Yvette, the dead woman. Had anyone at the station? Had the police?

"Of course, Beverly," I said, pretending I knew all about it. "Change can be so very difficult in so many ways."

"Thanks, Crystal. You're doing a good job. I love your red hair, and I love tonight's movie."

"Glad to hear it. Keep watching *Nightshades,* won't you?"

She promised she would, and I moved on to the next call.

"Hi, Crystal. This is Pamela."

"Do you have a question for me, Pamela?"

"I do. I've lost my watch. It was a gift from my husband." Her voice broke, and she sounded near tears. "I can't believe I was so careless. Please help me find it."

This one needs an answer from a real psychic. What would Ariel do?

I stalled for time. "Can you describe your watch?"

"It's gold, with some diamonds on the face."

I used the "eyes closed, forefinger and thumb on the forehead" pose I'd copied from Ariel.

"Think about the last time you wore it. Were you in the house or outside?"

"In the house, I'm pretty sure."

That helps narrow it down. Where do I take my watch off?

Eyes squeezed shut, I thought about that gold watch with its diamond face. And in my mind, suddenly I saw it! I sat up straight, eyes wide open, and leaned into the camera. I knew where the damned watch was! No doubt. Should I tell the woman what I was thinking? Sure. Why not?

"Do you have a place in your house where there's a bowl of little soaps, miniature shampoos, that sort of thing?"

"The guest bathroom. There's a glass bowl full of those little samples, like you get in hotels."

"That's it. Look in that bowl for your watch."

"I'm on the cordless phone. Wait a sec. I'll go in there and look."

No, don't do that. What if I'm wrong? My psychic cover will be blown.

"Just call me back sometime, Pamela." I prepared to end the call. Too late.

"Oh, my God! There it is. I must have taken it off when I cleaned the sink. Thank you, Crystal. You're amazing."

Yes, I am. And you're not half as amazed as I am.

Marty's sharp intake of breath indicated that she was surprised, as well. Pamela hung up, and the flasher blinked again. I seemed to be on a roll. I pressed the green button. "Hello, caller. Your first name and question please."

None of the other callers could compare with the surprise of Beverly's revelation that Evie was Yvette or with the "Oh my God, how did I do that?" shock of finding Pamela's watch.

A young widow was considering dating again. I could relate. I told her some of the things I'd been telling myself.

"Starting a new relationship scares you, doesn't it? There's no need to rush into anything serious right away. If you can get comfortable in a friendship with a man without feeling pressure, that may be enough for now."

I was relieved when the second half of *The Pit and the Pendulum* began to roll.

"That was a workout, kid," Marty said. "You did good, though."

"Thanks. Do I have to take more calls at the end?"

"Nope. This one's a tad longer than last night's flick. You have two more commercials to read, and you need to announce tomorrow night's movie. Someone said something about *Ghost*."

"*Ghost* is good. Do we have some notes I can look at?"

"Sure. Ariel kept notes on all the favorites. I'll print them out. Hey, Janice wants you to do an intro to run tomorrow. Tell 'em it's a special event. Uninterrupted movie. No calls. We'll load 'er up with a bunch of canned ads at the beginning and the end. Don't worry. It'll be all right."

"Okay. I wish I'd brought a change of clothes, though. It'll look like I'm wearing the same thing two days in a row."

"Oh, just grab one of Ariel's big velvet capes. She had a bunch of 'em. Good cover-up."

I remembered seeing some of the capes in Ariel's DVDs. "That'll work, I guess."

"You'll be fine. That was a surprise about Evie being Yvette, wasn't it? Evie used to call for advice all the time. Bad marriage, I guess."

I thought about what Jim Litka had said about the police looking for her ex. "I wonder if the police have located the husband yet."

"They did. Guess he has an alibi. Out of town all night."

"Quite a mystery."

"Not as mysterious as you finding that chick's watch. How the hell did you do that? I'm used to Ariel pulling off that stuff once in a while, but she was a friggin' witch."

"I tried to think of where a woman would take her watch off, and I know I take mine off if my hands are going to get wet. That means bathroom or kitchen to me. So I just closed my eyes and tried to visualize that watch in a bathroom. And darned if I didn't really *see* that little bowl with the watch in it. Freaked me out!"

"I'll bet. I'll go get those movie notes for you." She looked back at me over her shoulder. "Hey. Maybe you're channeling Ariel. Ever think of that?"

No. And I'll try not to think of it, thank you.

Another sprint between the set and the dressing room. I knew Aunt Ibby would be awake, watching the movie. I called her and caught her up on what was happening at the station and asked her to dig out a carry-on bag for me. I knew not only that she'd find the right-size bag, but also that the perfect clothes for me to pack, along with travel-size toothpaste and shampoo, would probably be neatly laid out on my bed when I got home.

"Thanks, Aunt Ibby. I don't know what I'd do without you."

I really didn't know what I'd do without her, and River's warning had frightened me. But what could I say? That a witch had told me that my aunt was in the middle of an unknown conflict between me and some nameless, faceless upside-down cardboard man from a deck of cards?

"How's O'Ryan doing with the idea of a litter box instead of the cat door?" I asked.

"He's not crazy about it. But he's a good sport. I told him it wasn't going to be forever. Just until we're sure he's safe."

"I worry about being away from the two of you."

"Nonsense. It'll only be for a day or so. We'll be fine," Aunt Ibby assured me.

"I know. I just worry. I have to do a little filming after tonight's show. I'll come home as soon as I can."

Back at the set Marty waited with three long capes. "Which one? Red, purple, or dark green?"

"Red, I guess. Purple was really Ariel's color."

"True." She handed me the red cape and, after opening a locker behind the camera, hung the others on hooks. Curious, I peered into the locker. A shelf held a wig stand, a clear plastic box, and the missing obsidian ball. I tried not to look at the ball, focusing instead on the box, its contents sparkling in the reflected studio lights.

"What's in there?" I asked, pointing.

"Those are quartz crystal necklaces. Ariel used to give them out once in a while. She got a good deal on a bunch of them from one of the sponsors. She liked to surprise callers sometimes by sending them one."

"That was nice," I said. "Do you think I should do that, too? Seems to be plenty of them here."

"Sure. Why not? You just tell whoever is running the board to get a name and address."

I put the cape on, adjusting it to cover my blouse and skirt. "How's this?"

"Good enough. Here are the notes on the movie. Let me know when you're ready, and we'll shoot this thing before the pendulum hits the pit, or however this thing ends."

I remembered *Ghost* pretty well—loved Patrick Swayze in it—so a quick read of Ariel's notes would be all I'd need to do the intro. I skimmed through the part about Molly and Sam's love affair, Sam's murder, and the realization that he was a ghost.

Even though I was comfortably warm in Ariel's velvet cape, I shivered when I read the description of Whoopi Goldberg's character, Oda Mae Brown.

Oda Mae Brown was a phony psychic who didn't even realize that her powers were real.

CHAPTER 23

I pulled the Buick into the dark, silent garage, grabbed my costume and a canvas bag stuffed with camera equipment, a few of Ariel's books, and another of Ariel's DVDs. I hurried toward the house, glad to see floodlights illuminating the courtyard. I'd given Janice the tickets to the Witches Ball and reminded Marty to see that the flower arrangement had enough water. I was quite sure I hadn't forgotten anything.

As I'd guessed, Aunt Ibby had produced a good-looking wheeled carry-on case, had filled a plastic bag with travel-size necessities, and had placed neatly folded jeans, T-shirts, and underwear on my bed.

"This reminds me of how you used to get me ready for summer camp," I told her as I added a pair of shorts, a bathing suit, and a sleeveless blouse to the pile. "I almost expected to see name labels sewn into my panties."

Despite O'Ryan batting at each item I put into the bag, I was packed, dressed, and ready with an hour to spare before George Valen was due to pick me up.

"Time for coffee before you leave?"

"Always," I said. "I need the caffeine."

A few minutes over coffee would give me a chance to remind her to be cautious while I was away, without explaining the strange, tarot-related reasons I had for worrying about her. Instead, I blamed O'Ryan's near abduction. After all, some creep in camouflage was still out there somewhere and knew where we lived.

"Don't you worry about us for a minute, Maralee," she said. "I've already arranged for an alarm security company to install everything we need to protect ourselves."

"I should have known you'd be way ahead of me. You always were."

She looked pleased. "Probably should have done it a long time ago. An old lady like me, living alone in this big old house, needs someone watching over her besides God and the angels. The alarm men will be here today."

"I'm glad. But you do have someone besides the angels. Me."

"I know. And that's a great blessing."

A plaintive meow from O'Ryan made us both laugh.

"Yes, O'Ryan. You're a fine watch cat!"

At 4:25 a.m. I stood by the front door, ready to dash outside as soon as I spotted George's car. He was right on time. A quick peck on the cheek for Aunt Ibby and a pat on the head for O'Ryan and I was on my way. George put the carry-on into the backseat. I climbed into the front, my handbag forming a separation of sorts between me and the driver.

"Got everything?" He smiled his nice smile.

"I hope so. This was quite the hurry-up affair."

"I know. You'll get used to it if you hang around the station for long. Got your boarding pass?"

I reached into the side pocket of the handbag. "Check," I said, then laughed aloud when I realized that Aunt Ibby had tucked a couple of granola bars in with the paperwork.

"What?"

"Oh, it's just my aunt." I pulled out one of the bars. "Look at this. Sometimes I wonder if she still thinks I'm six years old."

"That's kind of nice, you know?"

"It is, and to tell you the truth, I've always enjoyed the spoiling."

"Your aunt raised you?"

"She did. I lost both my parents when I was little."

"I know how that is. Janice and I were pretty young when our mother died, and we haven't seen the old man since the funeral."

"I'm sorry," I said. "So who took care of you?" I thought again of how lucky I'd been to have Aunt Ibby.

"I was over twenty and had a job. Old enough to take care of a thirteen-year-old. We did okay. How old were you when your folks died?"

"Only five."

"Practically still a baby."

"It wasn't so bad, really. I barely remember them, and I had a good childhood."

"You grew up in Salem?"

"Right there on Winter Street."

"Wow." He shook his head. "I can't even imagine it. Staying in one place that long."

"You really like moving around?"

"Sure. I can work just about anywhere, and I've already photographed New England in all four seasons." A shrug of the slim shoulders.

"It's all about the pictures?"

"It is. I sell to a bunch of big travel magazines. I've even done a couple of coffee table books."

"That's wonderful. Congratulations."

"Thanks. I love my work. Sold my first photo when I was just a kid."

Nude pictures of Mom?

I tried hard to erase the mental image. "Really?"

"It was a shot of an old church tower. Took it with a camera my mother gave me on my twelfth birthday. From then on I knew I wanted to be a photographer."

"I was in my first school play when I was nine," I told him. "That's when I decided I wanted to act."

"Well, you're acting just fine on *Nightshades*," he said. "From what I've seen, you make a convincing psychic."

"Thanks. Being a call-in TV psychic wasn't exactly what I had in mind when I was nine, though."

He shrugged. "It adds another dimension to your work experience. And this news gig in Florida is a big plus. Say, you ought to let me do some publicity photos for you. With your talent, I'm pretty sure you won't stay at WICH-TV for very long, and you'll need to update your résumé."

That nude picture reappeared in my mind. "Thanks," I said, mentally crossing my fingers. "Maybe I'll take you up on that."

I'd been concerned that the ride to Boston with George might be awkward, considering that I'd been in his living room, looked into his bureau drawers, and viewed photos that were undoubtedly meant to be private—all without his permission or knowledge. But the ride was not unpleasant. We compared educations and work histories. His story sounded a lot more interesting than mine.

While I'd moved from Salem High to Boston's Emerson College to TV work in Florida in a fairly straight line, George had accumulated credits from schools all over the United States and even from several in Europe. He'd started work as a newspaper photographer before he was twenty, and later his photos had appeared regularly in books and magazines.

Our childhoods were quite different. I'd been blessed with a loving, supportive environment for all my formative years—and then some. George recounted bouncing around from army base to army base, school to school. When his father was at home, he said, his parents argued loudly and often. When his father was away, his mother "drank like a fish."

"They finally divorced." His tone was flat, emotionless. "I took my camera and a backpack full of clothes and left Cincinnati as soon as I got out of high school."

"What became of Janice?" I asked.

He seemed surprised by the question. "Oh, I had to leave the kid there. I didn't know where I was going myself. It was okay, though. The old lady fell down the stairs and broke her neck after a couple of years. Drunk." I saw his hands tighten on the steering wheel. "I came right home and took the kid away with me."

"It must have been a terrible time for both of you. And Janice, just a little girl."

"Not so little. Just turned thirteen. And smart as a whip." There was pride in his voice. "I think she turned out pretty well, don't you?"

"Absolutely," I agreed. "She has a lot of responsibility at the station, and nothing seems to faze her."

"I know. Sometimes she amazes me."

George stopped talking and concentrated on the road ahead. I looked out the window at nothing in particular and thought about how difficult it must have been for the man to raise a teenage girl and still progress as he had in his own profession. I was, I realized, revising once again my opinion of George Valen. By the time we reached Revere, I'd convinced myself that there was probably some logical reason for the nude photo, and when we reached the maze of ramps and overpasses leading to Boston's Logan Airport, I'd gone all the way back to the impression he'd made when we first met in front of the elevator doors.

Nice guy.

Had that really been only a few days ago?

We pulled up in front of the terminal. In typical airport-rush fashion, I grabbed my carry-on, thanked George for the early morning ride, and hurried toward the revolving-door entrance. Turning up my jacket collar against the predawn chill, I knew how good that Florida sunshine was going to feel.

The shuttle was fast, the security lines were unusually short, and I was at airside with time to spare. I opened the outside pocket of my luggage and pulled out one of Ariel's books. All the caffeine I'd absorbed had done its job. Wide awake, I planned to get a little psychic homework done.

Dissociative Disorders. It was the book Pete Mondello had found between the cushions on Ariel's couch. I guessed that she must have been reading it while the movie was running, before she'd gone outside for a smoke. That one seemed advanced for a novice, and *Past Life Therapy in Action* didn't seem much better. My third selection was *Mysteries of the Tarot.* Bingo. *Mysteries of the Tarot* looked just right. At the last minute I also chose a slim black-covered paperback. *Glossary of Occult Terminology* might come in handy. I put the two books into my handbag and returned the others to the carry-on just as the boarding call for my flight to Tampa sounded.

I settled into my window seat, happy that the Doans had opted to fly me business class. Coffee was offered and accepted; a cello-wrapped Danish was rejected in favor of one of Aunt Ibby's granola bars. I began to read.

Within minutes I found myself immersed in the history of the colorful cards with the strange illustrations. I learned about the ancient Egyptians, the Gypsies, oracles, sorcerers, enchanters, soothsayers, magicians, and wizards who over many centuries have used the seventy-eight cards to explain the past and explore the future.

After about an hour of studying *Mysteries of the Tarot,* I began to see why River was so concerned about me and my aunt. If someone truly believed the cards could give accurate warnings about things that might happen in the future, the cards she'd read for me were pretty damned scary!

I closed the book and looked out the window as we passed over the Outer Banks of North Carolina, and tried to sort out some of the happenings of the past week.

We'd adopted a cat who'd been a pet of a practicing Salem witch, a witch whose drowned body I'd discovered. Marty had told me that Ariel had believed that O'Ryan was a "familiar." A quick check of the black-covered glossary provided a brief, but troubling idea of just what that might mean:

> *The familiar acts as a link between the physical and the spiritual worlds. A witch's cat can communicate with the dead. This is because, of all the animals on earth, the cat is the most sensitive to such spirits. The familiar can be used for good or for evil. It doesn't matter to the cat. It all depends on the mission the cat is sent on. Familiars are always cats with intelligence and attitude, not ordinary house cats.*

The Queen of Wands, the card River had chosen to represent me, had a cat in the foreground. I'd just read in *Mysteries of the Tarot* that the cat represented "the sinister aspects of Venus."

Was it possible that O'Ryan, the cat with intelligence and attitude, the cat my aunt and I had already come to love, had sinister aspects, too?

CHAPTER 24

We arrived in Tampa on time. A good sign. TPA is a remarkably efficiently designed place, so moving via escalator and shuttle, I quickly reached the outdoor area designated for picking up arriving passengers. Curbside, searching for the limo that would take me to the veterans' hospital, I removed my jacket, reveling in the soft, warm Florida air caressing my skin like the touch of a friendly kitten.

Spotting a sleek white Cadillac displaying a window sign lettered with my name, I waved. A smiling driver maneuvered the big car into a space right in front of me. Within what seemed like seconds, my luggage and I were riding in air-conditioned comfort across a long bridge spanning the sparkling turquoise waters of Tampa Bay.

"I'm taking you to the VA hospital, right, Ms. Barrett?"

"Yes. That's right."

"You got family there?"

Oops. How was I supposed to answer questions about my

*visit to the old soldier? I'd had no prep about that. I didn't
even know his name yet!*

"Umm . . . not exactly," I stammered. "I'm delivering some papers for a friend."

It was sort of true. Anyway, the driver seemed satisfied.

"That's nice. Those vets sure appreciate having vis-
itors. Specially pretty ones like you." He winked into
the mirror. "You from around here? You look familiar."

I gave him a quick rundown on my stint at the
shopping channel and suggested that was probably
where he'd seen me. It was, and for the rest of the ride
to St. Petersburg, I answered questions about the various movie and television stars whose jewelry, dolls,
perfume, and fashions I'd featured on the show.

We pulled into the parking lot in front of the im-
posing sprawl of hospital and administration buildings. Palm trees and flowering hibiscus gave the place
a tropical look.

The driver looked at me expectantly. "Want to get
out here?"

"I . . . I need to wait for a phone call," I said. "My . . .
um . . . friend will be calling to tell me . . . uh . . . what
building to go to."

He looked puzzled. "I think they can tell you that
at the desk."

*They probably know me at the desk. I've been here so many
times with Johnny.*

"My friend told me to wait."

"Suit yourself."

Tucking my cell phone into my jeans pocket, I
opened the carry-on and pulled out the camcorder.

"I'm going to get out and take a few pictures while I wait for my call." It was just an excuse to get away from questions I couldn't answer, but it might make a good lead for the interview.

I focused on a red hibiscus, then pulled back and panned slowly across the main entrance. I walked down a tree-shaded path, showing viewers a small lake where a family of wood ducks swam. More hospital buildings loomed in the background. My cell phone vibrated. I shut off the camera and sat on a nearby bench.

"Hello. Lee Barrett here."

"Hi, Lee. It's Rhonda. Mr. Doan wants to talk to you. How's the weather down there?"

"Gorgeous, as usual."

"It's cold and rainy here. Boy, are you lucky! Hold for Mr. Doan, please."

I hope I'm lucky. I hope I can pull this interview off. I hope George is right and it will lead to bigger things.

"Hello, Lee. Bruce Doan. How was your flight?"

"Fine, thanks."

"You're at the hospital now?"

"Right outside. I'm taking a few exterior shots for the lead-in."

"Good." There was a long pause. "I have the name of the man you're going to interview. The name of the owner of the murder weapon."

"Yes?"

"Lee, are you sitting down?"

"Yes, I am. Why?"

Another pause. "Bear in mind this may just be a big coincidence. . . ."

"What do you mean? What's his name?"

"Valen. Sergeant Major William Joseph Valen."

It was my turn for a long pause. An "Alice tumbling down the rabbit hole" kind of pause.

I found my voice. "Valen? No kidding? Have you asked Janice or George about it?"

"No. They know about it, of course. Both of them. Haven't made a peep. Neither have the cops. Not yet."

"The police have questioned them about it?"

"Sure. Hey, it's probably just some kind of weird co-incidence." He didn't sound convinced. "Anyway, there's a Salem PD detective down there now. He'll find out if there's any connection."

"Right. Well, then, I'd better get going. It's Sergeant Major Valen, you said?"

"Yep."

"Mr. Doan, George told me that they always called their father Sarge."

"I know. Listen, Lee. You just get in there and get that interview. Friendship be damned. It is what it is. Let the chips fall where they may and all that stuff. I want to know how the hell his straight razor got to Salem. I want to know if one of his kids had it." I heard a thump, which probably meant he'd pounded on his desk. "And I really want to know how the son of a bitchin' thing wound up in a Dumpster, with a dead woman's blood all over it, wrapped up in a raincoat with *my* station's call letters on it!"

He sounded like the Bruce Doan I'd seen that first day at the station. I pictured his red-faced outrage, re-membering the horrible things he'd said about Ariel. When he grew silent and the thumping stopped, I ventured another question.

"Do you happen to know what building he's in,

sir? I know my way around here, but this place is enormous."

He gave me the name of the building and the sergeant major's room number.

"Say, Lee," he added. "Don't include yourself in the shot while you're doing the interview. I'll have Phil Archer voice over the questions."

"Really? Why?"

"Think about it. Can't have the viewers mixing up Lee Barrett and Crystal Moon now, can we?"

"I guess you're right," I said, trying to hide my disappointment. So Phil Archer would get credit for my work. I was useful only because I was known to the higher-ups at the VA hospital, who'd hardly welcome an out-of-state, camera-toting stranger bothering one of their patients. George's optimistic idea that this assignment would advance my career was just wishful thinking. Apparently, as far as WICH-TV was concerned, I was only a second-string psychic.

"You sure you can handle this, Lee? I could send Palmer down to take over."

If I'd had a desk handy, I might have balled up *my* fist and pounded it.

Like hell I want Palmer to take over. Why would I? So he can snatch another job out from under me?

I remained cool. "No thanks, Mr. Doan," I answered, masking my anger. "Don't worry. I can handle it just fine. I'll send the video this afternoon."

"Oh, yeah. About the video. You can send it to me. I'm not sure I want George to edit it, after all."

"I understand. I'll be in touch as soon as I finish here." Gathering up camera and phone, I headed across the lawn to the waiting limo.

"I've got all the info now," I told the driver. "You don't have to wait if you have something else to do for an hour or so."

"Okay. Maybe I'll just drive over to the beach and grab something to eat. Want to take your stuff or leave it in the car?"

"I'll take some of it." I'd packed a folded WICH-TV bag, which was big enough to hold my purse, along with the camera and the envelope containing the photo of the razor. I tucked the phone back into my jeans pocket, left the carry-on in the backseat of the Cadillac, tossed the canvas bag over my shoulder, and headed for the main entrance.

A gentleman wearing a volunteer's badge gave me a visitor's pass, along with directions to where I might find William Joseph Valen, sergeant major retired. He summoned a golf cart, which was operated by a volunteer who remembered me. After a fast ride to the proper building, I showed my pass to a male nurse at a desk in the lobby. He remembered me, too.

"Old Sarge is going to be so glad to see you, Ms. Barrett," he said. "We've all missed you and Johnny coming around like you used to. Sorry about him dyin' like that."

"Thanks. Johnny always loved coming here, talking cars with everyone."

"Well, old Sarge will be thrilled. He hasn't had a visitor in months, and today he's got two."

"Two?"

"Yep. You and the cop who's sitting in a chair outside of his room."

"Outside his room? Why? Is he under guard or something?"

"Dunno. I asked. It's one of those plainclothes detectives. Not local. Anyway, he just said he's part of an investigation. That's all."

"I hope he'll let me in."

I'd hate to come all this way and be left standing in the hospital corridor outside the old soldier's room!

"Oh, sure he will." The man gave a short laugh. "Poor Sarge can't be under arrest for anything. I mean, what could he do? He's eighty years old with one leg!"

I clipped the visitor's pass to the collar of my blouse and started for the elevator. As soon as I stepped out into the third-floor corridor, I saw the room I was looking for. The number Doan had given me was plainly marked on the wall next to an open door. And just as the nurse had told me, a man, looking uncomfortable in suit and tie, sat in a straight-backed chair just outside the room.

But what nobody had told me was that the cop by the door was Salem detective Pete Mondello.

"Lee?"

"Pete?"

He stood up so quickly, he knocked the chair over. "What are you doing here?" he said as he retrieved the chair with one hand and extended the other to me.

Ignoring the question, I shook his hand. "What a surprise! I heard the chief say he was sending a detective down here, but nobody told me it was you!"

"It was a surprise to me, too. Didn't even have time

to pack." He pulled at his shirt collar. "Is it always this hot here in October?"

I laughed. "This isn't hot. You should be here in August!"

"No thanks. I'll be glad to leave tomorrow. Looks like the real story is back in Salem, anyway. Not much point in hanging around here."

"The sergeant wasn't any help?"

"Not really."

"Funny about the last name, though, isn't it?" I pressed for information. He must have talked to the old fellow about the Salem Valens. Or had he?

No answer. Just a raised eyebrow. I knew he wasn't about to discuss police business with me. But, hey, it was worth a try. I shrugged and gave up trying to out cop a cop.

"Well, nice seeing you again, Pete."

"Nice seeing you, too, Lee. Say, what *are* you doing here, anyway? You know him?" He gestured toward the open door.

Was it okay to tell him I was here on assignment? Or, because the old soldier was involved somehow in a police matter, could Pete prevent me from talking to him? My mind raced as I edged toward the doorway.

Sergeant Major William Joseph Valen himself bailed me out of that particular dilemma.

"Is that you, Ms. Barrett? Where you been? You're a sight for these old eyes. Get your cute little self right on in here!"

With scarcely a glance in the detective's direction, I hurried to the bedside.

"How're you doing, Sarge?" I shamelessly adopted the nickname everybody seemed to use, hoping it added to the illusion that I had some personal connection with the man. And since he obviously recognized me, perhaps, in some sense, I did.

"Doin' fine for a gimpy old fart, darlin'," he said. "Gosh, it's good to see you again. Sorry about your man. Everybody here felt awful about that." A smile lit up his wrinkled face. "But at least you're back to visitin' us."

"I moved out of state, Sarge," I said. "But I'm going to try to get down to see you guys more often." As I spoke the words, I vowed to make them come true. Johnny would want me to.

"Out of state, huh? Where'd you go?"

"Back to my hometown. Salem, Massachusetts."

"Oh, oh. Salem's where *he* comes from." He jerked a thumb toward Mondello, who'd turned the chair so that he was looking into the room. Bill Valen dropped his voice. "You didn't become a lady cop or something, did ya, honey?"

"Nope. I'm still on TV. But I'm trying to be a reporter. They sent me down here to get an interview with you about this old straight razor." I pulled the glossy photo out of the envelope and showed it to him, then tilted my head in Pete's direction. "I guess he told you what happened."

"He told me some lady went and got her throat cut with it. That's what he told me. And I told him I haven't seen that old thing in years. Not since I got back from Nam." He held up his right hand, as though taking an oath. "Honest."

"I believe you," I said.

"Oh, the detective does, too. Just can't leave till he

gets the say-so from his CO." He gave a mock salute. "I know that drill."

I glanced back to where Pete sat, clearly listening to our conversation while pretending to read the *Tampa Bay Times*. He looked uncomfortable and out of place in his dark suit.

Poor Pete.

I reached into the canvas bag and showed the old man my camcorder. "Do you mind if I ask you some questions with my little camera here running?"

"Go for it. If I can help you get the job you want, ask away."

There was a movable tray table at the foot of the bed. It would make a good flat surface for the camera. I focused the lens on Bill Valen and adjusted the sound.

"How do I look, honey?" He ran a heavily veined hand through thin white hair.

"Handsome as ever," I said and began the interview.

CHAPTER 25

"Ladies and gentlemen of the WICH-TV audience, we're here in St. Petersburg, Florida, at the VA hospital, talking with Sergeant Major William Valen."

"You can call me Bill, honey."

They'll have to delete that "honey."

"The Salem Police Department has traced the straight razor that is believed to be the weapon used in the recent murder of Yvette Pelletier in her Derby Street apartment to the sergeant major. His service number was scratched onto the blade. I believe you've seen a photo of the razor, Bill. Is it yours?"

"It is. I mean, it was. I left it in my old footlocker with a bunch of other stuff after I got back from Nam."

"I see. What became of the footlocker? Do you know?"

"Nope. Left it at my ex-wife's place in Cincinnati. Don't know what she did with it."

"Is your ex-wife still there in Cincinnati?" I was pretty sure I knew the answer.

"Marlena? No. She's dead. Been gone near twenty years, I reckon."

"Perhaps your children know where it is. Do you have children, Bill?"

"Yep. Two of 'em. But I don't know where they are, either." The rheumy eyes filled with sudden tears.

"Do you want to stop for a minute, Bill? I can turn the camera off."

"Yes, please." He wiped his eyes with the edge of a sheet. "Sorry. I don't like to talk about the kids. I should have tried harder to keep track of 'em."

I know where they are. But I'm not supposed to tell you.

I glanced toward the doorway, where Pete sat, newspaper neatly folded in his lap, his attention now plainly focused on me and Bill Valen. He shook his head ever so slightly. I got the message. The police weren't yet ready to connect the Salem Valens with the soldier. And as Mr. Doan had said, maybe it was all just some kind of weird coincidence.

"Sorry. I'm just a silly old fool. Give me a minute. I'll be okay."

"Take as long as you want to, Bill. I don't have too many more questions."

That was true. It should be pretty clear to anyone that Bill had no idea how or when his old razor had wound up in that Dumpster. But I wanted to talk about his war injuries. It would be important for the viewers, as well as the police, to know for sure that this old, bedridden veteran could not possibly have anything to do with a murder fifteen hundred miles away.

"It's just that I never should have left them with her. But the judge ordered it. I was away so much, and they were used to her, you know? And I made sure the government sent the allotment check every month. Even after she died, I had them send it to my oldest boy."

"Your oldest boy?"

"Yep. Georgie. I knew he'd take good care of the young one. But after a while the checks came back. No forwarding address."

So. His oldest boy is named George. We're well past the co-incidence stage now. His Valens and our Valens are one and the same. No doubt.

I glanced back toward Pete. Surely he already knew all this. He was on his cell phone.

"You ready for the camera again, Bill?" I asked.

"Sure, honey. Shoot me!"

I turned the camcorder back on. "Have you ever been to Salem, Bill?"

"Nope. Can't say as I have. Though I hear it's a right interestin' place."

"It is. But you've been to lots of interesting places, too, during your many years of service to America."

"I have. To Europe. To Korea. All over the States, too. The place that sucked the most . . . Oops, excuse the language. The only place that was really bad was Vietnam. I guess that's mostly because I left my leg there."

"You're a hero, Bill. Thank you for your service."

"Nah. I'm no hero. Got a couple, two, three medals, that's all. They're probably in that old foot-locker, along with all the other junk."

"Can you remember what else might be in it, Bill?"

"Oh, jeez. It's been so long. Probably some old clothes, shoes, boots, pictures of my kids. Just the usual stuff a soldier carts around."

"And your old razor?"

"That too. Last I knew, it was all back in Cincinnati."

"Thank you, Bill. It's been good talking to you. If you happen to remember anything else, anything at all, about that razor, please contact the Salem, Massachusetts, Police Department." I repeated the number.

"You're welcome. Sorry I couldn't be more help." He waved into the camera and smiled. He had a nice smile. A lot like George's.

I shut off the camcorder and put it back into the canvas bag.

"What does that say?" Bill pointed at the bag.

I turned it so the logo was plainly visible. "WICH-TV. Those are the call letters for the station I work for. Why?"

"Nothing, I guess. I just feel like I've seen those letters before."

"We have a good signal," I said. "But not that good! It doesn't reach Florida. There are lots of similar call letters. I mix them up myself sometimes."

"Anyway, darlin', it was great to see you, even if it was business. Don't be such a stranger. You going to visit some of the other guys and gals today?"

"Absolutely," I said, ashamed that I hadn't thought of it myself. "And as soon as I get some time off, I'll be back for a real visit." I meant it.

"I'll look forward to it. And you might send an old man a postcard once in a while. Let me know how you are. What you're doing."

"I will."

"Good. I love postcards. Got a little collection of 'em there on the bulletin board."

He pointed to a corkboard mounted on a closet door. "My youngest used to send me one every so often. Never any return address, but at least I knew everything was okay, you know? Haven't had one for a real long time, though."

I looked closely at the colorful array of postcards. Pete would be interested in this.

"These are nice, Bill. Do you remember where she sent the last one from?"

"She? No, I mean my youngest boy, Willie. Named after me. Didn't have no girls."

Tumbling a little farther down the rabbit hole! No girls? Then where did Janice come from?

I motioned for Pete to join us.

"Pete," I said, "these postcards are from one of the sergeant major's children." I wasn't ready yet to grapple with the possibility that Janice might not even be a Valen. I decided to stick to the mystery of the missing footlocker for now. Mistaken identities could come later. "Maybe there's something here to tell you where the footlocker could have traveled after Bill left it with his ex."

I was pretty sure Pete already knew about Bill's youngest son. After all, the detective had been here questioning the old fellow long before I'd arrived. I was also pretty sure he wasn't going to tell me a darned thing about what he'd learned.

Pete and I stood together, facing the display of postcards.

"Good work, Lee," he said softly. "I didn't notice these."

He turned and faced Bill Valen. "Sir, would you let us take a few pictures of your cards, front and back?

Maybe the postmarks will help us figure out where that trunk of yours has been all this time."

"Glad to help, but like I told her, they ain't really recent. There's years in between some of them."

Carefully, Pete removed the postcards from the bulletin board. He pulled a small digital camera from an inside suit pocket, revealing, as he did so, a holstered gun. One at a time, he placed the cards on a small nightstand, photographing the front, then the back, of each one. He moved quickly, not stopping to study the illustrations or to read the messages.

"Want to put these back, Lee?" He handed me the stack of postcards.

"Sure." I turned to the old soldier. "Were they in any particular order, Bill?"

"No. No special way. I take them down and read them once in a while, and then I just kind of arrange them so the colors look pretty. Know what I mean?"

"I'll do my best," I promised and began a random arrangement of the colorful scenes, tacking them up from left to right. I was beginning the second row when something about one of them grabbed my attention. It was a nighttime shot of a city street, buildings ablaze with neon, a Photoshopped full moon above. It was the pink and violet neon sign on the building in the foreground that had stopped me.

THE PURPLE DRAGON.

I knew right away where I'd seen that name before. It was on the framed nightclub photo on Janice's desk. Turning the card over, I read the message and noted the dated postmark.

I beckoned to Pete to join me in front of the closet door and lowered my voice.

"Did you ever notice the photo that Janice keeps on her desk?"

"The showgirl shot? Sure did."

"Look at this." I tapped the postcard.

"The Purple Dragon. Piccadilly Circus, London," he read, then flipped it over, studied it for a moment, then turned to the man in the bed.

"Could we borrow just one of these cards, sir?" he asked. "I'll personally guarantee we'll return it soon and that it'll be perfectly safe."

"Well . . ." Valen was hesitant. "Those cards mean a lot to me, young fella." He looked in my direction. "What do you say, honey? Can this boy be trusted?"

"I'm sure he can," I told him.

Pete had already slipped the postcard into his pocket by the time the old soldier answered.

"Okay. If you say so."

I finished arranging the bulletin board display, then stepped back to get the effect. Bill nodded his approval.

"It was sure good seein' you again, doll. Don't be such a stranger. Come back soon. Y'know, I ain't getting any younger here."

"I will, and I'm sorry I stayed away so long."

"Aw, we understood. Losin' your man and all. Now, don't forget to stop and say hey to some of the others."

"I'll do it right now," I promised and gave him a quick hug.

"Made my day, babe!" he said, waving as Pete and I left the room. "Take good care of her, young fella!"

Pete took my arm and guided me toward the elevators. "I'm off duty. Can I give you a ride somewhere?"

"Thanks a lot," I said, "but I want to visit a few of the other patients. I promised. Anyway, the station provided me with a limo. The poor driver has been cooling his heels outside ever since I got here."

"Nobody's cooling anything out there!" Pete wiped imaginary sweat from his forehead. "It's damn hot!"

"You need some Florida clothes, Pete."

"I know. Want to take me shopping?"

"I'd like to," I said, "but after I do my visiting, I have to figure out where I'm going to stay tonight."

"I lucked out with a nice place right on the beach," he said. "I'll bet they still have some vacancies."

He mentioned a motel Johnny and I had stayed in once or twice. He was right about it being a nice place. "Thanks. I'll check it out."

"Good. Maybe I'll see you later then. When are you going home?"

"Tomorrow afternoon. Three thirty on Delta. Have to be back for the late show."

"Three thirty? Looks like we're booked on the same flight."

The thought was not unappealing.

I kept my word to Bill Valen and was glad I had. The veterans were happy to have company, and I promised myself that I'd fly south to see them again soon.

The Cadillac was parked exactly where I'd last seen it, the driver patiently listening to a Santana CD and reading the *Wall Street Journal.*

"Have a good visit, Ms. Barrett? I'll bet your friend's friend was glad to see you." He sprang from his seat, held the back door open, and tucked the canvas bag neatly next to the carry-on.

"He was, thank you, and I stopped to see a few of my own old friends. I hope I didn't keep you waiting too long. Did you get some lunch?"

"Sure did. A grouper sandwich. Where to now?"

"I guess I need to find a place to stay." I mentioned the motel Pete Mondello had suggested. "Let's check it out and see if they have room for me."

"You're the boss."

There was a vacancy, and within a half hour, dressed in shorts and a T-shirt, I was settled in a spacious beachfront efficiency with a refrigerator, microwave, big flat-screen TV, and a comfortable king-size bed. If my mind hadn't been busy trying to make sense out of the overwhelming jumble of information I'd stuffed into my brain since George Valen had picked me up at four in the morning, I'd have felt as though I was on an all-expenses-paid Florida vacation.

I was sure now that the Valens at WICH-TV were closely related to Bill Valen. At least George was. But if Bill had no daughters, who was Janice? Did Bill's ex-wife have a little girl he didn't know about? That didn't seem likely. And what had become of young Willie, who'd kept in touch with his father over the years with a series of postcards? Did the Purple Dragon postcard mean that Willie and Janice had been in London together?

Where was the footlocker? Who had taken the straight razor? When? Why? What did Yvette Pelletier have to do with the Valens? How did Ariel fit into the puzzle? And O'Ryan? Why would anyone want to harm the yellow cat?

The thoughts spun around like some macabre carousel. I tried to shake them off. Hooking up my laptop, I downloaded all the video I'd shot at the hospital and sent it to Mr. Doan, just as I'd been instructed to do. I knew he'd be disappointed. Especially if he'd been hoping I'd find some crazed vet who'd sneaked out the hospital window, traveled to Salem, and murdered an old girlfriend with his razor.

I called Aunt Ibby, told her I'd arrived okay. I told her, too, about the Valen connection. "Want to put on your research librarian hat and do a little sleuthing for me?"

"Absolutely. What can I do?"

"You said that one of your Facebook friends was a policeman in London?"

"Yes. Nigel. He's with New Scotland Yard."

"Do you think he could find out if there was a George Valen, a Janice Valen, or a William Joseph Valen Jr. living in the London area around the late 1990s?"

"Consider it done," she said.

"Oh, and one more thing. Do you have access to old newspapers?"

"Sure. The microfiche at the library goes all the way back to newspapers from the seventeenth century."

"Great. Can you check obituaries in the *Cincinnati Enquirer* for a notice of the death of a Marlena Valen? It would be around twenty years ago."

She promised to get to work on both requests right away. We said our good-byes, and I realized about then that all I'd eaten since yesterday was a granola bar. No wonder I felt confused. Remembering what the driver had said about his lunch, I slipped the room key into the pocket of my shorts, along with my wallet, and headed out in search of a grouper sandwich of my own. One thing there is no shortage of along Florida's gulf beaches is seafood restaurants. I knew I wouldn't have to walk far to find one.

A rustic-looking beach bar with outdoor tables was practically across the street from the motel. It even had a sign advertising fresh grouper. Perfect. I headed for it with visions of a golden-brown chunk of flaky white fish resting on crisp lettuce and smothered in freshly made tartar sauce, all nestled in a soft sourdough bun. Pickles on the side. And maybe a nice cold beer. I began to cross Gulf Boulevard, and for the second time that day, a firm guiding hand grasped my arm.

"You hungry, too?" Pete Mondello looked cool and comfortable. He wore khaki shorts, and his short-sleeved white shirt fit so snugly across his well-muscled chest, it was obvious that he was no longer carrying a gun. Dark hair, wet from a recent shower or swim, curled slightly across his forehead.

"Starving," I admitted. "Grouper sandwich, here I come."

"Never had grouper," he said. "Anything like haddock?"

"Not really. Try it. You'll like it."

Pete was easy to be with. We sat together at a round table with a blue- and white-striped umbrella shielding us from the October sun.

"You did some fast shopping," I said. "You look much more comfortable."

"Thanks. I feel better, too." He studied the menu briefly, then ordered us a couple of light beers and two grouper sandwiches. "Lee, you were a big help at the hospital. I completely missed those postcards when I questioned the old gent."

"I don't know what they mean," I said, "but maybe they're a clue to something."

He smiled. "You sound like Nancy Drew. Looking for clues."

"I do, don't I? But there are so many questions, and everything has happened so fast ever since I came home to Salem."

His expression became serious. "I wasn't making fun of you. It can't have been easy, finding Ariel Constellation's body the way you did, then landing right in the middle of a crime investigation. Old soldiers, dead seagulls, kidnapped cats and all."

Our food arrived, and we both grew silent, enjoying the meal and the sunshine.

"Pete," I said when I was about halfway through with my sandwich, "did you see the body of the Pelletier woman?"

"Sure I did. Why?"

"Was she wearing a crystal necklace, by any chance?"

The relaxed look was gone. The cop face was in place. He put his sandwich down, looking at me intently. "How did you know about that?"

"I didn't. But I found out that Yvette Pelletier was a regular caller to *Nightshades*. And Marty told me that Ariel used to reward callers with those necklaces. I was just wondering if there's some connection. What do you think?" I wasn't ready to tell him, or anyone, about the vision of the camouflage-uniformed murderer stepping on Ariel's fingers.

"Could be. I'll run it by the chief." He took a sip of beer. "You ever think about becoming a detective? I think you'd be good at it."

"Not me. I still want to be a news reporter when I grow up."

He raised his glass in salute, and I raised mine to meet it.

"Cheers," we toasted in unison.

Pete and I spent the rest of the afternoon together. The evening too. At sunset, as the sky turned to improbable shades of pink and gold and magenta, we joined a group of turtle watchers waiting for baby loggerheads to hatch. We stopped at another beach bar and listened to bad karaoke. We strolled to the end of a long pier and watched the fishermen casting their lines into the moonlit gulf. It was nearly midnight when we returned to the motel.

"This was fun, Lee," he said.

"For me too."

He stood very close as I fished the key from my pocket and pushed it into the lock. He smelled good. *Like sunshine,* I thought. I made no attempt to move away. Maybe I even stepped a little closer.

It was one hell of a good-night kiss.

CHAPTER 26

Going to sleep just then was out of the question. Wide awake, I pulled the Ariel DVD out of my bag and popped it into the player attached to the TV. Might as well study Ariel's psychic technique a little more. Maybe it would help clear my mind of naughty thoughts about Pete Mondello.

Maybe not.

The date on the cover indicated that this DVD was newer than the one I'd viewed earlier. Ariel's hair was a little poofier; her jewelry a little glitzier. O'Ryan was there, sprawled along the back of the couch, looking relaxed and handsome. I wondered if the big cat would ever be willing to come back into the studio. It would be fun to have him as part of my show, and I was sure the viewers would love it.

The first call was from Linda, a Leo, who'd recently broken up with Ray, a Taurus. She wondered if she'd made the right choice. Ariel advised her not to give up on Ray entirely and told her that a more compatible friend might be coming into her life in the near future. *Harmless advice that sounded good and didn't really promise a darned thing.*

The next call was from a woman who was sure she was being haunted by the spirit of her dead mother-in-law. Ariel told her to sage the house and burn red candles.

How do you sage a house? And what do red candles have to do with anything? I need more studying!

A call from a woman who'd misplaced her husband's wallet brought a suggestion to meditate, visualize the wallet, then expand her field of vision until she could recognize the surroundings. Pretty much what I'd done when I searched for that lost watch for *my* caller.

Except that I'd really found the stupid thing!

A kid named Billy called to say his big brother was always spying on him. "I'm pretty sure the dude follows me around, y'know?" he said. "Like what's up with that? Is he nuts?"

Ariel hit the finger-on-the-forehead pose and told him not to worry, that his brother was just being protective, and to choose his friends carefully so that his family wouldn't have reason to worry about him so much.

I began to yawn, feeling sleepy, and shut off the TV. I got ready for bed, thinking about Ariel and the way she handled calls. I was becoming confident that, with a little more study, I could do just as well with the *Nightshades* audience.

I lay there quietly in the darkness, listening to the gentle sound of the surf on the beach. Something about the show I'd just watched nibbled at the corners of my mind. I knew I hadn't watched this particular DVD before, but somehow it was familiar. Maybe one of the callers was a regular, and maybe I'd heard the voice on the other DVD or on Aunt Ibby's *Dark Shadows* shows.

But reflections about Ariel and the *Nightshades* callers kept drifting away, replaced by thoughts of the handsome Salem detective I'd so recently, and whole-heartedly, kissed good night.

It had been a very long time since I'd felt attracted to men at all. When Johnny died, it seemed as though that part of me died, too. But I certainly felt something for Pete. To make it more confusing, I had to admit that I'd recently felt a tiny something for Scott.

I pulled a pillow over my head and tried to make the thoughts go away.

Scott is a job snatcher. Pete might be married.

But I sure hope he isn't.

I awoke to predawn light and the raucous calls of gulls greeting the sunrise. I bolted upright, realizing what had been familiar about that Ariel DVD. It was the kid. Billy. The one with the snoopy sibling. Billy had the same voice, the same inflections, the same whiny tone as another kid caller, the one whose mother didn't want him to buy a car. I'd have to remember to tell whoever screened my calls to watch out for a youngster who apparently made up problems because he liked to hear himself on TV.

Wide awake, in spite of the early hour and my recent sleep-deprived days and nights, I pulled on shorts and a sweatshirt and headed outside. Early morning on the gulf beaches is a lovely time, and there's nothing better than a brisk walk along the water's edge to clear the mind and get the day off to a good start. I walked about a mile down the beach, then turned and headed back. I'd worked up an appetite, and the fresh coffee and warm blueberry muffins offered in the motel lobby smelled wonderful. I carried mine outside to enjoy in the comfort of a bright red Adirondack chair facing the gulf.

I heard the scrape of the blue chair next to mine moving on sand, and I knew without looking up that Pete Mondello had joined me.

"You're an early riser, too," he said.

"I am. Always have been."

"Best part of the day."

"I know."

A nice thing about morning people is that they don't talk a lot. Pete and I sat there, enjoying our coffee, without feeling the need to make conversation. I watched the gulls cartwheeling gracefully just above the waves and thought of those poor poisoned birds under the police tarpaulin. I thought, too, about my interview with the old soldier and about the kiss I'd shared with the man sitting beside me.

I finished my muffin, brushed the crumbs onto the sand, and tried to brush away the thoughts. The birds were collateral damage. Someone had tried to kill the cat. The interview had proven nothing and would be credited to Phil Archer, anyway. The kiss could probably be chalked up to a couple of beers and the Florida moonlight.

I stood up and tossed my paper cup and muffin wrapper into a nearby trash barrel.

"Guess I might as well start packing. Checkout time is eleven o'clock."

"Our flight isn't until three thirty," Pete said. "You

have any good ideas for killing time between now and then?"

I checked my watch. "If you happened to buy a bathing suit on your shopping trip yesterday, I think we have time for a swim right now."

"I did, and we do."

"Meet you back here in five," I promised, glad that I'd packed a really cute hot-pink two-piece.

"Make it three. It might be a long time before I get to swim in the gulf again."

I didn't actually check, but it couldn't have been more than five minutes before we were both at the water's edge. I'd thought he looked hot in his khaki shorts and white shirt the day before, but he looked even better in swim trunks and no shirt. We swam for nearly an hour, then spread a couple of motel towels on the warm sand and flopped down on our bellies, facing each other. I shared my tube of sunscreen with him but didn't offer to help him apply it.

"You're a good swimmer," he said.

"You too."

If Ariel had been able to swim, could she have escaped from her killer?

We lay there for a while, careful to turn occasionally so his New England skin wouldn't burn. My tan was pretty well established, but I never like to overdo it. We chatted about the weather, the plane trip, my job at the station. I found out he wasn't married. We each avoided any mention of the evening before, or of the serious police business that had brought both of us there.

"Can I give you a lift to the airport, or is that limo guy coming back?" he asked.

"Limo guy," I said. "I'm supposed to call when I'm ready to leave."

"Can't you call and tell him not to come? That you already have a ride with an old friend from home?"

"Oh, Pete. I don't know. Mr. Doan has already arranged—"

"Come on. You can show me the sights around here."

"We do have a few hours to kill before flight time. I guess maybe it would be okay."

He stood and reached for my hand, pulling me to my feet. "Great. Let's get started."

I laughed. "All right. Give me a little while, though. I have to check with the station and then call the limo guy. And I need to dry my hair."

Back in the room I aimed the hair dryer with one hand and speed dialed the station with the other. Rhonda answered.

"Hi, Lee. How's Florida? And what's that noise?"

"Hair dryer. Been swimming."

"Oh, rub it in, why don't you? You want to talk to the boss?"

"Yes, please."

I shut off the dryer when the station manager answered. "Yes, Lee. What's up?"

I asked if it was all right if I canceled the limo ride, and told him I'd be with a Salem detective.

"All right? It's a great idea. Save us a few bucks on the ride, and maybe you can sweet-talk the cop into giving us some inside info on the case. Didn't get much from the old fellow, did we?"

"Not much. Sorry, Mr. Doan."

"Not your fault. At least our viewers will know what

he looks like," he said. "By the way, did Palmer set it up to get plenty of shots of you at that Witches Ball shindig?"

Publicity shots! That weasel! And I'd been dumb enough to think he was asking me for a date!

"Publicity shots. Sure thing. All set, sir."

"Good. Use that credit card Janice gave you and pick out something nice and sexy. The Boston stations will be there, too. The more shots of you, the better for *Nightshades*."

I called the limo service and canceled my afternoon ride, then punched in Aunt Ibby's number. I'd shoved the bad thoughts away for quite a while, but the worry was back. I wanted to be sure that the alarm system was being installed and that O'Ryan was safely inside the house.

My aunt answered on the third ring. Yes, the man was there to install the alarm system. Yes, O'Ryan was fine, pacing back and forth in the front hall, as though he was waiting for someone. No, she hadn't had a chance to go to the library to check the microfiche for the death notice of Marlena Valen. Yes, she had e-mailed Nigel in London but hadn't heard from him yet. And would I please stop being such a fussbudget? She'd been taking care of herself just fine for sixty-odd years, thank you very much.

There wasn't much I could say to all that, so I said my "Good-byes" and "I love yous" to my aunt and cat and hung up.

Soon, hair dry and brushed into some sort of order, bathing suit plastic-bagged and packed with my other belongings, I was ready to check out and start my stint as tour guide. We'd agreed to meet in front of the motel at nine, and I was right on time. Pete was already there, rental car engine running and trunk open. He put my bag alongside his, held the passenger door for me, and off we went. I'd decided that a ride through a few of the gulf beach towns was a good starting point.

"Lots of motels and restaurants," he said.

"Sure. Tourism is a big part of the economy here."

"Salem too," he said. "Seems like everybody's interested in witches these days."

"Seems that way," I agreed. "Especially around Halloween."

I know I'm a lot more interested in them than I used to be. I've been seeing a dead witch in a black ball, and I seem to have acquired a witch's familiar for a pet.

We rode through St. Pete Beach and crossed the bridge to Fort DeSoto Park. Got out of the car and walked around the old fort for a few minutes, then headed back toward the city.

"Have you been to Florida before, Pete?" I asked as we approached downtown St. Petersburg.

"Once. When I was a kid, the whole family went to Disney World."

"I bet that was more fun than sitting in a hospital corridor."

"In a suit and tie," he said. "Mickey Mouse was great, but I think I like spending the day with you better."

I was pretty sure I blushed. It wasn't every day I got to trump an American icon.

"Thank you. I'm having a nice day, too."

Let's not go there, please. I don't want to talk about yesterday. Or last night. Or even this morning.

We made a quick tour of St. Petersburg. I pointed out the modern Dali Museum and the old Tropicana Field, the USF waterfront campus and the vintage Vinoy Hotel. We cruised past the yacht club and the marina, the shuffleboard courts and the souvenir shops. We stopped so that Pete could buy a Tampa Bay Rays cap.

"You a Rays fan?" I asked.

"Not really. Just want to bug the chief. He's a big Red Sox fan."

"He doesn't seem to have much of a sense of humor. He sure was deadly serious when he questioned me about where I was when Ariel died."

"But he had to question you about all that." He gave me a serious look. "After all, you found the body, left some blood at the scene, and got the dead woman's job!"

"True. What about you? Did you think I had something to do with all this mess?" I could feel my anger beginning to rise. "Well, did you?"

"Never, Lee. Not for one minute."

"Really? You didn't?"

"Of course not. I mean, not after I found out you were on a plane at the time." He smiled. And I had to laugh.

We had lunch alfresco in the tree-shaded Garden Restaurant, then started for the airport, with plenty of time to spare before our flight. Conversation came easily then. He told me a little about himself, how he'd come to chase criminals for a living. He'd wanted to be an attorney, but there wasn't enough money for law school, so he'd followed his dad's footsteps and joined the Salem Police Department after two years at the local junior college.

"Have you thought about going back to school?"

"I'm taking an online criminology course."

"Good for you."

Criminology, huh? How could he not have at least thought about the possibility that I might have had something to do with Ariel's death?

We turned in Pete's rental car, passed through security, and rode the shuttle to airside.

"Your ticket is business class?" he asked.

"Right."

"Mine's coach. City budget constraints, you know." He smiled. "So I probably won't see you again until we land in Boston. Got a ride home?"

"George Valen is picking me up."

"George? That could make for an awkward ride home."

"I'll be okay," I said "I can handle it."

I hope I'll be okay. I hope I can handle it.

"I know you can. Listen, Lee, we've only got a few minutes before boarding, and there's something I need to ask you about."

"Okay. Shoot."

"Please understand that I'm only asking because it's my job."

I had a sinking feeling. "Go ahead."

"It's about that crystal necklace. You seemed to think the Pelletier woman might be wearing one."

"Right."

"The chief is wondering how you knew that Yvette Pelletier had that necklace. Tell me again, will you? How did you know that?"

CHAPTER 27

What makes me so trusting? I should have learned something when Scott took me to a football game so he could ask me how I knew Yvette Pelletier had died in her kitchen. Then he'd made a date with me for the Witches Ball only because Mr. Doan had told him to. Had Pete wormed his way into my confidence just so he could find out what I knew about the dead woman's necklace?

Which was actually nothing. I knew the crystal necklaces existed and Ariel gave them away to favored callers. Period. The reason I'd asked about it was that I was positive the two deaths were connected and that the neckace might be the link between them. I couldn't very well tell him the *other* reason I was sure of a connection—that I'd seen a vision in the obsidian ball of the camouflage-suited killer stepping on Ariel's hands—could I?

I took a deep breath. "Look. You told me yesterday that I sounded like Nancy Drew, looking for clues," I said. "Maybe I do. Maybe I should take one of those online criminology courses. Maybe someday I'll be an investigative reporter. I don't know. I'm just interested in what's going on. That crystal necklace might explain the connection between Evie . . . Yvette and Ariel. You can't tell me that I'm the only one who thinks the same man killed both of them!"

"Lee, you know I can't tell you anything about an ongoing investigation, don't you? And you do believe me when I tell you that I don't think now, nor have I ever for one second thought, you had anything to do with anybody dying, ever?" He'd put his suitcase on the floor and placed both hands on my shoulders, looking directly into my eyes. "The thing is, Lee, sometimes people know things that they don't know that they know. You know?"

I had to laugh. The sentence was so goofy, and the tone so sincere. "I think I know what you mean," I told him. "And if I think of anything at all, even if I don't know that I know it, I'll call you right away."

Pete laughed, too. "Exactly," he said. "See you in Boston."

Once again I drew a window seat, and I pressed my face against the pane like a little kid as we lifted off over the blue expanse of Tampa Bay. My choice of reading material this time was *The Witchcraft Delusion in Old Salem Village.* The book, like those I'd been assigned in middle school, told of poor innocent souls, mostly women, who'd been subjected to dreadful accusations and horribly intrusive physical examinations, all carried out by the town's most pious religious leaders. Their final indignity was a public hanging at Gallows Hill.

Several of the books I'd borrowed from Ariel's library

contained highlighted paragraphs and underlined words and sentences. I'd often marked college textbooks that way myself. But in this book, Ariel, or whoever had used it, had made copious notes in the margins of nearly every page in cramped, but legible handwriting.

The book detailed the court proceedings for each of the people accused of witchcraft. In the margin beside each case description were handwritten notes. Next to the paragraph about Sarah Good, an accused witch who was hanged at Gallows Hill, someone had written "S.G. was a practicing witch," even though the book treated her sympathetically. A paragraph about Rebecca Nurse, who was pronounced not guilty and was usually regarded as an innocent victim of mass hysteria, also had margin notes, which stated, "The court was wrong. Nurse was absolutely a witch." Page after page spelled out the margin writer's conclusions as to the guilt or innocence of the accused. I was surprised to see that Ariel, or whoever the margin writer was, most often agreed that the long-ago court had it right in the first place. Old Salem Village was a nest of pin-sticking, image-making, fit-throwing evil hags who consorted with the devil and his minions and delighted in torturing their neighbors.

The hanged witch whose trial received the most coverage, both in the text and in the marginal notations, was Bridget Bishop, whose apparition reportedly haunted the restaurant where I'd recently had that memorable lunch. The book, which treated most of the accused as innocent victims, hinted that perhaps Bishop was actually a practitioner of the black arts. The margin writer was more specific. "An extremely skillful witch" was underlined. "We have so much to learn from her!" said another note. Particularly chilling was the sentence printed in large black letters: "Her spell book is the Holy Grail."

That spell book sounded intriguing. I flipped to the bibliography in the back of the book. My *Nightshades* audience would love to hear some real witch spells. I planned to run *I Married a Witch* with Veronica Lake later in the week. A harmless spell or two would be a good lead-in. I ran my finger down the page listing primary sources. No spell book there. Surprising. It should have been an important reference. Surely some enterprising publisher had produced a paperback reprint. It was just the kind of thing Salem tourists love. I'd look for a copy in one of the souvenir shops when I went shopping, per Doan's orders, for something glitzy and sexy.

The thought of shopping reminded me of Scott Palmer and that phony-baloney semi-invitation to the Witches Ball. I'd show him. I'd glitz his eyeballs out, then ignore him for the rest of the evening. I smiled at the thought, closed the book, and settled in to enjoy the rest of the flight to Boston.

We landed on schedule, greeted by gray skies and rain falling in a fine, biting cold mist. Rhonda hadn't been kidding about the lousy weather. I called George right away. He said he was parked nearby and promised to be at the terminal in five minutes. I huddled in my jacket, jamming my hands into my pockets, wishing I'd brought a warm hat. As I watched for George's car in the passing parade of buses and taxis, I glanced around at the crowd of arriving passengers, thinking I might see Pete.

"Looking for me?" George skidded the car to a halt at the curb, and in seconds we were speeding away toward Salem.

"How was your trip? Bet the weather was nicer than this gunk."

Are we going to discuss the weather? Surely he knows that I interviewed his father, that he and his sister are positively connected to the weapon that killed Yvette Pelletier.

"The weather was lovely," I said. "Even went for a swim this morning."

If he doesn't want to talk about what I really was doing in Florida, that's all right with me.

"A swim, eh? Sure wouldn't want to go for a swim around here this time of year." He gestured toward Boston Harbor, a dark gray line in the distance. "Brrr. A body wouldn't last long in these waters."

Is that a casual observation or a veiled threat?

Or am I taking this girl detective thing a little too far?

I took a sideways glance at his profile. He looked the same as he usually did. Calm. Pleasant. Nothing nervous or menacing there. Was he just going to carry on as though nothing had happened? As though nobody knew about Sarge's razor? As though the police weren't investigating his connection to the case right this minute?

The man had nerves of titanium. Maybe other body parts, as well. I wondered how Janice was faring. I hoped she hadn't turned to pills and booze, but I was afraid she might have.

"It'll be nice to be home," I said. "Bad weather or not."

"Like Dorothy says, there's no place like it."

"Right." My mind raced, searching for small talk. I

couldn't think of a thing, so I settled for looking out the window, listening to the *swish-swish* of the wipers.

George broke the silence. "The cops searched our condo."

"Oh?"

"I know you're wondering what's going on." He turned and faced me briefly, smiling. "But you're too polite to ask."

"You don't have to talk about it if you don't want to."

"You'll hear it all when you get to the station tonight, anyway."

"Is Janice okay?" I asked. "Will she be screening my calls tonight?"

"Afraid not. She came down with one of her bad headaches."

"Not surprising. Considering all the . . . stuff going on."

"Yeah." His smile was gone. "They were looking for the old man's footlocker."

"The police?"

"Yeah. I told them where it was."

"You knew?"

He laughed. A short, unfunny sound. "Sure. It was right in my living room. Been there all along."

I thought about the glimpse I'd had of George's living room when Janice had brought me in there while she rifled through his bureau drawers. In a moment I realized that I'd seen the footlocker. This was one of those things Pete meant about people knowing things they don't know that they know. It didn't seem so goofy anymore. The missing footlocker was the base of George's glass-topped coffee table, and probably the inspiration for his khaki and navy color scheme.

I couldn't very well admit that I'd been snooping around in his place, so again I said, "Oh?"

"I use the old thing as a base for my coffee table. When I was a kid, I thought it was kind of cool. Then I just got used to it and carted it around whenever we moved."

"When I talked to your dad in Florida," I said, "he told me that he remembered the razor being in it. I know it's none of my business, but did you know it was there?"

"The cops asked me that, too. But, no, I don't remember it. I hadn't looked inside the thing in years. Cops had to break the lock. The key is long gone. All I remember being in there was some old clothes and shoes and stuff and the old man's medals. I always meant to take the medals out and get one of those shadow box things done with them. Too late now."

"I'm sure the police will give it back as soon as they're through with it."

"Doesn't matter. Darn thing was empty."

"Empty?"

"Yep. Not a damn thing in it except a couple of mothballs rolling around."

I'd barely had time to react to the fact that the footlocker was empty when we turned the corner onto Winter Street.

"But how can that be?" I asked. "Where could everything have gone?"

"Beats me." He shrugged. "We've moved at least three times, maybe four, since I remember it being opened. So the stuff could have been lost, could have strayed, or could have been stolen anytime. Anyplace."

We pulled up in front of Aunt Ibby's house. George hurried around the car, opened my door, and picked up my carry-on.

"Well, here you are. Home again, safe and sound."

"Thanks so much for the chauffeuring, George. I really appreciate it."

"My pleasure, Lee. I'll see you later tonight."

"I hope Janice will be feeling better."

"Hope so." He waved and drove away.

Poor George. He had way too much on his plate. On top of the police hounding him, his regular work at the station, his sister pitching a sick headache every other day, and having to ferry me around, now he'd drawn the late-show call-screening duty.

I'd just retrieved the house key from my purse when the front door flew open. A smiling Aunt Ibby offered a welcoming hug, and O'Ryan made figure eights around my ankles.

"Maralee, we missed you," said the aunt.

"Mmruff," said the cat, which I took to mean something similar.

"I missed you both, too," I said. "It's good to be home."

"Come on in and tell me everything." She picked up my bag and placed it on the bottom step of the curved staircase. "Take off your jacket. I've made tea. I want to hear all about your interview."

I followed her into the living room. She gestured toward the TV.

"You didn't even get credit for it, you know. They

doctored it up somehow so it looked as though old Phil Archer had asked the questions."

After taking off my jacket and boots, I relaxed in the big chair, wiggling my toes and accepting the pink china cup of hot tea and honey. O'Ryan sat, watching, then carefully climbed onto the arm of the chair and settled quietly beside me.

"I knew about that. Mr. Doan said he didn't want the viewers to get confused between Lee Barrett and Crystal Moon."

I'm just glad if somebody else was going to get credit for my work, it was Archer and not Scott Palmer!

Aunt Ibby nodded. "Makes sense, I guess. Anyway, what was the old soldier like? He seemed nice." She paused for breath, bright eyes curious. "Tell me everything."

I tried not to leave anything out as I described my visit to the VA hospital and my conversations with Bill Valen, both on and off camera.

She was silent for a moment when I'd finished. "So," she said, "apparently, there's another child? Willie? The boy who sends the postcards?"

"Quite a surprise, isn't it? And if it's true that the sergeant and Marlena had only the two boys, where does Janice fit in?"

Aunt Ibby put down her teacup. "I've wondered from the start if it was possible that she's the girlfriend, not the sister. What with the shared living space and all."

"I've wondered about that, too," I admitted.

"So now that the police know about the connection between Sergeant Major Valen and the TV station

Valens, are they being investigated? WICH-TV hasn't mentioned anything about it yet, but the *Salem News* and the *Globe* are both on it."

"Not surprising," I said. "And it seems that the missing footlocker has been in George's living room all along."

"No kidding? And did he know the razor was in it?"

"He says not. And even stranger, when the police broke the lock, they found the footlocker empty. Nothing in it at all."

"Empty?"

"Empty," I repeated. "Nothing in it but a couple of mothballs."

"Mothballs," she said. "That's the second time mothballs have been mentioned here lately."

"It is?"

"Didn't Mr. Litka tell us that the person who tried to steal O'Ryan smelled like mothballs?"

"You're right. He did."

Again, we know something without knowing we know it.

Our tea finished, my aunt stood and picked up the tea tray. "Why don't you see if you can get a little sleep before you go to the station? I know you haven't had time to shop, so I've put together another attic costume creation for you. It's hanging on your closet door. I'm going to go over to the library for a while to see what I can dig up about Marlena Valen."

"Thanks, Aunt Ibby. What would I do without you?"

"Nonsense. I'm having fun. Makes me feel needed."

"You are needed, and a nap seems like a good idea."

"And Maralee?"

"Yes?"

"Did George say that the trunk had been moved several times since he'd looked inside?"

"That's right. He says the key's been lost for years."

"It seems to me that at some point during moving, he would have noticed that it felt lighter or that he could hear those mothballs rolling around inside."

"That would mean it'd been emptied after he put it in his living room when they moved here."

An imaginary lightbulb turned on over my head.

"Uh-huh." She paused on her way to the kitchen. "Unless, of course, they used professional people who put the furniture in place before they moved in."

Right down to the books in the bookcase and the color-coordinated magazines on the coffee table.

My imaginary lightbulb clicked off. I was back to square one.

CHAPTER 28

Before she left for the library, Aunt Ibby explained about arming and disarming the new alarm system. She'd also had video cameras installed on the front and back of the house, as well as on the garage and in the courtyard.

"Couldn't resist it," she said. "You know how I love my electronic gadgets! Don't know why I didn't do this long ago."

"I'm glad you've done it now. I admit I worried about you while I was away."

O'Ryan, who was sitting on the stairs, next to my luggage and purse, said something that sounded like "Mmehhe?"

"Yes, you too." I stooped to pat him. "Let's go upstairs and unpack."

"I'll be back soon," Aunt Ibby promised. "This shouldn't take too long. Don't forget to disarm the system when you open an outside door. The instructions are right on the control pad."

"I'll be careful, but I don't expect to be opening any doors."

A blue circular skirt and a yellow satin blouse hung on padded hangers against the closet door. An embroidered vest completed the outfit, and long strings of blue and yellow beads were arranged on the dresser.

I am so spoiled! She thinks of everything.

Unpacking could wait until later. I hung up my jacket, put the boots in the closet and, taking the cell phone out of my purse, sat cross-legged on the bed and called Pete Mondello's number.

My call went directly to his voice mail.

"Hi. This is Nancy Drew," I said. "This might not be important, but I promised I'd call if I thought of anything. Did the police report about the footlocker note that there were a couple of mothballs in it? The guy who tried to grab my cat smelled of mothballs. Just thought I'd mention it. Bye."

I really wanted to add "Call me" but resisted the temptation. The next phone call, if there was to be one, would be up to him.

I called River North. She answered on the first ring.

"I'm so glad you're back safely," she said. "I've been worried about you."

I assured her I was fine, and told her about the new alarm system.

She said she felt relieved. "Look, Crystal," she said, "I'm taking part in a candlelight tea-leaf reading tomorrow evening at the Lyceum. You had to miss the one on the common, so I hope you can come to this one. It's for charity. I can reserve a ticket for you. It'll give us a chance to talk a little more about what the tarot told me. If your aunt would like to come, too, I think she'd enjoy it."

The candlelight tea-leaf reading, it turned out, was a fund-raiser for a new bookmobile for low-income neighborhoods, one of Aunt Ibby's favorite projects. I asked River to reserve two tickets and promised to be at the Lyceum at six the next evening. I was curious about the tarot message, and I wanted to ask about that spell book.

"I'll see you then. And, Crystal, I have big news! I've been invited to join Ariel's coven. They need another member to balance the power, and out of all the witches they could have chosen, they picked me!"

"Congratulations," I said, hoping that was the correct response to news of a coven joining.

"Thanks," she said. "Blessed be. I'll be watching tonight."

"Bye, River. See you tomorrow."

I plumped up my pillows and lay down, O'Ryan stretched out full length beside me, his throaty purr providing a soothing, melodic sound. I was asleep in a matter of minutes.

Apparently, however, uninterrupted sleep wasn't in my future. Within an hour the insistent buzz of the cell phone roused me from a silly dream about Ariel chasing O'Ryan up a flight of stairs.

"Hello, Maralee dear. I hope I didn't wake you, but I think you'll want to hear this." My aunt was using her quiet, calling-from-the-library voice, but even so, she sounded excited.

"That's okay," I said, struggling to sound wide awake. "What did you find?"

"I didn't have to look far," she said. "Marlena Valen's death made the front page!"

"Front page? Why?"

"Seems she died under what they called 'unusual circumstances.'"

"How so?"

"Here. I'll read some of it to you. Listen. 'Police were called to a suburban Cincinnati home this morning, where they discovered the body of Marlena Valen, forty-two, at the foot of a staircase in the three-story town house. Mrs. Valen had sustained a broken neck and other injuries. She was nude. The police have indicated that alcohol may have been involved. Due to the unusual circumstances, the possibility of foul play has not been eliminated. The only other person on the premises was a minor child, whose name is being withheld. The child apparently discovered the body early this morning and ran to a neighbor for help.'"

"Wow!" was all I could think of to say. "I knew that she'd fallen down stairs, but I didn't know she was nude or that one of her kids found her."

"Wow indeed. I'll read further and see what I can learn from reports in the days following this one. I'll print all this out for you if you like."

"Yes, please. As Alice said, 'Curiouser and curiouser.'"

Going back to sleep was out of the question.

So Marlena Valen had died sans clothing. And she'd posed for naked photos, taken by her own teenage son. It occurred to me just then that perhaps Marlena Valen was simply a nudist. I'd known several people in Florida who favored that lifestyle, men and women comfortable enough in their skin to bare it all. From the photo I'd seen of Marlena, she had good reason to feel comfortable in hers.

If that was the case, young George had simply photographed someone he saw every day. Maybe the whole family ran around in the buff. As strange a mental image as that produced, I liked it better than some of the creepy scenarios I'd contemplated earlier. But what about the "possibility of foul play" aspect of the fall down the stairs? I'd have to wait for Aunt Ibby to complete her newspaper research before I'd learn what had actually happened to Marlena.

What about the minor child who'd found the body? Did the article refer to Willie? Or had Janice made the terrifying discovery? George had said he had come home after his mother's death and had taken thirteen-year-old Janice away with him. But how had Janice come into the picture in the first place? Had Marlena taken her in for some reason? Was she a foster child or the daughter of a relative? And why hadn't George taken Willie with him, too? Or had he?

Was the relationship between George and a thirteen-year-old girl something he needed to hide?

Now I was all the way back to creepy George again.

That unpleasant thought process was interrupted by another phone call. Caller ID showed VETERANS ADMINISTRATION. Had something happened to Sarge? I hoped not.

"Hello. Lee Barrett here."

"Oh, hello, darlin'. Glad I caught you in."

I was relieved when I heard the old soldier's voice. "Hello, Sarge. What's up?"

"You said I could call you if anything happened here that I thought you should know about."

"Absolutely. What's going on?"

"Well, honey, it's the darnedest thing."

"What's happened? You okay?"

"Oh, sure. I'm fine. But listen, babe. I got another one of them postcards. From my boy."

"From Willie?"

"It's from Willie, all right. I know his writing. But the thing is, it's got a picture of a witch on it. It's from right where you live. From Salem, Massachusetts."

So Willie was here. Or had been recently. Why hadn't George mentioned that his kid brother was in town? Or did he even know it?

"Want to read it to me, Sarge?"

"Sure. It says 'I saw you on TV, Dad. You look good. I am fine. If that lady said anything bad about me, it is not true. I did not steal her cat. Love, your son Willie.' Does that make any sense to you, honey? Did you lose a cat?"

"My cat is right here beside me, Sarge. Somebody did try to take him a while back, but why would Willie have anything to do with it?"

"Don't rightly know, babe, but do you think I should call that cop about it?"

"I think so." I was sure Pete would want to know about Willie being in Salem. Or was he really here at all?

"Sarge," I said, "look at the postmark. Does it say Salem or someplace else?"

"Funny you should ask about that. I was just going to tell you. It has those letters on it. You know, like the letters on that bag of yours. WICH-TV. One of the other postcards he sent me had that mark, too. Remember I told you I'd seen them letters before?"

That postmark came from the postage machine next to Rhonda's desk.

"I remember, and, Sarge, when you talk to Detective Mondello, be sure to tell him about that, too. Okay?"

After he promised he'd tell Pete the whole story, we said our good-byes. O'Ryan's ears had perked up when he heard me mention the word *cat*, and now he sat up straight, fully alert, with his head tilted at a "What's going on?" angle. I scratched his neck, and he responded with a happy "Mrruff."

"Who has access to the postage machine, O'Ryan?" I asked aloud, then answered my own question. Everybody at the station. And anybody in the whole building. And when Rhonda took her frequent breaks, anybody wandering in off the street who knew how to operate a vintage Pitney Bowes machine.

Another thought occurred to me. How did Willie know it was a "lady" who'd interviewed the old soldier? Aunt Ibby had said that the report gave the impression that Phil Archer had conducted the interview.

How many people at the station knew I'd been sent to Florida? Doan had seemed quite secretive about the whole thing, not wanting rival stations to get the idea. Mrs. Doan knew, of course, and Janice and Marty. Rhonda and Phil Archer were in on it, and then there was George. Things always seemed to come back to George.

"Did George send the postcard?" I asked the cat.

O'Ryan had gone back to sleep, or was at least pretending to snooze.

But no. Sarge had said that he recognized Willie's handwriting and the postcards had spanned many years. How could that be? Had George and Willie switched places somewhere along the line? Was that why George never went to see his father? Because he'd be recognized as Willie?

No. That didn't make any sense, unless both Willie and George were professional photographers.

"I give up," I told the cat, who opened his eyes briefly, then squeezed them shut. "I guess I'll go to work early and see what I can find out. I'll start with Marty. She seems to know everything that goes on there."

O'Ryan reached out a paw and patted my hand. "Rrritt," he said.

Since Aunt Ibby wasn't back from the library yet, I wrote a quick note telling her where I was going, and that I'd get a cab home. I stuck the blue-and-yellow outfit into a garment bag and called Jim Litka. Within ten minutes the green-and-white taxi pulled up in front of the house and the cabdriver rang the doorbell.

I disarmed the alarm system and let him in.

"No luggage or lost cats today, Jim," I said. "I just need a ride to the station."

"You're early," he said, reaching for the garment bag, which I'd draped over the newel post at the bottom of the stairs. "Let me help you with that."

O'Ryan, hearing the masculine voice, came running. He rubbed against Jim's denim-clad leg and purred a greeting.

"He's sure friendly. Hi there, big boy."

"He knows you're a friend. After all, you saved him from who knows what."

"My pleasure. Glad I was there to help. Did they catch the guy yet?"

"Not that I've heard." I punched the code into the keypad.

"Got an alarm system, huh? Good idea."

We walked to the cab. Jim opened the door for me and hung the bag on the backseat hook. There was plenty of pedestrian traffic along the route to Derby Street. Lighted storefronts and lines in front of restaurants indicated that business was thriving in downtown Salem.

"Gonna need a ride home tonight?" he asked when we arrived at the station.

"Don't know yet," I said. "I'll call if I do."

"Anytime, Ms. Barrett. Anytime at all."

"Thanks, Jim." I hurried up the stairs and into the warmth of the building.

Rhonda wasn't at her desk, so I went directly to the black-walled studio, passing darkened sets all the way to the back of the cavernous room, then headed for the dressing room, where I could hang the costume du jour.

I was about to turn the knob when I heard voices inside.

Who would be doing wardrobe or makeup at this time of day? Network programming would be running until the late news came on at eleven.

I stepped back into the shadows and listened.

"Why are you here? George said you were gone. That I didn't have to listen to you anymore." It was Janice's voice.

What's she doing here? George said that she was at home, with one of her bad headaches.

Another voice, one I couldn't identify. The tone was mocking, unpleasant. "Shut up and listen, you stupid cow. You'll do what I tell you to. The same as always."

Janice's voice again. Almost a whisper. "You shouldn't be here. What if someone sees you?"

A harsh laugh. "You'll make sure that doesn't happen. Where did you put my clothes?"

"Clothes?"

"Don't play dumb with me. You know what I mean. And I can throw *you* down a flight of stairs anytime I want."

I put my hand over my mouth to muffle an involuntary gasp.

"I think the police took them. They took some sheets and pillowcases, too."

"They didn't take the clothes. The trunk is empty. You took them. Don't you remember, cow slut?"

"I . . . I really don't know. Sometimes I can't remember things. Ever since . . ."

"Yeah, yeah, I know all about it. I was there. You were glad she was dead. Remember?"

"No. No. I don't know what you're talking about." Janice sounded close to tears.

"I wish I'd broken the other one's neck, but I saved her kids, didn't I? They'd thank me if they could."

"I don't know what you're talking about. You'd better go away. I'll try to find the clothes. I really will."

"Quiet, cow. I hear something. Look outside and see who's there."

I scampered behind the refrigerator on the *Cool Weather Cooking with Wanda the Weather Girl* set. I heard the door open and the *click-click* of Janice's high heels.

"There's nobody here. Probably just a rat."

The door closed. All was quiet. Carefully, I crept

along the far edge of the studio, finally reaching the door to the parking lot. I pushed it open inch by inch and, taking a deep breath of cold, salty air, made my way around the building. For the second time that evening I entered the front door of WICH-TV. Almost at a run, I crossed the black-and-white tile floor, punched the UP button, and began the slow, clanking ride to the second floor.

I hurried from the elevator and pushed open the glass door. Rhonda was at her desk. The security guard/cleaning man leaned on a broom, in conversation with the receptionist. Mr. Doan stood beside the fax machine. Everything was back in place. Where had they all been a few minutes ago? Had I wandered into some kind of twilight zone? Was Janice really down there in the dressing room, being threatened, or was I so overtired that my mind was playing tricks on me?

Mr. Doan spotted me first. "Well, well. Look who's here! Welcome back, Lee. How was your trip?"

"Fine, thanks."

"Hey, Lee," Rhonda said. "Your tan is darker. Got in a little beach time, huh?"

"A little."

"Yeah, Wanda and I were talking about you being down there while we're freezing our tails off up here. Lucky stiff! Why can't we get special assignments like that, huh, Mr. Doan?"

The station manager ignored her question and looked at the sunburst clock on the wall. "You're early, Lee."

"I know. But I missed a day. Thought I'd look over the movie notes and the commercial docket for tonight's show, and I have some questions about the screening." I tried hard to sound casual. "Is Janice around?"

"No. Went home sick again." He didn't sound pleased.

"How about George? Is he here, Rhonda?"

Was Janice really here in the building or not? If she was in danger, I had to tell George. If he thought I was nuts, that was the chance I had to take.

"I think so," she said. "I saw his car in the lot when I came back from dinner. Spaghetti night at the Pig's Eye."

"He's in the building," said Doan. "We had a brief meeting in my office a short while ago."

"Want me to page him?" Rhonda offered.

"Yes, thanks."

"No problem." She tapped a few buttons and reported. "He's in the control room, fixing stuff. Go on down."

I hurried through the green door, still carrying the garment bag. I'd just have to keep carrying it for a while. There was no way I was going into the dressing room. Not until I was sure no one else was in there. The more I thought about it, the surer I became that what I'd heard behind the closed door wasn't my imagination.

I knocked on the control room door. The red "on the air" light was off, so I entered as soon as I heard George's muffled "Come in."

"Hello? George?"

He was on his back, with his head inside the cabinet where, Janice had told me, the mess of wires connected to the outdoor cameras was housed, his legs and feet extending into the small room.

"Hi, Lee. Excuse my big feet. Doan wants the surveillance cameras fixed pronto. What brings you here so early?" He bent his knees and scooted himself away from the cabinet.

"I had stuff to do. Nothing important. Look, George, I'm worried about Janice."

"Nice of you to be concerned, Lee." He stood up. "But don't worry. She has these headaches every so often. Has pills for them. She'll be right as rain. I left her sound asleep. Dead to the world."

"That's just it, George. I don't think she's home asleep. I'm quite sure she's here. In the building."

"What do you mean?" He took a step toward me, and I took an involuntary step back. "You saw her here?"

"No," I admitted, still backing away from him. "I didn't actually see her. But I heard her voice. She was over in the dressing room. Talking to . . . somebody."

His eyes narrowed. "Who was she talking to?"

"I don't know."

"A man? Was Janice meeting with a man?" George looked angry. "Could you hear a man speaking in there, or could she have been talking to someone on the telephone?"

I hadn't thought of that. "Speakerphone maybe," I offered. "I didn't recognize his voice. But, George, he called her names. Threatened her. I think you'd better see if she's all right."

George's expression made me think that maybe his relationship with Janice was something other than brother and sister, as Aunt Ibby had suggested. Jealousy

might account for the look of fury. But no matter if he
was jealous or not, I wanted him to get to the dressing
room to help the frightened woman.

"Okay then," he said, opening the door. "Come on.
Let's go."

"Me?" I squeaked. "You want me to come with you?"

"Come on!"

He approached a large panel and, one at a time,
flipped all the switches to the ON position. One by one
the studio lights came on, illuminating each set.

"See? All clear. Nothing to be afraid of here." We
arrived at the dressing room door. The garment bag
had grown heavy on my shoulder. George threw the
door open.

The room was empty. Just as empty as an old army
footlocker. I hung my costume on the rack, then sat
on the bench in front of the vanity.

"There's nobody here." I stated the obvious.

"Not now," said George. "Nobody here now."

He pulled a phone from his pocket. A very high-
tech, very expensive phone. He pushed a couple of
buttons, moved his fingers over the screen, then
turned the device toward me. The illuminated oblong
showed a big bed beneath a rosy chintz-patterned
comforter, I saw Janice. She appeared to be asleep.

It was comforting to know that Janice was safe at
home. At the same time it was disturbing to know that
her brother—or her lover or whoever he was—had a
camera focused on her bed.

And had George noticed, as I had, that in the dressing room there lingered the faint fragrance of J'adore?

CHAPTER 29

We left the dressing room, George walking ahead through the lighted studio with quick, angry steps. I deliberately slowed my pace, stopping before I got to the *Nightshades* set, where I saw Marty already at work.

What I'd overheard amounted to a confession of murder. I needed to tell Pete, even though I had no way of proving that it had happened at all. Apparently, no one had actually noticed me entering the building earlier. But they'd all seen me the second time. Mr. Doan had even checked the time on the sunburst clock. I couldn't identify the man who'd confessed. I'd never even seen him. And Janice, who'd been threatened so cruelly, was apparently safe at home, in her bed. I called Pete's number, anyway. Again the voice mail.

"Call me. It's important." Next call was to the police department number I'd given to Sarge.

"This is Lee Barrett. May I speak to Detective Mondello?"

"Sorry. He's not here. Wanna leave a message?"

"Yes, please. Would you ask him to call Lee Barrett

as soon as possible?" I repeated my number. "It's important," I said again and headed for the *Nightshades* set.

"Hi, kid," Marty called. "Glad to see you got back okay. That interview was pretty good, even if Archer got the credit for it."

"Can't have the late-show audience confusing Crystal Moon with Lee Barrett." I parroted Mr. Doan's sentiment.

"Yeah, I guess. Here. Take a look at tonight's bumper shot. Like it? We're showing *The Witches,* so I'm using the witch hat for the centerpiece, along with the plastic tombstone and the flying bat and some of the flowers from your arrangement. Cute, huh?"

I tried to focus on what she was saying. Tried to put aside what I'd just heard.

"Looks good to me. Got notes on the movie? I remember watching it over and over when I was a kid, but that was a long time ago."

"Got notes," she said. "It's a kid flick, I know, but everyone seems to like it. Say, did you borrow the pumpkin we used the other night?"

"No, I didn't. You said it was George's. Maybe he took it home."

"Nope. I asked. Oh, well, somebody probably grabbed it. It's an antique, you know. Made of papier-mâché. They don't make them like that anymore. Fire hazard."

"I'm sure it will turn up." I kept my tone light. "Janice might know where it is. Have you seen her tonight?"

"Janice? Nope. Haven't seen her. Though when Rhonda and I were leaving the Pig's Eye after dinner—

it's spaghetti night—Rhonda thought she saw Janice's little red Porsche going by." She gave the witch hat a final pat. "But it couldn't have been her, because George says she's home with a headache. Migraine, I guess."

"Too bad. She seems to really suffer from those things."

"That's a fact. Though when they first came to work here, she was hardly ever out sick. This is all pretty recent."

"How recent?"

"Oh, about a couple of months."

Was the man with Janice in the dressing room the cause of the headaches? *Come on, Pete! Call me! For all I know, there might be a murderer still hiding somewhere in the building!*

Marty gave me the neatly typed sheets containing a synopsis of *The Witches,* a list of the night's scheduled commercials, and the triple-spaced script for the ones I'd be reading from the teleprompter.

"Looks like we've picked up a couple of new sponsors." I was surprised and pleased.

"Doan's wicked happy about that. He never liked Ariel, you know, but he liked her ratings. He seems to like you, though. Mrs. Doan does, too. But then, she and Ariel were great pals at one time."

"Really?" I remembered how Mrs. Doan had behaved when the witch coven boat had arrived. "She seemed glad Ariel is dead. What happened between them?"

"Don't know, exactly. It happened right after Ariel and Doan had a big row. The missus got the idea that Ariel had put a witch spell on her husband. She begged Ariel to take it away." Marty ducked behind her camera, then reappeared. "Naturally, Ariel swore there was no such spell."

"What kind of spell was it supposed to be?"

Marty smothered a snicker. "It seems that Mr. Doan hadn't been performing his husbandly duties as well as he used to, and Mrs. Doan was convinced that Ariel had made his whatsit malfunction, if you know what I mean." She shrugged. "Maybe she did, for all I know. She did a lot of weird shit lately."

I had no desire to comment on the state of the boss's whatsit.

It was getting close to the time I'd have to put on my Crystal Moon outfit, and I didn't look forward to going back into that dressing room.

"Guess I'll go get into character," I said. "Be right back."

She had ducked behind the camera again and gave me a brief wave. "Okay. See you in a few."

I didn't hurry.

Maybe if Rhonda is still here, I can ask her to come down and help me with my hair and makeup so I don't have to be alone in there.

I reached for my phone. The ring tone sounded as soon as I touched it.

Oh my God! I hadn't turned my phone off when I was listening outside the dressing room door. What if it had rung then?

I shook away the bad thought and looked at the caller ID.

Pete Mondello.

"Oh, Pete. I'm so glad it's you!"

"Wow!" I could hear the smile in his voice. "Thanks. I was glad to hear from you, too. What's going on?"

"Pete, something really strange has happened here at the station. I think I might have overheard a murder confession."

His tone immediately became serious. "What murder? Who confessed?"

"I don't know exactly. A man. He threatened Janice. Only, she might not have been here. . . ."

"Slow down, Lee. I can't follow what you're saying."

"I know. I'm sorry to sound so rattled, but, Pete, I'm scared."

"Are you doing your show tonight?"

"Yes." I looked at my watch. "In about an hour."

"I'm coming over. You can tell me the whole story then."

"Thank you, Pete."

I hung up and pushed the door of the dressing room open. I sat at the vanity and looked into the mirror. Pete was coming. I felt better already.

The lighted vanity mirror intensified the shadows in the room. I was alone, yet the feeling of someone— something—being nearby was almost suffocating. I dressed quickly in the blue-and-yellow outfit. My makeup was a hurry-up affair, too. I put my street clothes into the garment bag and took it out of the room with me. I didn't want to go back in there after the show, when the whole building would be virtually empty.

The studio lights were still off as I hurried up the darkened aisle toward the *Nightshades* set, nearly bumping into Pete Mondello.

"Pete! I'm glad you're here."

"Is there someplace we can talk? So you can tell me what's going on that's got you so upset."

He put an arm around my shoulders, steering me back toward the dressing room. "Here. How about this little room?"

I suppressed a shudder. "I guess it would be okay."

I sat on the vanity bench, facing Pete, who'd pulled up a folding chair opposite me. He took both of my hands in his. "Now, what's going on?"

"Can it be off the record?"

"You know I can't do that, Lee. I'm sorry."

"I know. Okay. I'll tell you, but I warn you, you might think I'm crazy."

"I promise not to think you're crazy." He smiled and gently squeezed my hands.

"All right. But first, did Sarge—Bill Valen—call you about the new postcard?"

"He did. It was definitely mailed from here."

"And he told you that the WICH-TV postmark was on one of the other postcards?"

"He did. The postmark was faded and blurred, but once he called it to our attention, we recognized what it was. It was mailed two years ago. Had a nice picture of snow in Vermont."

"Do you think the missing kid, Willie, was here? *Is* here in Salem?"

"It's beginning to look as though that's possible. Now tell me what's going on that's got you so spooked."

I related the conversation I'd overheard, trying hard to recall the exact words. "The man was so mean, and poor Janice sounded terrified."

He had the cop face on again. He reached into his

pocket for notebook and pencil. "You're sure the female voice was Janice's?"

I was.

"You said on the phone that Janice might not have actually been here. What did you mean?"

I explained about George's security cameras at the condo, including the one he had in Janice's room. "George showed me pictures of Janice asleep in her bed."

"He monitors his sister's bed?"

"Apparently. I found that strange, too."

"I'm not making a judgment." His voice was suddenly gruff. "Just making sure that was what you meant. Now tell me about the man's voice. Have you heard it before?"

"I'm not sure. It seemed sort of familiar. Like someone I've heard before, but not exactly. I just can't place it. I'm sorry."

"That's okay." His nice voice was back. "And you say nobody else that you know of witnessed this?"

I shook my head.

"And no one even knew you were in the building at the time?"

"I'm pretty sure. At least I didn't see anyone. And I've checked around a little, and nobody saw Janice here, either. But I'm sure I didn't imagine it. I was here. Janice was here. And a man was here."

Pete leaned back in the folding chair and looked at me intently. After a long moment he said, "I don't think you're crazy, Lee. I think you heard just what you say you heard. But now we have to prove it." He stuffed the notebook back into his pocket and put the pencil behind his ear. "How far from the station is the Valen place?"

"Not far at all," I said. "Closer than my house. Just on the opposite side of the common. It's one of those beautiful old Federal houses."

"How long would you say it takes to drive from here to there at night?"

"Oh, I don't know. Five or six minutes. Maybe less." I saw where he was going with that train of thought. I snapped my fingers. "And Rhonda and Marty thought they saw Janice's car go by on Derby Street at around the time I was inside the station."

He pulled the notebook out again. "What does Janice drive?"

I thought for a moment. "A little 2012 red Porsche Cayman. Six-cylinder, six-speed manual. Two-seater. Goes from zero to sixty in five point five seconds."

Pete put the notebook down, smiling. "A bit of a gearhead, are you?"

I returned the smile. "Can't help it. I was married to Johnny Barrett for five years. Hung around cars a lot."

"Impressive." He made a few notes. "So I think we can safely assume that Janice could easily have been home in bed within minutes of the time you heard her speaking to a man in this room."

"Yes, she could. And if nobody saw me in here, then maybe they didn't see her, either."

"That car wouldn't go unnoticed, though. We'll check it out." This time the notebook and pencil went into his inside pocket, and once again the gun was noticeable. "Meanwhile, you think hard about that other voice, will you? And, Lee, do you have a ride home?"

"No. I was going to call a cab."

"I'm going to hang around. Do a little snooping. I'll drive you home, okay?"

It was more than okay. A ride home with a police escort was exactly what I needed just then. "Thanks, Pete. I'd really appreciate that."

"No problem. Come on. I'll walk you back to the set."

Marty looked comfortable on the turquoise couch, feet up on the coffee table. "Oh, there you are. Listen, you want to run through the movie intro so I can time it?"

"Sure. What would you like it to be?"

"Minute and a half is good."

I'd read the notes Marty had given me, and that, coupled with my memories of the good old Anjelica Huston film, provided an easy ninety-second recitation of Luke's adventures with witches who turn children into mice.

"Perfect," Marty said. "Minute and a half on the button. You're good at figuring time."

"Logged lots of hours with a stopwatch on the racing circuit. After a while it gets automatic."

Pete gave a wave and walked toward the door leading to the control room, where George Valen would be preparing to field calls from the *Nightshades* faithful. Maybe Pete, with his powers of persuasion, not to mention the power of the badge, could get George to fill in some of the blanks in the strange happenings that centered around WICH-TV.

CHAPTER 30

It was time for me to concentrate on the show, on becoming the Gypsy psychic the viewers expected, on solving the unsolvable, predicting the unpredictable, and at the same time selling the sponsors' products.

The theme music played, the witch hat bumper appeared on the screen, and the teleprompter displayed my first commercial of the night. We were off to a good start. A couple of canned commercials, a station promo, my movie intro, and it was time to relax while the first half of *The Witches* ran.

"Want to watch?" Marty asked.

"Not tonight," I said. "Too much on my mind."

"Anything I can help with?"

"I don't know," I said. "Something really strange happened tonight, and I'm trying to sort it out."

"Plenty of strange stuff around here lately, that's for sure."

"Anybody besides me hearing voices?"

"Voices? What kind?"

I described briefly what I'd heard from outside the

dressing room. Pete hadn't thought I was crazy. I took a chance that Marty wouldn't think so, either.

"I'm sure it was Janice's voice," I told her, "but I didn't recognize the man's. It sounded familiar, but I can't quite place it. Of course I never saw either one of them, and George says it couldn't have been Janice, because she's home in bed with a migraine. Any bright ideas? Or am I just losing it?"

"You know," she said, "you just may be onto something." She tossed a cover over the camera and sat beside me. "You aren't the only one who's heard those voices."

"Glad to hear that. Who else?"

She tapped her chest. "Me. It was before you came here. Before Ariel died. I didn't tell anybody about it. I mean, it wasn't a creepy conversation like you heard, but it was . . . odd."

"What happened?"

"I was looking for some duct tape to secure some wires, and I knew there was some in the control room. I didn't know anyone was in there, so I was surprised when I heard Janice's voice. It sounded like she was arguing with somebody. Arguing about those crystal things Ariel liked to give away sometimes."

"Did you see who she was arguing with?"

She shook her head. "I don't walk in on arguments. The duct tape wasn't all that important, anyhow. But I did hear the guy's voice, too. He sounded mad. And mean."

"Do you remember what they were saying?"

"Kind of. The man wanted her to deliver the crystal necklaces instead of mailing them. Said he wanted to be sure the right women got them."

"And Janice didn't want to?"

"Not at all. It sounded like she was crying. She just kept saying no."

"Then what happened?"

"Don't know. I had to get back to work. But here's the strange thing. It was Janice's day off. She wasn't even supposed to be here."

"Did you ever ask her about it?"

"Nope. None of my business." She looked at her watch. "Oops. Almost time for another commercial. Ready?"

"Yes. But, Marty, do you have any idea who the man was?"

"Nope. Like you said, he sounded familiar. I thought it might be one of Ariel's regulars."

One of Ariel's regulars.

Of course. That was exactly why the voice sounded familiar to me, too. In fact, I'd heard that voice recently. I was pretty sure it had been the youngish-sounding man who'd said his name was William. The one who was going to get his mother a cat.

Get his mother a cat!

What was the matter with me? The cat he meant to get was O'Ryan! And his name was William! *Willie?* What was his mother's name? *Lena? Short for Marlena?*

I looked around the darkened room for Pete. I had to tell him that it was Willie who'd been threatening Janice and that Marty had heard him once, too, talking about delivering the crystal necklaces. But Pete was nowhere in sight, and it was time for me to read the next commercial. I forced a smile, faced the camera, and somehow managed to deliver a more or less sincere pitch for a local auto dealership.

The movie had reached the midway point. Luke and his grandma had managed to put the magic potion into the witches' soup. It was time for Crystal Moon to work her Gypsy magic and solve the problems of the *Nightshades* audience. There was no time to tell Pete what I'd just learned.

"Hello, caller. Your first name and your question please."

I worked my way through three calls, dreading the reply to that "Hello, caller" greeting each time, fearful that the answering voice would be that of the man I was sure was the long-missing Willie Valen.

Thankfully, all the calls were from ordinary people who wanted advice on love or loss or money. George, whatever else he might be, was an excellent call screener. When it was time for the movie to resume, I told Marty about my suspicion that the caller named William was the man who'd tried to steal O'Ryan and that he might be the one who'd cut Yvette Pelletier's throat and crushed Ariel's hands.

I wanted to tell her that he had probably thrown his own mother down the stairs. But I wasn't ready to go there yet.

"I'm going up to the control room to find Detective Mondello," I told her. "I'll bring him right back here. I don't like leaving you alone."

"Don't worry about me, Moon. I'll be fine."

Her voice wasn't quite as strong and confident as it usually was, though, and I hurried on my way to the control room.

The door was closed, but I could hear male voices.

Should I knock? Or just walk in? Or stand here and listen?

Nope. No more listening at doorways for me. I was afraid of what I might hear. I knocked with one hand and pushed the door open with the other.

Pete and George stood side by side, watching a divided screen set apart from the long bank of monitors showing a range of camera shots. I recognized it as a surveillance monitor. There were four sections, each one displaying a grainy black-and-white exterior view of the WICH-TV property. The parking lot and the street in front of the station were easily recognizable. A few cars moved along Derby Street, and the sidewalk was clear of pedestrians. The cameras mounted on the sides of the building showed no activity at all.

Pete looked up when I entered. "Hi, Lee. Look. George has the outside cameras working again."

"That's good. Have they found the missing footage?"

"Not yet, but they will," Pete said. "They took the hard drive apart this morning."

"Pete, could I talk to you for a moment?" I said.

"Sure. What's up?"

"Could we go back to the studio? Marty's alone there."

"Of course." He held the door open for me. "We'll talk again later, George."

"Sure," George said. "I'm not going anywhere. Good show, Lee."

"Thanks for the easy calls, George."

I kept my voice steady, my tone pleasant, but I really wanted to scream, "George, for God's sake, what is wrong with you? Your brother's here in Salem. He's threatening your sister—or whoever she is. He may be a killer, and you're sitting here, fooling around with stupid phone calls and an old surveillance camera."

As soon as the door closed behind us and Pete and I were alone, the words came tumbling out. By the time we reached the set, I'd told him about William, the caller who'd promised his mother a cat on the same night that the camo guy had tried to steal O'Ryan, and who'd said his mother's name was Lena, which could be short for Marlena. I told him that I was sure the man was Willie Valen, and that I was sure Janice was in real danger.

We reached the *Nightshades* set, where Marty was pacing between her camera and the star-flecked blue backdrop. It was the only time I'd ever seen the woman look nervous.

"Marty will tell you, Pete. She's heard the same man arguing with Janice, haven't you, Marty?"

Marty repeated the story she'd told me. Pete wrote in his notebook.

I couldn't seem to stop talking, asking questions. "Pete, do you think George even knows that his younger brother is here in Salem?"

"I don't know, Lee." Pete sounded serious. "But we'll get to the bottom of all this, Willie or no Willie."

"Who's Willie?" Marty wanted to know.

"When we were in Florida, we found out that George and Janice might have a younger brother named Willie. But nobody seems to know where he is."

"I wish Ariel was here," Marty said. "She'd probably be able to figure everything out about this Willie character and solve the murders. Even her own."

Pete put the notebook down and faced Marty. "What makes you say that?"

"It's kind of weird, really. I worked with Ariel for years, you know? And she always answered the questions from callers with that mystical malarkey talk, like you do, Crystal. I mean, just plain, commonsense answers with some kind of horoscope bull. Nothing anyone with a brain would take seriously." She gave an apologetic nod in my direction. "No offense intended."

"None taken, Marty. But what makes you think she could solve the murders?"

"The last month or so, her answers to callers started to get more specific. She started finding lost stuff for them. I mean, telling them exactly where the thing was." She pointed a finger at me. "Just like you found that lady's watch in her bathroom. How the hell did you do that, anyway?"

"I don't know. I really don't. But what about Ariel?"

"Well, I asked her about it. She was really getting into the witch bit. I mean, she had always *said* she was a witch, but it was part of the act. She didn't really believe it herself. Until all of a sudden, she changed. She could do . . . things. Magic things."

"What does that mean?" Pete wore his skeptical cop face. "Can you be specific? What exactly did she do?"

"First, it was little stuff—almost like practical jokes. Like she made Rhonda's makeup kit disappear. I don't know how she did it. It was there on Rhonda's desk, like always. Then *poof!* It disappeared. I saw it with my own eyes. Ariel just laughed and wouldn't tell how she did it. Rhonda was really pissed, too, because she never did get it back."

"Anything else?" Pete asked. "Maybe she just took a magician's course somewhere."

"That's what we all thought. Then she started fooling around with cars in the parking lot. She just put her hands on the hood of George's car one day, and it started up all by itself, even though the doors were locked. She just laughed that time, too."

Pete scribbled in his notebook. "And you say her answers to callers were getting more accurate? She was finding things?"

"Not all the time. But she was 'seeing' the callers more. You know what I mean?"

"No," Pete said. "I don't."

"I do," I said, recalling the times I'd heard Ariel tell a caller, "I see you" doing this or that. "Marty, do you think she was actually seeing them?"

"Maybe."

Pete snapped the notebook shut. "That's all kind of hard to prove. Listen, Lee. I need to check out a couple of things with George. After the show is over, I'll drive you home."

"Okay. The movie will be over pretty soon, and I'll take a couple of calls after that."

I took my place on the couch, and Marty positioned herself behind the camera.

"Marty," I said, "do you think Ariel was really practicing some kind of magic? Some kind of spells?"

"Looked that way to me. I know it sounds crazy. I'm sure that cop thinks I'm nuts. You ready? Counting. Ten. Nine. Eight . . ."

We'd reached the end of the movie, the part where Luke and his grandmother find the addresses of all the witches in America and plan a kind of "seek and destroy" mission. If the movie were real, would Luke and his grandma have found Ariel Constellation's name on the list? Would they have found and destroyed her?

But life wasn't a movie. Someone had sought and destroyed Ariel, and I might have overheard her killer's confession. Maybe Pete Mondello didn't believe me. Maybe the police department had to ignore things like witches and magic spells. But I didn't. I *knew* Janice was in danger, and if no one else was going to help her, I knew I'd have to.

Somehow I finished the show without messing up.

Still wary about going into the dressing room alone, I decided to change into my street clothes in the cramped ladies' powder room in the station's reception area. I made sure that the cleaning man/security guard was on duty before leaving Marty in the studio, then grabbed my garment bag and said good night to the camerawoman.

"If Detective Mondello is looking for me, would you tell him I'll meet him down by the elevator?"

"Sure thing. Good night, kid."

Getting undressed in the pink and lavender confines of the tiny bathroom wasn't easy. I stuffed the Gypsy outfit and gold sandals into the garment bag and wiggled into my jeans and sweater. I sat on the purple plastic toilet seat and pulled on my boots. I took a quick glance at the star-shaped mirror, deciding that there wasn't time or space to fix my hair or makeup.

I was about to unlock the door when I heard footsteps. Was it Pete, looking for me? I couldn't be sure. What if Willie Valen was out there? Did he know I'd heard him talking to Janice? Was he waiting for me? I held my breath.

"Hello. Are you all right?"

It was George Valen's voice. Was he talking to me? How did he know where I was? I didn't answer.

"Janice? Is that you? Did I wake you?" His voice was warm, concerned.

He was on the phone, calling his sister. I began to breathe again. But now I had a new problem. Did I come bursting out of the bathroom or stay put? Would Pete come looking for me if I kept him waiting in the downstairs lobby much longer? I sat on the toilet and listened.

George's voice changed to a harsh whisper.

"Willie! You little son of a bitch! Leave her alone! What do you want?"

CHAPTER 31

I didn't dare budge. I just sat there on the hideous purple toilet seat, eavesdropping. After what seemed like an hour, but was probably only a minute or two, I heard the slam of the heavy metal door. Was he gone? Did I dare to creep out of this claustrophobic closet?

I took a deep breath, grabbed the bag of clothes, burst out of the bathroom, and raced for the lobby. Should I get into the slow-moving elevator or take my chances in the dark, winding stairwell? I opted for the elevator and punched the DOWN button.

Thankfully, Pete was there when the doors clanked open.

"Hey, where've you been?" There was real concern in his voice. "I was getting worried about you."

"I was getting worried about me, too," I told him. "Let's get out of here."

Tossing the garment bag over my shoulder, I practically raced him to the street.

"In a rush to get home, Lee? Come on. My car's right here." He held the door of the unmarked police car open, and I climbed in, feeling safe for the first time since I'd overheard that chilling exchange from outside the dressing room.

"It's not that, Pete," I told him. "I just wanted to get out of there. Listen, I was in the bathroom and I heard George on his phone." The words tumbled out in an excited rush. "He was talking to Willie. I heard him. He called Willie a little son of a bitch and told him to leave Janice alone. And, Pete, Willie was in George and Janice's condo! Let's go over there, and you can arrest him."

"That's not the way it works, Lee. You know that. I'd need a warrant. And we don't know if there really is a Willie."

"Someone is sending those postcards to Bill Valen," I pointed out. "And we know the most recent ones came from here."

"Sure. Someone. But has anyone actually seen this mysterious Willie? Hearing conversations from behind closed doors doesn't count."

"You don't believe me."

"Yes, I believe you heard something . . . someone. But, Lee, I'm a cop. I need facts. Eyewitnesses. Real people. No witch tricks or sound effects."

"At least can we drive by the Valens' condo? George told Willie to get out. Maybe we'll see him leave."

"Okay. It's on the way to your place, anyway. I guess we can do that." His tone was a little condescending, but I decided to let that pass. "Now," he said, "tell me exactly what you think you heard George say on the phone."

"It's not what I *think* I heard. It's what I heard."

"Sorry. That's what I meant."

"That's all right. He thought he was talking to

Janice. He said 'Hello' and 'Did I wake you?' Then, I guess, someone answered, because he was quiet for a minute. Then he said, 'Willie! You little son of a bitch! Leave her alone!' Then he said, 'We got rid of you before, and we can do it again.'"

"And you heard all this through the bathroom door?"

"Yes, I did."

"Is that all he said?"

"No. He said that it was too bad about something that happened to Willie back in Cincinnati, but that whatever it was wasn't Janice's fault."

Washington Square was eerily still when we cruised to a stop in front of the big old house turned condos.

"Looks quiet enough," Pete said.

"Maybe too quiet," I whispered. "I'm worried about Janice, Pete. That man, that Willie, if that's who it was, threatened her. I heard what I heard."

"You know I can't do a darned thing officially here, Lee. But would it make you feel better if I knock on the door and ask George if everything is all right in there?"

"Oh, would you?"

"Sure. I'll be right back." He opened his door.

"Are you kidding? I'm not staying out here alone! I'm coming with you."

I was sure he wanted to object but probably figured it would be a waste of time. Which it would have been. I joined him, and together we approached the Valens' front door.

Pete consulted the glass-covered directory and pressed a combination of buttons.

George answered immediately. "Yes, Pete. I see you. What's up?"

I looked around and spotted a small camera above the door.

"George, sorry to bother you at this hour," Pete said, "but Lee is worried about you folks. Is everything okay in there?"

"Sure. Why wouldn't it be?"

"Are you sure Janice is all right?" I asked.

"Oh, hi, Lee. Janice is fine. Sleeping like a baby," came the quick reply. "Go home and get some rest, you two. We're fine. Thanks for asking. Good night."

"Good night, George," Pete said. "See you later."

"But, Pete," I whispered. "What if they're not okay? What if Willie has a gun pointed at them? What if . . . ?"

"Shhh." He took my arm with a firm grip and led me back to the car. "We've done all we can for now. I'm going to get you home. Your aunt will be worried. Then I'll radio for a cruiser to do an extra patrol around the neighborhood for the rest of the night."

What a nice guy.

"Thanks, Pete," I said. "That makes me feel a little better."

He smiled. "Just a little?"

"I'm still worried about Janice. But you're right. We've done all we can for now."

It was just a short distance to Winter Street from the east side of Washington Square. We pulled up in front of the house in minutes. Pete picked up the garment bag and walked to the front door with me, much as Scott Palmer had a couple of nights ago. But there was no long, deep-in-the-eyes look from Pete Mondello.

Instead, without a second's hesitation, with his free arm he pulled me close and delivered another one of those knee-weakening, toe-curling, heart-pounding kisses. And this time beer and Florida moonlight had nothing to do with it.

He handed me the garment bag. "Good night, Lee. I'll call you tomorrow."

I just stood there, surprised and pleased at the same time, probably looking like a goof, while he walked down the steps, then turned and waved. "Good night," he said again.

I managed a wave and then unlocked the door. I thought that Aunt Ibby would be up waiting for me, and I was right.

"I'm glad you're home, Maralee," she said. "You did so well with all the questions tonight, and I enjoyed the movie, too. And you looked so pretty. But, dear, were you a bit nervous?" She took my hand, leading me into the den. "I don't think anyone but me noticed, but is something wrong?"

"Yes, something is very wrong." I told her about the disturbing conversation I'd overheard between Janice and the man behind the dressing room door. I didn't leave anything out. I told her about Marty hearing an argument between the two. I related the telephone call between George and someone he called Willie.

She sat quietly and let me pour it all out. "So you believe that Willie, George's younger brother, is here in Salem and, for some reason, means to harm Janice?"

"I do. I'm really frightened for her. Pete and I went over to the Valens' place after I finished the show so that we could check with George and be sure they were all right. He said they were, but I'm still worried. What do you think?"

"I think you did well to tell the detective all about it. That was the responsible thing to do. Meanwhile, you and I will learn everything we can about this Willie person. You keep your ears open around the station, and I'll do some more research online."

"Have you turned up anything interesting so far?"

"Well, for one thing, the police in Cincinnati declared Marlena's death an accident with alcohol involved. Also, I heard from my Facebook friend Nigel. Remember I told you about him? He's with New Scotland Yard."

"What did he say?"

"So far, he's found information on both George and William Valen. They had valid passports and traveled between the United States and England. They arrived in London from the U.S. together and departed together about six years later. He says that George worked in London as a freelance photographer for several of the London tabloids. Sort of a paparazzo, apparently."

"What about Janice?"

"Nothing on a Janice Valen so far. But there were three women with the first name Janice on the plane they flew home on, and he's looking into that."

"You have some great Facebook friends. Nigel seems to be going all out for us."

"Yes. Nigel is a very special friend. We met last year, when he was here on sabbatical."

"Oh?" Was my staid and proper aunt blushing? "A *special* friend?"

"We went out to dinner together a few times. Don't look so surprised."

I didn't press the subject. "Well, he's certainly been very helpful. Did he say anything more?"

"He looked into that nightclub—the Purple Dragon. He says it closed years ago. And, Maralee, he says it was one of those female impersonator clubs. You know, where men dress up like women and sing and dance and such."

"That's strange. I'm sure the Purple Dragon was the name I read on Janice's photo."

"Nigel says there was no Janice Valen listed as an employee there. But there was a Billie Jo Vale. Do you think that could have been a stage name that Willie Valen might have used? William Joseph . . . Billie Jo?"

"You may be right. I'm going to call George in the morning and ask some questions. He can tell me it's none of my business, but I'm going to at least try to get some answers."

My aunt looked at her watch. "It's been morning for quite a while already, my dear. Let's go to bed and think about all this later."

"You're right. Where's O'Ryan?"

"I think he's already up in your room, waiting for you."

"I won't keep him waiting any longer. Good night."

The cat was on the bed, just as Aunt Ibby had said he would be. He opened his eyes briefly when I turned on the light, then settled back onto the pillow with what looked like a contented smile on his face.

I could hardly wait to join him. Exhaustion hit me like a giant wave, and I hurried through the face-washing, tooth-brushing, pajama-donning ritual and tumbled into bed.

"Good night, O'Ryan," I mumbled.

"Gnufff," he answered.

In seconds I was sound asleep.

But not for long. I awoke with a start. As if in a dream, I heard once again the plaintive voice of Paul, the boy who wanted to get a job instead of studying. His speech pattern was the same as Billy's, the kid who thought his brother was spying on him. I'd connected the two voices before, when I was at the motel in Florida. But the reason for the sudden awakening this time wasn't just the connection between the two calls. It was the realization that Paul was not even a real kid. He was one of the callers on my own audition tape.

And all the voices on that tape belonged to Janice Valen.

At least, I'd thought they did.

CHAPTER 32

I tried to recall the details of that day not so very long ago. I remembered that I'd wanted to thank Janice for helping with the audition. But she'd told Marty that she couldn't come down to the studio, because she was calling from home. So had the voices really been Janice's? Or had Willie been there even then? Taking the telephone from her and pretending to be a teenage kid? How many other voices on *Nightshades* had Willie provided? And had Ariel been tricked the same way I'd been? Just how had Willie achieved such control over the program director, who had, at our first meeting, seemed to be such a confident, take-charge woman?

Too many questions. Too many difficult things to figure out—especially at four o'clock in the morning. I rolled over, careful not to disturb the cat, and went back to sleep.

When I awoke a few hours later, O'Ryan had already left to join Aunt Ibby in the kitchen, where the melded aromas of coffee, bacon, and apple muffins promised a delicious, if caloric, breakfast—just what I needed to fortify myself for the busy day ahead.

I needed to shop for a few more outfits for Crystal Moon, along with something glitzy and sexy for the Witches Ball. The station's credit card was about to get a good workout. Salem at Halloween is probably as good as New Orleans for great masquerade wear.

I'd see River at the Lyceum for the evening tea-leaf reading, and somehow during this day I'd find the time—and the courage—to confront George Valen about what was going on with the elusive Willie. He could tell me it was none of my business. He could probably get me fired. But if Willie was responsible for trying to steal O'Ryan, it was my business, and I intended to get some answers.

If it was Willie who was running around after dark in Salem, wearing a camouflage outfit, stabbing one woman and drowning another, and if it was Willie who'd threatened Janice so cruelly, and who'd hidden in the yard at Winter Street and stuffed my poor cat into a pillowcase, then George needed to do something about it, younger brother or not. And he needed to do it now. Before someone else got hurt.

Was Willie the King of Cups reversed? Was he my secret enemy? What would River think if I told her everything? If I told her about finding Ariel's body, about seeing visions in the obsidian ball, about hearing voices behind closed doors, about my fears for Janice Valen's safety, and about the growing mystery of Willie Valen? Maybe a witch would be the perfect person to talk to. But do witches have a confidentiality agreement, like doctors and lawyers? I had to smile at that idea.

I hurried downstairs, and Aunt Ibby greeted me with a hug and a glass of freshly squeezed orange juice.

"Sit down and have a good breakfast, Maralee," she said. "Most important meal of the day, you know. You've been running yourself ragged with this crazy job and murders and mysterious voices and whatnot." She waved a spatula. "Now sit."

I did as she said, and between bites of perfectly crisp bacon and warm apple muffin, I told her about my realization that Willie's voice had come from Janice's home phone.

"What do you think, Aunt Ibby? Could Willie be stalking her after all these years? And is Janice Valen one of the Janices who flew home from London with George and Willie?"

"I don't know, Maralee. Nigel didn't say that any of the three Janices was *with* them. Those are big planes. Chances are that there're at least one or two Janices on any of them."

I sighed, more confused than ever. "You're right. Thanks for breakfast. I'd better get moving. I have some serious shopping to do."

"Want the car?"

"No thanks. I'm sure I'll find what I need on Essex Street. It's nice out, and I can walk off some of this food. I'll take a cab home if I'm weighted down with bags and boxes."

I put my wallet into the pocket of the NASCAR jacket and set out to spend the station's money. There were plenty of shops in downtown Salem, and I was pretty sure most of them would be featuring costumes and accessories this month. I was right. Within the first hour I found three Gypsyish skirts, which I could mix and match with the ones I already had. In a vintage fashion store I found two beautifully embroidered blouses, sufficiently low-necked to please Mr. Doan. I was about to leave when I thought to ask about the dress I'd need for the Witches Ball.

"Got anything with lots of sparkle? Something really glitzy?" I asked. Maybe I could save the station a little money, I thought, by buying vintage instead of new.

"I have something in the back you might like," said the woman. "Wait a sec."

She returned, carrying a large cardboard box. "This just came in." She opened the lid, pushing aside blue tissue paper. "Take a look. It's a 1980s vintage Bob Mackie."

It was gorgeous. Silver and crystal beads sparkled across fabric so sheer, it was almost invisible. The bead design on the bodice was gracefully constructed to cover strategic areas, and the long, pencil-slim skirt was divided with a thigh-high slit.

"Try it on. It's just your size."

She was right. It fit as though it had been made for me. I turned in front of the full-length mirror.

"How much is it?"

"One thousand seven hundred. It's a steal at that price."

So much for saving the station a little money. I knew Doan would love the dress, but would he love it seventeen hundred dollars' worth?

I did one more turn, admiring my own reflection. "I think that might be more than the station's budget allows."

"The station?" The woman smiled into the mirror. "The TV station?"

"Right."

"I thought you looked familiar. You're the new *Nightshades* girl."

"That's me. I'm supposed to find something fabulous to wear to the Witches Ball. This is fabulous enough, but I doubt that my boss will want to pay that much."

"Bruce Doan's the boss over there, right?"

"You know him?" I asked.

"He comes in with the missus once in a while. I call her if anything nice in purple comes in. If it's something he likes on her, he doesn't question the price. Why don't you take it over to the station and model it? See if he likes it." She handed me a vintage French telephone. "Here. Call and see if that's okay."

I took another turn in front of the mirror.

Oh, he'll like it, all right.

I accepted the phone and dialed the station's number. I was surprised when Janice answered. She sounded cheerful, unaffected by the events of the night before.

"How are you feeling, Janice?" I asked. "You okay?"

"Sure. Why wouldn't I be? What's up?"

How could she be so calm? So normal? So untouched by the threats she'd received just hours ago? I wanted to tell her that I knew she was in danger. To tell her to be careful.

Instead, I just told her about the vintage Mackie. And the price. "It's lovely," I said. "But awfully expensive. They say I can take it over and show it to Mr. Doan. I'll need a ride, though. I walked here."

"Hold on. I'll check."

In less than a minute she was back. "Okay, Lee. All set. I'm sending George to pick you and the dress up. You can model it for Doan, and if he likes it, it's a go."

By the time I'd changed and the gown had been carefully repacked, George's car pulled up in front of the store. Carrying the dress box and all my other packages, I climbed in.

"Wow! Are you buying out the city?" He sounded perfectly normal, just as Janice had, with no hint in his voice or appearance that anything out of the ordinary had happened to either of them.

Was there going to be more of the "small talk" George and Janice seemed to favor, or was this the time for me to come right out and tell him what I knew about Willie?

There's never going to be a right time to tell a guy that you think his little brother is a serial killer. Just do it.

CHAPTER 33

"George," I said, "it's time to get serious. You didn't think it was odd that I showed up on your doorstep with a cop at two o'clock in the morning? You're not just a little concerned that I overheard a man threaten your sister? That the man is your own brother and might be a killer?"

His hands tightened on the steering wheel, but he didn't speak.

I kept right on talking. "Is Willie at your house? We know he's in Salem. Sarge got a postcard from him. It was mailed from the station."

"Willie's going away," he said, speaking so softly that I had to lean toward him to hear. "And Janice will be all right. I've made an appointment with a specialist in Boston."

"A doctor? For Janice? Has he injured her? My God, George! Why are you protecting him?"

"You don't understand, Lee. Nobody does."

"Try me," I said. "I want to understand—to help, if I can."

He turned and faced me, not loosening his grip on

the wheel. "I want so much for her to be all right. Maybe this new specialist can do something for her."

"Is Janice injured somehow?" I repeated my question. "Has Willie hurt her?"

"She's not hurt that way. I mean, not her body. It's her mind. He's messed up her mind again."

Again? He's messed up her mind again?

I remembered the woman's frightened look when I mentioned plastic surgery. "Janice is afraid of doctors. Has she agreed to go?"

"I haven't told her yet. I'll get her there somehow. This doctor says he thinks he can help. That what she has is just a psychosomatic problem."

I knew I'd seen or heard that term somewhere very recently. I searched my memory as we approached the station. George wheeled the car into the parking lot, coming to a halt close to the seawall. The engine continued to run, and he made no attempt to open the doors.

"I hope the doctor can help, George. But what about Willie? Surely you know he's dangerous. That he may even be a killer. You have to turn him in to the police."

"Oh, I would if I could ever catch the little bastard!" He pounded on the dashboard. "He manages to disappear every time I get close to him."

"You mean he *wasn't* at your house last night?"

"Oh, he was there, all right. I even talked to him on the phone." He spread his hands in a helpless gesture. "But, as usual, by the time I got home, he was gone."

"Where could he go?" I wanted to know. "Does he know anyone in Salem who'd shelter him?"

George dropped his hands, and his shoulders

began to shake. Was he crying? I didn't know what I should do or say. I froze, feeling helpless as he made strange gasping sounds. In the face of the fact that his brother was suspected of murder and that his sister might be in grave danger, the man was laughing.

That little voice we all have inside our heads but usually ignore was telling me, *The guy is cracking up. Exit stage right.*

This time I listened, opened the passenger door, and stepped out next to the seawall. In full fleeing mode, I was ready to dash for the station's back entrance.

You can't leave all those packages in the backseat, dummy. Especially the seventeen-hundred-dollar one.

I tried the back door, but, of course, it was locked. There was nothing to do except knock on the window and motion to the driver, who had apparently recovered from his badly timed fit of hilarity. He rolled the window down.

"Sorry, Lee. You must think I've lost my mind." He patted the seat beside him. "Come on back in. I'll try to explain."

Yeah. Fat chance of that happening!

"Uh, that's okay, George," I said. "We'll talk some more later. Right now I have to get my stuff out of the backseat. Mr. Doan is waiting for me."

The back door lock clicked open, and I reached in, grabbing the dress box first, then piling the bags on top of it.

"Thanks for the ride," I said, knowing as I spoke how inane that sounded.

If poor Janice has a psychosomatic problem, you've got one, too, Buster.

Hurrying toward the studio, I balanced the packages with one arm and pushed the door open. At that moment I remembered where I'd seen that term before. It had been highlighted in one of Ariel's witchcraft books.

The seventeenth-century medical doctor was likely to attribute symptoms he could not explain to witchcraft, much the way today's physician is apt to characterize whatever he cannot understand as a psychosomatic problem.

CHAPTER 34

There were areas of bright light within the usually dark studio. Both the news desk and the weather set were illuminated, and a glance at my watch told me it was nearly time for the noon news show. The anchorman rummaged through a stack of papers, while Wanda the Weather Girl searched for a place to clip a mike to the very low neckline of a tight red sweater. The ON AIR signs weren't yet lighted, so with the pile of packages nearly at my eye level, I hurried across the room to the door leading to the upstairs offices.

Rhonda helped me dump my assorted bags onto one of the chrome and purple chairs, and I put the dress box on the counter.

"Janice says you got a real Bob Mackie!" She sounded breathless. "Can I see it?"

"Sure." I opened the box, pushed aside the blue tissue, and lifted the delicate bodice. "What do you think?"

"Jeez. I think if you even lost a couple of those shiny crystals, you'd be kind of exposed."

"I know. If Mr. Doan wants me to wear it, I'll have to be really careful."

The door to Janice's office swung open, and the program director joined us. "Is that it? The million-dollar dress?"

"This is it," I said, studying Janice's expression, her body language, her tone of voice with much more attention than ever before.

What does a person with psychosomatic problems look like, anyway?

Janice glanced at the dress, gave me an up-and-down appraisal, and nodded her approval. "It'll be spectacular on you. Doan's in his office, waiting for the fashion show. Put it on."

"You can use the little powder room right here," Rhonda said, pointing toward the closed door. "I'm dying to see how it looks on you."

Janice objected. "No. Use my office, Lee. That dinky little bathroom is useless. There's barely room to take a whiz in there."

Yeah. Tell me about it.

I lifted the dress carefully from its tissue cocoon and started for the open office.

"There's a full-length mirror inside the closet, Lee," Janice said. "Take your time. It'll have to look perfect if Doan's going to spend big bucks."

"Thanks," I said, carefully closing the door behind me. For a moment I stood in the center of the room, admiring the soft golden color of the walls, the spare but elegant lines of the Scandinavian modern furniture, a calming contrast to the garish decor of the reception area.

I opened the closet and gingerly arranged the dress

on a black satin-padded hanger. There were only a few other things there—a couple of Janice's business suits in plastic dry cleaner bags and a plain gray jogging outfit. I smiled when I saw a pale blue fairy princess costume, complete with silver wings and a shimmering tiara. Janice must have decided to go to the Witches Ball, after all. Next to the princess getup was a man's suit and a black derby hat. In a small plastic bag attached to the pocket was a fake mustache and a bow tie. A wooden cane completed the look.

I'll bet Janice picked out the Charlie Chaplin outfit for George. He probably sees himself as Han Solo or Indiana Jones. I don't know how I see him anymore, after that meltdown in the car.

The Mackie dress required that I strip down to bikini panties. I hesitated and looked around the room for cameras. After all, if George had a camera in Janice's bedroom, he might have one in here, as well, and I most certainly didn't want to be displayed in the buff on his cell phone. Janice had told me to take my time, so I did. I walked around the perimeter of the room, peeking behind draperies and picture frames. Satisfied that I wasn't being watched, I undressed quickly and slipped the pricey creation over my head.

The mirror reflected a glamorous me. Johnny would have loved this look. I checked my makeup and smoothed my hair a little, turned a couple of times, then realized I hadn't brought proper shoes. Maybe Janice had shoes to go with the fairy princess thing. Bingo! A pair of silvery sandals were neatly lined up on the floor, below the blue dress, next to a pair of men's shoes with slightly turned-up toes, just right for the Little Tramp.

I slipped the silver sandals on. Too big, but the general effect was okay, and I was sure she wouldn't mind my wearing them. I was ready for Doan's inspection.

Leaving my own clothes folded on Janice's closet shelf, I stepped back into the reception area, posing in the doorway for a second for dramatic effect. It was a wasted effort. No one was looking at me.

The TV monitor over Rhonda's desk was tuned to the noon newscast. Rhonda and Janice, their backs turned to me, watched.

"Looks like George and Scott got there in time," Janice said. "Hey, there's the chief."

"What's going on?" I asked.

"Hey, Lee. While you were changing, the chief called a presser. More news about the murders, I guess. George and Scott took off like a couple of bats out of hell."

I gave up the posing and joined the two women. The craggy face of the Salem police chief filled the screen.

"This will be a brief update on our progress with the investigation into the deaths of Yvette Pelletier and the woman known as Ariel Constellation," he announced. "We are now actively searching for the man in the camouflage outfit who showed up on various surveillance videos along Derby Street on the night of the murders. The missing data from the cameras located outside the WICH-TV building has now been recovered. The same man who was observed near the Pelletier home was also filmed approaching Ms. Constellation in the television station's parking lot. This man, who was at first considered a person of interest, is now a suspect. We have obtained a DNA sample from an article of clothing that, we believe, belongs to the suspect."

A grainy video in black and gray tones showed a tall figure in camouflage pants and shirt, a ski mask covering most of his face. I recognized a bit of the seawall. I didn't see Ariel, but I was sure I saw the shadowy figure of a cat following close behind the man as he disappeared behind the building.

"We are asking for the help of the community," the chief continued. "If anyone recognizes this person or happened to see him on Derby Street late on the night in question, or has any information that might be helpful in this investigation, please call the number at the top of your screen. That's all."

He turned and headed back into the police station, obviously hurrying, avoiding shouted questions from the press.

Scott Palmer appeared next. "Guess that'll be all from the chief for now, folks," he said, "but a source has told WICH-TV that the article of clothing in question is the suspect's ski mask, which was recovered at the scene of an attempted burglary at another location in the city."

That would be at the scene of an attempted cat *burglary. And all this is getting entirely too close to home.*

CHAPTER 35

The noon news had made my grand entrance fall kind of flat, but Janice and Rhonda each made the appropriate oohs and aahs the Mackie gown deserved. If the fact that Camo Guy was now officially a suspect in a double murder held any special meaning for Janice, there was nothing in her behavior to indicate it.

If she thought her own brother was killing people, wouldn't she react somehow?

"That dress is worth every cent," Janice declared. "Doan won't be able to say no."

Rhonda agreed. "You look like a movie star on the red carpet."

Janice approved of the borrowed silver sandals and quickly propelled me toward the station manager's office door. "Go on in," she said. "You'll knock his socks off."

"Are you coming with me?"

"Sure. If you want me to."

"I do," I said, and together we approached the huge stainless-steel desk. Mrs. Doan had clearly had a hand in decorating her husband's space. The shades of purple here were of a darker hue, a bit more masculine perhaps, but purple just the same.

Bruce Doan rose from his chair when we entered. Out of courtesy or just to get a better view of my scantily covered self, I couldn't tell. Without speaking, he gave a circular hand motion, indicating that I should turn. Slowly. So I did.

Janice broke the silence. "Well? What do you think?"

"This shindig draws big coverage," he said. "I think every TV station in the state will be running shots of the gorgeous red-haired psychic from Salem, Crystal Moon!" he said. "You'll be the belle of the Halloween Ball. And sponsors will be falling all over themselves to buy time on *Nightshades*. Am I a marketing genius or what?"

"Yeah. No doubt," Janice said without much enthusiasm. "So I can okay the invoice? It's worth seventeen hundred bucks?"

"Oh, sure. Pay it. When is the big event, anyway? This weekend?"

"Friday night," I said. "Before the show."

"Day after tomorrow. Good. Listen, Lee. Just leave the dress at the station, all right? You get dressed here and ride over to the party with Palmer so George can get a shot of you as soon as you arrive at the door of the place. Palmer will be wearing some kind of costume, too, so you'll look like a regular couple. He'll be miked so he can tell our audience what's going on, what bigwigs are there, and all that crap. Then you get seen schmoozing around the hall, getting as much face time as you can from the other stations. Maybe even some national."

He rubbed his hands together. "Then you both come back here with plenty of time to do *Nightshades*, and Palmer might have time to do a piece on the new basketball coach at the high school for the eleven o'clock news. Got it?"

"Got it," I said. He certainly had it all figured out. Scott, the Mackie dress, and I would serve as a kind of animated billboard for WICH-TV for an hour or so, then would do our regular jobs. And I wouldn't be a bit surprised if the gown got sold later on eBay at a profit.

Yes, Bruce Doan was a marketing genius.

"Oh, Lee. By the way, buy yourself some better shoes," he continued. "Those don't seem to fit right."

"Yes, sir. I will."

"And turn around one more time, will you?"

I did as he asked.

"Who did you say that designer is?"

Janice answered, "Bob Mackie. Very famous. Dressed the beautiful people, from Cher to Barbie."

"It's pretty clever, isn't it? How everything important is really covered up, but it looks like she's showing a lot of skin. I wonder if I can get one of those for Mrs. Doan."

We left on that interesting thought, and I hurried back to Janice's office. I returned the gown to the padded hanger in the closet, replaced the fairy princess sandals beside the Little Tramp shoes, got dressed in my own clothes, and mentally checked off *Buy costumes* and proceeded to the next item on my to-do list.

Find the Bridget Bishop spell book Ariel recommended in her margin notes.

The noon newscast had ended, and an old *Seinfeld* ran on the monitor over Rhonda's desk.

"Did they have any more about that ski mask on the news?" I asked the receptionist.

"Nope. Look. This is where Elaine tries to bribe the old people to give her an egg roll. I love this part."

"Yeah. Me too."

If I was going to find out any more about DNA on the ski mask, it looked as though I'd have to wait until the evening news. Or until Pete called.

If he called.

"Rhonda, do you mind if I leave my shopping bags here while I do a quick errand?"

"No problem. What did you buy?"

"Just a couple of Crystal Moon outfits. You can look at them if you want to."

I left the station and headed down Derby Street to the shops on Pickering Wharf, confident that this wouldn't take long. I was sure there'd be a bookshop there, as well as plenty of places featuring witchy stuff.

I was right about the shops. Witchy stuff abounded, but no one seemed to know what I was talking about when I asked for Bridget Bishop's spell book. But I'd be seeing River North later. She'd know where to get it.

On to the next thing on the list. Which had actually been the first thing but hadn't worked out all that well.

Talk to George about Janice.

I'd already made up my mind to try again. I'd just have to get past George's peculiar outburst. What had

I said to trigger a fit of laughter in such a decidedly unfunny situation, anyway? I went over the conversation in my mind. I was sure all I'd asked was whether he knew of anyone who might shelter Willie.

What's so laughable about that?

I wasn't ready to give up on trying my best to help Janice. But if the police couldn't protect her, if even her big brother didn't know what to do, and if Janice herself seemed oblivious to the whole weird situation, exactly what could *I* do? I'd have to arrange another one-on-one conversation with George.

It turned out that I didn't have to do any arranging at all. When I returned to the station—without a spell book but with a nice postcard to send to Bill Valen—the first person I ran into was George. Couldn't miss him. He was right in front of the building, holding a clipboard and looking up toward the roof.

When you see somebody doing that, you have to look up, too. So I stood there next to him, staring at the rain gutter, where there was nothing to see but a few silent seagulls standing in an orderly row.

"Oh, hi, Lee," he said.

"Hi, George. What are we looking at?"

"Surveillance cameras. Taking inventory. Doan wants to know if they all look secure."

"Do they?"

"Don't know yet. Want to walk around the building with me?"

It was the opportunity I'd been looking for.

"Okay," I said. I tucked the tiny bag containing the postcard into my pocket, and together we began slowly walking the perimeter of the old brick structure.

"I owe you an apology, Lee," he said. "You must think I'm an insensitive boob. Laughing like that when you're just trying to help us." He shook his head. "It's pretty complicated. You probably wouldn't understand."

"Try me," I said. "I've dealt with some pretty complicated stuff myself."

Especially lately.

He paused, looked up at the roofline, and made a note on a yellow pad attached to the clipboard. We resumed walking. "Well, here goes. You wanted to know who would protect Willie."

"Right," I replied. "He may be really dangerous! I know he's family, and maybe you and Janice don't want to think he'd really hurt anyone, but, George, the evidence is piling up. We know that somebody took all of your dad's things out of that trunk in your living room. The police say that Yvette Pelletier was killed with his razor." I waved toward the cameras overhead. "Some cameras on the street showed a man in what looks like army gear. Sarge's clothes? Sarge's boots?"

He stopped walking and looked at the ground. He spoke so softly, I had to move closer to hear him. "Maybe. Probably. And you're right. Willie is dangerous. Has been for a long time. But it's not all his fault." His eyes welled with tears. "He was such a nice little kid. So cute and smart."

"What happened to him, George? What made him

change? I mean, if it *is* Willie the police are looking for."

"I'm afraid it is. But I never thought he could be violent, you know? I knew he had a lot of anger in him, but nothing like . . . like what's been going on around here."

We started walking again, slowly heading toward the seawall. "So," I asked again, "what happened to him?"

His expression changed. No tears now. His jaw tightened; his eyes narrowed.

"It was the abuse." We'd reached the seawall. He slammed the clipboard on the granite slab, letting it fall on the ground. "I should have figured it out. I should have been there to protect him. An innocent little kid like that."

"Abuse?"

"Yeah. But we thought . . . I thought . . . he was finally at peace with it. That he was in some kind of a safe place now, where nothing could hurt him anymore. You know what I mean?"

"No, I don't know what you mean. At peace? It sounds as though you thought Willie was dead."

A mirthless laugh. "In a way, that's how I've thought of him for a long time. I didn't expect to see him again . . . not in this life, anyway." He picked up the clipboard, and together we rounded the corner of the building. "The doctor said he probably wouldn't ever be able to come back."

"I don't understand, George. Is the safe place some kind of hospital? Is that where Willie's been?"

We were behind the station now, where the back of

the building faced the harbor. A narrow wooden structure with flaking and faded gray paint was attached to the brick wall.

Doan's secret staircase.

George had stopped talking. Scanning the roofline and window ledges, he made notes on the yellow pad. Maybe he didn't want to tell me anything more. And it was, after all, none of my business. But if I was going to help Janice, I needed information. The wind whipping across the water had turned cold. I jammed my hands into my pockets.

"Why is Willie tormenting Janice? I can't believe *she* abused him."

"Of course she didn't!" He sounded indignant at the suggestion. He dropped his voice to a whisper, even though there was no one around to hear except me. "The abuse was sexual. And it was awful. But I thought I was the only one who'd been singled out. I ran away."

Oh boy. I don't want to hear this.

My first thought was of Sarge. I clutched the postcard in my pocket. That dear old man in the veterans' hospital couldn't be guilty of anything so heinous. Could he?

"Not Sarge!" I blurted.

"No. Not Sarge. It was her. Our beautiful mother. Marlena."

CHAPTER 36

"There aren't any here." George made another note on his pad.

"Huh? Aren't any what? Sexual predators? What are you talking about?"

He gestured with the pen toward the roof: "Cameras."

"Are there supposed to be?"

"Guess not." He put the pen in his pocket. "Let's go inside."

The man was a master at changing the subject. And when the subject was his child-abusing mother, I couldn't blame him. I didn't really want to hear the gory details, anyway. But I still didn't have the answer to my original question.

Who was protecting Willie?

So I asked again. "George, I don't want to pry into your personal business, but who do you think *is* protecting Willie?"

"Protecting him? Why, it's Janice. She's always protected him. Come on. Let's go in. It's getting cold out here." He grabbed my hand, steering me toward the parking lot, then led the way to the street with long strides. I almost had to run to keep up with him.

Janice? Janice was protecting the man who'd threatened her? Called her terrible names? Made her cry? It made no sense.

I caught up with George in the front entryway. He'd already pushed the elevator button, and the doors had begun their noisy opening slide. Janice Valen, stunning in a long, A-line white leather coat, stepped out.

"Oh, there you are." George linked his arm into hers and started back toward the street entrance. "Ready to go?"

"Ready, big brother," Janice said. "We're going to Boston, Lee. See you tonight. I'll be back in time for *Nightshades.*"

"See you later, Lee." George aimed a brief wave in my direction. "Have a good day."

So the Valen siblings were heading for Boston but would be back in time for the show. This must be about the appointment George had made with the doctor who'd be treating Janice for "psychosomatic problems."

I mumbled, "See you later," and took the elevator up to the second floor, wondering if Janice knew yet where her brother was taking her. I was pretty sure he hadn't told her the truth, and I felt even sorrier for her than I had in the first place.

Poor Janice. No wonder she takes a drink once in a while.

Rhonda was at her desk, peering into a small compact mirror, carefully applying mauve lipstick in a shade nearly matching that of a nearby arrangement of silk lilacs.

She looked up. "Oh, hi, Lee. You caught me. The cops were here taking spit samples from everybody, and my lipstick got a little messed up."

"You look fine. That's a pretty color on you."

"Thanks. The cute cop was here, too, looking for George."

"Mondello?"

"Yeah. I told him George was outside checking cameras, so we looked out the window to see where he was." She clicked the compact shut and smiled. "We saw you and him holding hands and running out from behind the building. What's up with that?"

"Holding hands? Me? We were not! I mean . . . not like that." I remembered how George had pulled me along when I couldn't keep up with him. "George was in a hurry. He needed to take Janice . . . someplace."

"Yeah. To Boston. He's taking her to Bella Luna for an early dinner. It's her favorite restaurant."

Will the trip to the doctor's office be the appetizer or dessert?

"So Pete . . . Detective Mondello . . . has left?" *Now Pete thinks he saw me holding hands with George.*

"Yeah. He said that they could get George's spit later and that they already had yours from before."

"That's true. Well, see you later, Rhonda. Got my bags?"

She reached beneath the counter. "Here you go. I put them into one of the company canvas bags for you. Easier to carry that way. The outfits are cute."

"Thanks, Rhonda. That was thoughtful of you. You working tonight?"

"Not unless I have to cover for someone."

With a silent prayer that if she did, it wouldn't be as

my call screener, and with the canvas bag slung over my shoulder, I started walking home. I could have called a cab, but without the bulky dress box, and with the blouses and skirts all in one bag, walking was an easy enough option. Anyway, it would give me some time and space for thinking.

The information George had shared with me hadn't really cleared anything up. In fact, it had further complicated an already muddy situation. The elusive Willie was almost certainly involved somehow in two murders. Did Willie have the missing key to Sarge's old footlocker? He apparently had access to the Valens' condo. I was sure he'd been there when I overheard George talking to him. He must have been at the station at some time, too, because the most recent postcard to his father had been postmarked from there. Most disturbing was George's revelation that the Valen children had endured sexual abuse from their own mother.

I still felt strongly that Janice was in danger, but how could I help her if it was true that she was the one protecting Willie? George had said that she'd *always* protected him. Did that mean from childhood? And if they'd been children together, why would Sarge deny her?

I was concentrating so hard on the thoughts spinning around in my mind that I didn't notice the car moving along slowly beside me until the driver tapped the horn.

"Want a lift?" A smiling Pete Mondello leaned across the seat and opened the passenger door.

I did—especially from him. I climbed into the car,

a little bit surprised by how very pleased I was to see him, and probably grinning like an idiot.

"Thanks, Pete. It's starting to get a little nippy out."

"Not much like Florida," he agreed. "I'm glad I caught up with you. I looked for you back at the station, but I guess you were out checking cameras with Valen."

"George was checking them, but he was in a big hurry and was just dragging me along for company. He and Janice had a dinner date in Boston." I hoped the "dragging me along" part explained the momentary hand-holding. "Did you know there are no cameras on the back of the building?"

"Sure. Your boss says he never saw any need to go to the expense of installing them, because there's nothing to see but the seawall and the old fire escape."

"Mr. Doan's priorities are hard to figure out sometimes," I said, thinking about the seventeen-hundred-dollar dress hanging in Janice's closet, "but I wish we could have seen what Camo Guy was doing when he ducked back there."

"Camo Guy?"

"Rhonda named him. Seems to fit."

"It'll do until we've got his real name, and I think we're getting close."

"No kidding?" Was Pete actually going to share some information? "What's going on?"

He looked over at me and nodded his head. "I think it'll be okay to tell you this, since you helped a lot in getting some important evidence."

"Me? I did?"

"It is the stamp on the old postcard from London.

It's the kind you have to lick. We got the DNA from the back of the stamp, and it matched the DNA from the hood the guy dropped when he tried to grab your cat." Again the big smile. "You were the one who noticed the postcards. Not me."

"Wow! That means now you can arrest Willie, and Janice will be safe!"

"Not so fast. Doesn't work that way." His cop face was back. "What we have is a postcard signed by somebody who calls himself Willie. And we have a hood the same person wore while allegedly trying to steal a cat. Hardly the stuff murder convictions are made of."

CHAPTER 37

All too soon we were in front of the house on Winter Street. Pete walked me to the door, insisting on carrying the canvas bag, No kiss this time, but a quick "I'll call you" sounded good to me.

Aunt Ibby and O'Ryan greeted me in the front hall, O'Ryan with deep-throated purrs and Aunt Ibby with a quick hug and an excited "What did you buy?"

"A couple of outfits for Crystal Moon and a fabulous dress for the Witches Ball, except I can't show you that one, because Mr. Doan made me leave it at the station." We headed into the den, and I dumped the contents of the canvas bag onto the couch. "And I learned some more about Willie and George and Janice."

"I did, too," she said, unfolding skirts and blouses and arranging them against the couch cushions. "Nigel called. These are cute. I found some more jewelry for you, too. Why did you have to leave the dress there? Tell me everything."

There was a lot to tell. It had, after all, been a very busy morning. I started with the shopping part, mostly describing the Bob Mackie dress, then moved right into the creepy ride back to the station with George.

"You mean he started laughing even though he knew his sister was in terrible danger?"

"He did," I said. "At first I thought he was crying."

"What did you do then?"

"I got out of the car as fast as I could, thanked him for the ride, and ran inside the station. A pretty chicken reaction, I guess."

I launched into a description of Mr. Doan's reaction to the million-dollar dress, as Janice had called it. I told her about the costumes in Janice's closet and about how I'd checked around for cameras in her office before I tried the Mackie on.

"I don't blame you for that," she said. "But I really wish you'd been able to bring it home. I'd love to see it on you."

"I know. But you'll see it soon, I promise. The ball is Friday, and I'll get Scott to drive by here before we go so you can see it in person before we go to the party."

"Scott?"

I explained about Doan's plans to make our "date" a publicity stunt for the station.

"It does make a certain amount of sense," she said. "If that gown is as spectacular on you as I think it must be, you'll be the most photographed person there." She cocked her head to one side and looked at me intently. "But I'll bet you wish you were just going there on a regular date with somebody special."

"Yeah, well, that's not happening. Let me tell you about what else I learned from George."

"You talked to him again? After the laughing jag?"

"Sure did. I ran into him outside the station. He was checking the outside surveillance cameras. He apologized for what had happened before, and I finally worked up the courage to ask some really pointed questions about Willie."

"I can tell by your expression that you got some answers." Her bright eyes sparked, and even O'Ryan seemed to have developed a sudden interest in the conversation. He stopped playing with imaginary creatures on the rug and jumped up onto the couch, being careful to avoid stepping on Crystal Moon's new outfits.

"I did. And the story gets even weirder. Apparently, according to George, the Valen children were abused. Sexually."

Her reaction was exactly what mine had been. "No. Not Bill Valen!"

"Not Sarge. It was the mother. Marlena."

"Oh dear. How terrible. It's hard to even imagine such a thing. But what about Willie? Does George believe his brother is responsible somehow for these Salem murders?"

"I'm afraid he does. And the strange thing is, he says it's Janice who's protecting Willie."

"Janice? I thought you said Willie torments her. Makes her cry."

"That's right. Doesn't make a lot of sense. Does it?"

"So perhaps Janice knows where Willie is. Could she be hiding him somehow? What else did he tell you?"

"Not much. By that time Janice had joined us, looking fabulous, and they were off to Boston for dinner. At least she *thinks* they're just going to dinner."

"The plot thickens?"

"Yep. George told me he'd made an appointment with some kind of doctor who's going to treat her for 'psychosomatic problems.'"

"That could mean anything."

"I know. Ariel's book says that in the old days psychosomatic problems were called witchcraft."

O'Ryan's ears perked up. Did he hear the name Ariel or the word *witchcraft?* Hard to tell. I patted his head and explained to Aunt Ibby how frightened Janice seemed to be of doctors.

"I'm sure she has no idea of where he's taking her. She doesn't need any more stress. I want so much to help her. I think she's in real danger, and I don't know what I can do."

She reached over and patted my knee. "I know you care about her very much. But you may be dabbling in a situation that's way over your head. I think you need to step aside and let the police handle this." She gave me a sidelong glance. "Speaking of police, wasn't that the nice young detective who brought you home just now?"

"Detective Mondello? Yes. He saw me walking and offered me a ride."

"Did you tell him the things you told me? About Janice protecting Willie? And about the child abuse?"

"Not yet," I admitted. "I wanted to, but I'm sure George told me those things in confidence. Anyway, things that happened in their childhood are pretty far removed from the current murder investigation, don't you agree?"

"I think he'd be interested, anyway, but do what you think is best. Anything else, before I tell you about Nigel's call?"

I'd almost forgotten about the call from my aunt's British friend. "Not much. I went down to check the shops at Pickering Wharf," I said. "I was looking for a book Ariel mentioned in some margin notes, but they didn't have it."

"Maybe we have it upstairs. We'll check later. I love those shops. Did you buy anything?"

"Just a postcard to send to Bill Valen. He likes to get postcards. And Pete . . . Detective Mondello . . . shared a little information with me."

I told her about the DNA on the old postcard Willie had sent from London, and how it matched the sample on the ski mask the cat stealer had dropped.

"I suppose they'll be checking everyone at the TV station, looking for a match."

"They already have," I told her. "They've checked everybody except George Valen."

CHAPTER 38

By that time Aunt Ibby had waited long enough to tell me about the telephone call from Nigel, her detective friend from New Scotland Yard.

"First of all," she said, "none of the Janices on that plane could have been *our* Janice." She counted off on her fingers. "One was an infant, and the other two were women over fifty. So the only Valens on that particular flight from London were George and William Jr."

"You know, I halfway expected that."

"Uh-huh. Me too. But Nigel did get some more information on the Billie Jo Vale who worked at the Purple Dragon."

"No kidding? What?"

"He interviewed some of the performers who'd worked there with Billie Jo, and they remembered quite a few details about goings-on at that club."

"Is Nigel pretty sure Billie Jo Vale is related to our Valens?"

"He believes Billie Jo *is* one of our Valens."

"Who? Which one?"

"I'm not sure, but according to Nigel, one of the dancers at the club, a fellow named Alfred, remembers Billie Jo, who he called B.J., as kind of a loner."

"A loner in a nightclub?"

"Yes. B.J. didn't date the patrons, didn't hang around with the others after work, and was always escorted home by a man who claimed to be an older brother."

"I guess that would be George. So that would mean B.J. is either Janice or Willie. Did this guy have a good description?"

"Better than that. This Alfred's going to give Nigel a picture. He'll e-mail it to me as soon as he gets it, and if he learns anything more, he'll call right away."

"Good work, Aunt Ibby. Between us we'll figure this out."

"I think eventually we will. But for right now, if we're going to have a session with your witch friend this evening, we'd better grab a bite to eat and then start getting ready."

She was right. The day was moving much too fast, and I was looking forward to seeing River. I'd already decided to share with her the secret of the images I'd seen in the black ball. I was sure she'd understand better than anyone else I could think of. By five o'clock we were fed, showered, appropriately dressed, and on our way to the candlelight tea-leaf reading. I'd asked Aunt Ibby if we could leave a little early, because I hoped to get a few minutes alone with River before the event began.

There was a line of people, mostly women, waiting in front of the lovely old hall on Church Street. There was one space left on the bench next to the door, and

I led Aunt Ibby to it. I guessed I wouldn't get to see River before the readings began, after all. Disappointed, I walked the short distance to the corner of the building. I heard a tapping sound and, shading my eyes, peered into an arched window. A smiling River North looked back at me, gesturing toward the side of the building. She mouthed the words "Around back."

I nodded understanding, told Aunt Ibby I'd be back in a few minutes, and walked down a narrow path to the kitchen entrance, where River waited, shivering in flowing midnight-blue taffeta. Her single thick braid of black hair was dotted with silver moons and gold stars.

"You look lovely, River," I said, meaning it. "The hair accents remind me of Ariel."

"Thanks, Crystal," she said. "Actually, they *were* Ariel's. The coven invited me to help them clean out Ariel's apartment, and they said it would be all right for me to have these."

"Cleaning out her apartment already?"

"Yeah. End of the month, you know, and the landlord is anxious to rent it. Anyway, it's a tiny place. We all pitched in to rent a storage locker. We'll go through the stuff later."

"The TV said she didn't have any relatives around here. What will become of her things?"

She shrugged. "Dunno. Come on in, will you? I'm freezing out here. Anyway, I want to talk to you before they open the doors. My teapot is ready, so I have a few minutes."

"I wanted to talk to you, too, River."

She held the door open, and good kitchen smells

warmed the chill air. "Oh. Crystal, as long as we're back here, look over there at that square patch of land with nothing on it."

"I noticed that," I said. "What's it for?"

"It isn't for anything. Nothing will grow on it. Ariel said it was the spot where Bridget Bishop's house once stood."

"Interesting," I said. "Maybe that's why the legend says her ghost appears here. By the way, that reminds me. One of the things I wanted to ask you about is Bridget Bishop's spell book. Do you happen to have a copy I could borrow?"

River's look was one of disbelief. She stopped abruptly, facing me, hands on her hips. "How do you know about that?" she demanded. "Damn it! The twelve of us spent all day tearing that stupid apartment to pieces, looking for it!"

CHAPTER 39

It didn't take long to explain about Ariel's margin notes. "I thought it must be just a souvenir book, something I'd find easily in a shop. What's so special about it?"

"Don't you get it?" She dropped her voice. "It's Bridget Bishop's *real* spell book! From back in sixteen ninety-two!"

"You mean you think Ariel had a three-hundred-year-old book? Written by a witch?" I didn't believe it.

"Oh, Ariel had it, all right. She'd started using it, too. All of a sudden she could do amazing things. Impossible things." She led the way to a table in the corner of the dining room. "So naturally, everyone wants that book."

I remembered what Marty had told me about Ariel's sudden ability to make things disappear, to start cars without keys, and to literally see the callers. What River said seemed to confirm those strange events.

The lights were dim, and candles in pewter candlestick holders gave the room a pretty glow. "Here. Sit down," River ordered. "Before your aunt and the others come in, I need to tell you something. I read your cards again. Something new showed up."

"I guess it isn't anything good."

"It may or may not be. The cards tell the truth, but some things might look bad at first and then turn out to be okay, you know?"

"I think you're trying to make me feel better, and I hope you're right." I sat at the table and watched the candle flame before me. "I need to tell you about something that's been happening to me lately, and I have no idea whether it's bad or okay."

"The cards will help you to understand," she promised. "Here's what I saw. The Ten of Cups is reversed between the Queen of Wands, which is you, and the Queen of Cups, which is your aunt. This usually means that one of you is facing a loss of a friendship or even a betrayal. And here's the part I've been worried about. There can be damage coming to your home." She leaned forward, looking into my eyes. "Be careful, Crystal. And here's another thing. The Enchantress card, with the number eight, is between you and the bad guy now. . . . Remember that reversed King of Cups I told you about? The eight means balance. I think you are going to be able to bring two sides of your nature into harmony. Does that make sense?"

I thought of the side of my nature I'd long ago forgotten about—the side of me with the ability to see disturbing pictures in a black ball.

"Maybe. A little bit. Listen, River. Do you know what a scryer is?"

There was a little commotion near the front door of the restaurant as the first of the patrons filed in.

"Sure. It's a person who sees things in mirrors or hubcaps or something."

I had to smile at the hubcap idea.

Why not? Especially if they're black and shiny.

Aunt Ibby, looking relaxed and happy, approached us. I was surprised to see that behind her, heading for a nearby table, was Mrs. Doan, resplendent in purple and lavender plaid with a matching fedora.

"Apparently, I am one," I whispered, "and I've been seeing some scary things. I'll tell you later. Here comes my aunt."

If River was surprised by my revelation, she controlled it well. She stood and greeted Aunt Ibby with a handshake. "Good evening. Thank you for coming."

I made a quick introduction, and we all sat down, my aunt and I side by side, facing River across the table. A chintz-patterned teapot on an electric warmer stood at the table's center, next to the candle, and a matching pair of dainty china cups and saucers were arranged in front of us.

"Excuse me. Aren't you Lee Barrett?" came a voice from behind me. I knew without turning that it came from Mrs. Doan.

I stood and extended my hand. "I am," I said. "How do you do?"

"I recognized you from the television," she said. "I'm Buffy Doan."

Buffy?

"I'm so happy to meet you, Mrs. Doan," I said. "This is my aunt, Isobel Russell, and my friend River North."

Oh boy. Will River and Mrs. Doan recognize one another

from that unfortunate telecast on the day of Ariel's "crossing over" ceremony? I hope not.

If they did, neither one acknowledged it, but instead nodded politely and murmured the usual pleasantries.

"Would it be all right if I joined you?" asked the station manager's wife. "They seem to have overbooked the event, and all the other tables are full."

"Oh, please do," Aunt Ibby said. "Here. Have my chair, Buffy. River, could you find someone to bring another, along with a teacup?"

In minutes, the four of us were gathered around our table. Four of us in the semidarkness, a flickering candle and a steaming teapot reflected in the tall arched window overlooking a vacant patch of ground.

Double, double toil and trouble;
Fire burn, and cauldron bubble.

River filled our cups. Loose tea leaves floated in the fragrant, hot liquid. The room grew quiet as the guests sipped their tea and studied the tea leaf readers they'd chosen, hoping perhaps to learn of coming good fortune or love or riches.

"Leave a tiny amount of tea at the bottom of your cup," River advised. "Then swirl it around three times and turn the cup upside down on the saucer."

There was a chorus of clinking sounds around the room as each of the guests obeyed the instructions of his or her reader. A few self-conscious giggles sounded here and there as all of us prepared to hear what the tea leaves might foretell.

River read Aunt Ibby's cup first. "Look, here's a

kettle. An old friend will call. And here I see a bird. That means important news is coming toward you." She pointed to a pear-shaped leaf. "A closed bag," she said. "That can mean a trap. Be careful."

Aunt Ibby looked skeptical. "I like the old friend part."

River nodded. "Here's a little broom. See it? It shows a new era in your life. Be happy. But be careful."

Mrs. Doan was next. River frowned as she peered into the cup. "I see a broken necklace. It can mean a broken friendship." She looked up at the woman. "Have you broken with a friend? Someone you trusted?"

"Why, you're right! I have. But she wronged me. I'm sure she did."

River shook her head. "No. See the question mark here?"

We all looked into Buffy Doan's cup. The question mark was clear, unlike some of the other symbols River had described so far.

"Does that mean I was mistaken? She didn't do . . . the thing I accused her of?"

"'Fraid not," said River. "You might need to apologize."

"Oh dear." Mrs. Doan wiped a teary eye. "It's too late. She died."

River patted the woman's hand. "It's never too late. She will hear your apology."

"She will? Are you sure?"

"Absolutely," River promised and reached for my cup.

It held an assortment of pictures inside its chintz-patterned shell. At least River seemed to think so. She saw a man with an umbrella, which she interpreted as protection for me.

Pete Mondello?

There was a lion on the edge of the cup. "An important male," River declared, "or maybe someone born under the sign of Leo."

Or maybe just a big yellow cat.

"Look," she said, pointing. "There's a hat. Means a change of roles for you."

From what to what? Fake psychic to news anchor? I wish!

"The leaves act like an Earl Grey Rorschach test, don't they?" my aunt asked. "Like tasty little inkblots."

"Pretty much," River agreed. "But did you all enjoy the readings?"

Aunt Ibby and I assured her that we had. The sounds of chairs being pushed back indicated that the evening's entertainment had come to an end. We stood there together for a moment, chatting about the bookmobile program, which would benefit from the proceeds of the event. That is, Aunt Ibby and I chatted about it. Mrs. Doan had been silent since River had told her that whoever she had wrongfully accused would forgive her. She'd accused Ariel of interfering with her love life. Tampering with Mr. Doan's whatsit. I wondered if that was the person River had been referring to.

As I pushed my chair up to the table's edge, I glanced out the window beside me. It was dark outside, and the glass reflected only blackness. Too swiftly to look away, I saw the pinpoints of light, the swirling colors. The empty patch of land behind the restaurant came into focus. But it wasn't empty anymore. Ariel Constellation stood there, blond beehive perfectly stiff despite the wind whipping at her satin gown. She smiled, lifting a hand in greeting, then disappeared.

I felt, rather than saw, the slight motion behind me as Mrs. Doan waved toward the window.

Her voice was calm. Controlled.

"Oh, isn't that nice. She forgives me. But she must be cold. She should have worn her cape."

I whirled and stood face-to-face with Buffy Doan. Her expression was almost what you might call serene. A far cry from the angry, distorted face the viewers of WICH-TV had seen when she stood with the witch protestors.

I found my voice. "Did you say something, Mrs. Doan?"

"Oh, Lee. Did I speak out loud? You must think I'm a loon." She smiled. "I imagined that I saw Ariel out in the yard there, waving to me. I think it was a sign that River is right. Ariel forgives me. She accepts my apology." She dabbed at her eyes with a lavender hankie. "Maybe I need to apologize to the witches, too," she said. "Perhaps I was wrong about all of them. Good-bye now. I so enjoyed meeting all of you." She moved, trancelike, toward the exit.

River tugged at my sleeve and whispered, "Did you hear that? She saw Ariel."

"Oh, dear." Aunt Ibby frowned. "Do you think she's all right? I'll walk with her to the door." She hurried to catch up with the plaid-suited woman.

"River," I said, "if she's loony, I am, too. I saw Ariel out there. I thought she was waving to me."

"Wow. I wish I could have seen her. But I guess if she wanted me to, I would have."

"You mean, you think Ariel can cause these . . . apparitions . . . or whatever they are . . . from the grave?"

"I don't see why not. I told you. She has the spell book, wherever she is. But what's this about you being a scryer?"

I gave her a brief rundown on what had been happening to me ever since I first looked at the obsidian ball. I told her about the pictures in the Mary Janes, too, and how I'd forgotten about that childhood trauma until it had all come crashing back in the attic.

Had that just been a couple of weeks ago?

"Hmmm." River put her hand to her forehead, much the way Ariel used to. "I'm just wondering. Do you think it's possible, just maybe, that your scryer thing hasn't really come back? That maybe you're just seeing what Ariel wants you to see? After all, it's *her* black ball. And you *did* find the body .And if you have a background of seeing stuff, why, you'd be just a perfect receiver!"

What was it that Marty had said when I found that woman's watch? "Maybe you're channeling Ariel," she'd said. "Ever think of that?"

Aunt Ibby had come back to the table in time to hear River's theory. Her expression mirrored her skepticism. "Shall we get along home now, Maralee? Thank you for an interesting evening, River. I've thoroughly enjoyed it."

"Thank you, Miss Russell," River said. "I hope to see you again. Crystal, is your real name Maralee? Would you prefer that I call you that?"

"It is my real name," I said. "But I'm becoming quite comfortable with Crystal."

"Okay, then, Crystal. We'll talk again soon. Think about what I've told you."

Sure. Why not? I'll add ghostly apparitions, a change of roles, damage to the house, and Aunt Ibby falling into a tea leaf trap to all the other things I'm supposed to be thinking about.

I picked up my purse, took my aunt's arm, and headed outdoors, into the darkness.

CHAPTER 40

At around nine thirty I dressed in one of the new Crystal Moon outfits, added a long wool cardigan sweater, and called Jim Litka for a ride to the station. I planned to get to the *Nightshades* set early. I wanted to look through Ariel's books for some witchcraft lore to sprinkle into my introductory monologue leading into the night's feature movie—*I Married a Witch*. I'd hoped to use Bridget Bishop's spell book, but clearly, that wasn't going to happen.

I didn't tell Aunt Ibby about seeing Ariel standing on the site of Bishop's house. I needed to think about what River had said. Was it possible that I was being haunted by a dead witch? That these *visions,* or whatever they were, weren't coming from my mind, but hers?

Marty was already on the set when I arrived—no surprise there. She'd found more Halloween-themed decorations, and bouncing spiders had joined the bats suspended from the ceiling on invisible threads, and a large stuffed black cat took up about a third of the space on the turquoise couch.

"Hi, Moon," she called as soon as she saw me. "How do you like the big cat?"

"Cute," I said. "O'Ryan will be jealous. I'm going to grab one or two of Ariel's books and find someplace quiet to curl up and study some Salem witchery. I'll be back in plenty of time to run through the intro and look over the commercials. Okay?"

"Sure. And, Moon, George was looking for you."

"Oh, they're back? Good." I selected a small chamber of commerce booklet called *Bewitched in 1692* from the pile on the table. "This ought to be all I'll need. Where is George now?"

Marty shrugged. "Who knows? That boy moves around a lot."

"Well, if you see him before I do, tell him I'll be in the break room."

"Gotcha."

The break room was unoccupied, but the coffee was still hot. I poured a mugful and settled down in the tattered recliner and began to leaf through the pages. I read of the terrible death of poor Giles Corey. The old man had refused to plead one way or the other, so he was taken out into a field, where, one at a time, heavy weights were piled onto his naked body. The pressure was so great that his tongue was forced out of his mouth, and the sheriff, with his cane, forced it back in while the anguished man was dying. Pretty gory stuff, but the *Nightshades* faithful could handle it.

I made a few notes on index cards, then finished my coffee. I was rinsing out my mug when George Valen appeared.

"Lee. Glad I found you. Have you heard anything from Janice?"

"No. Last time I saw her, she was with you, heading for Boston. Why? What's wrong?"

He sat opposite me on a folding chair, his face ashen. "I made a mistake taking her to that doctor. Now she's gone. Run away."

"Are you sure? Has she ever done this before?"

"Not for a long time. I'm really worried." He put his head in his hands. "She seemed to get along with the doctor all right. I mean, I wasn't in on their discussion, of course, but she didn't scream or try to run out of the office or do anything like she used to. She was quiet at dinner, but that's not unusual."

"Then what makes you think she's run away? Maybe she just had some errands to do before work."

"She took my car. Left hers in the driveway." He looked about to cry.

Or laugh, God forbid.

"Maybe hers didn't start. Did you use it to get here? Did you call her cell?"

He shook his head, looking down at the floor. "Went right to voice mail. I walked over here. Her car is a stick shift. I've never driven one. Always afraid I'd tear the clutch out or something if I used that fancy little red car of hers."

I looked at my watch. "I can drive one. We have some time before the late news. Do you have keys?"

"There's a set in her desk." He stood up. "Let's go. We'll borrow one of the company trucks. And thanks, Lee."

I still didn't see what was such a big deal about a girl borrowing her brother's car, but I followed him into Janice's office. I glanced around the room while George opened and closed several drawers. The closet door stood ajar, and I peeked inside before pushing it closed to check on the million-dollar dress. It was there on the hanger, just as I'd left it, right next to the fairy princess costume, Janice's silver sandals neatly lined up just below. As the door clicked shut, it occurred to me that the Little Tramp shoes weren't there. George had probably reneged on playing Charlie Chaplin. I didn't blame him.

"Got 'em," George said, slamming a drawer shut. "Let's go. Have to get you back in time for your show."

I shrugged back into my sweater as we dashed for the parking lot. Carefully lifting the skirt and petticoat, I climbed into the truck's high passenger seat. Tires squealing, we lurched out of the parking lot and onto Derby Street.

Good thing Doan isn't watching. Tires cost money.

We pulled up and parked in front of George and Janice's condo. George tossed the key on its heart-shaped silver key ring to me. "The car's in the driveway on the side of the house. You try to start the thing. I'm going to run inside and see if maybe she's come home."

It was dark back there, but as I approached the red Porsche, outdoor floodlights illuminated the space. George must have turned on the lights for me. Unlocking the door, I slid into the driver's seat and started the engine. It purred sweetly to life. I checked the gauges. More than half a tank of gas. Everything else looked normal.

A Porsche was much more fun than an old Buick. I could imagine myself opening her up on an open road. I was about to reluctantly shut off the engine when I noticed something on the seat next to me. A piece of folded fabric. I switched on the interior lights and knew without touching the thing exactly what it was.

I was looking at the mate to the pillowcase O'Ryan had been trapped in.

CHAPTER 41

I knew I needed to tell Pete Mondello right away about the pillowcase. Too late, I realized I'd left my purse—phone, wallet, and all—back at the station. After all, I hadn't expected to be wandering around Salem, looking for my missing call screener in the middle of the night.

George's tap on the glass startled me, and I quickly turned off the interior lights and opened the window. "All okay here," I told him. "She started right up. Plenty of gas, and all the gauges look normal."

"Janice isn't in the house," he said. "Want to drive this thing back to the station for me?"

"Love to," I said, meaning it. "See you back there."

In what seemed like minutes I pulled the Porsche into Janice's parking space at the TV station. Now, what was I going to do about the piece of percale evidence on the seat next to me? If I picked it up, I might be compromising evidence. If I left it in plain sight, whoever put it there might take it. I locked the car, put the key in my sweater pocket, and ran for the studio door.

I didn't even speak to a surprised-looking Marty as I grabbed the phone from my purse. Pete answered on the first ring.

"Pete," I said, "I've found a pillowcase. I'm pretty sure is the mate to the one the cat stealer used. It's in Janice's car out in the parking lot here, and no one seems to know where Janice is. I'm afraid something may have happened to her."

"Is the car locked?" he asked.

"Yes. I have the key right here."

"Hang on to it," he ordered. "I'm coming."

George and Pete arrived on the *Nightshades* set at the same time.

"Good that you're here, Valen," Pete said. "Saves me getting a warrant. I'll need permission to search your sister's vehicle. I understand she's missing."

"Sure. Anything you want. Just find my sister before . . ." He looked down at the floor. "Before someone else does."

"The key?" Pete held out his hand, and I dropped the silver key ring into it. "Can you come outside with me, Lee . . . er . . . Ms. Barrett?"

I checked the studio clock. The late news would be on in a few minutes.

"Yes, Detective. I can."

Together we hurried out to where I'd parked Janice's car. Pete unlocked it. He opened the door and aimed a flashlight toward the passenger seat.

There was nothing there.

"Who else has a key?" Pete asked.

"Janice, I guess, "I said, "but I'm sure the pillowcase was right there less than fifteen minutes ago."

"I'm sure it was, too," Pete said. "And I'm pretty sure Janice Valen grabbed it."

"Janice? But why?"

"Look, I know Janice is a friend of yours, but I'm afraid she's pretty deep into this mess."

"Pete, I'm sure Janice is in danger!"

"Remember the night you heard Janice talking to someone in the dressing room?"

"I'll never forget it. She was so scared."

"That same night Marty and Rhonda said they thought they saw her car speeding down Derby Street when they were coming back to the station after dinner."

I nodded. "Spaghetti night at the Pig's Eye."

"Right. We checked around to see if anyone else had seen her." He closed the door of the Porsche.

"Had anyone?"

"We didn't make the connection right away, but one of the shop owners in that little strip mall"—he pointed down Derby Street—"calls us all the time if anybody she doesn't know uses the Dumpster out back. She's a nuisance caller, actually."

"She saw Janice?"

"She called the desk that evening. What she said was that some 'rich bitch in a fancy car' was dumping her trash out of a big cloth bag into their Dumpster."

"You think it was Janice? Using somebody else's Dumpster isn't a big crime."

"Usually we wouldn't give it very high priority, but it was the same one Bill Valen's razor turned up in. So the chief sent a uniform over to check the next day. Sometimes people who do that leave a piece of mail or something with their name and address on it."

"And?"

"We were too late. There was no mail, nothing interesting at all. An old homeless guy, the woman said, was out there first thing in the morning, rooting through the trash."

"Vergil Henry," I said.

"Right. It took a couple of days to locate him, and by then he'd already sold some of what he found. But he was really proud of his new boots."

"Sarge's boots?"

"Most likely. We talked him into letting us take the boots and what he had left of the rest. We're checking the pawnshops where he remembers selling some of it."

"You think Janice threw the contents of Sarge's trunk into the trash?" I asked.

"Looks that way."

"And took the pillowcase out of her car tonight."

"Probably."

"She's still protecting him then."

"Who's protecting who?"

"Janice. Protecting Willie. George told me she always protects him."

He locked the car. "I'll give the key back to George," he said as we started back toward the station. "Let's get you back inside. Almost time for your show. I'll talk to Janice."

"If you can find her."

"She can't be far away if she was here taking the pillowcase a few minutes ago."

I looked around the lot. "Then George's car must be here somewhere, too. She was driving it. Pete, the cameras are working again. Can't you look and see if Janice opened her car?"

"I can do that."

"But, anyway," I said, "I guess she has a right to open her own car if she wants to."

"Maybe. Maybe not. I'm going to stick around for a while. I'll be here if you need a ride home."

"Thanks. That would be nice."

I did a fast makeup job, reread my notes about old Giles Corey getting squashed, rehearsed the intro to *I Married a Witch,* and took my seat beside the large fuzzy black cat.

"You're in luck," Marty announced. "You don't get Rhonda for call screener. Janice got back in the nick of time."

Janice is here. Safe.

I was surprised by the intensity of the wave of relief I felt. But I just said, "Cool."

"By the way, Doan called. Wants you to stay awhile after the show so George can get a few still shots of you in the fancy dress on the *Nightshades* set for Friday's papers."

"Can't that wait until tomorrow, when we go to the party? I'm sure all the papers will be there."

She gave a "Who knows?" hand gesture. "He says he wants to be sure the papers have really good pictures. George's pictures." She ducked behind her camera. "Showtime. Counting. Four . . . three . . . two . . ."

CHAPTER 42

I started the show with the Giles Corey story. It gave me a chance to be a bit dramatic, and it even drew early comments from callers. One man said he'd heard that whenever there was a disaster in Salem, the old man's ghost appeared. Said his grandfather saw it, fully clothed and unsquished, standing in a cemetery the night before the Great Salem Fire.

I tended to believe it. Seeing ghosts in Salem seems to be a fairly common occurrence. It was the Salem Fire reference, though, that made me think about the old wooden fire escape on the back of the building. At the next commercial break I asked Marty about it.

"Does anyone besides Mr. Doan have a key to the secret staircase?"

"I don't know for sure," she said. "But I suppose someone must have one. In case of an emergency, you know."

What if whoever killed Yvette Pelletier and stepped on Ariel's hands and disappeared behind this building simply unlocked that door and ran up the stairs into Doan's office? Certainly the police must have checked that possibility.

Once *I Married a Witch* started, I'd find Pete and ask about those keys. I could hardly wait. By the time lightning had struck the tree where the witches' spirits were imprisoned and Veronica Lake had begun working her magic on Fredric March, I had dialed Pete's phone and was on my way upstairs to meet him.

"Pete, can I ask you a question?" I knew he probably wouldn't want to discuss police business, but he seemed to trust me more and more lately. "It's about the fire escape out back."

"Like, who had a key?" He smiled.

"Exactly. Do you think the killer could have ducked inside here that night?"

"We've checked that possibility."

"And . . . ?"

He held up three fingers. "Doan has one. Mrs. Doan has one. And the fire department has one."

"But someone could have a duplicate key."

"Doan says no, but the odds are someone does."

"Janice?"

"Probably. He keeps his in his desk. She's in and out of that office twenty times a day."

I thought about what George had told me about Janice always protecting Willie. "If Janice has a key, Willie must know where she keeps it."

"What does this Willie have on her, anyway? Is there anything more about this family you think I should know?"

"Did either of them tell you they were abused by their mother as children? Sexually, I mean."

"Jesus! Are you sure? Who told you that?"

"George."

His cop face was firmly in place. "Anything else?"

"Did George tell you that he took Janice to a doctor today? That she's afraid of doctors?"

"Is she sick? What's wrong with her?"

"I don't know. He said she's being treated for a psychosomatic disorder."

"That can mean anything. What else?"

How much could I tell him without sounding like a total kook? If I left out the things I'd seen in the obsidian ball and the stuff River had read in the tarot, what was left? Should I tell him about what Aunt Ibby and I had learned about Marlena's death? Did he have to know we'd been checking up on the Valens' life in London, thanks to Nigel? Was all this useful, or did we come off as just a couple of very nosy women?

I took a deep breath. "Okay. But I know you're going to think I'm taking this Nancy Drew thing a little too far."

"Try me."

I told him Marlena had died from a fall down a flight of stairs, that she'd been drunk and naked, and that the body had been found by a "minor child."

"Naked?" he asked. "Does that tie in with the sexual abuse somehow?"

"I have no idea," I said. "But they did call her death suspicious. There's another thing. Maybe it means something. Maybe not." I told him about the picture of Marlena that George had taken.

"You and your aunt have been busy. Anything else?"

"My aunt has an old friend at New Scotland Yard. She asked him to look into the time George and Janice spent in London." I told him what Nigel had learned about the Purple Dragon and how George and Willie had come back to the United States together.

"I think the chief would like to know about the New Scotland Yard contact," he said. "You have the guy's number?"

"No. But my aunt does. He's going to call her again soon. Nigel told my aunt that one of the Purple Dragon performers was called Billie Jo Vale. We're wondering if that was a stage name for William Joseph Valen. Willie."

"Lee, I wish you'd told me all this sooner." His expression was stern.

"I was just trying to figure out how to help Janice, Pete," I said. "We were looking into things that happened to the Valen kids a long time ago. It has nothing to do with Ariel or Mrs. Pelletier and how they died."

That doesn't really make a lot of sense right now, even to me.

He put his hands on my shoulders. "Listen to me, Lee. Stop trying to help. Let the department take it from here. Nancy Drew isn't real. You are." He pulled me close for an instant, then let go. "Now, go back to work. I need to talk to George and Janice. I'll drive you home."

I felt relieved. He was right, of course. Aunt Ibby and I needed to stop being so nosy.

Just as soon as we get that picture of Billie Jo Vale. And when we can be sure that it's safe for O'Ryan to go outside.

"I have to stick around for a while after the show," I told him. "Doan wants George to take some photos of me in the dress I'm wearing tomorrow night."

"I'll wait," he said. "I hear that dress is worth it."

I hurried back down to the *Nightshades* set. It was nearly time for the first round of callers. I pushed the large black cat over a little more and settled myself on the couch. If Janice's day had been as bad as George thought, it hadn't affected her call-screening ability. The calls were varied and pretty easy to handle. I coasted through the requests for help with romance, work, in-laws, and one lost parakeet.

During the second half of the movie I made some notes on the next night's program—a marathon of good old Halloween-themed *Twilight Zone*s and *Outer Limits* shows—rehearsed my closing commercials, and wondered how Pete was doing with his questioning of George and Janice Valen.

The end credits rolled. I patted the stuffed cat and said good night to Marty.

"If you don't mind, Moon, I'll stick around for a while."

"Fine with me."

"Good. I want to get the set looking nice. For the pictures."

"Thanks. And lose the big cat, okay?"

Smiling, she gave me a thumbs-up and began dusting and straightening the already straight book pile. She stashed the black cat behind the couch, opened a cupboard door, carefully removed the obsidian ball, and placed it almost reverently in the center of the table.

CHAPTER 43

The reception area was empty when I passed through on my way to Janice's office. Her door was closed, so I knocked a couple of times before pushing it open. The place was dark except for a pale beam from a streetlight filtering through partially closed draperies. I felt for a light switch on the wall and had a moment of uneasiness when I didn't find it right away.

Come on. Turn on the lights. Grab the dress. Pose for the stupid pictures and get out of here.

After a second or two of semi-frantic pawing at the wall, I hit the right button and welcome brightness filled the room. I was glad to see it. What I didn't expect to see was George sitting at Janice's desk.

I took a step back. "George? What are you doing here? Alone in the dark?"

"I thought Janice might have come in here." He shook his head. "She's gone again, Lee."

"But she was here all evening. She screened my calls. Did a good job of it, too."

"No," he said. "She wasn't. She was here for the first

few calls, then asked me to ride the board while she went to the bathroom. She never came back. I've looked all over the station. Detective Mondello is looking around outside."

Is Pete looking in the water next to the granite wall? Ariel went outside late at night, and in the morning I found her drowned body.

I shook away the unpleasant thought.

"Did you call your house? Maybe she didn't feel well and went home."

"I tried. No answer."

"What about her cell?"

"It's here. She left it." He lifted the slim phone, then slammed it down on the desk. "Damn it. She just keeps going away. I thought she'd be able to stay here with me. Safe. Forever. The doctors in Europe thought it was possible. Even likely. But no. He had to come back!" He pushed the chair back and stood, glowering in my direction. "There's nothing here for him! Nothing left of him, really!"

Again, a short burst of the strange laughter.

I backed up a little more and tried to speak calmly. "George," I said, "this isn't helping to find Janice. If she's in trouble, we need to figure out where she's gone."

"I'm sorry. Lee. You don't understand what's happening here. No one does." He looked down for a moment and seemed to regain control of himself. "Sorry," he said again. "Listen. Let's get those pictures taken while we figure out the best way to handle this."

"If that's what you think we should do," I said. "I'll just get the dress and take it down to the dressing room." I edged along the wall toward the closet. Getting

out of this office seemed like a really good idea.
"Marty's fixing up the set. You go on down. I'll see you
there, okay?"

I waited until he'd left the room before I popped
open the closet door, reached inside, and pulled the
dress from its hanger with far less care than the delicate fabric deserved. With the Mackie over my arm, I
dashed for the reception area and raced down the
stairs to the studio.

Marty had done some rearranging of the set. She'd
moved the couch and table to one side, revealing an
unobstructed portion of the star-spangled blue wall
backdrop. I could see what she had in mind. George's
pictures of me would be uncluttered, but would have
a definite *Nightshades* look.

She had borrowed a Doric column from the sports
set—I recognized it as the one that usually held a half-
size replica of the Stanley Cup—and had made a tight
arrangement on its top with the quartz crystal cluster,
a tall wooden candle holder with a half-melted white
candle, and the obsidian ball.

"How d'ya like it, Moon? Not bad, huh?"

"Very effective, Marty. What did George think?"

"George? Haven't seen him yet. But he'll like it.
You standing next to the pillar thing. That's a good
look. I figure that's a standing-up dress, not a sitting-
down dress. Am I right?"

"Absolutely right. I'm not sure I *can* sit down in it.
But I'd better put it on and get this done." I looked
down the long, dark aisle leading to the dressing
room. "Can you turn on a few lights? It's kind of
spooky down there."

"Sure." She pushed a series of buttons, and I hurried

along the welcome path of brightness provided by ceiling track lights. It had become impossible for me to be in that dressing room without thinking of the voices I'd heard there. Of the terror in Janice's voice and the cold threat in Willie's.

Trying to blot out the memory, I stripped to bikini panties and slithered into the beaded beauty. I fluffed my hair, added a squirt of hair spray, and reapplied eye makeup. Satisfied that the me in the mirror would probably photograph well, I returned to the revamped *Nightshades* set.

"Hot stuff, Moon." Marty's greeting was enthusiastic. "Not much to it, is there?"

"Mostly beads and thread," I admitted. "And I'm freezing."

"Yeah. Those goose bumps won't look good in the pictures." She opened one of the cabinets. "Here. Wear one of Ariel's capes until it's time for the shoot." She placed Ariel's long purple velvet cape around my shoulders. "Better?"

"Much better," I said, gathering the soft folds close, enjoying the immediate warmth of the thing.

"Looks good. That one was Ariel's favorite."

I still wasn't comfortable with the idea of sitting, so standing, I dialed Aunt Ibby's number. She answered right away.

"Hi," I said. "Just wanted to let you know I'm running a little late. Mr. Doan decided he wants some still pictures of me in the Mackie dress. George is going to do the shoot, and then Detective Mondello will take me home."

"I'm glad you called. O'Ryan is starting to pace in

the front hall. He always does that when he thinks you'll be home soon."

I smiled at the thought. "Well, you be sure to tell him everything is fine. I'll be home as soon as I can."

"I'll tell him," she promised. "And, Maralee, Nigel sent that picture of Billie Jo Vale."

"Really? Can you tell who it is?"

"Looks quite a lot like your friend Janice to me. Of course, there's a big, fancy headdress thing on her head and she isn't wearing much, but it does resemble her quite a bit."

Has Nigel sent a duplicate of the photo on Janice's desk?

"Set looks perfect, Marty. You ready, Lee?" George Valen spoke from behind me.

"Thanks, Aunt Ibby. We'll talk about that when I get home." A quick good-bye and I turned to face the photographer.

"Any luck?" I asked, knowing by George's worried expression that he hadn't found his sister.

He shook his head. "No. And my car is gone again. She left hers."

Marty looked up, bright eyes alert. "Janice took off?"

"Yeah. Pete's going to drive around and look for her."

"Mind if I do that, too?" the camerawoman asked. "You don't need me here for anything else, do you?"

"No. Everything here is good. Thanks, Marty. You're a pal."

"No problem. I've been worried about her lately. She seems a little . . . I don't know . . . a little spacey. Like she's been popping a lot of those pills she takes."

George didn't respond, and I couldn't think of

anything to say. Marty waved, shrugged into a quilted jacket, and left us.

The studio seemed very quiet. And very dark. The only sound was the click-clicking of a single switch as George focused a spotlight on the place where I was supposed to stand—next to the pillar, where the obsidian ball sparkled with reflected light.

I stood there, still wearing Ariel's cape, feeling increasingly uneasy.

George's voice seemed to come from a distance when he began to speak.

"It started, you know, when I was only twelve years old."

CHAPTER 44

"Twelve years old," he repeated. "That was the year I got my first camera. Did I tell you that?" He didn't wait for an answer. "It was a good one. A nice, expensive Ricoh. Extra lenses and all. Zoom, wide-angle, the works. She taught me how to use it, too. Knew a lot about photography, my beautiful mother did. Said she'd been a model when she was young. I don't know if that was true or not. She was such a liar."

He laughed then, a short, ugly sound. "I started with landscapes, then buildings. I'm still good at buildings. Salem's a good place for buildings. Don't you think so, Lee? Beautiful old buildings."

I nodded but didn't speak. Interrupting just then didn't seem like a good idea.

"When I was thirteen, she decided I was ready to photograph the human body. Her body."

He grew silent, then motioned for me to move into

the spotlight. "Drop the cape," he ordered. "Turn to your left."

I tossed the cape onto the couch and faced left.

"Good," he said. "You're very lovely, Lee."

This one-sided conversation was starting to creep me out. I looked around the studio, deciding which was the closest exit—just in case I might want to leave in a hurry.

"She was lovely, too, Lee. She took me out into the woods one day. I thought I'd be taking pictures of trees. I like trees. Did you know that once Salem had wonderful elm trees? They were all lost to a blight. A blight is a terrible thing."

Then, for a few minutes, the only sounds were the whirr of his camera and his brief commands.

"Smile.

"Turn right.

"Toss your hair. Nice."

I followed his directions and wished that Marty or Pete or the night watchman/security guard would interrupt us. No such luck.

"She knew about trees, too. She knew about a lot of things, I guess. 'That's an ash,' she'd say. 'And that one's an oak. The bark has a pretty texture, don't you think?' Then she did the most amazing thing. She took off all her clothes." Again the short laugh. "It didn't take very long. She wasn't wearing any underwear."

The camera stopped whirring, and George's voice turned into a high falsetto.

"'Oh, Georgie, before you take my picture, help me arrange my breasts the way you think they

should be. They're so big, I never know what to do
with them. Come on. You can touch them. I'm your
mother, after all.'"

Oh my God. Was this the way that picture of Marlena
had been set up? Could she really have told a thirteen-
year-old boy to touch her breasts?

The camera began whirring again. "What the hell
was I supposed to do? I was thirteen, for Christ's sake."

There was a long pause, then more directions.
"Turn your back toward me. Look over your shoulder.
Moisten your lips. Great. Look up a little. Perfect. I'll
tell you what I did, Lee. I squeezed off one shot of
my beautiful mother leaning against the beautiful
bark of that beautiful oak tree, and then I ran. I ran
out of the woods. I ran all the way home. Got into my
bed and pulled the covers over my head. Face forward, Lee. Can you turn so your leg shows through
that front slit? Good."

Then it was all professional directions for a while.
He knew his business; that was certain. I could tell already that the photos would be good. I struck pose
after pose, hoping that he was through telling me
things I didn't want to know about. He wasn't.

"She never mentioned that day again. Never even
asked to see the picture. But she wasn't through with
me. No. Not her. She waited a couple of years. She'd
started drinking pretty heavily by then. Started
coming into my room at night. Climbing into my bed.
Saying she'd had a nightmare, or she was cold or
lonely. Then one night she was naked. She started
touching me. She knew what she was doing to
me." Again the ugly laugh. "Know what I did, Lee? I

ran away again. The next day I talked a friend into letting me stay at his house. I was making enough money selling my pictures so I could pay his parents board. Stayed there all through high school. I only went home once in a while to see Willie."

Yes. Talk about Willie.

"See, I thought it was just me. I thought she'd singled me out for some sick reason. Willie was just a skinny little kid. I mean, when I was fifteen, he was only eight. A cute little third grader who loved the Ninja Turtles. You getting cold, Lee? Put the cape back on for a minute. I want to try a warmer filter on this spot."

I pulled the cape around me and looked at the studio clock. Had I been posing for only fifteen minutes? It seemed like hours. Again, I wished someone—anyone—would interrupt us. George fiddled with the tall lamp for a moment, and the circle of light took on a pinkish glow.

"Back to work, Lee. Just a little longer, I promise. You're a great model. I'll make up some prints for your portfolio."

"Thank you, George," I said, taking off the cape. "That would be nice."

"Anytime. No problem. Ahh. That light is better. Great on your hair. On the dress, too. Where was I? Oh, yeah. Willie. Poor little Willie. Left there all alone with a monster."

The quiet sounds of the camera were interspersed with George's staccato demands. "Turn right. No, just your head. That's good. Sexy look now. Gorgeous. Smile. Turn the other way."

Get back to Willie. What happened to him?

He answered my unspoken question.

"I guess she'd learned something from my reactions to her. She must have taken her time with Willie. The doctor said it had gone on for years. You know what a dissociative disorder is, Lee?"

"No, I don't," I said. "Ariel had a book with that title, but I haven't read it."

"Ah. Poor Ariel. Had a book on it, did she? She must have figured it out. That's probably why she's dead."

Why had Ariel died? What had happened to Willie? *There are so many questions. Pete says I need to stop playing girl detective. Let the department handle it.*

I asked, anyway. "What had Ariel figured out?"

"Look over your right shoulder now. Tilt your chin up. Good. Did you ever see the movie *Sybil?* Sally Field starred in it. Maybe you're too young to remember. Look at me. Smile. It was about a child who had been abused so horribly that she developed other personalities. She became other people, really, who could bear the pain for her. Her name was Sybil. And she wasn't aware of the other personalities, but they were aware of her. Put your hand on your hip. The other hand. Hard to believe, isn't it?"

I followed his directions while searching my mind for the old movie. "I think I saw it once on TV a long time ago. It was supposed to be a true story."

"Right. And what Sybil had was dissociative identity disorder. So does Willie. Sometimes it's called multiple personalities."

"Willie has multiple personalities?"

"At least one."

"One?"

"After our mother died and I got ready to take Willie to London with me, I noticed that he acted strange. Even his voice sounded different. Of course, he was the one who'd found her body at the foot of the stairs, so I chalked it up to that."

"That would be pretty shocking to a kid," I said. "Finding a body is frightening for anybody. I know."

"His behavior was so bizarre, he was so unlike the kid I remembered, that I took him to a doctor. A psychiatrist. Look to your left. Well, the doctor tried hypnosis. That's when we discovered Billie Jo."

"Billie Jo?"

"Yep. My little brother's extra personality was a girl. And that brave little girl had taken years of Marlena's abuse. See, that way, Willie didn't have to have sex with his mother. Billie Jo did it for him."

"But still . . . I mean . . . how . . ."

"I know. Sex is sex, and the whole thing makes no sense. But after Marlena was dead, probably after being pushed down the stairs by one of them—I don't know which one—it was up to me and the doctors to try to straighten things out."

I knew which one it was. I had heard Willie admit to it. And he had threatened to throw Janice down the stairs, too. I didn't tell George about that, though. Why complicate things even more? He kept talking.

"It turned out, according to the doctor, that neither personality wanted to be a boy. Anyway, Willie was appearing less and less as the Billie Jo personality took over. The doctor prescribed hormone treatments, along with the psychiatric sessions. By then Willie's

voice and looks had become completely feminine.
He'd started wearing girl's clothes, and before long, I
almost forgot that he was my brother, not my sister. I
guess he forgot it, too. Can you lean back a little? Push
your hips forward. Stick your leg through the slit.
There you go. Perfect. Hell, when he was seventeen,
he even got a job as a female impersonator! Billie Jo
Vale. Quite the local celebrity."

At the Purple Dragon. Willie sent Sarge a postcard
from there.

"Billie Jo was pretty young for a sex change opera-
tion, but we found a doctor in Barcelona who'd do it.
Only took a couple of hours and *voilà!* There she was.
Janice."

Willie is Janice. Janice is Willie.

I said it aloud. "Janice is Willie."

He nodded. "The Spanish doctor suggested the
new name. For Janus. You know, the Roman god with
two faces. Look to your left again. No. Look down a
little."

Following his instructions, I looked directly at the
obsidian ball. The colors swirled, the pinpoints of
light glowed, and I saw the front door of the house on
Winter Street.

I knew George was still talking, but I couldn't stay
focused on his words.

*Why is the ball showing me the front door of Aunt Ibby's
house? Or, if River's theory is correct, why is Ariel showing it
to me?*

I tried looking away. Tried to concentrate on what
George was saying. I didn't want to see pictures in the
damned thing anymore.

"Lee? You okay? Do you need to take a break?"

"What? Oh, no, George. I'm fine." I kept my head turned away from the obsidian. "You say the doctor gave Janice her name?"

"Yes. And Willie stayed away from her. From us. For years. At least I think he did. But lately—I don't know exactly when it started—lately he's been popping in and out. Like that grinning cat in *Alice in Wonderland*."

"Have you told the police any of this, George?"

"No. I can't. She's my sister. I'm supposed to protect her." The camera grew silent. "They'll come for her soon enough. As soon as the test on that stamp comes back, they'll know she's the one they're looking for. They'll know she killed that poor woman. And Ariel, too, I suppose."

"She killed Yvette Pelletier? *Why?*"

"I didn't know at first. But then I watched some old *Nightshades* tapes. Yvette was a regular. Ariel advised her to get rid of her husband, and she left him. She had two boys. Fifteen and eight. Just like us. That was all it took for Willie to want to get rid of her. He did it to save the boys, you see?"

"Janice stole the clothes from your trunk," I said, "and Willie wore them."

He nodded, and the camera began to click and whirr again. "Pete says she threw them away, though. Maybe she's trying to keep Willie from getting out again by getting rid of his clothes. Look left, Lee. Smile." He laughed. "It isn't as though he couldn't find something else to wear."

I followed his direction and looked left. But I didn't smile. The blackness of the obsidian glowed brightly with the image of the house on Winter Street. I knew what Willie had found to wear. The Little Tramp, carrying a lighted jack-o'-lantern, twirled his cane and climbed the front steps toward my aunt who stood, smiling, in the open doorway.

CHAPTER 45

I was surprised by how calm I sounded as I moved away from the spotlight.

"George," I said. "I have to go home. Willie is at my house, and my aunt is in danger." I grabbed my purse, threw Ariel's cape around my shoulders, and extended my open palm to the surprised cameraman. "Give me the keys to Janice's car and call 911. And find Pete."

George stuttered and sputtered half-formed questions. "What . . . how do you . . . what . . . ?" But at the same time he reached into his pocket and handed me the key on its heart-shaped silver ring.

"Call 911," I repeated as I raced toward the lit exit sign. "Send them to my house."

He nodded and was on the phone before I reached the door.

It was lucky that the streets were nearly empty while I proved that the Porsche really could go from zero to sixty in five point five seconds. *Eat your heart out, Danica Patrick.* I roared down Hawthorne Boulevard, pushing ninety, careened past the statue of Roger

Conant, rounded the Civil War monument, and with tires squealing, pulled up in front of the house and dashed up the front steps. The door was ajar; the house dark. I pressed the light switch. Nothing.

"Aunt Ibby?" I called. "Are you okay?"

My voice echoed in the high-ceilinged hallway as I listened for a reply. There was none.

"Willie, I know you're in here. Where is my aunt?"

A small gleam of light appeared at the head of the stairs. I squinted into the darkness and recognized the flickering orange glow and the eerie grin of a Halloween pumpkin.

"Is that you, gypsy woman?" The voice was the one I'd heard threatening Janice.

Wait a minute. It is *Janice.* It was hard to wrap my mind around this multiple personality thing.

"Yes. It's me. Are you here, too, Janice?"

He laughed. "She can't hear you, Gypsy. She can't do anything. I'm in control now."

"I see." Somehow I maintained my calm tone of voice. "What are you doing in my house? Where is my aunt? And what happened to the lights in here?"

"I put the old woman up in the attic," he said. "Then I threw the main switch. I'm waiting for the damned cat. It can see in the dark, you know, and I'm sure it will come looking for me, like Ariel told it to. Then I can kill it."

I fought back a rising panic.

What does he mean, he put her in the attic? Is she alive?

"Willie, is my aunt . . . safe up there?"

"The old woman? I guess so. I had to tie her up. Put a gag in her mouth, too."

I have to get past him somehow and get to the attic. Make sure Aunt Ibby is all right.

I put my purse on the floor and started slowly up the staircase. I kept talking.

"Why do you want to hurt the cat?"

"He wants to kill me. When I stomped on the witch's hands just before she went under the water, she called to him. 'Orion,' she said. 'Orion, revenge me!'" His voice dropped to a harsh whisper. "It's a witch's cat! It has to do what she says!"

I was close enough to see his face, illuminated by the candlelit pumpkin he held in his lap. He didn't look much like Janice. The features seemed coarser somehow, the eyes narrower, and the mouth was twisted into a downturned grimace.

Of course, I reasoned, *he isn't wearing Janice's carefully applied makeup, he has that fake mustache, and Janice's fine blond hair is tucked up under the Little Tramp's bowler hat.* Still, it was like looking at a complete stranger, someone I'd never seen before.

Keep him talking.

"Why did you push Ariel into the water, Willie?" I pulled the cape closer around me and tugged the hood over my hair. The dark purple color might make it harder for him to see me in the darkness, especially with that candle flickering just below his eyes. I pressed my back against the wall, creeping closer to the stair where he sat, not taking my eyes away from his face.

"I was in a hurry," he said. "Had to get into the station and change back into the stupid cow's clothes. I was kind of excited, you know? I'd just killed that evil bitch down the street. The one who was going to make her kids do bad things to her, you know? I saved those kids!" The tone of voice was smug, self-satisfied. "I told her I had one of those crystal necklaces for her. From Ariel. She let me right in. Even turned her back and asked me to fasten it for her! Made it so easy to use my nice sharp razor. My raincoat kept the blood off my good clothes."

I suppressed a shudder. "And Ariel saw you when you came back?"

"Worse." He put the pumpkin down on the stair next to him. "She called me Janice. Then she said, 'I guess you're using your other personality tonight. What's his name?' She knew about me! The witch knew about me. She was sitting there on the wall, so I just put my foot on her back and pushed her over. Easy!"

"She tried to get out of the water, though," I said, catching a flash of golden eyes in the dark hall, where O'Ryan silently stalked Ariel's killer. "The police said she tried to climb back out."

"Oh, she tried." He giggled. "But she was too fat. The water was too deep. The wall was too slippery. And I had my big boots on! Stomped on her hands real hard. After a while, she gave up. Then I went up the secret stairs, hid my clothes, took the disk thing out of the video machine, and yanked out a bunch of wires, too."

"The cat saw all this?"

"It did. And I knew it would come after me, you see? I tried to make it eat rat poison, but it wouldn't eat it. Then I grabbed it out of its yard, but it got away. Too bad. I had it in a big bag, and I was going to throw it in the water." He laughed. "So it could drown like Ariel did."

At that moment, O'Ryan made his move. He leaped onto Willie's back, clinging there as the killer spun around, struggling to shake him off. I dashed past the grinning pumpkin and reached the door to the attic. Slamming it shut behind me, I called Aunt Ibby's name and raced up the stairs. A muffled groan led me to where she lay behind a bureau. Pale beams from streetlamps filtered through the uncurtained attic window. The ropes around her wrists and ankles looked like worn clothesline, tied in simple, but tight knots. Her nightgown, twisted around her body, was torn and dirty. A rag was stuffed in her mouth, and she made gagging noises deep in her throat.

I pulled the rag out as gently as I could. "Shhh," I warned. "He's still out there. The police should be here any minute." She nodded, extending her arms toward me. I got to work on the wrist bonds, and in moments the clumsy square knot fell away.

"I thought it was you at the front door," she whispered. "The voice sounded just like you. 'Let me in, Aunt Ibby. I've forgotten my key.' Sounded exactly like you! He ran in and hit me with a cane and dragged me up here. Said he was going to kill O'Ryan!"

"I know," I said. "Janice is really good at voices. Can you undo the rope on your ankles?"

"Janice?" She bent to untie the knotted rope.

"Janice. Billy Jo Vale. Willie. All the same. I'll explain later. Listen. Hear that?" The welcome wail of police sirens sounded in the distance. "We're going to be okay. Here comes the cavalry!"

Our relief lasted only seconds. The attic door creaked

open. "Here, kitty, kitty," came a hoarse stage whisper. "Are you up here?"

The grinning pumpkin bobbed up and down as Willie climbed the stairs, the candle's glow casting his long, distorted shadow across the dusty floorboards. We ducked behind the bureau. The sirens' shrieks grew louder. Willie drew closer.

"Come, kitty, kitty. Uncle Willie has something for you."

The bowler hat was gone, and Janice's smartly styled blond hair was incongruous with Willie's crazed facial expression. The black mustache had become partially unglued, and it tilted at an odd angle on his upper lip. He balanced the lit pumpkin on the seat of the rocking chair, where just weeks ago I'd sorted costume jewelry. In his right hand a long knife glittered.

Too close to our hiding place, he looked from side to side. A scratching sound came from outside the window behind him. In the streetlight's glow I saw O'Ryan out there, hind legs on the slanted roof below the windowsill, paws on the glass pane. The cat meowed loudly and scratched again.

No! Run away, O'Ryan. He has a knife!

"How did you get out there, damned cat?" Willie put the knife down on the sill and struggled with layers of old paint, grunting and swearing as he pounded upward on the sash with both palms. The wooden frame gave suddenly, and O'Ryan leapt into the room, a yellow blur in the dim light, as the knife clattered to the floor. Willie quickly retrieved the knife, and whirled in the cat's direction.

I spread one side of the purple cape over my aunt's shoulders and pulled the other side close around me,

hoping the voluminous folds would protect us from
the killer's view. As I clutched the cape's edge, I felt
something beneath the velvet. Slowly, I ran my hand
along the soft fabric. There was an opening, a neatly
formed pocket, just inside the front panel. I slid my
hand into a narrow slit, then withdrew it quickly.
There was a small sound, like paper crackling.

Did Willie hear it, too?

The wail of sirens must have drowned out any other
noise he might have heard. But police out in front of
the house or not, my aunt and I were alone in a dark
attic with a knife-wielding killer and a witch's cat. I
dared to peek out from behind the velvet hood.

*Wait a minute. It's not as dark as it was. And there's
another crackling sound. Not paper. Fire.*

Orange plumes of fire and bright red sparks shot
up from the seat of the old rocking chair, where the
antique pumpkin lay on its side, the face half eaten
away by flames. I tugged at Aunt Ibby's arm and whispered, "Come on. We have to get out of here!"

Fire spreads quickly in an old, dusty attic, and ours
was packed with plenty of flammable stuff. As we
watched, a dress form, draped with sheets, formed a
hideous human-shaped pyre, and black smoke rose
from a stack of old *National Geographic*s.

Willie, standing between us and the stairway,
seemed oblivious to the growing conflagration
around him. Knife upraised, he faced the snarling
yellow cat. O'Ryan, fur bristling, teeth bared, stood on
top of a walnut bureau, eye to eye with the killer.

The sirens had stopped, and we heard the pound-
ing of feet in the house below. Drawing the cape
around us both, I again felt the little pocket and

pushed my fingers into it, withdrawing a brittle paper packet.

"You first," I told my aunt as we crawled toward the open window. "I'll be right behind you."

She pulled herself up to the sill and, feetfirst, wiggled out onto the second-story roof. My long cape caught on a nail, and I shook it off onto the floor. I was starting to follow my aunt when I heard Pete's voice calling from downstairs.

"Lee! Where are you? Where the hell are you?"

"We're here, Pete!" I yelled. "In the attic! It's on fire! And he has a knife!"

Willie whirled, first toward the sound of Pete's voice, then toward mine.

I heard the splintering of wood as the attic door burst open and, at the same time, the roaring *whoosh* of flames caught in the draft between the door and the open window. Willie screamed, and the knife fell to the floor as the sleeve of the Little Tramp costume caught fire.

I watched, terrified, as a yowling O'Ryan hurtled himself from the top of the bureau onto the back of the man, who tottered on the top stair.

"Maralee! Hurry!" my aunt called to me and reached a guiding hand through the window. The smoke and flames made it impossible to see across the room any longer. I took her hand and, kicking off the gold sandals, climbed over the sill, aware that the gossamer fabric of the beaded gown was shredding, catching on splinters of rough wood.

More sirens sounded as fire trucks approached. I couldn't hear Pete's voice any longer. Or Willie's screams. Or O'Ryan's yowls.

"Let's move over as close to the edge as we can get,"
I said. "The firemen will see us there."

I realized then that I still clutched the brittle paper
I'd pulled from the pocket of Ariel's cape. I held it
toward the streetlight. There were several thin pages
filled with cramped writing, sewn together on one
side to make a little book. On the cover, spidery letters in brownish ink spelled out the words *Bridget
Bishop. Her book.*

I didn't hesitate for a second. I threw the damned
thing back through the window, into the flames, and
followed my aunt to the edge of the roof.

CHAPTER 46

We slid on our fannies toward the edge of the slanted roof, yelling for help all the way. Rough granules coating the shingles tore at both dress and skin, and angry flames shot from the window behind us. I looked down, calculating just how far we might have to jump if the firefighters didn't reach us before the fire did.

We were on the back side of the house, and we could hear the fire equipment arriving out front, on the Winter Street side. Below the second-story roof was the walled garden off the kitchen, where O'Ryan did his business.

O'Ryan! Poor dear cat. Did you get away?

"If we have to," my aunt said in a remarkably calm voice, considering the circumstances, "we can probably hang onto the rain gutter and drop down to the top of that wall. After that, it's easy."

"Piece of cake," I said, thinking of Marty. "Let's hope we don't have to."

But, as it turned out, we did have to.

Our cries for help were heard, and men carrying

ladders ran toward the garden below. But by then, we were being bombarded with tiny hot embers and fiery pieces of debris had started to roll toward us.

"Come on," she said. "Let's go." And with my sixty-five-year-old aunt leading the way, I backed, feetfirst, facedown, over the edge of the roof. Grabbing the slippery but sturdy rain gutter, I dangled there, inches above the garden wall.

It was Pete Mondello who caught me. My arms were tight around his neck; my face was pressed against his shoulder. He made no attempt to put me down, holding me close. One of the firemen had rescued Aunt Ibby. She stood there in the garden, bunny slippers still amazingly intact, trying to arrange her torn and stained flannel nightgown into some semblance of modesty. She gazed upward as fire ate away at the top of the old house.

"Oh, dear. We're going to have quite a mess to clean up here, aren't we?" she said. "Are you all right, Maralee?"

"I think so," I said, reluctantly loosening my hold on Pete's neck. "But, Pete, did you get him? Did you arrest Willie?"

He frowned, lowering me gently until my bare feet touched the cold ground. "I've read Janice Valen her rights. She's under arrest. We're waiting now for the ambulance to take her to the hospital."

"Can I see her please, Pete? Talk to her?"

He hesitated. "I guess so. Come on. She's hurt pretty bad."

More sirens screamed, and flashing red lights reflected on darkened windows. The ambulance had arrived, but so had the news photographers. Pete tried his best to shield me from the cold and the cameras, draping his jacket around my shoulders as we ran toward the front of the house.

The murderer looked very small, lying there on the brick sidewalk. They'd cut the right sleeve of the costume off, and I had to look away, fighting nausea. From shoulder to wrist, the long, slim once-white arm had become a bulging chunk of raw red and yellow meat surrounded by charred black flesh. One leg stuck out at a strange angle, and blood streaked both face and hair. I reached for the undamaged left hand as paramedics lifted the stretcher, and a low moan escaped the cracked lips.

"Lee? Is that you?" The brown eyes opened wide, and despite the soot and blood and her singed lashes, I knew I was seeing Janice, not Willie. As always, she'd taken the pain for him.

"Yes. I'm here. They're taking you to the hospital."

"The man said I'm under arrest," she said. "Where's George?"

"I'm here, sweetheart. I'm here." George had pushed his way through the crowd of police and press and spectators. He elbowed me out of the way, knocking Pete's jacket to the ground, and grasped her hand. "Don't worry. Everything will be all right."

"George, there was a fire. And a cat jumped on me. And Willie threw me down the stairs, like he always said he would." Janice began to cry.

I backed away as the paramedics lifted her into the waiting ambulance. They let George go with her, and sirens blaring, they sped away.

It wasn't until then that I realized that the clicking

sound I heard was cameras. They were aimed at me. A quick downward glance told me why. Between racing up to the attic, crawling on splintering floorboards, sliding along on rough shingles, and dangling from the rain gutter, I'd literally destroyed the million-dollar dress. All the strategically placed beading on the bodice was gone. The knee-high slit now extended to my waist. I was, in fact, standing in front of my burning house, virtually naked. These were definitely not going to be the publicity photos Mr. Doan had in mind.

Pete wrapped me once more in his jacket and waved the photographers away. "Come on. You and your aunt can sit in my car until I finish up here. Then we'll see about finding you someplace to stay."

Aunt Ibby and I huddled together in the backseat of the police car, watching through the rear window as streams of water from fire hoses finally knocked down the flames. After what seemed like hours, Pete climbed into the front seat and handed me my purse.

"Found this at the bottom of the stairs. Thought you might need it."

"Thank you," I said. "Can we go inside and get some clothes?"

"Nope. Sorry. Not safe." He turned and faced us. "But look, I've got a couple of those WICH-TV rain-coats in my glove box. Those'll cover you for now. I've called the hotel, and they're expecting you."

"But what about O'Ryan? Did you see him at all? Did he get out of the house?" I asked.

He shook his head. "I didn't see him. But, hey! Cats

are smart. Especially that one. He'll be okay." He didn't sound convinced.

The hotel staff greeted us as though every night they checked in guests with bare feet or bunny slippers, and with oversize raincoats over torn nighties or ruined designer gowns.

"I'm going to need statements from both of you," Pete said. "I'll wait here while you get cleaned up, and then you can tell me exactly what went down at your place tonight."

After taking warm showers and wrapping ourselves in big, fluffy white Hawthorne Hotel bathrobes, we opened the suite door and invited Pete in. He sat on the sofa, all business, with notebook open, pencil poised.

Aunt Ibby spoke first, describing how Willie had tricked her into letting him in and how he had shut off the electricity and hit her with the cane, then dragged her up to the attic, binding her with the clothesline.

Holy crap! How am I going to tell him that I was looking at a black glass ball and I saw Aunt Ibby opening the door and that was how I knew I needed to get home?

I started by telling him everything George had told me about Janice and the multiple personality disorder. Aunt Ibby offered the information she'd received from Nigel about Billie Jo Vale. I told him what Willie had told us just a little while ago in the dark attic. I told how he'd confessed to killing both women. That he thought he was saving Yvette's children from the abuse he'd suffered from Marlena. And how he'd come there to kill O'Ryan.

"Why'd he want to kill the cat?" Pete asked.

"O'Ryan saw him push Ariel into the water. She told O'Ryan to avenge her death," I replied.

"She told the cat?"

"O'Ryan is a witch's cat," I explained. "He has to do what she says. Ask River about it some time. She'll fill you in."

He looked doubtful but continued to write in his notebook.

I told him about the papier-mâché pumpkin and the crystal necklace and the secret staircase. I told him every single thing I could think of that had anything to do with Janice Valen and the murders. I told him how neither Willie nor George could drive Janice's car, and how I'd had a strong feeling that my aunt was in danger, so I'd borrowed the Porsche and sped home. He seemed to buy it. I didn't tell him about the pictures in the obsidian ball. And I never told him, or anyone else, about Bridget Bishop's book. When he finally closed the notebook and stood to leave, I asked what would happen to Janice.

"She clearly has mental issues," he said. "I doubt that she'll ever go to trial. I imagine she'll be hospitalized."

"And George?"

"Accessory after the fact, maybe, though he's clearly got some mental issues, as well. That'll be up to the court. Walk me to the door?"

Aunt Ibby pretended a yawn and headed for the bedroom. "Good night, Detective. Don't stay up too late, Maralee."

Pete Mondello and I shared a very long good-night kiss. More than one, actually.

A gentle knock surprised us both. I adjusted the neckline of the bathrobe and, trying not to appear too flustered, ran a hand through my hair and peeked through the peephole.

The night desk clerk stood there, cradling a big, beautiful yellow cat in her arms. I threw the door open.

"O'Ryan! Where did you come from?"

"Isn't this Miss Russell's cat?" the desk clerk asked. "The security guard heard him scratching at the front door." She put the cat on the carpet. "I recognized him right away from her Facebook page. I wonder how he knew she was here."

"Well, I'll be damned," Pete said as O'Ryan, shaping his tail into a question mark, took a leisurely stroll around the edges of the room, yawned, and headed for bed.

I never did get to the Witches Ball. Mr. Doan talked Scott into adding the job of program director to his regular duties. Marty got promoted to head camera-man. When the news got out that both murders had been committed by a WICH-TV employee, and that *Nightshades* had been the start of it all, the show was canceled and my career as a TV call-in psychic was over, just as the tarot cards had predicted. *Nightshades* was replaced by *Tarot Time,* with River North as host, doing over-the-phone readings between vampire and zombie movies. I'm afraid some of the shots of me in the messed-up Mackie went viral. I'm still kind of avoiding looking at black, shiny objects, and so far, no problem.

There was a sad call from the VA hospital. Sarge passed away peacefully in his sleep the night before all the excitement. A blessing, really. He didn't have to learn how his boy Willie had ended up.

The Winter Street house isn't habitable yet, so Aunt Ibby, O'Ryan, and I are still living at the hotel. One thing I learned during my stint at WICH-TV—it's not a bad idea to be able to do more than one job. I've signed up for one of those online criminology courses Pete told me about. I'm looking forward to some interesting study dates, and I'm pretty sure he is, too.

It was the first white Christmas I'd seen in a long time. My recent winter holidays had featured lighted boat parades, palm trees, beach volleyball, and lawn flamingos decked out in Santa hats. But New England Christmases were the ones I'd grown up with, and Florida seemed very far away from Salem, Massachusetts.

I'd pulled a big wing chair up close to the window overlooking Winter Street as snow swirled in bright halos around the streetlamps and tree lights cast colorful dots onto wind-sculpted drifts. Snow-muffled church bells rang, calling the faithful to evensong at St. Peter's, just a few blocks away. O'Ryan was stretched out full length on the carpet beside me, tummy up, eyes squeezed shut, a cat smile on his face, large yellow paws clutching a damp purple catnip mouse.

I'm Lee Barrett, née Maralee Kowolski, thirty-one, red-haired, Salem born, orphaned early, married once, and widowed young. I'd been living in Florida for the past ten years, and since I'd returned to Salem

a few months back, my aunt Isobel Russell and I had
been sharing the fine old family home on Winter
Street . . . the same house where she'd raised me after
my parents died.

I'd been working in television, one way or another,
ever since I graduated from Emerson College. So far
I'd been a weather girl, a home shopping–show host,
and even a phone-in TV psychic. That last gig, a brief
stint at Salem's cable station WICH-TV, was on a show
called *Nightshades*. I dressed up like a Gypsy and, in between scary old movies, pretended to read minds, find
lost objects, and otherwise know the unknowable. I'd
been hired as a last-minute replacement for the previous host, Ariel Constellation, a practicing Salem witch
who apparently could *really* do all that psychic stuff.
Unfortunately, I'd been the one who'd discovered
Ariel's body floating facedown in Salem Harbor.

Not an auspicious start for a new job.

It didn't end well, either. Ariel's killer set a fire that
pretty much destroyed the top two floors of our
house, and if it hadn't been for O'Ryan's timely inter-
vention, Aunt Ibby and I might not be around to cel-
ebrate Christmas.

After the unpleasant publicity, *Nightshades* was canceled and I was once again unemployed. We're set
well enough financially so that being between jobs
wasn't a major problem, but I prefer being busy.

On a positive note, I was sure that when my sixty-
something, ball-of-energy aunt got through redesign-
ing the entire upstairs and driving contractors and
decorators nuts, the upper stories of the house would
once again be livable and we could stop tripping over
paint cans and fabric samples and wallpaper books.

I angled the wing chair a little to the right so that I could watch for headlights rounding the corner onto Winter Street. Not just any headlights. I was hoping for a Christmas night visit from a special friend. Well, maybe Detective Pete Mondello had become quite a bit more than just a friend . . . but I was trying to move slowly in that area of my life.

My aunt Ibby appeared in the doorway, bearing a tray with two chintz-patterned cups and a matching teapot.

"You and O'Ryan certainly look comfortable. Ready for a spot of tea?"

"Sounds good," I said, returning the chair to its original position. "I was just enjoying watching the snow. It's been a long time."

"Too long." She placed the tray on the antique drum table between us and sat in the wing chair facing mine. "And at last you're home for Christmas."

She filled our cups with fragrant jasmine tea, and we tapped them together in a toast.

"Here's to the end of a strange year," she said. "And let's hope that the next one is a lot less stressful."

"Amen," I said. "I'll drink to that."

Aunt Ibby smiled and gestured toward the sleeping cat. "Looks as though O'Ryan is enjoying his Christmas mouse."

O'Ryan opened one eye and rolled over, still hugging the mouse. "He loves it," I said. "And he seems to have quite a catnip buzz going on."

"Pete will be pleased that his gift was such a big hit," she said. "Too bad he couldn't have joined us for dinner."

We'd had the usual holiday houseful of relatives

and friends for the festive meal, but the gathering snowstorm had sent them all home early.

"He spent the day at his sister's, but he said he'd try to stop by later."

"I'll bet a little snow won't keep him away," she said with a knowing smile.

I turned my chair just enough so that I could still see the headlights on any car turning onto Winter Street. It wasn't often that Pete had a holiday off, and I was pretty sure he'd want to spend at least part of it with me . . . snow or no snow. We'd already exchanged Christmas gifts. I hadn't wanted to give him anything too personal at this early stage of our relationship, so I'd decided on a pair of tickets for good seats at an upcoming Bruins hockey game. His gift to me, a vintage brooch with an oval miniature painting of a yellow cat, was pinned to the deep V-neck of my white silk blouse. I wore dark green velvet jeans and had tucked a sprig of holly into random red curls escaping from my attempt at a French twist.

"You know, Maralee," Aunt Ibby said, "I have a very good feeling about the New Year. The house is coming along beautifully, and the fact that you're going to start January with a good deed for the community is an excellent omen."

"An *omen?*" I laughed. "Maybe you've watched too many episodes of *Nightshades!*"

My aunt was a recent, and still pretty skeptical, believer in things paranormal. We both had reason to know, though, that some things were just beyond our understanding. O'Ryan was an outstanding example of that knowledge. The handsome cat, snoozing happily at our feet, had once been Ariel Constellation's pet . . . some said her "familiar." As many folks in Salem will testify, a witch's familiar is far from being an ordinary house cat!

She shrugged. "Well, omen or not, your volunteering to help out at the new school will be such a blessing for the students."

"I hope so," I said. "I'm looking forward to it."

The Tabitha Trumbull Academy for the Arts was due to open just after the start of the New Year, and I'd been invited to be a guest instructor. The school was located in the sprawling old building that had once housed Trumbull's Department Store in downtown Salem. The store had been closed since the sixties and had been slated for demolition until government grants and an historical site designation had saved it from the wrecker's ball. Already dubbed The Tabby, the school would soon be bustling with the activities of aspiring dancers, poets, painters, actors, and, in my department, television performers and producers.

"Your mother and I used to go to Trumbull's with your Grandmother Russell when we were little girls," Aunt Ibby said. "We loved it. There was a grand staircase to the second floor with wide bannisters. I always wanted to slide down on one."

"Did you ever do it?"

"No, I never did."

"Now that I'm officially an instructor at The Tabby, I'll give you permission to slide whenever you want to."

O'Ryan's ears perked up, and yawning, he stood, stretched, and trotted toward the front hall.

"Someone's coming," Aunt Ibby said. "O'Ryan always knows before we do."

She was right. The gleam of headlights glinted on the frosted windowpane as a car rounded the corner from Washington Square.

"It's probably Pete," I said. When the door chime sounded, I followed O'Ryan into the hall and opened the front door. Pete Mondello stood there, smiling, hatless, holding a huge poinsettia plant under one arm while fat snowflakes fell all around him.

"Brrr. Cold out there." He hurried inside, pulled me close for a quick hug with his free arm, and stamped his feet on the woven rope mat. "Merry Christmas, Lee," he said, tossing his coat onto a hook on the tall hall tree. "You look good."

"You look good, too," I said, brushing a snowflake from his dark hair. An understatement. He looked wonderful. "How was your Christmas?"

"Fun," he said, bending to stroke O'Ryan's head. "My sister's kids had a ball opening presents."

"So did O'Ryan," I told him. "He had the wrapping off of his purple mouse before we were up this morning. He's been playing with it all day. I think he's still a little bit drunk. Come on inside and get warm."

Aunt Ibby greeted Pete with a welcoming smile, a "Merry Christmas, Pete," and an offer of pumpkin pie.

He patted perfectly flat abs, claiming he'd already eaten too much, wished her a Merry Christmas, and handed her the poinsettia.

"Thank you, dear. It's lovely." She placed the plant on the sideboard and stood back to admire the effect. "Pete, I was just telling my niece about the old Trumbull's Department Store."

"I've seen pictures of it," he said, "but I've never been inside."

"It was a beautiful store. All those gleaming hardwood floors and racks of the latest clothes, a great big book department, hardware and notions and linens and toys and jewelry and just about anything a person might want. There was a player piano on the mezzanine floor landing, and a man in a tuxedo played the popular tunes all day. But I guess the old stores just couldn't compete with the malls."

"I'm sure it looks quite different now," Pete said. "Empty."

"I guess it must," I said. "The school director, Rupert Pennington, says a lot of the old fixtures will be moved out by the time school starts. My classes will be in the old shoe department."

"I always got my back-to-school shoes at Trumbull's," my aunt said, reminiscing. "I wonder if the old bentwood chairs are still there. Thonet, I think."

"I've heard the city plans to reuse as much of the furniture and fixtures as they can," I said, "and some of the things will go to auction. A country store up in Vermont has already bid on the curved glass counters and old thread cases and wooden millinery stands."

"I suppose some of that old store stuff is pretty valuable these days," Pete said.

My aunt nodded. "Maralee, do you remember our handyman, Mr. Sullivan? He and his son were working on taking some of the smaller pieces to a storage locker today. On Christmas."

"How do you know that?" I asked.

"Mrs. Sullivan is one of my Facebook friends. The men went to work right after dinner. She's not pleased.

She seems concerned about them working there after dark."

"I remember being afraid to walk past the Trumbull's building at night," I said. "All the kids said it was haunted."

"I've heard those stories, too," Pete said. "Something about a lady in white in the upstairs window and strange lights flickering on and off. Down at the station they think it's just a trick the Trumbull family used to keep vandals away. I know they could never keep security guards very long."

A slight buzzing sound interrupted us, and Pete reached into his pocket for his phone. "Oops. Sorry. I'll take this in the hall."

When he came back into the room, his expression was serious. "Afraid I have to leave. Something's going on at your new school."

"What's wrong?" I asked.

"Don't know yet, exactly. Seems your Mr. Sullivan went down into the basement, and his son says he just disappeared. Never came back up the stairs."

Grab These Cozy Mysteries
from
Kensington Books

Catering and Capers with
Isis Crawford!